I0825377

OVER THE CLIFFS

OVER THE CLIFFS

CHARLOTTE CHANTER

Edited and with an introduction by
Gina R. Collia

Published by Nezu Press
Queensgate House,
48 Queen Street,
Exeter, Devon,
EX4 3SR,
United Kingdom.

This edition published 2024

Over the Cliffs first published by Smith, Elder and Co., 1860.

ISBN-13: 978-1-917113-00-7

PUBLISHER'S NOTE

Three editions of *Over the Cliffs* were published: the first UK edition of 1860 was contained in two volumes; a US edition appeared in one volume in 1861; and a single-volume UK edition appeared in 1866, with some text removed. This new Nezu Press edition contains the complete text of the 1860 first edition, but it contains one significant change. Within the 1860 edition, at the very end of chapter XXXII of the second volume—after the sentence ending 'and he sat and awaited his doom.'—the narrative shifts rather suddenly from the impending downfall of one of the story's villains to happy scenes involving other central characters which take place many years later (beginning 'What happy gatherings there used to be'). The description of these happy scenes is confusing, as—in addition to the sudden change in location, time and mood—it includes references to events which have not yet been revealed to the reader. The text containing these future scenes was omitted entirely from the 1861 US edition. It was then included in the 1866 edition, this time in the final chapter. In this Nezu Press edition, as with the 1866 edition, it has been placed at the end of the closing chapter, immediately before the final paragraph, which is where it appears it should have been all along.

CONTENTS

VOLUME I

VOLUME II

Charlotte Chanter
Fearless Fern-Hunter of Devonshire
by Gina R. Collia

Charlotte Kingsley was born on 24 December 1827 in Barnack, Cambridgeshire,[1] the sixth of seven children, to Charles Kingsley (1781-1860) and his wife, Mary (née Lucas, 1787-1873).[2] Charlotte's mother, an 'eminently practical' woman who was 'full of poetry and enthusiasm', was born in the West Indies; she was the daughter of Nathanial Lucas of Farley Hall, Barbados.[3] Charlotte's father claimed descent from Rannulph de Kingsley, who was granted the 'office of Bailiwick and Keeping in the Forest of Delamere in the twelfth century'.[4] Charles Kingsley was the only son of a wealthy man (also named Charles Kingsley, 1743-1786), and, though he was left an orphan when he was only five years old, he was brought up 'with good expectations as a country gentleman'.[5] Unfortunately, mismanagement of his inheritance by trustees during his minority soon diminished his fortune.[6] And, though he was a talented artist, naturalist and linguist, Charles Kingsley 'had every talent except that of using his talents.'[7] His fortune was squandered before he reached the age of thirty, and he found himself almost penniless and, for the first time in his life, in need of a profession.[8] Too old to join the army, he decided on the Church.

At the time of Charlotte's birth, Rev. Charles Kingsley was rector of Barnack.[9] She was born in the Great North Room of the fourteenth-century rectory, which was said to be haunted by Button Cap, an old rector of Barnack who defrauded a widow and orphan. According to Charlotte's eldest brother, also called Charles Kingsley (1819-1875)—who went on to become the well-known

Barnack Rectory (now Kingsley House), Charlotte's birthplace.

author of *Westward Ho!* and *The Water-Babies*—since death, the old rector had taken to wandering about wearing 'flopping slippers', 'a flowered dressing-gown, and a cap with a button on it'.[10] Rev. Kingsley had been offered the living at Barnack, one of the best in the diocese, by Bishop Herbert Marsh of Peterborough with a single condition attached: he was to give it up when Bishop Marsh's own son was old enough to be ordained and replace him.[11] Young Marsh was ordained in 1830, and Rev. Kingsley, having been advised to try the Devonshire climate for the benefit of his health—he had caught malaria whilst in the Fens—left Barnack and travelled with his family to Ilfracombe, on the North Devon coast,[12] with its 'rock-walled harbour, its little wood of masts within, its white terraces, rambling up the hills,' and 'its quiet nature and its quiet luxury, its rock fairy-land and its sea-walks, its downs and combes, its kind people, and, if possible, its still kinder climate'.[13]

It was while staying in lodgings in Ilfracombe that Rev. Kingsley was offered the position of curate of Clovelly, forty or so miles southwest along the Devonshire coast, by Sir James Hamlyn Williams of Clovelly Court.[14] At the time, the rector of Clovelly was Rev. Orlando Hamlyn Williams, Sir James's brother,[15] but in November 1831 Rev. Williams died at the young age of thirty,[16] and in the summer of the following year Rev. Kingsley was appointed the new rector of Clovelly,[17] with a living of £350 a year.[18] Over time, the reverend 'won the hearts of the stalwart Devonshire fishermen, because he feared no danger, and could manage a boat, shoot a herring-net, and haul a seine as one of themselves'.[19]

Clovelly sits perched on a 400-foot-high cliff, its high street winding its way down the hillside at such a steep angle that, within the whitewashed cottages that line it, the steepness 'causes one man's floor to be on the level of his neighbour's roof'.[20] On the subject of descending to the village, Charlotte later wrote:

Entrance to Clovelly, by Charlotte Chanter, from *Ferny Combes*. 1856.

'We proceed, slipping and sliding, till we pause at what is properly the head of "the street." On each side, tiny gardens or quaint terraced balconies project from the ground-floor of the houses. . . The sea breaks and shimmers below; over the bay the yellow sands gleam, and three or four poplars in the foreground cut the picture and add to the singularity of the scene. . . As we proceed, broad paved steps render the walking anything but agreeable; experience proves a short shuffling trot to be the most secure pace. Any one who ventures down Clovelly street must leave his dignity behind him, and get down as best he may, fortunate if he have not a hard tumble or two by the way.'[21]

Charlotte and the two youngest Kingsley boys were very close in age, with George having been born two years before his sister and Henry—who would go on to write *The Recollections of Geoffry Hamlyn* and *Ravenshoe*—two years after her. The three siblings spent a great deal of time together, and she appears to have been, in her younger years at least, 'one of the boys'. On one occasion, fuelled by jealousy and with the assistance of George—or perhaps by his instigation—she put the infant Henry into a wheelbarrow and proceeded to wheel him across the garden and into a pond, abandoning him there to be rescued by the gardener, who discovered him while searching for his barrow.[22] Charlotte's parents were keen naturalists and amateur conchologists, and they encouraged their children to take an interest in the natural world around them. As a child, Charlotte often accompanied her mother on explorations of Clovelly beach with George and Henry, [23] while the three oldest Kingsley boys—Charles, Herbert and Gerald—explored further afield with their father or went out in the herring boats with the local fishermen.

The Kingsleys were all keen readers. The rectory library contained many books that had been collected by Mrs Kingsley's Barbadian ancestors over the years, 'volume on volume of famous voyagers…Dampier, Rogers, Shelrocke, Byron, Cook… and the respectable Captain Charles Johnson, deeply interested and very properly shocked at the "the Robberies and Murders of the most Notorious Pyrates" '—books that fired the imagination of the young Kingsleys with tales of adventure and 'old sea heroes'.[24]

Mrs Kingsley often told her children tales of her home in Barbados, as did her father, Nathaniel Lucas, who was a great traveller.[25] He was also a member of the Barbados Assembly and, according to legend, a witness to the macabre events which took place in the Chase Vault in Barbados between 1912 and 1920—events which formed the basis of Isabella Linnæus Banks's supernatural short story 'The Pride of the Corbyns'.[26]

Tragedy struck in 1834, when Herbert, the Kingsleys' second son, who had been sent to Helston Grammar School in Cornwall to be educated, died at the young age of fourteen. Shortly before his death, he stole a silver spoon, sold it, and ran away from school. He was arrested the following day, put in handcuffs, and taken back to Helston Grammar.[27] After being locked in his room, he soon became ill with rheumatic fever and, despite showing signs of recovery, died suddenly from heart disease.[28] Following his death, there was some talk about the cause of it; it was suggested that he had drowned himself in Loe Pool, and his headstone in Helston churchyard, marked only with the letters 'H. K.', appeared to lend substance to the rumour.[29]

Two years after Herbert's death, in the spring of 1836, Rev. Kingsley was appointed rector of St. Luke's, Chelsea, and the Kingsleys were forced to exchange their idyllic seaside life amongst the fisherfolk of Devon for one of ceaseless parish work amongst the middle class of suburban London.[30] Rev. Kingsley and his wife were busy from morning till night, and their home was frequently the meeting place for various committees. How nature-loving Charlotte, then eight years old, must have missed exploring the Devonshire countryside on Dart, her Exmoor pony. Her eldest brother, Charles, complained to a schoolfellow that their society in Chelsea consisted entirely of clergymen, who talked of nothing but ‘parochial schools, and duties, and vestries, and curates’, and ‘silly women blown about by every wind’, who were forever ‘falling in love with the preacher instead of his sermon’.[31] The ‘filth, wretchedness, and indecency’ of London was something which Mrs Kingsley felt no young woman should be subjected to.[32]

Charlotte was sixteen years old when, in April 1844, Caroline Kohle, a twenty-three-year-old lady’s maid from Baden-Baden, Germany, was found dead at the Kingsleys’ home in Chelsea. The Kingsleys’ housemaid discovered her in Charlotte’s bedroom, lying face down on the floor beside the bed, her shoes having been removed.[33] Miss Kohle, who had been employed at the rectory for a year, had appeared to be in excellent health and good spirits prior to her death. Mr R. C. Gardiner, the surgeon who performed the postmortem, concluded that she had died from ‘a slight thickening of the valves of the heart, which had been caused by the tight lacing of a pair of stays, which had produced curvature of the spine, and thrown the heart out of position.’[34] The coroner pointed out that ‘tight lacing by females was a most baneful practice’, and that ‘the system pursued at ladies’ schools in this country was the most pernicious that could be conceived.’[35]

It is impossible to know for certain what effect this tragic event had upon young Charlotte, but a lady’s maid is a trusted personal servant, required to dress and undress her mistress, bring her breakfast in bed, draw her bath, mend her clothes, and so on, so the two young women would have spent a fair amount of time together. According to the evidence given at the inquest, Miss Kohle had dressed Charlotte shortly before her death.[36] We do know that Charlotte had a great affection for the German language and later in life carried out German to English translations for magazines, so it is likely she enjoyed contact with Caroline Kohle, as it afforded her the opportunity to converse in a language she so loved.[37] With regard to the effect of Miss Kohl's death on Charlotte's views concerning restrictive, potentially dangerous, female clothing, it is difficult to imagine, given what we do know of her interests and activities in adulthood, that she was a slave to fashion. And the heroine she created in *Over the Cliffs* is far from what you would call a 'fashion victim'; young Gratiana Dawson opts for simple clothing as she clambers about the Devon coast, and her style is considered 'quaint' and old-fashioned; others are afraid to imitate it, 'lest they should appear singular'.

In February 1845, the Kingsleys received the news that Gerald Kingsley was dead; he had died whilst serving on H. M. S. *Royalist* in the Torres Straits. Gerald had joined the Royal Navy in 1838 and had been promoted to the rank of mate on 2 June 1841.[38] At the end of 1844, H. M. S. *Royalist* reached Singapore from Port Essington, having received no official communication whatsoever from the Admiralty for more than a year and a half—she had been entirely forgotten.[39] During that time the ship's wretched crew had taken ill with fever, and one by one the men had died. Gerald, the last remaining officer, had lain 'in the little brig, roasting and pining, day after day' until he too had succumbed on 17 September 1844.[40] By the time the *Royalist* arrived in Singapore, having been brought into port by the acting second master, she was falling to pieces.[41] Rev. Kingsley received the news of his son's death during a visit to the local public library. He overheard a gentleman say, 'Dreadful bad business this about the *Royalist*—every single officer on board her dead—those who did not die of fever were eaten by cannibals.' Rev. Kingsley fell down in a dead faint.[42]

John Mill Chanter, the third son of Rev. William Chanter (1766-1859) and his wife, Mary (née Wolferstan, 1770-1824), was born on

25 March 1808 at the old-fashioned parsonage in Hartland, Devon,[43] where the scenery is 'grand, marvellous, and awful; the thunder of the Atlantic is for ever in one's ears; the salt spray in one's face, glorious, invigorating, and inspiring'.[44] And it was in Hartland, a next-door neighbour to Clovelly, that John spent his childhood days, in a land 'full of many a wild story of smuggling, wrecking, and the supernatural.'[45] When he was about ten or eleven years old, John was sent off to Blundell's School, Tiverton, and he remained a pupil there until he entered Oriel College, Oxford,[46] where he took his bachelor's degree in 1831.[47]

After leaving Oxford, he returned home to Hartland, where he acted as curate of Welcombe until 1834, when he took his master's degree and was ordained a priest.[48] From Welcombe he went to Pilton, Barnstaple, where he remained for the next two years. It was while he was at Pilton that his friend Rev. Kingsley suggested he take the position of curate in Chelsea, thinking it unwise that he should remain in the country.[49] So, John travelled by coach to

Ilfracombe Town and Harbour, published by Fisher, Son & Co., 1830.

Holy Trinity Church, from *Twenty-Four Views of Ilfracombe* by J. Gadsby, c. 1875.

London to see him, and the journey there turned out to be a fortuitous one; in conversation with a stranger he mentioned the reason for his visit, and the gentleman replied, 'The living of Ilfracombe is vacant… I wonder if you would care to have it?'.[50] John was appointed vicar of Ilfracombe in April 1836,[51] and on 8 May he 'read himself in'.[52] At the time, the parish church, Holy Trinity, was in a terrible state of repair; the pews were full of woodworm, the windows rattled in their frames at the slightest breeze, and the stones along the aisles had been so badly laid that the foul odour from those buried beneath found its way into the church itself.[53]

The Kingsleys had first made the acquaintance of John Mill Chanter in 1830.[54] During the following years, with the Kingsleys living in Clovelly and the Chanters residing in neighbouring Hartland, it was natural that they should see something of each other. During the Kingsleys' time in Chelsea, they continued to visit North Devon when the opportunity arose, and in January 1848 they travelled to Ilfracombe again.[55] Charlotte, then twenty years old, and John, twenty years her senior, had a great deal in common. They shared an intense love of nature and, along with Charlotte's brother Charles, spent a considerable amount of time exploring Ilfracombe and the surrounding areas.

> ' "I remember" (said a dear old friend) "…Miss Kingsley, had a class of girls; I was one of them, and Mr. Charles would often come in when we were there, and make us all laugh with his funny, quaint sayings. Long expeditions they took together, Miss Kingsley, Charles, and the Vicar, mostly on horseback (for they were all at home in the saddle) away to little Trentishoe, or beautiful Lynton and Lynmouth, or the other way to Braunton Burrows, on botanising excursions, or for a long stretching gallop across the yellow sands of Woollacombe to Croyde, with the fragrant scent from the brown seaweed in their faces. Pleasant days indeed they must have been." '[56]

The following year, on 10 May 1849, John and Charlotte were married at Clifton Church, Gloucestershire.[57] When the reverend and his young wife returned to Ilfracombe, many of his parishioners gathered to cheer them in; they 'chained' the road from Barnstaple into Ilfracombe and erected arches throughout the town, with flags flying and bells ringing. However, news of this somehow reached John Chanter, and he and Charlotte entered the town by a different road,[58] making their way to the vicarage unseen.

The vicarage was a 'long low house with a buff coloured face and deep finely slated roof, not always even, but gently undulating as if its old beams had wearied with keeping the horizontal for so

Ilfracombe Vicarage, by Gratiana Chanter, from *Wanderings in North Devon.*

many centuries, and had lowered their aching arms to a more restful position.'[59] Within the oldest part of the house—above the kitchen, which was thought to have been the original mansion house's entrance hall—there was a haunted room; it was used as a lumber room as all refused to sleep in it.[60] The ghosts were said to be those of two pretty children, murdered by their uncle for their money, who wandered the room and sighed.[61]

South Side of Vicarage, by Gratiana Chanter, from *Wanderings in North Devon.*

The life of the vicar of Ilfracombe was a busy one. In addition to providing services, directing the renovation of Holy Trinity, and raising funds for the construction of a new church for Ilfracombe's increasing population, John held classes at the vicarage for both girls and boys, day and Sunday school classes 'in the tumble-down room over the Market', and he had an infant school at the Quay.[62] He taught the schoolmistress himself, to so high a standard that she satisfied the school inspectors for forty years. When he first took on the living at Ilfracombe, the vicarage and its garden were in as sorry a state as the parish church. The house had been home to countless rodents for years; in fact, the very first soul to greet him when he arrived at his new home was a very large rat.[63] When it rained, the kitchen floor 'used to be an inch or two deep in water, so that the maids were obliged to trot about in pattens.'[64] And the garden was an overgrown wilderness, surrounded by derelict barns. John began work at once; the barns were removed, 'the rats were dismissed', and he planted every tree and shrub in the vicarage garden himself.[65]

The Chanters' first child and only son, Kingsley, was born on 24 March 1850.[66] Mary Geraldine arrived the following year, on 5 June.[67] Then came Louisa Cadogan (15 March 1853),[68] Mabilla (15 November 1854),[69] Gratiana (9 May 1857),[70] Katherine Stanley (19 February 1859),[71] and Charlotte Joyce (28 June 1863).[72] The vicar's 'quiet humour and power of telling a good story' made him a delightful companion for his children,[73] and Charlotte, who 'had an endless stock of delightful German legends and fairy-tales at her fingers' ends', captivated them with tales of goblins, water nymphs, and Devon pixies.[74] In 1858, the Chanters' collections of tales for children, *Jack Frost and Betty Snow*, was published by Griffith and Farran. The stories within the small volume, about 'the different dogs, cats, and birds, who had from time to time formed part of their household',[75] were dedicated to Kingsley, who was then eight years old, 'for whom they were written to enliven the weariness of a rainy week'.[76]

In 1856, two years before *Jack Frost and Betty Snow* was published, Charlotte's guide to collecting and identifying the ferns of Devonshire, *Ferny Combes: A Ramble After Ferns in the Glens and*

Valleys of Devonshire, was published by Lovell Reeve. The year before, her brother Charles had coined the term 'Pteridomania', to describe the fern-fever that had swept through the country, suggesting that, as pursuits for ladies went, it was preferable to 'novels and gossip, crochet and Berlin-wool' and that it had almost wiped out any interest in 'fancy-work'.[77] Two years before *Ferny Combes* was published, Charlotte and John discovered in Hartland woods a variety of fern that was unknown, and it was subsequently named after the former: 'Mrs Chanter's Prickly-Toothed Buckler Fern' (*Lastrea dilatata chanteriæ*).[78] In her preface to *Ferny Combes*, Charlotte explained that her decision to write the book had arisen out of a desire to share with others the happiness she enjoyed 'amid the wild scenes of Devonshire, hoping that they too may derive fresh life and joy from the breezy heaths and moorlands of their native country.' In order to find material for the book, Charlotte and John took a tour of the Devonshire countryside, travelling from one place to another in their little carriage, drawn by Ivanhoe, their white horse.[79]

Charlotte and John possessed an adventurous spirit, and neither was afraid to get their hands dirty; they enjoyed exploring uncharted territory, and their flower-hunts around the countryside often required that they 'rough it'.[80] During a tour around Wales, they pulled up at a place in the mountains and, hungry after their travels, asked for something to eat. The woman who greeted them said she had no food in the house, so the vicar picked up his rod and proceeded to the stream, returning with enough trout to provide them with a meal; Charlotte cooked the fish herself, for the woman 'professed total ignorance in the art of frying trout.'[81]

In the spring of 1859, John Chanter suffered a serious illness and was advised to travel abroad for the sake of his health. He and Charlotte travelled to Nice in southern France, and the couple remained there until the end of October.[82] Unfortunately, the trip was not as successful as his doctors had hoped. By December, his health had deteriorated, and he and Charlotte spent another six months in Nice, returning to Ilfracombe in the July of the following year.[83] Again, though there was some improvement, the trip failed to return him to anything approaching full health. While in France, the couple went flower hunting, and they put together quite a collection, including rare specimens, before returning home to the vicarage.[84]

Over the Cliffs, Charlotte's only fiction novel, was published in two volumes by Smith, Elder and Co. in the autumn of 1860. The story is set on the coast of Devon at the beginning of the nineteenth century. Its fearless heroine is Gratiana Dawson (also called Tye and Grace), the daughter of a brutal bully who hates his children and is prone to violent paroxysms of passion. Motherless, forced to live under the roof of a tyrant, and the victim of one indignity after another, she refuses to surrender to the abusive men around her. Edward Mountjoy, the hero of the story, says of her, when speaking to Captain Douglas of the Royal Navy, 'She has done things in her day that required from her more nerve than would be required of you in attacking an enemy.'

Gratiana's home is Harscourt, which stands in a lonely spot 'three or four hundred yards from the cliffs, at the head of a deep gully which runs down to the sea', and throughout the novel the rugged coastal landscape—the cliffs, the jagged rocks, the boiling, surging sea, and the sedgy moorlands—is as much a part of the story as the characters who dwell within it. It is a tale of murder, a stolen inheritance, smuggling, shipwrecks, blackmail, treachery, greed, plotting, counter-plotting… and love. There is even a hint of the supernatural in the form of a sighing ghost—much like those that inhabited Ilfracombe vicarage—for Gratiana Dawson sleeps in the very room where her mother lay after her death, 'and which popular superstition still considered she frequented.'

When writing *Over the Cliffs*, Charlotte included elements of her own life and experiences. Her heroine was named after her own daughter, as was another character in the story, Lily Fowler; her second daughter, Louisa, was referred to as Lily by her family and friends, and, as with her fictional counterpart, she had a very fine singing voice.[85] Like Charlotte's own mother, the character Agnes Mounjoy—who is like a mother to Gratiana Dawson—was born in the West Indies. The locations described within the novel were based on real places that she and her family were familiar with; for example, some of the more rugged scenery was inspired by the 'wild neighbourhood' of Morwenstow, located about ten miles to the south of Hartland, to which the Chanters were frequent visitors.[86] In fact, they were staying at Morwenstow for the summer when Charlotte wrote her novel.[87]

Tonacombe Manor, from a drawing by J. Ley Pethybridge, c. 1910.

Several years later, when describing a family holiday in Morwenstow that took place in October 1868, Gratiana Chanter described Tonacombe Manor, the fine medieval house where she and her family stayed, as 'suggestive of everything that was mysterious and delightful.'[88] One of the bedrooms was inhabited by a ghost called Zachary, 'a delightful place to creep to in the twilight, and peep through the keyhole, with the expectation of witnessing the ghostly Zachary performing ghostly deeds'.[89] During their visit, there were many storms, and 'miles inland could be heard the raging of the sea… a green black mountain of water, rounding and rolling on, ever gathering in force and size as it nears the bristling shore and boulder-laden beach.'[90] The Chanters spent most of their time on the cliffs or under them, looking for Cornish diamonds.[91]

Over the Cliffs was generally well received; the critic for the *Globe* wrote that Charlotte had produced a story 'whose incidents are of uncommon interest, and set as it is among the wild scenery of North Devon, close to the roar of the Atlantic wave, the natural features of the locality add both strength and beauty to the tale.'[92] *Over the Cliffs* was 'not among those books which are forgotten as soon as read.'[93] It sold well enough to warrant a US edition in 1861 and a second UK edition in 1866. And yet, Charlotte did not write another novel. She did, however, return to writing for children, and two of her morality tales were published in *Our Young Folks: An Illustrated Magazine for Boys and Girls*, an American periodical which ran from January 1865 to December 1873; 'The Swallow' appeared in September 1865, and 'The Rabbits and the Foxes' was published in October the following year.

On 25 June 1869, John bought the Millslade Inn, in the village of Brendon, near Lynton, at a public auction and converted it into a private residence.[94] The Chanters had stayed at the inn from time to time over the years, to have access to the nearby East Lyn river for trout fishing, and after their purchase of it their summer holidays were always 'passed amongst the wooded vales, and breezy

Millslade, by Gratiana Chanter, from *Wanderings in North Devon.*

moorlands with which it is surrounded';[95] much later, following the vicar's retirement, it became the family home. Gratiana described the house as 'not a handsome one, but a comfortable and cosy home, situated in a singularly beautiful position'.[96] The area was, and still is, very popular amongst anglers and artists.

On 2 December 1869, the Chanters' only son, Kingsley, enlisted in the Merchant Navy. One year later, he deserted.[97] He did not return to England, and the Chanters had not seen their son for more than five years when, in January 1875, while John was suffering from a severe attack of bronchitis,[98] the news came that Kingsley was dead.[99] He had been travelling on an American steamer when, having fallen or been washed overboard, he drowned 'in the element he always loved so well'; according to the *Ilfracombe Chronicle*, 'the free-hearted youth', who appears to have been well liked, was 'a victim to his too great love of adventure'.[100] Around the same time, Charlotte and her husband received news that her eldest brother, Charles, had also died.[101]

It appears that Charlotte ceased writing, for publication at least, following the death of her son. References to *Ferny Combes* and *Over the Cliffs* continued to appear in newspapers throughout the 1870s, but no mention was made of any other works by her. In November 1874, the *Ilfracombe Chronicle* ran an essay competition for local boys up to the age of seventeen; the subject was 'The Events of the Year in Ilfracombe, and their probable Effect on the future of the Town', and Charlotte was one of the judges;[102] this appears to have been her last appearance in print in the capacity of 'Authoress of "*Over the Cliffs, &c.*" '. Reports of the social activities of her husband and daughters made no reference to her after 1875. Aside from her appearance in the regular lists of residents and visitors printed in the *Ilfracombe Chronicle*, the only mention of Charlotte in the years just prior to her death was within a list of subscribers, published in February 1879, who had donated money for the widow of Richard Braund, who had drowned at Ilfracombe the previous month.[103] Charlotte's final visit to Millslade took place in the summer of 1877, after which the house was listed as 'to let'.[104]

Though Charlotte's retirement followed her son's death, it was most likely due to a deterioration in her health rather than a response to her bereavement. Charlotte was very ill during the last years of her life. She suffered from chronic myelitis—chronic inflammation of the spinal cord.[105] The common symptoms of the condition include sensations of numbness or tingling, pain, fatigue, and muscle weakness; at the end of the nineteenth century, chronic myelitis would usually result in complete paralysis and, after a prolonged and painful illness, death.[106] Her physician would have required her to 'keep in a horizontal position' and 'never lie on the back'.[107] Charlotte—used to drawing upon nature for inspiration—would have been unable to leave her bed, let alone leave her home to wander around her beloved Devonshire countryside. Gone were those glorious days of 'riding among the stony precipices of Trentishoe, fording rivers, scrambling over rocks, plunging into pathless thickets, and traversing the wilds of Dartmoor'.[108] And oh, how that must have pained her.

Charlotte died at Ilfracombe vicarage on 19 March 1882; she was fifty-four years old.[109] During the morning before her burial, which took place five days later, 'the bells of the Parish Church rang out muffled peals', and throughout the town shops were closed and blinds were drawn 'as a token of respect for the deceased lady's memory'.[110] During the funeral service the church was crowded,[111] and a hundred or so of the town's inhabitants attended the burial. She was buried 'amid general manifestation of sorrow' in a vault constructed 'in the new portion of the churchyard' at Holy Trinity.[112]

Notes

1 Barnack is a village and civil parish in the Peterborough unitary authority of the ceremonial county of Cambridgeshire.

2 Charlotte was baptised on 17 October 1828, see *England, Select Births and Christenings, 1538-1975.* According to her death certificate, she was fifty-four years old at the time of her death, on 19 March 1882. According to her daughter Gratiana, her birthday fell on Christmas Eve (see *Wanderings in North Devon*, p. 66). Therefore, Charlotte must have been born on 24 December 1827. There were seven Kingsley children in all. The Kingsley's fifth child, Louisa Mary, died in infancy on 14 May 1824, four years before Charlotte's birth (*Stamford Mercury*, 21 May 1824, p. 3).

3 Frances Eliza Kingsley, *Charles Kingsley: His Letters and Memories of His Life.* New York: Scribner, Armstrong & Company, 1877 (abridged from the London Edition), p. 22.

4 Lady Susan Chitty, *The Beast and the Monk: A Life of Charles Kingsley.* New York: Mason/Charter, 1975, p. 23.

5 Frances Kingsley, op. cit., p. 21.

6 William H. Scheuerle, *The Neglected Brother: A Study of Henry Kingsley.* Tallahassee: Florida State University Press, 1971, p. 6.

7 Chitty, op. cit., p. 24.

8 Frances Kingsley, op. cit., p. 21.

9 Ibid., p. 24.

10 Ibid., p. 25.

11 Ibid., p. 24.

12 Ibid., p. 30.

13 Charles Kingsley, *Prose Idylls: New and Old.* London: Macmillan & Co., 1873, pp. 254 and 255.

14 Frances Kingsley, op. cit., p. 30. Rev. Kingsley was curate from 1831 until he became rector in 1832 (see also Lady Susan Chitty, *Charles*

Kingsley's Landscape: His Letters and Memories of His Life. Newton Abbot: David & Charles, 1976, p. 8).

15 Joseph Foster, *Alumni Oxonienses: The Members of the University of Oxford, 1715-1886; Their Parentage, Birthplace, and Year of Birth, with a Record of Their Degrees*. Volume IV—Later Series. Oxford: James Parker & Co., 1891, p. 1568.

16 *Oxford Journal*, 17 December 1831, p. 3.

17 *Huntingdon, Bedford & Peterborough Gazette*, 11 August 1832, p. 3.

18 Chitty, op. cit., p. 34.

19 Mary Kingsley, introduction to George Kingsley's *Notes on Sport and Travel*. London: Macmillan & Co., 1900, p. 10. A 'seine' is a long fishing net which hangs vertically in the water (its bottom weighted to maintain its shape), the ends of which are drawn together to encircle the fish.

20 Charlotte Chanter, *Ferny Combes: A Ramble After Ferns in the Glens and Valleys of Devonshire*. Second edition. London: Lovell Reeve, 1856.

21 Ibid.

22 Mary Kingsley, op. cit., p. 5.

23 Chitty, op. cit., p. 39.

24 Mary Kingsley, op. cit., p.12.

25 Frances Kingsley, op. cit., p. 23.

26 *Folk-lore: A Quarterly Review*. Volume 18, 1907, pp. 389-390.

27 Chitty, op. cit., p. 45.

28 Frances Kingsley, op. cit., p. 33.

29 Chitty, op. cit., p. 45. Loe Pool is the largest freshwater lake in Cornwall. It is reputed to be the lake into which King Arthur's sword, Excalibur, was cast.

30 Frances Kingsley, op. cit., p. 39.

31 Ibid.

32 Ibid.

33 *Penzance Gazette*, 17 April 1844, p. 2.

34 *Gloucester Journal*, 13 April 1844, p. 4.

35 Ibid.

36 *Cork Examiner*, 17 April 1844, p. 4.

37 Gratiana Chanter, *Wanderings in North Devon: Being Records and Reminiscences in the Life of John Mill Chanter, M. A., Oxon, 51 Years Vicar of Ilfracombe.* Ilfracombe: Twiss & Son, 1888, p. 41.

38 *The Navy List, January 1843*, pp. 46 and 128. The rank of mate was the equivalent of sub-lieutenant.

39 William Laird Clowes, *The Royal Navy: A History from the Earliest Times to the Present.* Volume VI. London: S. Low, Marston & Co., 1897, p. 329.

40 Frances Kingsley, op. cit., p. 85

41 Clowes, op. cit., p. 329.

42 Mary Kingsley, op. cit., p. 4.

43 Gratiana Chanter, op. cit., p. 1.

44 Ibid., p. 3.

45 Ibid.

46 Ibid., p. 6.

47 Ibid., p. 7.

48 Ibid., p. 10.

49 Ibid., p. 11-12.

50 Ibid., p. 14.

51 *Oxford University and City Herald*, 30 April 1836, p. 3.

52 Gratiana Chanter, op. cit., p. 15

53 Ibid., pp. 15-16.

54 Ibid., p. 19.

55 Chitty, op. cit., p. 116.

56 Gratiana Chanter, op. cit., p. 20.

57 *Bristol, England, Church of England Marriages and Banns, 1754-1938,* Clifton, St. Andrew, Gloucestershire.

58 Gratiana Chanter, op. cit., p. 20.

59 Ibid., p. 36.

60 Ibid., p. 38.

61 Ibid., p. 43.

62 Ibid., pp. 33-34.

63 Ibid., p. 39.

64 Gratiana Chanter, op. cit., p. 39. Pattens: wooden clogs or overshoes that elevate the foot to aid the wearer when walking on muddy or wet ground.

65 Ibid., p. 39.

66 *Lady's Newspaper and Pictorial Times*, 6 April 1850, p. 30.

67 *Western Times*, 14 June 1851, p. 4

68 *North Devon Journal*, 17 March, p. 5.

69 *North Devon Journal*, 23 November 1854, p. 8.

70 *Italy, Find a Grave Index, 1800s-Present.*

71 *North Devon Journal*, 24 February 1859, p. 8.

72 *North Devon Journal*, 9 July 1863, p. 8.

73 Gratiana Chanter, op. cit., p. 40.

74 Ibid., p. 41.

75 Ibid., p. 40.

76 *Jack Frost and Betty Snow: With Other Tales for Wintry Nights and Rainy Days.* London: Griffith and Farran, 1858.

77 Charles Kingsley, *Glaucus; Or, The Wonders of the Shore.* Cambridge: Macmillan & Co., 1855, p. 4.

78 E. J. Lowe, *Our Native Ferns; Or, A History of the British Species and Their Varieties*, Volume I. London: Groombridge and Sons, 1865, p. 300.

79 Gratiana Chanter, op. cit., p. 44.

80 Gratiana Chanter, op. cit., p. 49.

81 Ibid., p. 50.

82 *North Devon Journal*, 3 November 1859, p. 8.

83 *North Devon Journal*, 5 July 1860, p. 3.

84 Gratiana Chanter, op. cit., p. 48-49.

85 *North Devon Journal*, 20 May 1880, p. 8.

86 Gratiana Chanter, op. cit., p. 56.

87 *North Devon Journal*, 19 March 1874, p. 6.

88 Gratiana Chanter, op. cit., p. 56. Tonacombe Manor was the home of the eccentric poet-priest Robert Stephen Hawker. He and Charlotte's

brother Charles had known each other for years; Gratiana thought Hawker kind and hospitable, and the vicar spent quite a bit of time with him.

89 Ibid., pp. 57-58.

90 Ibid., pp. 58-59.

91 Ibid., p. 59. 'Cornish diamonds' are quartz crystals.

92 *Globe*, 4 October 18060, p. 1.

93 Ibid.

94 The auction was held on 25 June 1869, by Mr Frederick Symons, at the Golden Lion Hotel, Barnstaple. See *North Devon Journal*, 17 June 1869, p. 1.

95 Gratiana Chanter, op. cit., p. 64.

96 Ibid., p. 77.

97 *UK, Apprentices Indentured in Merchant Navy, 1824-1910*. He was in Newcastle, New South Wales, Australia, when he deserted.

98 *Ilfracombe Chronicle*, 5 December 1974, p. 5.

99 *Ilfracombe Chronicle*, 23 January 1875, p. 5. He died on 1 August 1874 according to *England & Wales, National Probate Calendar (Index of Wills and Administrations), 1858-1995*.

100 *Ilfracombe Chronicle*, 23 January 1875, p. 5.

101 Charles Kingsley died on 23 January 1875. *UK and Ireland, Find a Grave Index, 1300s-Current*.

102 *Ilfracombe Chronicle*, 28 November 1874, p. 4.

103 *Ilfracombe Chronicle*, 1 February 1879, p. 2.

104 *Ilfracombe Chrinicle*, 11 August 1877, p. 5.

105 Death certificate, district of Ilfracombe, county of Devon, registered 22 March 1882. Causes of death: chronic myelitis and lardaceous disease of the liver (now known as amyloidosis).

106 Byrom Bramwell, M. D., F. R. C. P. (Edin.). *Diseases of the Spinal Cord.* Second edition. Edinburgh: Young J. Pentland, 1884, p. 250.

107 John King, M. D., *The Causes, Symptoms, Diagnosis, Pathology and Treatment of Chronic Diseases.* Cincinnati: Moore, Wilstach & Baldwin, 1867, p. 188.

108 *North Devon Journal*, 28 August 1856, p. 6.

109 UK and Ireland, Find a Grave Index, 1300s-Current.

110 Death certificate.

111 *North Devon Journal*, 30 March 1882, p. 8.

112 Ibid.

VOLUME I

CHAPTER I

THE HOME OF THE DAWSONS

AWAY in the west is the old home of the Dawsons—away by towering cliffs and raging waters.

The wind comes sighing over sedgy moorlands, the mist drives up from the sea, and mist and wind seem fit possessors of that desolate region.

No stately English mansion shut in by towering trees, no pretty villas with flowery lawns, no trim cottages with tiny gardens, smelling sweetly of woodbine and wall-flowers, are to be seen there; but in their stead, ruin, desolation and loneliness.

One looks around, in wonder that aught so dreary, so untrodden, should yet remain in this busy, active land: and yet there are signs that it was not always so.

See that great ghost of a house yonder on the hill, with walled-up windows and smokeless chimneys, and never a tree or a shrub near it. It was not always so!

Walk a little farther, and you find yourself on the brink of a deep ravine; see that long, low house, with its gabled windows and ancient terraced garden, where still a few myrtles and roses linger: the house is tenantless and in ruins. It was not always so!

The whole of the country in which are laid the scenes of the following chapters, gives one the idea of a region once much more thickly peopled than at present, or at least peopled by a greater number of men of substance than is now the case. Every here and there, on hill or in valley, you find a mansion once comfortable, and apparently intended for persons of a better class of life, now occupied by the small farmer, its spacious rooms turned into granaries, or quite shut up and deserted. Various reasons are given for this condition of things: one undoubtedly is, that the district is far removed from any towns and the conveniences necessary for life in the present day; so that almost all those who could afford it have gradually been drawn nearer to the centres of activity and commerce, and to the great advantages of society. Hence the neighbourhood is but thinly inhabited, and its larger houses, once the scenes of a somewhat free hospitality, are mostly abandoned.

To the lovers of natural beauty, however, the country is most attractive. A short distance inland, it is indeed bleak and exposed; the Atlantic blast sweeps unimpeded over the hills; but few trees are visible, and those that are seen turn their faces from the sea breeze, and bend crouchingly towards the east, as if to escape its bitterness. But draw nigh to the sea, and the most delicious sights burst on your view: deep velvety combes, with their sloping sides, of oak and furze, or heather; every combe possessing its own garrulous brook, and terminated by its triangular piece of blue ocean glittering in the sunshine, or darkened by passing clouds.[1]

We have said that the country is thinly inhabited. It was always so; but not to such an extent as at present. It was also far away from public observation, and the watchful oversight of authority; hence, wild and illegal acts took place not unfrequently, long after the period of our story, and justice was very slow in taking notice of them, if, indeed, they ever reached the ears of justice. Few of the gentry of that date paid duty to the king, either for their own port-wine, or for the silken garments of their wives. In a certain corporate town that we wot of, whenever a team of horses passed through with smuggled goods—a thing of no very rare occurrence—

[1] Combe: a steep, short valley running up from the sea.

all eyes were shut, and the chief magistrate generally found a handsome present from France in his garden, by way of thanks, next morning. And, perhaps, he was a wise man, for not only did he thus receive a plentiful supply of good wine, but he prevented the shedding of blood; a thing very likely to have happened, had he, or his officers, ventured to take the kegs instead of receiving them.

Those times have passed away, but all the memories of them have not. One such memory still clings around the old house of Harscourt.

In the days of which we write, Harscourt was not a very ancient structure; at least, not the principal and largest part. It stands even as it stood then, three or four hundred yards from the cliffs, at the head of a deep gully which runs down to the sea. Just round the house the trees are few and stunted, but in the glen to the right some fine timber is to be found.

The front, or new part of the house, had no pretensions to architectural beauty, but promised large and well-lit rooms. Behind was the old house, rambling and rather dilapidated, with the exception of a fine old hall, given over to the servants and the numerous hangers-on of the stables and home farm.

There was a small flower-garden on one side of the house, surrounded on three sides by high stone-walls, and opening, on the fourth, by a flight of steps, into a grass-field, bounded by the cliffs. Such was the neighbourhood and house of Harscourt. We must now take a glance at some of its inhabitant in their childish days.

CHAPTER II

"THE SEA-GULLS IN THEIR NEST"

"LET us go home over the cliff, Edward; the tide is rising fast." The speaker was a girl about ten years old, tall for her age, slender, with light brown hair, bleached from exposure and neglect, streaming over her shoulders. Her eyes were hazel-coloured, with long black lashes, and her complexion, naturally dark, was rendered many shades darker by the sun. Her small, well-formed bare feet, as they pressed the short turf, were the fairest thing about her. She was dressed in a coarse sort of smock-frock, of no particular fashion, and a hood with a deep cape hanging down to her waist.

She had two companions—lads—one three or four years older than herself, a sturdy, handsome fellow, the other much about her own age, and greatly resembling her.

"Oh, Tye!" exclaimed the younger boy, "the cliff is so much farther round, and the hill is so steep, and I'm so tired, let us go the shorter way, by the beach;" and seating himself on the turf, he laid a string of a dozen speckled trout beside him.

"If you go by the beach," said the elder lad, "you must come at once. Put on your shoes, Tye, and make haste. If you are quick we may manage it, but the waves run high."

In a few moments they were sliding down a low part of the cliff, over which the stream they had been rifling fell splashing into a deep pool on the beach.

The shore was composed of large round pebbles, no very easy walking for those little weary feet. But the girl kept up steadily by the side of her elder companion, in spite of many a stumble.

Presently they came to where the cliff rises into a precipice, and vast blocks of stone jutting out into the sea seem to prevent all further progress; but the children knew the coast well, and climbed like goats. See! now they stand all three on a great rock, pause, and look where next to spring. The eldest springs first, and calls to the girl to follow. She is over, her arms round the boy to steady herself. They totter for a moment, then regain their footing, and she slides off the rock to make way for Regie. Another spring, another totter, and they are over that danger, in a little cove, where, instead of rough stones and rugged rocks, small white pebbles form their path. However smooth the path, there is no time for loitering.

"We must run; we shall thus gain a few moments," said Edward, "and moments are of importance to us; the tide is higher than I thought."

They run as well as they are able, and now they reach another barrier, higher and more jagged than the first. They climb, they scramble, keeping as near the cliff as they can, for the tide is close upon them.

"The Blower!" muttered Edward; "if the tide is in it, we are in danger."

The younger boy caught the word: "The Blower, Edward! Oh, let us go back!"

"Impossible!" was the reply. "We could not pass the Foot, now. Courage! steady! be as quick as you can; we must leap the Blower!"

"We have leaped it before, you know, Edward," said the girl.

"Yes," thought Edward; "but not in such a tide as this."

They stood at the edge of the dreaded Blower, which is formed by several gigantic masses of rock thrown together. Under one of these the sea forces its way; it is not above three or four feet across, and about eight feet deep, and may easily be crossed at low tide; but it is a different thing when the sea, boiling and surging in the narrow channel, renders the head giddy and the foot unsteady.

Edward leaned over; the water was gurgling at the bottom. "We have time!" he cried; "quick!"—but as he spoke there came a booming and hissing, and a volume of water rushed up through the aperture, drenching them in a moment.

"Jump between the waves!" he cried, and suiting the action to the word, in a moment he was over.

"Come, Regie," and he held out his hands: the boy jumped clear and was safe.

"Now, Tye, quick!"

The child was over-tired; she paused, she trembled, she let the favourable moment pass, and then she jumped—jumped short, and was in the Blower. The wave receded: Tye stood supported by a small ledge of rock, clutching a projecting angle with both hands. She could not hope to buffet many waves—certain destruction seemed to await her.

"She must be saved, she shall be saved!" cried the frantic boy.

But only the helpless children heard him, and the sea-birds started from their nests at his cries.

Poor Tye! the seconds were like years to her! All the little incidents of her short life rose up before her, and in a moment she thought how sorry Edward and Regie would be, and how they would miss her.

A wave came: fortunately for her, not a strong one; but as it was, she only retained her hold by creeping closer between two of the rocks, while the water nearly suffocated her: as the wave went back Edward was at her side.

"Put your foot on my hand, and spring." The child obeyed, and in a few seconds she was on top of the rock; but her deliverer was still in the Blower. "Lie down, Regie, and put your hands over the rock, with the backs downwards;" and Tye called on Edward to hook his hands in theirs.

The ready wit of the girl saved the life of her friend; a violent wave at that moment burst through the Blower, and Edward was lifted by its force on a level with the rock.

"Pull towards you, Regie—pull hard!" and in spite of the dreadful surf, in a moment Edward was by their side, drenched to the skin, and tremendously bruised; as was poor little Tye; while the blood flowed in a stream from a deep cut on her temple.

Once again! over more rock, slipping and cutting themselves with the sharp edges of the slate, till they reach a broad open beach, where the sea beats less wildly. The cliffs here are lower again: it is the mouth of another of those combes with which that coast abounds. At the farther side a pretty trout-stream finds its way to the sea. The children were hurrying toward the stream, as its banks form the easiest path to the hills above, when a man suddenly appearing from behind a rock called on them to stop.

"Where do you come from? Who are you? Where are you going?"

"We come from Merscombe, and we are going to Harscourt—and now let us go on," said Edward; "the evening is closing in; we have a long way before us, and are late enough as it is."

"You must wait till it suits my pleasure to let you go, my man; and if it's my pleasure for you to stay here all night, you must stay."

"Oh, pray don't!" cried the child, coming forward—"pray don't! we shall be so beaten if you do."

"Beaten! who'll beat you?"

"Father."

"Why, bless the child, how did you get that ugly cut on your forehead? And you are dripping wet. What on earth have you been about?"

"I've been in the Blower," replied Tye, shuddering.

"In the Blower! and how did you get out again?"

"He got me out," was the reply, with a jerk of the head towards Edward. "But do let us go home, there's a dear good man! I am so cold!"

Now the little damsel did not at all like the looks of the rough man beside her, and she had her own suspicions of his goodness; but, child as she was, she knew the use of flattery.

The man seemed to hesitate, and a gleam of intelligence shot over Tye's face as she watched the man's eyes directed towards the opening of the glen, where the stream came down.

"I know all about it," said she, nodding her head mysteriously, "you are hiding or running something up there; but if you will let us go we will be blind, and if we chance to see anything we will not tell: we are accustomed not to speak of what we see. You can trust them, too," she added, pointing to the boys: "can't he, Edward and Regie?"

The man looked at her in astonishment.

"You're a queer article, at any rate," he muttered.

"On our honour, sir," began Edward—

"Your honour, indeed! Ha! ha! a good joke. But this child must not be kept here, she'll die of cold. Wait a bit;—I'll see what I can do."

The morning had been one of those bright sunny mornings so common in early spring, which tempt the fisherman and invalid out, and then as the day advances, the sky clouds over, and driving mist takes the place of sunshine. The three huddled together as close as they could to keep each other warm, but with poor success. The man went up by the stream, and in a quarter of an hour, which had seemed an age to the children, he reappeared.

"Come along," he said, "and if they speak to you, speak up for yourselves."

There was a strange party and a strange scene presented to their view, as they rounded the corner of the cliff and advanced about twenty paces up the glen. Four or five young men were seated in an angle of the rock, a meal spread out before them. There were long-necked wine-bottles from France, and squat, sturdy bottles of spirits from Holland, looking decidedly as if they had never paid the king's duty. And there was a bale or two lying near, looking suspicious of Lyons silk or Genoa velvet.

The principal personage seemed to be not more than four or five-and-twenty, with fair hair and a fair complexion, his eyes were grey and restless, and a smile seemed ever on his lips; yet it was not a natural, pleasant smile.

"Who are you, in the name of wonder?" he shouted to the little girl, who advanced in front of her companions.

"I'm Gratiana Dawson," was the reply.

"Whew!" whistled the young man, elevating his eyebrows; "what! Dawson of Harscourt's daughter? You look more like a beggar-girl than a gentleman's daughter."

"I've been out fishing, and tumbled into the Blower," answered Tye, apologetically, colouring deeply, and looking down at her shabby and bedrabbled attire.

"And who is the little fellow? Your brother?"

"Yes: he is Reginald."

"And the other?"

"Oh, that's Edward."

"Edward who?"

"Edward Mountjoy."

"What, Agnes Mountjoy's son? She who lives in the vale?"

"Yes."

"Tunny, you must see after that lad; there's good blood of our sort in his veins, if he takes after his father."

"I'll see to it, Mr. Martin; but now let the children go, it's getting late."

"You had better give them the password, Tunny; and mind, young ones, you've seen nobody."

The man addressed as Tunny, and whom the children knew by name, accompanied them a little way up the glen.

"If any one asks you if 'the moon is up,' say the 'seagulls are in their nests,' " said Tunny, as he turned back to take up his watch on the beach once more. And the trio went on their way through the mist.

CHAPTER III

LOOKING OUT FOAMWARD

WE have mentioned the house at Harscourt; now we will give a feint sketch of its master, such as he was at the commencement of our story.

He was a notorious person, possessed of one of the best estates in the neighbourhood, and inheriting a name that had more than once been distinguished in the annals of the country; he had been sent to Eton, from thence to college, and finally to make the grand tour of Europe. Mr. Dawson gained but little from these advantages. Left an orphan at an early age, he had never known control, and as he was naturally of a violent and morose temper, he had become so overbearing and dictatorial, that he was universally disliked; whilst continual indulgences in strong drink (a fault, alas! not uncommon in those days) had inflamed his passions, so that at times he lost all control over himself, and acted like a madman.

During his residence abroad, he had married a French lady, lovely, gentle and well born. Hers was a sad lot; transplanted from the sunny vineyards of the south of France, to that rude mansion on the Atlantic cliffs, she did not long survive the change: her youngest child was scarce a twelvemonth old, when she suddenly died. She had long been ailing and fading away, it is true; but her death, for all that, seemed too sudden to be accounted for. Strange things were whispered as to how there was an ugly bruise discovered on the pale corpse; but nothing ever came of the whispers, for Mr. Martin of Cross, who was in the house when she died, said she fell down in a fit and struck herself against the table; so the matter blew over, though a sort of vague impression remained on the minds of many, never to be effaced, that there had been unfair dealing in the business. The two children were given into the charge of Ages Mountjoy, the smuggler's widow, who had been Mrs. Dawson's chief companion (for she too was a stranger in the land), and spoke the French tongue purely and softly. For a while Mr. Dawson shut himself up, and withdrew from all society, save that of Mr. Martin.

After a time, he emerged a little from this seclusion, and would now and then attend the petty sessions, at Matton, eight miles off; and he soon became renowned as one of the most severe men on the bench: none escaped him; he seemed to rejoice in punishing guilty and innocent alike.

The principal entrance into Harscourt House was on one side, by a door which led directly into the hall, a fine room with a wide open chimney and carved chestnut roof. Within again was a smaller hall, connecting the two parts of the house, out of which the different passages and staircases led.

The great hall was the usual living room of Mr. Dawson and his companions. The two poor children on their return from the fishing expedition, with the dread of a beating before them for having long outstayed their usual time, had tried to make their entry unperceived, by a back door; but finding it locked, they were forced to enter by the hall, and found themselves at once face to face with "the Tyrant of Harscourt," as their father was commonly called.

A stout, coarse-looking man met them on the very threshold with an outburst of passion: the children, only too accustomed to such treatment, kept a respectful distance; words could not break bones, and as long as their father confined himself to words they did not particularly mind. It happened, however, unfortunately for them, that Mr. Dawson had been indulging in drink more than usual, and was just at that moment in one of those moods in which he was most dangerous.

"Why don't you speak, you obstinate jade? I'll teach you to hold your tongue when I want an answer!" he shouted at Grace, who had stood without uttering any reply to his repeated questions as to where she had been; and seizing a glass from the table, he hurled it at the child's head.[2]

Grace saw what was coming, and bent her head, while in a moment the glass was shivered to atoms against the wall behind her. The girl, overwrought, excited, frightened, burst into an hysterical laugh at her assailant's failure. He was by her in a moment, a heavy hunting-whip in his hand.

"Run, brother, run!" she cried, "or you'll be murdered as well as me."

The boy flew away, and his sister received all the weight of the whip across her face and shoulder, causing the wound on her forehead to burst out bleeding afresh.

"Dawson! I say, Dawson!" exclaimed a man, coming forward. "I'm not going to stand by, and see this child used in that way. Remember, we've had enough of that sort of thing here before now, Bed and supper are what she wants more than beating; let her go, I say!"

"I won't be interfered with in this house, I can tell you, Martin. Look after your own children, and I'll look after mine," blustered the drunken bully.

But Mr. Martin was not to be turned from his purpose, and he drew the brute back to the table; giving poor trembling Grace an opportunity of escape.

---

[2] Gratiana, a name of Italian origin, is a variant of Grace.

She was hardly past the door, when a new paroxysm of rage seized her father, and he attempted to follow her; but failing in his purpose, he consoled himself by ordering that the children should be kept on bread and water for a week, and not be allowed to stir outside the doors.

Gratiana had a spice of her father's temper in her: she was violent and wilful, but generous and devoted in her love. She would rather have had every bone in her body broken, than that Reginald should get into trouble; and she forgot her own heavier punishment in trying to comfort Reginald over his spare supper. For herself, she formed the great and heroic resolve of starving herself to death, rather than eat dry bread and be beaten; and long after Regie was in bed and asleep, she sat by the window looking out to sea, picturing to herself how horror-stricken her father would be when he found her stiff and stark from cold and hunger, and how he would repent and mourn over her body.

Then, again, she determined to run away; and imagined herself a very rich and grand lady (though how she was to become so was not very clear), driving in a fine coach with four horses along the streets of London, and passing a poor beggar-man, who was her father reduced by his wickedness to beg his bread; and how she said, "I am your daughter, whom you treated so cruelly, giving me dry bread, and beating me with a riding-whip."

She was too much absorbed in her meditations to notice that the door had been opened, and that some one stood near her.

"Miss Grace, are you not in bed yet?" asked the intruder.

"Oh! Damaris! how you frightened me!" cried the child, suddenly roused from her heroic dreams.

"Hush! don't make a noise; I know you don't like dry bread, so I managed to get you something else. Here, take it quick, or they'll miss me in the kitchen."

"And then they will beat you, as they beat me: you should not have come, Damaris. I don't mean to eat anything any more. I wish I was dead! oh, how I wish I hadn't got out of the Blower, and then he would have been sorry: the rocks ain't as hard as he is, nor the sea as fierce!"

"Hush, Tye! pray hush, or they will surely hear you. Good-night now," and Damaris, herself a child in years, strove to comfort her young mistress by a gentle caress, and then slid down the stairs again to her proper position among the pots and pans.

But the child still sat on the window-seat, looking out into the night, and weaving dreams for days yet to come; and a soft sighing noise went through the room (a sound the girl had so often heard that she feared it not), a sound as of a mother mourning over her child.

CHAPTER IV

HAY HARVEST

THE spring had ripened into summer, and in the sheltered valleys hay harvest had begun. The doors of Harscourt stood open, and the house was deserted by all, save the woman who rejoiced in the dignity of Mr. Dawson's housekeeper; an ugly, hard, ill-favoured woman, who bullied and tyrannized over all within her reach. "Hay harvest," as they call it in the west,—"haymaking time," as it is called elsewhere—was a busy, important affair at Harscourt. In those days furze and bracken flourished where now, with good management, you may see, rich hayfields and shocks of corn. Turnips and mangel were unknown; and on saving the hay depended the well-being of the live stock of the farm, to say nothing of the ten or dozen horses which the owner of Harscourt kept.[3]

For the last week or so there had been brewings of strong beer, and brewings of weak; and now there were extensive drinkings of both, along the slopes of Greenfield Glen, and in the meadows at the bottom of the Combe, where the grass was tall and high, and where still might be found a few remaining whitsundays, or sweet-scented narcissus, while in the hedges the larger periwinkle and columbine offered tempting treasures for a wild nosegay.

For several weeks after the fishing expedition to Merscombe, Reginald and Gratiana were kept strict prisoners. Mr. Dawson determined to take them in hand, and every day they were consigned to the care of a pedagogue, whose attainments were below the

---

[3] Mangel: mangelwurzel, a large, coarse, yellowish-coloured beet, cultivated as cattle feed.

average amount of knowledge that a lad would pick up in a second-class of a country national school at the present day; Grace seated at one end of the table, with a book before her, casting longing glances at the bright sun and fields, and Regie at the other, his hands and clothes stained and bespattered with ink, struggling hard to copy an immense flourishing D which headed the copy; "Due respect should be paid to superiors:" in Regie's scrawling hand, "Due respect should" was the extent that got into one line. The pedagogue, William Jenkins by name, was seated in a so-called easy chair, pipe in mouth and can in hand.

Such was the picture which might be seen in the garden room at Harscourt for some weeks. Wondrous little was the reading, and next to nothing the arithmetic, the juveniles acquired: they lost more than they gained, for they were deprived of the free air and rambles they loved so well, to say nothing of never seeing Edward. At such times as the pedagogue was not with them, they were vigilantly watched by the dragon before mentioned, who made nothing of turning the key on them for hours at a time. Many a pathetic appeal did the poor little prisoners make to their father in his sober moments, but in vain: he was determined they should learn, and not go gallivanting about the country like a couple of gipsies.

"But heaven soon granted what their sire denied."

The Harscourt ale was proverbially good; Mr. Jenkins, like all the world, thought so: he liked ale decidedly, and was apt to be thirsty. Mr. Jenkins did not admire the housekeeper, but he admired what she had in her keeping; so he made love to the lady for what she could bestow on him, and many was the can of prime October that he imbibed in the garden room at Harscourt. Now it so chanced one day that the learned and painstaking tutor having taken a little drop more than usual—not only of ale, but also of a long-necked, broad-bottomed bottle, for which the housekeeper had a peculiar affection—he became slightly stupid, and his legs refused to do the work usually required of legs. It happened that very day, some mischievous sprite put it into the mind of Mr. Dawson to visit the garden room, and see how the children progressed: not that he was any great judge in such matters, but being in want of someone to torment, he thought he might just as well turn his attention to the children. He could not have chosen a worse time for his visit; Jenkins was decidedly drunk; and however much Mr. Dawson liked to get drunk himself, he did not choose any dependant of his to follow in his footsteps

"What are you about, sir?" shouted the master of Harscourt, at the incapable pedagogue.

"Hold your tongue, sir, and learn your lessons," was the reply.

"Do you know to whom you are speaking, you drunken dog?" roared Mr. Dawson.

"Learn your lesson, and don't scream at me, sir," rejoined the pedagogue. "Due respect should be paid to superiors."

"Superiors, indeed!" shouted the frantic employer. "I'll teach you what's meant by superiors!" and without much ado, he ejected the unfortunate tutor headforemost out of Harscourt, and then returned to cuff and bully the children, as if they had been to blame for Jenkins's drunkenness.

But the hay harvest came, when every one was too busy to look after the two young ones, and so they were free once more.

Cautiously they used their liberty, for they knew what it was to be deprived of it, and contented themselves with little rambles along the pleasant downs, where now the pink thrift and many-tinted ladies'-fingers took the place of the tiny spring squill or mermaid's blue-bells; these would, as the summer advanced, be succeeded by the pale sea-lavender, the sweet-scented ladies'-tresses, and the dwarf centauries. Grace, who was the more fearless of the two, would crawl on her hands and knees to the edge of the most precipitous part of the cliff, and, dropping a stone over, send the wild sea birds screaming from the nest they had built in the little chinks and crannies of the rock; making the black cormorant, who had been standing on some jagged rock in the sea, take wing, and sail past with his long neck outstretched, looking like some messenger from a darker world.

But one bright summer morning, when all the folks were off to the hayfield, Grace incited her brother to undertake another fishing trip.

"We can go down through the fields to the Combe, Regie, and then on to the stream; no one will miss us; and perhaps we shall see Edward and mother Agnes."

Merrily they ran races through the grass fields till they reached Combe Wood, where, winding round the great white rock, they struck into a little track which led down the steep hill-sides to the meadows below, through which meandered a bright sparkling stream.

The scene was a busy one: the mowers in one place mowing down the long thick grass in rows; in another, troops of women and girls tossing it hither and thither, with many a joke and jest; and yonder the low truck carts without wheels waiting to cart it to the mow-yard when ready.

"Come, Regie, come along," cried Tye, impatiently.

"It is very peasant here, sister; let us stay."

"Oh, no! I do so want to go farther down! Do come, Regie!"

The boy cast a lingering look at the haymakers, and followed his sister, who sped on, brushing by the tall king fern and the scratching brambles with equal rapidity, till they reached a little hamlet, just where the brook, whose course they had been following, joined a good-sized stream that had its source in the moors above, flowing down a picturesque valley some three miles long, bordered on either side with deep woods. Where the two streams joined, and the woods ceased, stood a picturesque mill, with its usual accompaniments, a water lane, an aged orchard, and some large yew-trees. The miller came out, and greeted the children kindly as they passed along. The women pitied them for their lone and loveless life, and the men fancied them for their good looks, and the courage they knew them to possess. Below the mill the hills arose bare and bleak, and continued so to the sea, about three parts of a mile distant, while in the bottom lay rich water meadows, surrounded by loose stone walls.

"Ain't you going to grope, Gratiana?"[4]

"Yes; but not here: lower down will be better:" and on flew Tye almost as fleetly as the goats that bounded out of her way.

"Where are you going, Tye?" cried the lad, as his sister continued her headlong course.

"To the cottage, to be sure; where else did you suppose I meant to go?"

"But father said he would break every bone in your body, if you went with Edward again."

"I don't care; I'm going there: you may go back if you like."

"Pause awhile, Miss Tye; remember, 'Don't Care' came to a bad end."

But Tye heard no warning voice, and in a few minutes she was in the cottage with her arms round Agnes Mountjoy's neck.

"Dear child," said the woman, as she took off Gratiana's hood,

---

[4] Grope: to catch with the hands, to tickle trout.

and stroked back her hair, "I am so very glad to see you. You mustn't forget mother Agnes ever, will you?"

"Oh, no, mother dear; but it's such a long time since we have been here—and where is Edward?"

"I don't know, darling; he has been out all morning."

"Fishing?"

"I don't know; I think not," answered the woman, with a trembling voice, as she turned from her visitor to do some little housekeeping business.

She was a striking-looking person, the mistress of that little cottage; tall, above the usual height of woman, every limb was beautifully moulded and proportioned; her hands, in spite of her daily labours, were small and white; her face a perfect oval, her features small, the complexion like a lily. No one could help asking, as they looked on her, how came she in that poor cottage? If she had been a princess, you would have said, "Look how good blood shows."

"Mother, are you angry with me?" inquired Tye, going up to Agnes, whose silence rather surprised her.

"Angry, dearest! angry with you! no. But, Tye, listen to me." And Agnes seated herself, and drew the child close to her. "Edward is going away—is going to leave me. When he is gone, I shall have only you. Don't forget me, Tye, when I'm alone."

The child's great brown eyes filled with tears and her bosom heaved.

"Where is he going, mother Agnes?" she inquired, in a low voice.

"He is going to sea."

"To sea! Ah! that comes of looking at the waves so and watching the ships! Regie will go next, I suppose. But it's very cruel of Edward—very!"

"Hush, Tye, here he comes."

As she spoke Edward and Regie entered, followed by the sailor Tunny.

"Is it possible, Edward, you are going to sea?" cried Grace, rushing up to the lad as he came in, the tears on her cheeks.

"Yes, Tye," answered the boy, stoutly.

"To be sure, Miss Grace," interrupted Tunny. "What else can a lad do? Isn't it better to be pacing the planks of as nice and trim a vessel as you'll find in the four seas, than to be setting potatoes or reaping corn?"

"No!" cried Grace passionately, "it isn't half so good! We were all so happy! Why should you come and slock Edward away?"[5]

"I slock him away? Why, what should make you say I did it? he goes of his own free will, to be sure."

"It is you, I say; it is all your doing!" cried Grace, vehemently, "Didn't I hear that——"

Tunny scowled at her, and held up his finger, and Edward gave her a warning glance. She was silent in a moment.

"You might have spared me my son, Tunny; I have but him. Ain't there others as likely lads in the country, and better, too?"

"Now, Mistress Mountjoy, you don't believe that. You know you think your boy the best and handsomest in all the country round; and so do I, and that's just why I want him."

"If he had fallen into any hands but yours, I wouldn't have minded it half as much."

"But it's a fine business, is seafaring," rejoined the man, "and this is a fine opening for the lad: it isn't every day he could get such a berth as he will have on board the *Seamew*. Why, in a few years

[5] Slock: lure, entice, tempt (to wrong).

he will be back with lots of money, and be able to live in a grand house like Harscourt."

"It's no good having a grand house if you ain't happy," said Grace; "and I'm sure the cottage, and the garden, and the field, and the goats, are much better than Harscourt."

"That's what you think now, young lady, but you'll tell a different tale one of these days: a few years and you'll turn your back on your friend Edward as quick as anybody, if he ain't rich."

Edward looked at his little friend, and his lip quivered. The child's arms were round his neck in a minute.

"Never, Edward, never: Tye will never turn her back on you. You are her own dear, best friend, and if she were the greatest lady in the land to-morrow, she would say Edward is my friend always."

Two great tears dropped from the boy's eyes, and mingled with little Tye's.

"Don't forget me when I'm away, Tye, and be kind to my mother—promise, Tye."

The child promised.

In less than a week Edward was on the wide sea, and the widow was alone in her cottage.

CHAPTER V

REGINALD'S NEW ERA

TIME flew on, and Reginald grew a tall, good-looking lad, but with an uncommonly small amount of learning; being wholly ignorant of the mysteries of Latin and Greek, and having but faint ideas on the important subjects of spelling and summing: he could stammer through a page and scrawl his name, but there his knowledge ended. And there it would have ended for the term of his natural life, had not Fate willed it otherwise; so she commenced operations, as most operations in Harscourt house usually commenced, namely, by a quarrel.

Everything at Harscourt either began or ended in a "row;" sometimes it both began and ended in that pleasant manner.

Grace was quick in her temper, like her father, and soon excited. Reginald was not so quickly moved: he was lazy, and did not like the annoyance and risks of a quarrel, and avoided it when he could; but yet there was the family temper at the bottom, and when deeply stirred he was capable of great violence. He hated to be interfered with, and there was generally an explosion after any unwonted interference on his father's part. In fact, both the young Dawsons were sorely tried, and had long discovered that half the scoldings they got were unjust; for while real faults passed unobserved, the merest nothings would raise most awful storms if Mr. Dawson's temper happened to be ruffled.

Now it chanced one day that Master Regie—as many other young lads, both before his time and since, have done—got a tremendous fall, and a ducking into the bargain; and returning home with a very bloody face and extremely wet clothes, as fate would have it, he met his father and two or three gentlemen on horseback, face to face. Mr. Dawson troubled himself little about his children's appearance in general, not caring how dirty or shabby they looked; but as his companions caught sight of Regie, they began to commiserate the poor boy, and one took a shilling out of his purse and tossed it to him. Mr. Dawson's rage knew no bounds, and he struck the boy across his shoulder with his whip.

"Hold hard there, I say!" cried one of his companions. "What business on earth have you to whip the poor little fellow like that?"

"I'll do what I like to my own son, and I'd like to see the man that could prevent me!"

"Your own son! why I took him for a beggar lad. Why on earth don't you clothe him like a gentleman and send him to school?"

Mr. Dawson had his own reasons for not quarrelling with his friends; and, notwithstanding his passion, he managed to command himself. Reginald, limping home, poured the tale of his wrongs into Tye's ears; at which she ranted, and raved, and vowed vengeance, and strutted up and down the room, exclaiming against the miseries and injustice to which they were subject.

A new era in Reginald's life was to date its commencement from that day. The hint about school was not thrown away on Mr. Dawson: he cared little whether the boy learnt or not, but it was a new species of torment—a new punishment; and before he met his son again, he had resolved to send him to the grammar school at Torford.

Reginald received the announcement very philosophically; he didn't care to learn; but then there would be lots of boys to play with (he had been rather dull since Edward went to sea), and it was something new; so, though he shed a few tears at the idea of parting with his sister and the dogs, on the whole he considered it a rather good move than otherwise. Grace, however, was in bitter trouble at losing him, but she kept her sorrow in her own heart; she had no one to share it. Edward gone, and now Regie: what should she do?

Her heart was like to burst when she saw her brother, mounted on the grey pony that was their common property, disappear along the road to Torford (the metropolis of the West, about twenty miles off): she stood and watched the spot where she had last seen him, long after he was out of sight, and then, bursting into a violent fit of crying, set off full speed to mother Agnes to be comforted. The wild girl was ever welcome at the cottage in Combe, and while there, her fierceness and violence seemed to be quenched; she would sit for hours at the feet of that pale, beautiful woman, learning little tasks that she would set her, and which were always readily performed, or listening to tales of imagination or romances of real life, in relating which Agnes excelled. They had few books, but in days long passed the sailor's widow had been highly educated, and had read much; and being possessed of a remarkable memory, Grace got the benefit of her knowledge. There was a strong tinge of superstition in Agnes' mind, and this she communicated to the girl; but it was a fanciful ideal superstition in many respects, and rendered the mind poetical without materially injuring it.

Meanwhile Reginald rode on, well pleased, over a bleak barren country; to the right a wild moory, boggy region, with the sluggish Tor winding in and out among the dark heather or tall rushes like a gigantic serpent; while on the left the broad blue bay of Torford stretched for miles, with its projecting headlands, and miles and miles of sandhills, and the roaring, surging bar where the Tor emptied itself into the sea.[6] In all that twenty miles they did not pass twenty

[6] Bar: a build up of sand where a river or harbour meets the open sea.

houses; their halting-place being at a lone wayside inn, a rather noted place in those days as a resting-place for smugglers.

Reginald's great sleepy eyes lit up with pleasure as from the top of the last hill they came in sight of Torford, with its old irregular bridge and broad stream, its numberless vessels and boats, its quaint houses on either side of the river, which to the left, towards the sea, wound along past pleasant scenes, with many a cosy home dotted about here and there. As their horses' hoofs clattered over the pavement, the people came out at their doors to look at them, and Regie felt himself a person of no small importance. They rode down the precipitous High Street, along the quay, crowded by sailors and porters busily lading and unlading the vessels that lay alongside, and, turning up a broad paved street with substantial-looking houses on either hand, stopped before the most respectable of all those respectable habitations—at least, if respectability consists in size, for it was twice as large as it neighbours. Mr. Dawson and his son dismounted, and were shown into a large parlour, on one side of the entrance. You descended a step into the room, which was panelled, with three windows looking towards the street. Round the room hung pictures, indifferently executed, of ships, with their names painted in large letters in the corner; and over the high carved chimney-piece was a very large one containing the portraits of a whole fleet of merchantmen, while from a house as high as St. Paul's the owner was represented as contemplating them, with a pipe in his mouth and a glass by his side.

"Law! Mr. Dawson, is that you?" exclaimed a round buxom ball of a woman, who burst open the door in no gentle manner, and tramped, or rather waddled, across the room with so heavy a tread, that the poor old boards sank and creaked again. "And this is your son. Bless his pretty face! The very image of his mother, poor dear!"

and she lifted her eyes to the ceiling, and shook her head. "But do, Mr. Dawson, sit down; let me take your hat and whip;" and she bustled about, calling to Jenny to bring some glasses, and tell Master William to come there that instant minute, for Mr. Dawson and his son were come. Then puffing and wheezing, she took her seat by the table, resting one plump elbow on the shining mahogany table that stood in the centre of the room, and commenced a regular fire of questions against her visitor; much to his disgust, for he did not like talking, especially to women: he shifted about from chair to chair, and looked at the pictures, and out of the window, returning, when required to speak, a vert curt answer.

But his hostess went on, not the least observing that he was rude, or that she was boring him, till at last, his patience thoroughly exhausted, he inquired roughly when Mr. Fowler wold be in.

"It's just dinner-time," quoth Mrs. Fowler, "and he is sure to be in then: trust Jack Fowler for not letting his dinner get cold. He has been busy this morning; one of his vessels has come in with a valuable cargo, and he is down at the Quay seeing after it."

As she finished speaking, the street door flew open, and a loud voice inquired if dinner was ready.

"There he is!" cried the stout lady, rising with difficulty; "I told you he wouldn't forget his dinner in a hurry;" and off she went to meet her lord and master.

In a few seconds Captain Fowler entered the room. He was a very large, burly man, almost as fat as his wife, but tall in proportion. He was a pleasant-looking person; his manners were frank and hearty, and he greeted his visitor with honest cordiality.

In early life he had risen to the command of a trading vessel, and by hook or by crook had amassed money, till he was now the owner of the fleet portrayed above the mantel-shelf, and one of the wealthiest merchants in Torford. He was the kindliest, most indulgent husband and father, as might clearly be seen in the joyous way he was received by three or four bouncing girls who rushed to welcome him as he entered the dining parlour, and the way he joked his wife as she stumbled over the step into the room. "Bless me," she cried, "I always forget that step:" which was certainly true, as Mrs. Fowler had never failed to stumble over it on an average six times a day, for the last ten years past, yet still remained forgetful of it.

"Well, Dawson, how are you?" shouted the burly captain, as he nearly dislocated the stranger's wrist; "so you are going to put your boy to school, and the missus here is to take care of him. She'll do that, trust her; there isn't a kinder soul within the four seas than she is, though she be a little fat."

The captain roared at his own wit, and his wife cried, "Lor, Captain Jack, how you do talk!"

"He'll have a capital friend in our William," continued the captain; "he is a strong lad, and doesn't stand any nonsense, so he'll see the lad isn't used too ill, just at first; but sooner or later, my boy, you must fight your own battles, and show if you have any pluck in you, otherwise you will never do at school, and never get on as a man; a man can't get on now-a-days, nor any other days that ever I heard of, if he hasn't pluck. But come along, I'm starving. Hey, Will, are you there? here's young Dawson; mind you take care of him."

And for the first time, Reginald met the lad who, when grown a man, was to influence his life for weal or woe. He was two years older than Reginald, being just fifteen, a tall, sturdy-built fellow, very like his father, but with a cunning, sly expression deeply imprinted on his face.

There is one other member of the family deserving peculiar

notice: a spiritual-looking little child, at this time about five years old, younger by many years than her elder sisters, and cast in a totally different mould from them. Small of limb, and light as a fairy, she seemed as if she was a being from another sphere. She was the pet and darling of all. The captain couldn't drink his after-dinner glass, if Lily did not drop in the sugar; nobody found "the missis' keys" so quickly, or unravelled the skein which the fat hands of Miss Sally had tangled into a perfect Penelope's web, or smoothed the ruffled temper of brother William, so well as Lily. She was ever cheerful, flitting up and down the old oak staircase, and making the panelled room resound with her clear warbling voice.

This was the family into which Reginald was introduced: a striking contrast to his own cheerless home.

On the morrow Mr. Dawson departed, and left Reginald to be introduced as best he might to his school-life. At this portion of his existence little is recorded in the family archives of the house of Harscourt: for being, as we have seen, an indifferent scribe, he did not often indulge in letter writing; and all the authentic information that can be derived are tales of certain battles in which he always won, and of which he informed Tye, who no doubt recorded them in her own memory, as other sisters remember their brothers's schoolday feats.

CHAPTER VI
A CHILD OF SONG

THE back of Mr. Fowler's house was more pleasant and cheerful looking than the front. The entrance hall—to speak in modern phraseology—was not six foot wide; with the eating parlour on one hand, and the best parlour on the other. But passing the entrances into these two rooms, you came to a wide light hall, with a glass door opening into the garden, and a broad oak staircase, with a large window about half-way up looking across the salt marshes down the river. Opposite the staircase was a door leading into the kitchen and back premises of the house. The garden was old-fashioned, with tiny beds edged with thick box borders, while within the evergreen frame, fairy rose-de-mouse stocks, gillyflowers, and the sweet-scented narcissus flourished. The back of the house was covered with honeysuckles and roses, among which blazed the scarce scarlet and yellow Austrian briar.

But the fairest flower in all the garden was the fairy Lily that stepped so lightly over the gravel, and went kissing the flowers as they turned their beauties towards her.

"They are my out-of-doors sisters," she would say, as she passed from bed to bed, pulling up an intruding weed here, propping a drooping flower there; making a pleasant murmuring like the bees singing in the flower-bells. But when the weather was cold and stormy, so that the flowers drooped, and perished under the cold blast; or when the sun shone dazzling and hot, making the earth quake and shiver from his beams; then she took her place on the old oak staircase, singing till the panelled walls echoed again,—singing of pleasant breezes and murmuring streams, of odorous flowers and happy birds flitting among them, till the heron, sailing by in melancholy majesty, seemed as if he paused on his wing to listen; and one might fancy that the seagulls called to her to come and sing them her joyous song.

But most of all, she loved the time when the straight, heavy summer rain dropped echoing on the thirsty ground, that sent pleasant, refreshing odour up to heaven as its thanks, and the flowers, weary and worn like mourning children, raised their heads as if thanking their Father for his mercy. Then the blackbirds and the thrushes came and sat upon the dripping shrubs, and sang such songs that the child's heart swelled within her: she longed to interpret their magic notes, and tears gathered in her eyes, as the mist rises from the sand after summer rain. Oh, but she loved the birds! Oh, but she loved the flowers! The quiet gurgling of the river, the dancing, merry streamlet, the rushing of the mighty ocean, the clear blue of the summer sky! She loved them, she dreamed about them till her life became one long song of joy—one long, deep feeling of blessedness and music!

And those around her felt and knew that she was different, yet their greatest treasure. But she knew no difference, saw not that she was cast in a different mould, and felt no pride that she was not as others, but went on her way singing the wild songs the birds taught her, on the old oak staircase.

She sat one day in her usual seat on the top stair by the window, her face turned toward the sky, her work lying neglected on her lap, while she sang softly to herself. Reginald sat at the bottom of the stairs leaning against the banisters, with his book on the step above him making believe to learn his lesson, but in reality listening to and looking at Lily.

"I wish I could sing as you do, Lily," said the boy at last.

"Ah! Regie, you would never sing the same song as I do; you don't love the birds and the flowers."

"I love the seagulls, Lily."

"Ah! but they are wild ocean birds, not gentle home birds."

"They are wiser than your thrushes and blackbirds; they don't stay at home in leafless hedges, but go sailing over the blue sea. But sing on, Lily, I like your music."

"I cannot sing when I am bidden, Regie—it must come of itself—I cannot make it come," and the child sighed, and lifting up her neglected work, plied her needle busily for some minutes in silence.

"Don't you ever want to go away from this place—to change, Lily?"

"Change my home! Go away from Torford? Oh, no, Regie; why should I wish that?"

"I don't know why: only I am always longing—I don't want to go from here, at least, not altogether; but I should like to see some of the beautiful places one hears of over the sea."

"Oh, I could never go!"

"You don't love the sea, Lily?"

"No! no! no! the sea makes people false and cruel—I see it every day."

"Your father is not cruel, Lily, yet he was a sailor once."

"Oh, he is different," said the child, turning her soft blue eyes upon the boy: "he is not cruel, he is not false; but all are not like him!" and the tears gathered in the forget-me-not eyes of Lily, as she thought of one she loved so much as her father.

"I mean to be a sailor, Lily, one of these days," said the boy stoutly, after a pause, looking up to the child; "and I won't be false and cruel, never."

"Not a sailor, Regie! please not," and the tears that had gathered in the blue eyes fell like the heavy summer rain that was falling outside.

"I must be a sailor, Lily; I can't help it: what else could I be? I don't like riding and farming, and I couldn't live at home with my father: I must be a sailor, Lily, indeed I must."

"Be a soldier, Regie, a soldier; that would be so much better," cried the child, as if a sudden hope had flashed over her heart; and she descended the stairs, and seating herself just above the boy, put her arm round his neck, and looked imploringly in his face.

"No, Lily, that won't do: I must—I will be a sailor!" replied the lad with unwonted energy.

"Then you will join a king's ship, Regie?"

"No! Just think, Lily, how long Captain Clive has had to wait before he got a ship of his own: even now he has to obey orders; and some day she will not be his any longer, and another man will have her. I couldn't bear that, Lily: my ship shall be my very own, and I will make her sail where I will, and obey me in everything; and she shall take me to the lands where the orange grows, and the myrtles are trees, not bushes; and then, Lily, you shall come too, and Tye, and I shall have Edward to help me to manage my ship, and we will sail away, far away." Here the boy laid his head down on Lily's knee, and happy tears swelled beneath his drooping lashes at the delights he dreamed of.

The tears fell down the fair cheeks of Lily; but they were tears of sorrow: she saw that some day she should lose her friend and companion, and again sit alone on the old staircase. Since the day that Reginald had first been brought to that house by his father, now near four years, those two had been stanch friends and loving companions; more especially during the last two years, during which time young Fowler had been to sea.

But by degrees, Reginald came to consider Lily rather beneath him; to look upon her as a child, fancying himself a man, and to seek other society than hers—though he remained gentle and affectionate to her. Lily had felt this weaning process, and had felt it deeply; for he was her hero of romance; he seemed a handsome courtly gentleman, boy as he was, among the rough boisterous men she most commonly saw. There was an extreme loving gentleness in his manner, a winning softness in his voice, a pleasant lazy fun about his large dark eyes, that made him a universal favourite among women; and to Lily who loved all things beautiful, his wonderful good looks acted like a spell.

Reginald had his full share of natural ability, and with a little judicious training he might have made a figure in the world; but the position in which he had been placed at Torford called forth none of his energies, stimulated him to no exertion. His education, if the little bad Latin he picked up at Torford grammar-school could be so designated, had but slightly raised his standard of ideas; whilst the companions he had had, and the friendships he had formed, all tended to drag him down from the rank in life in which he had been born. Properly looked after and cared for, he might have taken his stand, both as regarded wealth and birth, with the rulers of the land; but without education, and cast among associates far below him, how could it happen otherwise than that he should sink to their level and think as they thought?

The little singing child had been his best, his most purifying friend; for she was so pure and simple herself, that those who were much with her could hardly fail to catch a little of her spirit. Many a schoolboy scrape had she helped him out of, more than one bad habit had her quiet entreaties broken, and gradually Reginald became almost as quiet and gentle as herself, when with her.

But the love of adventure was strong within him, and everything and everybody seemed to tempt him to try his luck upon the sea.

Those were stirring, active times; folks had not time to sleep. There were commotions at home and a strong enemy not far off: men were sailors or soldiers of necessity. The sailors of the seaport towns, if they escaped the press-gang, were obliged to enrol themselves in a corps to defend their immediate neighbourhood; this corps had a commanding or inspecting officer, who took charge of a certain district, and who was generally a captain in the navy. More than one on our old navy list could trace his rise from commanding some little coaster, to the favour of his commanding officer, who kept his eyes about him, and when he saw a clever sailor, recommended him for promotion. Those were days when men rose to command from before the mast.

Even now one hears tales of those times that seem scarcely credible in these apparently more secure days: of estates being sold for a mere song, because the French were coming, and it was as well to get something for them as nothing; of women and children escaping inland in the dead of night because the enemy had landed; of cannon pointed to command entrances to the harbours; of a troop of volunteers destroying a luckless French vessel and her crew which had stranded accidentally, believing that she formed part of an invading force. In those days, too, seaports now nearly deserted sent out many a gallant ship, built in the shipyards of the town by men of the town—the very sails and cordage made in the town—so that the ships seemed part and parcel of the people, so many had had a hand in them.

The shipyard at Torford was a favourite lounge of young Dawson's. He delighted to watch the vessels as they slowly grew beneath the hands of their makers: first the keel, then the ghostlike ribs, then great planks bent and bowed to the will of the workmen, then the broad even deck; and at last, the giant put in motion and launched into the deep, mid the shouts of men who cheered her on in her pride!

After awhile her appearance changes: no longer a great log on the waters; towering poles rise from her deck, and countless ropes and snowy canvas; and then she sails out into the wide sea!

The boy had a great taste for carpentering; not displayed as boys generally display that taste, in making rabbit-hutches, &c., but by really learning what he could as he watched the men at work, or coaxed them to let him try his hand.

Of how much use this boyish fancy afterwards proved, will be seen as the story advances.

CHAPTER VII
THE VICAR OF CARDEN

WHILE Reginald was a schoolboy at Torford, Edward Mountjoy was pursuing the calling he had chosen, under the superintendence of the man Tunny. Mother Agnes he seldom saw, for his time was fully employed; and the head-quarters of the vessel to which he belonged were at some distance from Harscourt—at the quaint, secluded fishing town of Carden, which has since become a much-frequented watering-place in consequence of the extreme beauty of its situation. But in the days of which we are writing it consisted only of a cluster of old-fashioned houses round the picturesque harbour, and a straggling street nearly a mile in length, extending along the slope of a hill and terminating in a second cluster of houses nestling at the foot of a steep acclivity, on which stood the fine old parish church.

The people were a wild race, like their neighbours, employed in shipbuilding or trading, and forming a little community among themselves almost entirely isolated from the rest of the country round; for there were few roads, and those of the very worst description, leading up and down such tremendous hills as to be almost impassable for wheels; the inland traffic being carried on by means of pack-horses.

Tunny, captain of the *Seamew*, and those with whom Edward Mountjoy was thrown, were some of the very roughest set in Carden; and the lad shrank as much as he could from their company while on shore; but at sea no sailor could be more active and energetic, and praise was lavished on him. He was a great favourite with all those with whom he was brought in contact, and the old hands, as they watched his daring deeds and feats of agility, pointed him out as a lad likely to distinguish himself as a seaman.

But no pressing or compulsion would induce him to join in the orgies—scenes of debauchery and drunkenness—in which his companions indulged while on shore: they were utterly distasteful to him; and many a night he spent wandering about the cliffs, or keeping his solitary watch on board his vessel, rather than join in the revels that were held in the numerous houses of entertainment near the harbour.

Often a long spell of westerly wind would prevent the *Seamew* from getting out of the landlocked harbour for weeks together, and then the lad would betake himself to one or other of the many little streams in the neighbourhood, and pass away his day in luring from their haunts the speckled trout with which every brook abounds.

It was on one of these expeditions that he met a lad with whom he soon struck up a friendship.

He was seated beneath some broad-spreading oaks that clothed a rocky knoll overhanging a bubbling, sparkling stream, when the bushes were hastily put aside, and a tall awkward-looking youth about his own age pushed through them. He evidently had not expected to meet with any one in that secluded spot, for he started, and let a book fall close to Edward's feet.

Edward picked up the book, and handed it to him, saying, "I am afraid I alarmed you; but for goodness' sake don't look so scared: if you have a fancy for this pretty nook, which is a great favourite of mine, come and sit down a bit, and tell us who you are; for to my knowledge I never saw you before."

"Nor I you," was the reply. "I suppose you belong to one of the vessels in the harbour, judging by your dress; and perhaps, as a stranger, you are not aware that Mr. Law, to whom this ground belongs, does not allow people to fish here."

Edward lifted his eyebrows, and replied with a merry laugh, "I'm not 'people,' and I don't think Mr. Law, or any one else, would hinder a poor chap like me amusing himself a bit; but as it happens, I sail in one of Mr. Law's vessels, and in all likelihood Mr. Law will condescend to eat some of my fish; so never trouble about that, but tell us who and what you are, for you don't talk like a Carden chap."

"Nor you either," was the rejoinder, as the new-comer seated himself on the bank beside Edward.

"Oh, no! I'm a stranger," replied Edward; "but you—are you a stranger too?"

"My name is Frank Dawson," said his companion, in a haughty tone.

"Dawson! that's queer," returned Edward, looking up at him, curiously. "Are you any relation of the Dawsons of Harscourt, or are you only of the same name?"

"We are nearly related," was the reply in the same haughty voice; "but how do you know anything of them?"

"Oh! I know them well enough," said Edward, amused at the idea of fancied superiority which he detected in his companion's tone. "We were brought up together, and my mother is the only mother the young ones have ever known."

"Does your father live near Harscourt?" inquired Frank Dawson.

"I have no father," replied Edward, colouring up; "he was drowned."

There was something so sad in the tone in which he mentioned the father whom he had never known, that young Dawson felt that he had struck a chord which he had no right to touch, and he apologized in a confused manner for his thoughtless question.

"Never mind, lad," replied Edward, in a moment himself again; "you couldn't guess he was gone. But don't think he was a gentleman, or a rich man like Mr. Dawson of Harscourt: nothing of the kind; they say he was captain of a privateer, or whatever you choose to call her, and his ship, the *Ocean Wave*, was the most beautiful schooner ever seen in the Channel."

Whether Frank Dawson was much edified at hearing the parentage of his new acquaintance, we cannot say; but he made no comment, merely adding, after a moment's pause, "And my father is vicar of Carden."

"I've seen him two or three times," said Edward, "and knew his name; but somehow I never heard he had anything to do with the people at Harscourt; though when you said you were called Dawson, I couldn't help fancying you must be some relation; there's such a look of Grace in you every now and then."

And so in truth there was, though it was the likeness of an ugly to a handsome person. Frank Dawson became interested at the mention of his cousins, whom he had never seen, and the two lads chatted on till the lengthening shadows warned them that it was time to turn homeward.

The contrast between the two, as they walked along side by side was very striking. Edward Mountjoy was strongly but lightly built, with a strikingly graceful carriage, and remarkably handsome face: in fact, quite a model of a noble-looking lad. Frank Dawson, on the contrary, was lanky and awkward, with long, ungainly limbs and shuffling gait, while his face was only redeemed from positive ugliness by a broad open forehead, and large, brilliant grey eyes; but withal there was a something about him which no one could be long in his company without feeling: it was a force and power such as few possess—the force and power of a really commanding intellect.

By the time the two lads reached the vicarage, which stood at the very entrance of Carden, they were as intimate as if they had known each other for years, and Edward, without ceremony, accepted the invitation of his new friend to come in with him and see his father.

Carden vicarage in those days was a ruinous, dilapidated place, hardly fit for human habitation, certainly not for the residence of a gentleman and a scholar, such as Mr. Dawson; but he had not been very fortunate in life, and he was glad to accept the tumble-down house and seventy pounds a year in the out-of-the-way town of Carden, where, if he lived poorly, no one would notice it, and where he could find leisure for his beloved studies.

He had another inducement, too, when he accepted the little vicarage: it enabled him to offer a home to the simple-minded country-girl who had managed to captivate the scholar's heart; but she was dead and gone now, and a troop of uncared-for and undisciplined children rendered the ruinous vicarage still more uncomfortable and uninviting. One room the worthy vicar kept for himself and his books, but the rest of the house and premises were given over to utter confusion and disorder. Frank Dawson, who inherited his father's love of books, was fain to betake himself to the cliffs and woods to obtain that quiet which all true scholars love, and thus he and Mountjoy had chanced to stumble on one another.

As the two lads paused at the humble gate which led into the orchard that separated the vicarage from the lane, a little bright-eyed girl of some six years old sprang out with a merry welcome to young Dawson.

"Oh, Frank, where have you been this long while? Mala is so angry; she has put away all the dinner, and declares you shan't have one bit! unkind Mala! Ocean Margaret is very angry!"

"Never mind, little mermaid," replied the lad, smiling and lifting the little creature in his arms. "Here, let me introduce you to a new acquaintance of mine: I found him in the wood, Ocean Margaret, as I found you on the shore."

"In the ocean, Frank! in the ocean: you should always speak the exact truth. You know," she continued, turning to Mountjoy, "that he saved me from being drowned when I was quite a little baby. I was washed off a wreck, and every one was drowned but me, and so I am called Ocean Margaret, and I am Frank's darling. But see, Mala is coming; and she is so angry with me, because I stole the key of the larder. Put me down, Frank, and let me run."

The irate serving-made made an attempt to catch the tiny thief; but she was off like a shot, and high above her pursuer's head, on the roof of the tithe barn which stretched away on one side of the house, before Mala had a chance to overtake her.

The two lads stood laughing heartily at the scene, while Mr. Dawson, roused from his studies by the noise and the angry tones of Mala, emerged from his retreat and stood in the porch, as much amused as any one at the position of Ocean Margaret and the discomfiture of Mala

"Leave the poor child alone, Mala; you mustn't vex her: remember she had no one to care for her—you must really be gentle."

"No one to care for her, indeed! as if there isn't more fuss made about that strange child than all your ten real children. It's a sin and a shame: and now she has been and stolen my key. Ah! when I catch her, won't I pay her off, that's all!" and Mala retreated, grumbling at the little creature, whom no one loved more truly than she did.

"You must come and speak to my father," said Frank, as he held open the gate; "he will be pleased to see any one that knows

Harscourt. He used to be there a good deal as a boy; and you know, he is the next heir."

The vicar bore a striking resemblance to Reginald: he had the same large lazy eyes and indolent manner, so different from Grace's quick, active movement. He had been a very handsome man, but years and cares had changed him much. His hair was grey and much off his forehead, while his sedentary life and inactive habits had given him a stooping, slouching gait, not unlike his son's. His dress was untidy and shabby, but about him still clung the air of a polished gentleman.

He greeted Mountjoy with as much politeness as if he had been a prince, instead of the simple sailor his dress bespoke him; and as soon as he knew that the stranger knew Harscourt and the young Dawsons, he pressed him warmly to come in at once, and, as he expressed it, "have a talk over the dear old place."

From that day forward, Mountjoy always found a place of refuge at the vicarage; many a book was entrusted to him, and many an hour on shipboard did he wile away with treasures from the poor vicar's beloved library.

Mother Agnes had taught her son a great deal more than most lads in those days ever learnt, and Mountjoy, without having any particular turn for literature, was thankful for some employment, and had sense enough to wish to improve.

To Frank Dawson the acquaintance was of still greater value. It took him away from his books, and taught him that there were other pursuits in the world besides reading. He became more manly and less awkward; he learned to shoot, and swim, and row; and more than once, when Mountjoy went for a visit to the cottage in the Combe, Frank Dawson was his companion; and there he learnt to know his cousins, whose acquaintance he would in all probability never have made, but for his chance meeting with the sailor lad.

Grace was to him the impersonation of all that was lovely and charming, and she, in return, thought him very wise and good; but while she formed the thread of romance which ran through his uneventful life—the being who was to exert a powerful influence on his destiny—he was nothing to her but "poor cousin Frank;" Mountjoy being the idol at whose shrine, child as she was, she worshipped.

The doors of Harscourt were never opened to Frank Dawson; a bitter feud between the quiet vicar and his fiery cousin prevented all intercourse; and Frank's visits to Combe and his acquaintance with Grace and Edward were unknown to Dawson of Harcourt.

CHAPTER VIII
THE STORM-FIEND

HOMEWARD bound! Favouring winds and good seamanship have guided yon great vessel safely across the Atlantic. Many a heart beats high at the thoughts of soon again treading their native shores, and once more beholding beloved faces.

Land is in sight, old England's cliffs looming out of the mist that spreads along the horizon. The tedium of the voyage is forgotten, none but glad thoughts are in the minds of those who crowd together on the deck of that gallant ship.

"When shall we reach our port?" they ask, as they gather round the captain.

"By noon to-morrow we shall be in Southampton Water, if this breeze continues," is the reply, and then they begin eagerly to count hours and moments, as hitherto they have counted days.

A merry party are gathered in the cabin of the West Indiaman that night; toasts are drunk, and thanks voted to the captain for his skill and good management in guiding them safely to their journey's end; the young wife puts her hand into her husband's, and says, "To-morrow at noon we shall be safe—quite safe;" a father says, "To-morrow I shall see my children;" and the captain thinks gently to himself, "To-morrow I shall see my wife." The passengers retire early, thinking that on the morrow they must rise early and be ready to land; and rocked by the billows they fall asleep with the words "to-morrow at noon" sounding in their ears.

As the evening deepened into night, heavy masses of cloud rose and covered the sky, till by midnight it was so pitchy dark that a man could not see his hand before him; the wind, which had been blowing softly but steadily, burst in fitful gusts, and moaned and whistled over the long low sandhills, and through the blue-green sandgrass with which they were covered.

"There will be wild work in the Channel to-night if the wind continues to rise," said a sailor to his companion, as they sat in the public-house of a long. straggling village that nestled by the side of a small stream that wound its way among the sandhills. "There will be wild work to-night. Maybe the captain will be sorry he declined my services as pilot, before the night is over," resumed the man. "There ought to be a fine levied on those fellows who think they are able to take a vessel anywhere, and keep a poor chap out of an honest penny. It's easy enough to sail a vessel in the broad sea, where there is nothing for her to run her head against, but it's a different thing when you get such a great lumbering thing as she is into narrow channels; then you want a steady, skilful hand, and a man who knows every rock and shoal, and I might say every wave that breaks and every breath that blows. He isn't up to his work: he took the wrong tack this afternoon, or I should not have been up here so long before him. Ugh! what a blast! Well for him if he weathers out this night."

The wind came eddying round the house in fitful squalls, and then, as if suddenly gaining strength, it shook the house to its very foundations, and tearing the creaking sign-board from its place, sent it full against the window of the room where the two sailors were sitting, shivering the antique casement to atoms, and extinguishing the solitary light that stood between them.

"She's in for it, take my word, Tunny," said the disappointed pilot to his companion. "The captain will have more on his hands before morning that he will care for. Hush! listen! surely there was a gun!"

"Who's to hear anything in such a row as this?" returned Tunny. "Come along, man, into the kitchen; we must settle out business some other time. I like plenty of company such nights as these."

The men groped their way into the outer room of the building, where round the fire were seated ten or a dozen men whose garb bespoke them sailors. One, sitting a little apart from the rest, with a book in his hand, was none other than Edward Mountjoy.

The storm now raged in all its fury, and seemed every moment to threaten the destruction of the frail tenement in which the smugglers—for such were the whole party—had assembled.

Towards dawn the wind abated in a measure, and again the pilot's practised ear detected above the storm the booming of a gun.

There was no mistake now. Clearly, at distinct intervals, came that terrible sound, like the cry of many voices calling for succour—the succour that no human arm could give.

"She's on shore, for twenty guineas," cried the pilot. "Up, lads, let's lend a hand, bearing no malice. Poor chap, he has got his punishment by this time! I make sure it is that Indiaman; there was no other vessel bearing guns in the offing this evening."

The men needed no second appeal, and in a few moments the whole number were making their way amid the sandhills, staggering against the wind, which now blew with redoubled fury, driving the blinding flakes of foam far inland, and covering the hollows with quivering masses of briny snow.

The darkness was passing away, and the grey light of dawn was breaking through the flying masses of black clouds that hurried across the sky, as Mountjoy, followed by his companions, gained the beach—a broad expanse of sand stretching on either hand as far as the eye could see. Heaven knows which is most awful, a wreck on rocks, or on broad open sands: who shall say which is most terrible, to be dashed against the pitiless crags, or suffocated whilst battling against the waves, as they march in regular order, beating down their wretched victims at every attempt to rise?

So the waves advanced on that wild March morning, toying with their prey; now floating some poor wretch far up on the shore, now dragging him back to their murderous embrace.

The guns had long ceased to boom over the water, the ship was now past all human guidance, and the surf burst over her in fury, at every blow tearing from her, now a mast, now a plank, or hurrying some shrieking human being into eternity.

On the shore, as the day advanced, were to be seen groups of women huddled together in little knots, watching with parted lips and tearful eyes the destruction of the noble ship and her crew; for, though from childhood accustomed to such scenes, still every fresh wreck stood out in fearful distinctness, and each had its own tale of horrors.

There too were the carts, strewn deep with straw, which, from fearful experience, those who watched the wreck knew would be necessary to transport the mangled bodies to their last resting-place. Few escaped with life from that luckless ship. The fair young bride lay there cold and pale, and near by lay her husband: the waves were merciful in their case, at any rate. Women's hands lifted them with tender care, and, unmindful of the storm, took off their own cloaks to cover the bodies from rude gazers.

But all were not so gently treated: hard hearts were there, as well as tender ones, and those more ready to claim salvage than to rescue lives.

While Mountjoy and some of his comrades were straining every nerve, and risking their own lives to save those of others, Tunny, like an evil spirit, wandered up and down the shore, gazing with unmoved countenance on the dead, and watching with eager eye for any article of value that chance might throw in his way. He did not seem likely to be rewarded in his unhallowed search, for most of the unfortunate passengers had been in bed when the vessel ran upon the sands; but suddenly he espied a body lying apart from the rest, and at the same moment his evil eye rested on a magnificent chain which lay across the chest of the man. He looked cautiously around, and then swiftly seized the prize. The man was not dead, and opening his eyes, he called the robber by name:—

"Tunny," he said feebly, "Tunny, help to save an old messmate, and forgive old grudges! I am not drowned, man, as you see, but grievously hurt."

The devil had entered into Tunny: the chain glittered with every movement of its half-dead owner, and tempted him like a serpent; he looked for a moment in the upturned eyes of the man, and then clenching his teeth, he struck him with full force across his eyes. He had the chain in a moment, and a valuable watch to which it was attached; but as swiftly came the dread of detection. Suppose, in spite of that blow, the man should revive, he would assuredly deliver him up to justice; he must finish what he had begun, and drawing the short dagger he always carried about him, he dealt his victim two or three stabs in quick succession, and then fled with hasty steps away from the sea.

CHAPTER IX

SNARED IN HIS GUILT

AS the murderer, still holding in his hand the treasure for which he had bartered his soul, pursued his headlong course, in one of the dips in one of the sandhills he came upon a party, among whom was Mountjoy, tenderly caring for an aged man, who, for some mysterious purpose, had been saved, while so many younger had perished.

Ah! wretched man, had you withstood the temptation offered you but a few moments ago—had you dared to lift your head, and face your fellow-man—had you ventured to look in the face of the old man, and into the bright, honest eyes of Edward Mountjoy, you would have had wealth enough and to spare, honestly gained; but you have lost your chance, and your crime will cause many others to be committed. That poor man who lies a bloody corpse yonder, is but one among many who will be brought to destruction through that deed.

But Tunny only heeded that Mountjoy recognized him, and called to him by name; and again, like a guilty creature as he was, he fled away in fear, till, catching his foot in the tough, tangled grass, he fell forward, and the watch escaped from his grasp. Now that it was gone, he felt as if some portion of the guilt was gone too, and overjoyed to find, as he imagined, a cure for the terrors he had in that brief time experienced, he hastily dug a hole in the drifting sand and buried the watch, and then once more he hurried towards land.

Again, as ill-luck would have it, he came face to face with Edward; and again Mountjoy spoke to him, and inquired where he was hurrying, and why he was not helping at the wreck.

Tunny answered with a fierce oath, and kept on his way. The young man mentally determined that, on the first opportunity, he would break for ever from a man whom he disliked more and more every day. Still it was no easy matter to get out of the hands of so deep and unscrupulous a man as Tunny, who knew Mountjoy's value, and had no mind to part with him.

Well it would have been for the widow's son if he had never met the smuggler captain, who, while he kept the young man near him for his own purposes, disliked him as cordially as he was disliked by Edward, and only wanted an opportunity to do him some deadly injury.

Not many hours after Mountjoy's encounter with the smuggler, a yell of execration sounded along the shore. The body of the captain had been discovered some little way from the wreck, and it was but too evident that the wretched man had been most foully murdered; for the weapon, all discoloured with his blood, lay close at hand. Tunny, in his haste to escape, had thoughtlessly let fall his dagger, and thus unwittingly had left evidence of the most conclusive kind against himself.

Yes, Tunny was fairly in a trap at last. Most lawless among the lawless, he had now fallen even below them. His crime had put him beyond the pale of humanity. Yet he comforted himself with the assurance that none of his men would identify the dagger if found; for they were as much in his power as he in theirs: unless, indeed, it was Edward Mountjoy—him he could not trust, never had trusted; and, at the thought, the wretched man ground his teeth with rage, and, unheeding the direction he took, hurried onward.

The Crew of the *Seamew* had been off the Hampshire coast, engaged on some smuggling affair; and as soon as the first excitement of the wreck was over, they thought it prudent to retire from the conspicuous position in which accident had placed them, and seek refuge on board their vessel, which was not far off; but when they came together their captain was missing, as well as one of their number.

They were not long in ascertaining the cause. The murder of the captain of the Indiaman, the finding of the dagger—which had been identified by the missing man as belonging to Tunny—and the imminent danger which they ran of being mixed up in the transaction, or betrayed by their commander for his own ends, should he be captured, made them resolve to seek safety at once; therefore, taking their ship into safe quarters, they dispersed in different directions: Edward Mountjoy making his was to the west.

CHAPTER X
TYE'S ADVENTURES

"HARSCOURT is a fine place, but Cross is a finer," was a saying among the country people. It had been true once on a time, but the glory of Cross was departed, or departing; while Harscourt still looked like a gentleman's house, however rough and rude might be the manners and habits of its owner. Cross was farther inland than Harscourt, standing on bare upland country, swept by every blast.

A miserable little village had risen up around its gates, which were now in a rather dilapidated condition, whilst the small cottages on either side, which were exalted into lodges, were the residence of about a dozen of the dirtiest children in the country; and ten to one when you approached the gate, you would find that it had been turned into a drying-ground for the rags of the young hopefuls.

Such was the case when Mr. Dawson and his daughter rode through, one day, on a visit to the Martins of Cross.

It was Tye's first party: for a party there was to be, and Mr. Dawson had willed that his daughter should accompany him. She was just sixteen, and as bonny a lass, with her great brown eyes, rosy cheeks, and dark hair, as could be seen all the country round; yet Tye was as much a child as when she fell into the Blower and Edward Mountjoy fished her out. Of the Martin ladies, old or young, she knew positively nothing, though they lived within three miles of her father's house. Mr. Dawson never invited ladies to Harscourt, and Tye's farthest excursions were confined to the cottage in Combe; she had seen Mrs. Martin and her daughters, it is true, but only on an occasional visit to church at Moorstowe with mother Agnes.

Tye rode on a pillion behind a man-servant; she was dressed in what she considered her best frock, a white gown of her mother's altered to suit her, but, even with its alterations, of a fashion long out of date. Tye did not want to go; she would much rather have had her afternoon with Reginald, who was come home from school for the summer; but Mr. Dawson willed it, and Gratiana had found that in the long run it was better to obey him sometimes. Reginald managed to excuse himself, and went to Merscombe stream instead.

Poor Gratiana! she felt exceedingly uncomfortable as she was ushered alone (for her father had gone off with Mr. Martin to see some farm operations) into the drawing-room at Cross, where six or seven young ladies were assembled discussing the fashions and their lovers, as young ladies ever have done and ever will do.

She met with no very cordial reception; for she was not one of their set, and could not understand their innuendoes.

She sat by the window, not knowing what to do with her hands, and longing to make her escape. Half-an-hour passed by, and the tedium became intolerable; she must go: it was impossible to bear any longer these increasing whispers and giggles in which she had no share; so, rising quietly, she left the room, and went, like Don Quixote, in search of adventures.

Her voyage of discovery first led her into the dining-room, which was immediately opposite the room where the giggling girls were ensconced. There she examined the appointments of the table, the snowy linen from the looms of Holland, the massive silver, and the old oak sideboard with its antique ornaments; then she set forth again.

She next came to a room which in modern times would be called the housekeeper's room in moderate families, and in great ones, the still-room. Fifty years ago the mistress had almost as much to do in that room as the housekeeper, and there was Mrs. Martin up to her elbows in jellies, confectionery, creams, and other delicacies for the appetite.

Gratiana looked in, and in a moment saw that the lady had more on her hands than she could well manage, and that the country maidens who went and came at her bidding were rather confused than aided by her directions.

"Mrs. Martin, if you would let me, I should be so glad to help you," said Tye, humbly.

"You!" exclaimed Mrs. Martin, turning sharply round: "Miss Dawson, there is no room for you here; you had better join the other young ladies in the drawing-room."

"I've been there, and it is very stupid: I had much rather stay with you here; and I really know how to help, if you will let me," and Tye tied round her slim waist a white apron, which hung over a chain hard by.

"What can *you* do? Who taught *you* to do anything?"

"Never mind; only tell me what to do, and I'll see if I can't do it."

"Why, there's a junket to have the cream put on it——" but before Mrs. Martin could finish her sentence, the delicate china bowl of junket was in Tye's hands, and on its way to the dairy, whence it emerged in ten minutes with an unbroken crinkly skin of sealed cream all over it.[7] "Well done!" exclaimed Mrs. Martin, as she received the precious burden from Tye's hands: "the best dairymaid in all the country could not have creamed a junket better."

"What can I do next?" inquired the girl.

---

[7] Junket: a dessert made from sweetened milk curdled with rennet.

"Oh, there's a cream to whip, and the cheesecakes to fill, and all sorts of things besides."

Tye turned to with right good-will, and Mrs. Martin soon found that her amateur helper could do more than her three girls, whom she had always kept to work, but who always took to gossiping when they were really wanted, or than all her servants put together.

"It is all ready now," said Mrs. Martin, at last, as she surveyed her preparations with matronly pride. "I'll just go into the kitchen, and see how things get on there, and then we will wash our hands, and be ready for the company. Dear me! there's Mrs. Hamlyn at the door; we must be quick. Bless me, child, you are the very image of your mother; and you have done just what she would have done, if she had been here—always so kind and considerate."

Tears sprang into Gratiana's eyes. She had never seen her own mother; she only knew Agnes, to whom she had been confided when her mother lay dying; yet there was a feeling in the depth of her heart, which often seemed to draw her somewhere, she knew not whither, in search, as it were, of some great want; and then she would exclaim, "Oh, had I a mother!"

The party was a grand one. There were the Hamlyns from Mullworthy, and the Suffords from the Haven, and the Roes from Hall, besides many minor stars. It was fine weather, and there was a moon: everybody living in the country knows that these are necessary to a general merry-making.

Hours were early in those days: by five o'clock the dinner was despatched, and the ladies once more in the drawing-room. Tye's miseries now recommenced:—

"Where *did* you get that gown?" inquired one of the young lades. "It is so old-fashioned."

"As old as the hills, *I* should say," laughed another.

"It was my mother's," said Tye, getting very red and looking down.

"*I* wouldn't wear out my mother's old gowns!" put in a third; "I'd let her wear them out herself. Why don't you?"

"Hush!" said another, "hush! her mother is dead."

Tye did not raise her eyes, for there were heavy drops on the lashes which she did not care to have seen.

"But you could work yourself a dress," said another, by way of mending matters. "See! I worked this I have on, and it is considered very handsome," and Miss Roe turned herself round to display her handiwork.

"I don't think it is very pretty," said Tye.

"Well, but it is very fashionable, I can tell you," was the reply. "In London, all the ladies wear just such."

"Have you ever been to London?" inquired Tye, rather maliciously.

"No, I have not; but the Misses Hamlyn have; and they say since Madame de, de, de—Oh, dear! how stupid I am—you know, the maid of honour to Marie Thérèse—don't you remember her name?"

"I suppose you mean Marie Antoinette," said Gratiana, with a sneer on her lip.

"Oh, yes! that is it: well, you know this lady works so wonderfully well, and she works dresses for all the great ladies, and they pay her for them, poor thing: she is a real lady, but very poor; and so, since she has done that, all the ladies have taken to work dresses."

"And get paid for them?" inquired Tye, innocently.

"Paid! oh, dear, no! they only make them for themselves. Now, do try and work one, Miss Dawson. I will lend you my pattern."

"Thank you, I can't work!"

"Not work? Then I suppose you can draw; and that cabinet work in black and white is very pretty."

"I can't draw, thank you."

"But you play on some instrument, or sing"

"Neither."

"Dear me! why, you can do nothing. What a stupid girl you must be!" cried a vivacious damsel.

A laugh followed, at Tye's expense, and she, colouring and drooping her head, slunk into a corner. Presently she arose and gently left the room. This time she paused neither at the dining-room door, whence proceeded sounds by no means gentle, nor at the housekeeper's room; but passing through a door she observed at the end of the passage, she made her way to the stable-yard.

"I'll show these young ladies I can do something," she muttered to herself, as she opened the stable-door.

It was a fine stable: seven stalls, each with its occupant, well groomed and well fed; not over-clothed, but carefully attended to, and well worked. The stable was deserted, for the men were feasting on the remains of the dinner; so Tye was free to do what seemed good to her little ladyship.

She began a systematic inspection. "You won't do," she said to the horse in the first stall. "I don't like a chestnut: hot in temper, fidgety about the mouth. Nor you," to a fine black horse, who kept striking one of his hind feet impatiently against the ground; "you are either sluggish or over fiery, you blacks: I suspect you are the latter. Light bay, four white legs; not my sort: besides, your head is tied up, that looks as if you were a crib-biter; you won't do." And Gratiana went from stall to stall, till she stopped suddenly, and exclaimed,—

"Oh, you beauty! you are the one for me." Tye's choice showed she was a judge of horse-flesh; the animal that called forth her admiration was of a dark brown colour, with tan legs and a tan muzzle.

He was a beautifully formed creature, with a small, well-shaped head, showing his African blood by his broad *nez retroussé*; which, however ugly in a woman, is a great beauty in a horse.[8] His legs were clean and muscular, and his coat remarkably short, fine, and silky.

"Are you gentle, you beauty?" said Tye, as with a handful of oats she approached the horse. The horse sniffed what was coming, and turned towards the side of his stall to make way for her, whinnying, and almost speaking to her. "You are a darling," said the girl, as she held her hand to the horse, who carefully picked the corn from her outstretched palm, only touching it with his lips.

Tye retreated cautiously, caressing the horse as she did so. In the next stall stood a fiery-looking roan, who made room for Tye just as the brown had done; but she was too wise to venture near him, for she saw how his eye turned round in his head, and how he kept pawing the ground. As she turned away, he leaned all his weight on the halter, as if to break it, and finding his efforts unavailing, he launched forth viciously with his heels.

Now, Miss Tye, what are you going to do next? Why, the fact is, the young lady is bent on a ride, and intends saddling her steed herself; which she accordingly does, selecting from the saddle-room the saddle she deems most fit. It is astonishing how quickly and well she throws the saddle on the horse's back: he is fourteen hands high, but Tye is grown a tall girl of her age. How knowingly she cries, "Quiet there! quiet, I say," as the brown turns his little head, and makes believe he intends to bite her for girthing him up so tight. Then she chooses a bridle, a pretty sharp one, and loosening the halter, calls on the horse to turn round; which he does in a moment.

---

[8] *Nez retroussé*: a turned-up nose.

Now comes the mounting; she leads him to the block outside the door, and in a minute she is in the saddle, with no habit but the despised white gown, and no covering on her head but her rich brown hair.

"Now, be a good horse, and do what I tell you: let us show the young ladies we can do something."

Tye guided her steed into a field at the back of the house, where she had noticed a leaping-bar; but the moment the horse felt turf beneath his feet he became restive. Tye kept a firm hand, and prevented him breaking into a canter; in a few moments he seemed to become more accustomed to his rider, and comparatively quiet. The girl now put him into a canter and took him twice round the field, then put him at the leaping-bar. The horse went over it in first-rate style.

"You'll do," said Tye; "but my petticoats won't: I must go and find a train."

She returned to the stable-yard, where she found their own servant lounging on the horse-block.

"Good gracious, Miss Tye, is that you? what in the name of all that is wonderful are you about?"

"Never mind, Will: quick, give me a horsecloth, or cloak, or something."

The man obeyed, and she was decked in a horsecloth train.

"Now, Will, open the gate into that park paddock—quick!"

The man did her bidding. "Bless the girl, if she aren't mad sometimes: what on earth is she going to do now?"

The horse was fresh, and galloped pretty briskly along the bottom of the meadow, which, as the ground sloped, could not be seen from the lower windows. Tye kept him in hand well, knowing that if she once allowed him to go his full pace, she would not be able to rein him in again. Now she turns up the slope to the house, between her and which is a fence. She gallops, keeping her horse well in, and nears the fence. The ladies in the drawing-room catch sight of her and scream. The fence is higher than the leaping-bar, but she clears it splendidly; on she comes, close past the window, startling the gentlemen at their wine and frightening the ladies into fits. Now she makes a sweep, she is over the fence again, and making the circuit of the field. Once more she nears the fence, and once more she is over; but her horse's hoofs just touching the upper bar, warn her to desist, and she draws rein at the hall-door. Men and women are there to meet her.

"Bravo, Miss Tye!" cry the men with one voice, and many a hand, old and young, is stretched out to help her from her seat.

"You said I could do nothing," said Tye, turning to the women. "Can you ride like that?"

CHAPTER XI
THE YOUNG ANGLERS

"I NEVER saw anything like it, never," said Will, after he had detailed Miss Tye's riding achievements to the men and maids assembled in Harscourt kitchen. "Parson Courtney himself couldn't have ridden better; and to see how her eye sparkled, and how proud she looked when she stopped at the door, and how all the gentlemen got round her! My belief is, young Jack Martin fell head over ears in love with her in one minute, there and then—*that's* my opinion."

The maids cried, "Law, you don't say so," and nudged one another; while Will stretched out his legs, leaned back, and looked important.

"Well, I must say," remarked Will, "that Miss Tye do beat all young ladies *I* ever saw in all the days of *my* life."

Will considered himself an authority. He was in the habit of attending Mr. Dawson when he went to the sessions at Matton, and once or twice he had been as far as Torford; and people did say that Will had even visited the county town, but under circumstances which caused him never to allude to that journey.

"Just see how she rides!" resumed Will: "now, who taught her? that's what I ask."

"I am sure *we* don't know," whispered the maids.

"Nor any one else either," said Will, authoritatively. "It comes natural to her. Certainly she is in and out of the stable all hours of the day, and sees *me* manage the horses, which has been a help to her, doubtless; but then to ride in *that* fashion: *I* never taught her. To be sure she has ridden the cream-coloured pony about the ground, when she fancied it; but I have my own opinion about

Miss Tye:" and Will shook his head and looked mysterious.

"What is it, Will? out with it man," exclaimed one of the men in the chimney-corner.

Will continued his speech without heeding the interruption: "I seed her in the housekeeper's room at Cross, with Mrs. Martin; and I heard what the maids said, how she did more in five minutes than all the rest of them in ten: now, who taught Miss Tye to whip creams, and all that sort of thing? Why, no one, to be sure!" continued Will, answering his own question. "It's like the riding: it comes natural to her. My belief is," said Will, by way of finish, leaning forward and speaking in a solemn whisper, "that Miss Tye is a kind of pixie."

"Who's talking of the good people to-night, of all nights in the year?" cried Tye, who had entered the kitchen unperceived; "have you forgotten what day it is and how

Pixies are ever most clearly seen
Dancing in circles on midsummer e'en?

But come, Damaris, I want you."

Damaris had grown a comely maid since the night she interrupted Tye's meditations and suicidal intentions, and had been promoted from the pot-and-pan department to be Miss Dawson's own waiting-maid, or to speak more correctly, her friend and ally.

"Any news, Damaris?" was Tye's question.

"He is come," was the reply.

"Have you seen him"

"No; but Master Regie told me."

"Call me early to-morrow, there's a good Damaris. I must go to the stream; let me have my rod and all the rest ready. Don't be late, my good Damaris."

"No, ma'am," answered the waiting-maid, as she closed the

door. "Well, Will may say what he likes about the riding, and the creams; but, for my part, *I* consider the fishing the greatest wonder of the whole matter. There, when the sun shines very bright, she remains all day long, with those bits of feathers and silk, and little hooks, and makes those odd-looking things which she calls flies; and then, when the weather is lowering and dull, or the wind stirs the water, she flings a line of twisted horsehair over the pools, and brings home a whole basketful of fish. It *is* very strange; and I know she got it all out of a book. I do really think it isn't all right with her—or that, as Will says, she is a pixie."

Poor Damaris had no sooner uttered the unlucky word than she repented it. A shadow passed by her; she dropped the light and screamed: presently she heard a haw, haw, haw, and a chuckle in the dark.

"Ah, you shameful fellow!" she said; "I know you: how could you frighten me so?"

It was Will, who, as a novel mode of making love, had been playing the hobgoblin, and almost threw Miss Damaris into fits.

Regie was off at break of day; but Tye could not manage to get away so early. Her ride, or dissipation, had tired her, and she slept heavily.

She was worth looking at as she walked down to the stream. Her simple cotton gown and hood became her wonderfully; and the short dress showed the pretty foot and ankle to perfection. Lightly yet firmly she walked; her rod already put together, and her basket slung over her shoulder. Though it was midsummer-time, it was fine fishing weather, for the streams were high from recent rains, and the air was close and warm; the morning shower still left traces of itself on the ferns and brambles, glistening in drops of crystal, and every now and then a sailing cloud drew a veil over the sunlight and aided the fisher's guile.

Oh, the gallant fisher's life,
    It is the best of any,
'Tis full of pleasure, void of strife,
    And 'tis beloved of many.
Other joys are but toys,
Only this lawful is;
For our skill breeds no ill,
But content and pleasure.

Thus sang Tye as she stopped by the bank of the stream to adjust her line and select her flies.

In the morning up we rise,
    Ere Aurora's peeping,
Drink a cup to wash our eyes,
    Leave the sluggard sleeping.
Then we go, to and fro,
With our knacks on our backs,
To such streams as the Thames,
If we have the leisure.

"I don't believe in the Thames," said Tye; "it's all very well, but give me a stream I can fling my line across. There's the Baldson with its sluggish, muddy water: well, you can't catch anything there, unless the weather is rough and squally; and then those bogs——"

Gratiana had a troublesome collar to deal with—not the collar of muslin and open-work, the usual property of young ladies—but the collar on which her flies were fastened, made of silkworm gut, and familiar to fishermen. Now this same collar kept "kinking." and otherwise annoying her, and she was losing her temper rapidly; when some thought changed her mood, and she sang out, in a clear, musical voice, the end of a verse of the old song that was in her mind:—

None do here use to swear;
Oaths do fray fish away;
We sit still, mind no ill:
Fishers must not wrangle.

The tangled collar is made straight, the flies are to her fancy, and Tye, after wetting her line in the running stream, flings it artistically across a deep pool, drawing the flies with a gentle motion towards her. A rise—a fish on her hook—he struggles in vain, and after a little skilful manoeuvring, she lands her prize, a jolly spotted trout, on the bank.

"No use trying that pool any more, now you have made such a splash, my friend; but I'll come back again by-and-by." And the girl walks on down the meadows, throwing her line in likely places, and capturing many a fine fish. But somehow she every now and then withdraws her attention from the stream in a very unfisherman-like manner. Whom is she observing? or whom does he expect to see? The fact is, she knows of Edward Mountjoy's return home. But why does she not walk straight to mother Agnes' cottage?—ah! that is a mystery.

It is just six years ago that Tye was introduced to us; just six years almost to a day that Edward first went to sea; since then, he has been home three or four times, and each time Regie and Tye and the young sailor have been companions, as in times gone by. They are indeed great friends, but somehow Tye grows shyer as she grows older, and shakes hands with Edward instead of putting her arms round his neck; and sometimes she calls him Mr. Mountjoy, at which Edward and Regie laugh immensely, and call her the little duchess. Then she blushes and pouts, and holds up her head, and doesn't speak for ever so long; till Edward is obliged to make friends with her, and say, "Dearest Tye, don't be vexed with me," and then they are greater friends than ever.

Ah, that blush! Do you then, Miss Tye, perceive the person you are expecting?

The girl tries to look unconcerned, and throws out her line; but she is not attending to it, and her fly catches in a great plant of the flowering fern which grows in bushes on the opposite bank, and which, by experience, she knows to be so tough as to make it useless to pull, since she would only break her line. But she takes it very philosophically, for she just seats herself down on the bank and allows the line to shift for itself.

"I'll unhitch it," cried Edward, who at this moment appeared on the bank opposite, and the line ere long was floating on the water. "Now for a jump," said the sailor: retreating a few paces, he ran and jumped the river, and seated himself at Tye's side.

The girl turned her head one moment towards her companion, then dropped her long lashes, and put her hand in his. Not a word was spoken, but by some magical influence each knew the other's heart.

Young Mountjoy was a model of a sailor; handsome, open-looking, bronzed, strong, and lithe of limb. It was not much wonder that Tye lost her heart to him.

And there they sat, hand in hand, happy and hopeful; just as they have so often sat on that same bank since the time mother Agnes first trusted the three out without her guardian eye upon them: the same, yet different—man and woman now, in thoughts and feelings. Down in the distance, mother Agnes stands at the door of her cottage watching them. There are tears in her eyes, and her hands are clasped. She guesses what they are thinking of; she remembers the time when she sat hand-in-hand with just such a gallant-looking sailor as that, and she remembers a bruised and battered corpse flung by the angry waves upon the shore. May they be happier then she has been; may they be more fortunate.

The love Tye bore Edward was not the work of a moment: it was no sudden romantic passion. It had grown with her growth, and strengthened with her strength. For several years had their affection been quietly increasing, till it pervaded her whole being, and became at length a woman's love. Had she been asked, as a young girl, if she loved Edward better than her brother, she would have answered, "Not better, only differently." Now she felt she loved him not only differently, but better; and in loving him, she loved everything better.

The couple at last look up and spy mother Agnes.

"Let us go," said Tye, rising, and slowly they wend their way along the margin of the stream to the cottage.

"Hollo, Edward! is that you? why, where have you been hiding all this while? See what a splendid lot of govers I have caught," and Regie held out a dish full of a peculiar kind of whiting which abound among the rocks of the west of England, and which are caught with lines baited with worms or small fish. "And Tye! why bless me, how red you look; what have you been about?"

"Nothing," muttered Ty, entering the cottage.

Mother Agnes looked inquiringly at Edward, and then followed the girl.

"See what a beautiful shawl Edward has brought me?" said Agnes, displaying a really handsome Indian shawl, "and a gown, too—black Mode. Won't it be nice for a Sunday dress? And he has got something for you, I suspect."

"Hush, mother! you have no business to tell tales," replied her son, at the same time pulling a parcel from his pocket. "I brought one or two little things from abroad; if Tye will accept them I shall be glad;" and the sailor thrust the parcel into the girl's hands.

"Let us see," said Regie, pushing forward.

Somehow Tye's fingers tremble very much, and she says, very pettishly—

"Pray, Regie, don't be troublesome.

But the packet is opened at last, and a long gold chain of Indian workmanship glitters in Tye's outstretched hand.

"Oh, Edward, how very—very kind of you! What a beauty! Please put it round my neck. I will always wear it for your sake." Tye's tearful eyes are turned toward the young man, who looks supremely happy.

"I am so glad you like it; I hoped you would." And the sailor thrusts his hands into his pockets, and begins whistling, to hide how really glad he is.

A merry party sit down to dine on Tye's trout and Reginald's govers. Edward declares the trout are the most delicious he ever tasted, and despises the govers. This offends Regie, who growls out that of course everything that Tye has to do with is always sure to be best. Then Tye puts both her arms round Regie's neck and gives him a kiss, and begs him not to think a cross thought this happy day when Edward is come back, and declares she likes govers best, till Regie's good temper is restored.

After dinner, Tye coaxes Mrs. Mountjoy down to the beach, and there, on either side of their sailor, they listen to the tales he has to tell them of distant countries, storms, and perilous adventures. Regie all the time lying in front of them, supporting his chin on his hands and kicking his feet up and down, devours every word, and meditates how *he* can manage to get away and go to sea like his friend.

While the young lovers live on in their happy day-dreams, meeting at every opportunity, and anticipating no ill, we must turn to a distant part of the country, and follow for a while the fortunes of another of the actors in our story.

CHAPTER XII

A MYSTERIOUS ERRAND

A PRISONER! yes, a prisoner! No free air, no joyous sunlight, no sight of the blue summer sky, save that narrow little strip that can be seen through grated bars!

Nothing but blank bare walls and clanking irons: nothing to break the monotony of time, but the daily visits of the gaoler, and the twittering sparrows that flirt and quarrel on the window-ledge.

"Oh, to be free!" groaned the prisoner. But there was no chance for him. *Murder!* It is an ugly word—an ugly deed, and that was the deed which this prisoner had done. He tried to push it off, to drive it from him, that hideous fact; but ever as the day waned, and night came on, came that ghastly spectre, the murdered man, standing steadily, immovably, in the corner of the narrow cell.

Ah! how he dreaded the night! how he trembled, and hid his head beneath the scanty coverlet! But it was no use: still, through everything that phantom was clearly visible; each well-known feature so marked, so distinct, and those glassy eyes with that look of horror and dismay: the very look the murdered man had turned on his old friend and companion the moment he struck him down, lest he should reveal a secret—a secret that but endangered his liberty. Now his life was in jeopardy.

"I will be free! I will be free!" cried the wretched man in agony, striving to reach the grated window. "Four days and no answer! It is hopeless: and yet there may have been some delay, some accident; he may be in time yet. Let me see: how did I word my letter?—'A prisoner in Newport gaol has a secret of the most vital importance to communicate to——. Fortune and honour depend upon his coming at once.' That was strong enough, I should think, to bring him immediately, knowing what I do of his former history. Well, I have had this secret in my keeping for some years, little as he suspected it when he used me as a tool; but it may save my life now. But why does he delay? he will be too late! too late!" and the unhappy being ground his teeth, and clenched his manacled hands together.

The summer sun was gradually dipping towards the wooded horizon, when a traveller, well mounted, but bearing the evidences of a long journey, in his dusty dress and heated horse, rode through the arched gateway that spans the High Street of Southampton. He cast a hurried glance along the street, and seeing it thronged with gay promenaders, he drew his hat down over his face and took the first by-street to the left, threading his way by narrow lanes to the shore; where, entering a low inn, he ordered his horse to be well cared for, and inquired the time the next skiff would leave for Cowes.[9]

"There won't be another to-night, sir," replied the landlord.

"I must get across somehow, immediately," said the traveller in a decided tone.

"If the gentleman would not mind the expense, he could hire a boat to himself," suggested the man.

"I don't care for expense," exclaimed the stranger, "only the men must be quick: and you can send me up some refreshment meanwhile."

The landlord left the room, and then, for the first time, the stranger removed his hat, passing his hands through his long luxuriant hair, and grinning in a rather crooked mirror to examine

[9] Cowes: a seaport town on the north coast of the Isle of Wight.

his teeth, which, with the exception of his hair, were the only beauty he possessed. He was rather tall, with a great stoop, which made him look almost deformed. His mouth was small, his lips thin, the small round eyes bright and deeply set. His forehead was low and contracted, with deep lines across it, and his hands were peculiarly thin and long. He was not a pleasant-looking man, and as he turned away from the glass, when he had finished the examination of his great white teeth, he looked as if his thoughts were as little pleasant as his face. It was but a sorry meal he made; the viands were none of the best; but if they had been the daintiest in the land he would have been little the wiser, so quickly did he bolt the coarse bread and cheese a slatternly maid had brought him.[10]

"The boat's ready when you are, sir," said the landlord; "better not delay, or you'll lose the good of the tide."

"All right," cried the traveller, as he hastily left the inn. "Take care of my horse, and when I come back to-morrow, I'll give you a sovereign; and, if I don't come back, why, he's worth a hundred any day." And stepping into the boat, he seated himself in the stern, and took the tiller to steer.

"The gentleman understands how to manage a boat, I see," said one of the boatmen.

"None better," was the reply; "but now, no talking, if you please, but unfurl your sail, and be off."

A light breeze was up, just curling the water, and the little bark flew swiftly onwards, cutting her way, now mounting a wave, now dipping down and springing up again, sending the spray flying as she darted along.

---

[10] Viands: food.

It was dark ere they reached Cowes, but the traveller still pushed on; and he had not been in the town half an hour, before he might have been seen leaving the inn mounted on a sturdy horse at full gallop.

"Nothing like making friends, be they high or low," soliloquized the horseman, as he approached Newport; "only always try and know something about them which they would rather not have made public, and then you can bend them which way you will: that's my plan.[11] I'll see if I can't get in and out of Newport gaol when I will and how I will. I wonder what this secret is, and who the fellow is who sent me that note? It may all be a hoax, but still one never ought to shrink from knowing a secret; it may prove of use some day. I half suspect Tunny to be the writer: but why didn't he put his name to it?"

As he wondered, he passed over the river, and ascended the rise to the town of Newport. It was late; only a light here and there told of some wakeful watcher, and occasionally a burst of wild merriment indicated the whereabouts of some low drinking shop.

The traveller paused a moment before the great inn in the square, from the balcony of which men who were ambitious of entering parliament made grand speeches and promises, never intended to be fulfilled; while the great red lion, from which the inn took its name, elevated his tail and showed his fangs, as if ready to devour all who would not vote for the estimable gentleman whom the landlord supported.

"Better not be recognized, if possible," muttered the horseman; so relinquishing a pleasant dream of a good supper and bottle of wine, he continued his way along the High Street, and turning to

[11] Newport: a town around five miles south of Cowes.

the left, entered a broad, deserted street, bordered on either side by houses of all sizes and patterns, the beloved abodes of numberless spinsters, of various ages, each of whom kept a maid (who would, in spite of her mistress's endeavours, be always flirting with some horrid man or other), and either a cat or a dog. It was rather a lively place just in the morning, when the pets were sent out for their daily walk—when Miss Jones's grimalkin set up her back and used bad language to Miss Smith's poodle, and Miss Dobbs's pug was knocked over and rolled in the mud by Miss Parker's dog, a rude, ill-behaved spaniel, of a doubtful character, which gossip whispered had been presented to her "by an officer;" and when the maids, in their white caps and snowy aprons, had to make little excursions into the street to capture the rebels, while all the mistresses looked out of their windows to see they spoke to no one. This, I say, was the only time any life appeared in Broad Street, where the grass grew undisturbed.

The horse's hoofs rattled on the pitched road and echoed through the streets, startling more than one ancient maiden, who was just laying aside her front, and betaking herself to the strange swathing-bands and monstrous cap with which her head was adorned during the darker hours, and frightening a timid damsel of eight-and-thirty almost to death. She was returning home from a quiet whist party, with her aunt, a staid lady of sixty, and escorted by the dancing-master of the place, an *émigré* who was a marquis, but who now possessed nothing but a gold snuff-box, the last remnant of his once magnificent property.[12] By the by, it is curious how few French marquises seem to have retained anything except

[12] Émigré: someone who has left their home country and settled in another, usually for political reasons.

snuff-boxes—sans chemise, sans culottes, they might be; but the snuff-box was ever present.

"He is a highwayman," whispered the damsel, in a trembling voice, to the dancing-master.

"An assassin! a brigand! a citoyen!" muttered the *émigré*, laying his hand where his sword should have been.[13]

"Protect us!" cried the elderly lady.

"With my life!" exclaimed the poor little Frenchman, shivering in every limb.

But his courage was not tried, for the stranger rode straight on till he came to the river-side; where, turning again to the left, he entered a narrow street, whose ancient red-brick houses were built along its banks; while in front, the high garden-walls of the Broad Street ladies rendered the street dark and gloomy.

Before one of the houses the traveller drew rein. It was taller by two stories than most of its neighbours, and had once, to all appearance, been the abode of some one well-to-do in the world. It had a flight of broad stone steps up to the front door, with handsome iron balustrades on either hand. The windows were nearly flush with the wall, and the glass was set in the heavy wooden frames so commonly used in the reign of Anne and the first Georges. Where a garden had originally been, now stood lumbering outbuildings, nominally lofts for sails and ropes; while between the house and the main body of these buildings was a large wooden door, with a small wicket for foot passengers. A half-obliterated signboard indicated that it was a house of entertainment; but no cheery light shone through the windows, no buxom landlady or jovial host

---

[13] *Citoyen*: a 'citizen'. Used during the French Revolution to promote equality. In this instance, a revolutionary, as opposed to someone loyal to the old regime.

made their appearance to welcome the stranger, who knocked more than once at the great gate before he received any answer to his summons. At length the wicket-gate was cautiously opened, but not more than a few inches, and a rough-looking man asked his business.

"My business is a night's lodgings—and yours, to give it; so I guess by your sign yonder: so open the gate and let me in."

The man hesitated.

"Don't you remember me?" asked the stranger in a low voice, dismounting and coming close to the gate.

The man, who held the door ajar, started and mutter an oath, but undid the fastenings without more delay, drawing back many a stout bolt and bar.

"You need not be in the least alarmed," said the unwelcome visitor, blandly; "I only want to make use of you for a night. Here, take the horse; I am going to sup with a friend, and shall not be back for an hour or two;" and he passed through the wicket, and out again into the dull street. "That shows the use of knowing a person's secrets. If I hadn't known that that fellow smuggled through his back door, I don't know where I should have slept to-night. Now, I'll see if another secret I know will help me or not."

And he proceeded by the river-side towards the gaol.

CHAPTER XIII

HOW TO USE A SECRET

THE traveller walked swiftly on till he reached the gaol, round a large portion of whose base glided the sluggish, muddy stream, with trailing water-weeds swaying hither and thither as it flowed languidly on, and the branches of the willow dipping themselves into its foul, brackish waves: a meet companion for those dreary walls! Close by the prison a small footbridge was thrown across the stream, from which a footpath wound through the meadows. As one stood on the bridge, and watched the slimy current eddying and whirling round the gloomy walls, it made strange noises like the sobs and groans of prisoners, as though it had caught the infection and mourned like them.

The stranger took a turn or two ere he approached the gaol gate. He was making up his mind as to the best course to pursue. He nocked twice before he gained admittance, or rather before the door was opened; when, not wishing a parley, he quickly extinguished the light which the woman who had answered his summons held in her hand, and pushed past her into a little room close to the door.

"Hollo there! who's that?" shouted a burly-looking man, springing up from a table, which he nearly upset. "Who are you, making such a piece of work here at this time of night?" and he clutched the collar of his visitor's coat firmly, and gave him a rather rough shake.

"That'll do, thank you: that's quite enough of that sort of thing," said the intruder. "Now tell Mrs. Phillips to shut the door, and give me some supper. You did not recognize me at first, eh? Don't distress yourself; you know I never bear malice."

The man had gradually relaxed his hold, and stood respectfully on one side, while the stranger seated himself without hesitation in the easiest chair in the room, and proceeded to examine the supper on the table, to see if it was according to his taste.

"I see you have spirits here—at your old drinking ways again, eh?"

"No, indeed, sir! Only a man must have a little comfort now and then."

"Well, I want some comfort now, that's certain; for all I've had since morning has been some execrable cheese and villainous beer. Have you any wine handy?"

"A bottle or two at your service," said the gaoler.

"Well, bring me some then. This pasty seems tempting. Is it one of your making, Ailsey?"

"Yes, sir," replied the woman who had opened the door, "and it is as good venison as you would taste within many miles."

She was a middle-sized, middle-aged woman, with traces of beauty yet remaining, but with a worn, haggard expression—a suffering, enduring face.

"How has he been going on lately?" inquired the intruder, as Phillips left the room. "No drinking, I hope?"

"He has been steady this long while," was the reply, and the woman turned away to put a chair in its place, and bring a clean plate. It was evident she did not wish to converse with her visitor.

The gaoler returned with a couple of bottles, and placed them before his guest, pointing out their divers qualities, while the woman gently left the room, whispering as she closed the door,—

"More mischief! more mischief! When will the wicked cease from troubling, and the weary be at rest?"

"Sit down, Phillips, and finish your supper," said the intruder, in a patronizing tone.

It is not pleasant to be patronized in your own house, and so

Phillips felt; but he said nothing, and took his seat at the table.

"Many prisoners in now?" inquired the stranger, after a while.

"Only three," answered the gaoler, shortly.

"What are they in for?"

"One is a deserter, another has been stealing potatoes."

"And the third?"

"Oh, the third is only in here on remand: I expect he'll be sent to trial for murder."

"Murder! that's a serious charge: what's the story?"

"He's a smuggling fellow, and had a quarrel with one of his friends, and gave him rather too hard a knock on his head."

"Smuggler, eh? I suppose he's the chap I want. You see, being in the Customs, one wants a secret now and then, and I fancy this fellow can tell me something worth knowing."

The gaoler looked up uneasily; somehow he did not like this preface.

"I'll get you to let me see him directly," continued his companion.

"It's impossible, Mr. Erlingham; it's against rules to admit any one after dark."

"I *must* see him," returned Mr. Erlingham; "and what is more, I *will*: and it must be to-night."

"I shall be ruined if you persist."

"*Be* ruined. Who put you here?—please remember that! Who saved you from being transported?—remember that!"

The wretched man winced, and bowed his head.

"Remember that at any moment I could denounce you as a notorious villain; so do what I ask you without hesitation. I wish to go now, at once."

He rose as he spoke, and the gaoler, unhooking a large key from the wall, and lighting a lamp, proceeded towards that part of the building in which the murderer was confined. It was the tower that was washed by the river. They ascended a flight of narrow stairs, and stopped at a small, pointed doorway. The key grated in the rusty lock, and Mr. Erlingham entered the cell. The prisoner started up, exclaiming that he was saved.

"You can leave us the light awhile, Phillips, and come back in ten minutes: and you can leave the key in the door, if you can trust me; if not, I suppose, I must be locked in."

The gaoler preferred securing his prisoner, and a shudder passed over the gentleman in the Customs when he found himself alone, face to face with a murderer!

"Tunny, I see," he began, when Phillips had withdrawn: "I thought as much. What on earth do you want of me? I don't see how I am to help you out of your present scrape."

"You can if you will," was the reply.

"Impossible! In a case like yours the law must take its course. There is no help for you."

"If the law takes its course in my case, it shall take it in yours too, I can tell you," replied the prisoner, savagely.

"Ha! condescend to explain how the law can touch me."

"In many ways: deep and cunning as you are, you have been playing a desperate game these many years. Remember you *may* lose."

"A desperate game, indeed! I have made too many good hauls in my day, for those above me to scrutinize my conduct very narrowly. Besides, I flatter myself I am above suspicion."

"I've nothing to do with your conduct in office; it is in your private life you are playing the desperate game I mean."

The prisoner fixed his eyes on his visitor, who shrank and dropped his eyes before that look, but tried to rebut all suspicion.

"You speak in riddles," he said at length.

"I will be plain, then," replied the prisoner. "If I am not out of this place in four-and-twenty hours, you may take a last look at the wealth you so much covet."

"You use high language, my man; but I fancy you will find it difficult to prove what you assert."

"Not so difficult as you imagine. I have been in the West Indies, and know your history well. You are no more heir to that Jamaica property than I am."

"I am my uncle's nearest relation. Who has a right to his money, if I have not?"

"You are not his nearest relation. He has a daughter."

"She has been dead and gone these twenty years."

"You are mistaken; and what is more, her son is nearly of age. A word to them, and where would you be?"

"I don't believe a word of your story. You have no proofs. You have merely trumped up this tale in hopes of getting yourself out of prison."

"It is no trumped-up story," replied the man, vehemently. "I have undeniable proofs; and unless you agree to aid me, both your uncle and his daughter shall know the truth in two day's time."

"Why didn't you send to them in the first place?"

"Because they have no power to get me out of this hole; you have."

"How am I to do it" inquired the plotter, arranging in his own mind the man's escape if it should be worth his while.

"You have ways and means of doing most things, if they suit your convenience," replied the prisoner, testily.

"But granting that this woman you know was Agnes Erlingham, and that her son is legitimate, and all that, what good is this knowledge to me?"

"I could put him in your power."

"You have some spite against him, I suspect."

"Well, he is the principal witness against me in this matter, and it would be a good thing for both of us, if we could get rid of him."

"Both of *us*, indeed!" exclaimed Erlingham, with a sneer; and pray what is the youth's name?"

"That you shall not know till I'm at liberty."

"I do not consider your secret worth knowing," was the reply. "You might have spared yourself the trouble of writing, and me the trouble of coming. The whole thing is an imposition."

"Stop, Mr. Erlingham, consider!" cried the unfortunate man, seizing hold of his arm. "Only consider that you may save a man from the gallows, and yourself from poverty!"

"Two things well worth considering, certainly; but the fact is, I can't save you and you can't affect my fortune one way or the other."

"Fool!" shrieked the prisoner. "But I will have my revenge! The day that sees me die, sees you fall! Mark my words: I know more than one secret about you, and I will publish them all!"

"Tell me the name of Agnes Erlingham's son, and I will think over the matter," continued the official coolly.

"Yes! and when you know his name, you will have a clue, and go ferreting him out, and leave me to perish here! No—no! I'm too deep for that."

At this moment Phillips approached the door, and Mr. Erlingham made a feint of leaving the cell.

"Not yet, pray not yet: just consider!" cried the prisoner.

"Will you tell me the name?" whispered Erlingham.

"Yes, yes!"

"You must leave us again, Phillips, I have a long story to hear," said Mr. Erlingham, and again they were alone.

"The name?"

"But how am I to know that you will get me out, when I have told you?"

"No parleying, or I am gone. I will make no promise till I hear the name."

"Edward Mountjoy," muttered the smuggler, in a low voice.

"Then she married that pirate captain who used to be about among the islands so much, years ago?"

"The same."

"And where are Agnes and her son to be found?"

"Nay, I've said enough; will you promise now?"

"I will see what I can do," relied Erlingham, doubtfully.

The murderer's heart misgave him; he did not believe in Mr. Erlingham.

"When I am out I will tell you all, and get this youngster put out of the way for good and all. He has broken the laws times and oft; there will be no difficulty in catching him."

"Possibly not."

Tunny began to feel that Mr. Erlingham had no intention of procuring his release.

"You love money, Mr. Erlingham?"

"Not more than most men, I suppose."

"I don't know how that may be, I'm sure; but I fancy you would do almost anything for money."

"Money is power."

"If you will get me out of prison, you shall have money."

"Where is it to come from, my friend?"

"Never mind: when I'm out I'll tell you. I know where several thousand pounds' worth of goods are concealed, and when I am safe I'll help you to the lion's share, and give you an opportunity of sending Edward Mountjoy beyond the sea for good and all."

"It's worth considering, certainly, if I can believe you," muttered Mr. Erlingham, allured by the chance of gain.

"I'll take my oath on it," exclaimed the smuggler.

"*Your* oath!" replied Erlingham, with a sneer. "But I'll see what I can do. If you deceive me, you will just find yourself within these walls again, pretty quickly, I can tell you. Good-bye for the present; you shall hear from me soon," and Mr. Erlingham quitted the cell in great haste.

"If any one comes to see that fellow, you will be good enough to admit them," said the unwelcome guest as he entered the gaoler's parlour.

"Mr. Erlingham, have you no mercy?" exclaimed Ailsey Phillips, as she stood between her husband and the visitor.

"How, Ailsey?"

"Cannot you leave him in peace" she cried, pointing to her husband. "He has been quiet and steady these three years, and now you come and make him do a thing he knows is wrong; and then you will have more hold on him than ever, and drag him down soul and body!"

"My dear Ailsey, like all women, you are unreasonable. Only think where Phillips would have been if I had prosecuted him for that money. I did him a kindness then, and now I ask a favour in return."

Ailey shook her head. "If it is found out that he has been tampering with that man he will be dismissed, and perhaps severely punished; and then he will sink lower and lower till he is destroyed."

"But, woman, you are imagining griefs that don't exist. If he gets turned out, I must find something else for him, that's all. I'll wish you good-night now: mind what I say about letting his friends see him; but remember, if you are questioned about anything, that you have never seen, and know nothing about me." And Mr. Erlingham left the gaol, and returned to his lodgings in the dull old house by the river.

"Always plotting! always in mischief!" moaned the gaoler's wife, as he departed. "Oh, that he would leave us at peace!"

"He calls me a villain," muttered the gaoler. "What better is he? Ailsey, girl, lift up your head: we must hope."

"Hope! there is no hope left," sobbed the poor woman. "He made believe to be so kind; and no doubt it was just to suit his own ends. Are you sure, Phillips, quite sure, that you never took that money?"

"I swear to you, Ailsey, I never saw a farthing of it. I believe he himself put it in my box. I've often thought so; but then, you see, I was drunk, and I have no proofs."

The wife rose, and leaned against her husband.

"It always does me good," she said, "to hear you say you did not take that money. So far, thank heaven! you are innocent."

CHAPTER XIV

LIFE AND DEATH

THE Dun Cow was not, as we have seen, a very cheerful abode, but it had many frequenters. Dark boats stealing up the river by night landed their cargoes on the wharf behind the house; and many a man lodged there who had never been seen to enter from the street.

Mr. Erlingham passed through the gate, and, crossing the courtyard with the air of one perfectly familiar with the place, entered a long low building abutting on the river. It seemed a sort of public room, and when he went in, about a dozen men were seated at two or three small tables near the wide, open hearth; on which, though near midsummer, a fire smouldered. There was a little commotion at his entrance, and the landlord tried to persuade him to adjourn to a room in the house; but he declined, and seating himself at a table near the fire, called for some wine, and invited the landlord to join him.

"You have had a murder somewhere down here lately, haven't you?" he inquired, addressing the room generally, and no one in particular.

"You can't call it a murder," cried two or three rough-looking men at once; "it was an accident."

"So! I have heard a good deal about it, and I am afraid poor Tunny's case is judged already."

"That's a shame," growled the men. "Tunny is a hot chap, and any one might be unlucky some time or other."

In truth, the men present were half afraid lest during Tunny's examination something should come out about their own doings.

They had not themselves seen the murder committed; they knew not the temptation, or the real depravity of the man; and as it was not for their interest that Tunny should remain in prison, they had come to the conclusion, even before Mr. Erlingham's arrival, that he ought not to be there, and that something should be done to aid his escape. They were, therefore, not unprepared for Mr. Erlingham's next remark:—

"I wonder a set of men like you don't storm the gaol and rescue him, if you admire him so."

The men eyed the new-comer suspiciously.

"You need not suspect *me*," said Mr. Erlingham, noting the look they gave him: "the fact is, I am interested in this man, and whoever gets him out will be well paid."

The men gave a low cheer.

"But how is it to be managed?" inquired one of them: "there are soldiers at hand, who would be down on us in no time."

"If you did it quietly, though, who's to know anything about it? Haven't you got pockets, and can't you put files and ropes into them?" suggested Erlingham.

"Yes: but how are we to get them to the prisoner?"

"Knock at the door, that is the most approved way of getting into people's houses."

"But Phillips won't let any of us in: he refused the other day."

"Go and try to-morrow, and see if he refuses."

"Perhaps it's only a trap to get hold of one of us," muttered more than one voice.

"Not a bit," was the rejoinder: "any one may go: a woman, perhaps, would be best to send."

The whole party laid their heads together, and began devising plans for Tunny's escape from prison, and also from the island.

"It must be done soon—at once," said Mr. Erlingham, as he retired, not for the night, but for the morning; for the light of the sun was rising above the horizon as he crossed the courtyard to the dull old house.

It is morning: a bright, sunny, summer morning; and the dogs and cats in Broad Street are quarrelling as usual, and the maids are chasing the culprits, while their mistresses keep guard. The little French *émigré*, who trips along with his violin under his arm, to give his daily lessons, stops for a moment before the house of his last night's companions to kiss the tips of his fingers to them. Now he has vanished, and the last rebel is captured. Each lady draws down every blind in her house, carefully excluding every ray of sunshine, so that a person unfamiliar with the daily habits of the dwellers in Broad Street would conclude there was a general mourning among the inhabitants; whereas it was only to preserve the precious furniture, which is cherished by each householder: carpets long innocent of colour, chairs with the longest of legs, the hardest of seats, and the most upright of backs. Very precious are these treasures in the eyes of their possessors: "This belonged to my uncle the bishop; that, to my grandfather, Sir——," &c., &c., &c.

So the whole street goes to sleep.

But hark! On the soft summer air floats the sound of instruments: the shrill fife, the rolling drum: nearer and nearer, louder and louder: till first one blind is put a little on one side, and then another; then one is drawn up, now many, and Broad Street looks broad awake again.

Now round the corner come three or four ragged urchins, followed by half a dozen girls and a dog or two. The music grows louder, and more rabble make their appearance, till at last the band comes fairly round the corner, and marches through Broad Street to "The British Grenadiers." It is a pretty sight: the colours flying, the bayonets glancing; and the old ladies admire till they think of some brother, friend, or lover, who, long, long ago looked just as gay and bright as those lads yonder, as full of health and hope; then tears course down many a wrinkled cheek, and they ask, "Where are they now?" Far, far away, in lonely, unknown graves, such as many of those gallant lads will soon fill; for they sail to-morrow for the seat of war, and most are looking their last at things familiar.

The last soldier, the last straggler has disappeared, the music sounds fainter and fainter, and the spinsters, drying their eyes, turn to Miss Burney's last volume, or an ancient newspaper. They draw down their blinds no more that day, for the sun is gone.

After a while, as the day grows cooler, walking parties of twos and threes pass down the quiet street into the pleasant fields; and, as evening closes in, and the curfew sounds from the old church-tower, they recross the foot-bridge by the gaol, and come home to piquet, cassino, scandal, and supper.

In the cell in the tower of the gaol all that bright sunny day the prisoner has been busy. He has filed and rasped and fretted his irons till one wrench will break them; but he looks angrily at the light, and longs for darkness, for he has still those thick window bars to manage. In the parlour in the gaol all that bright summer day, the gaoler had sat, the fatal bottle beside him: sometimes moping, sometimes wild with excitement, while the wife looks on and trembles.

So the day wears on. The last rays of the sun have disappeared, the rosy clouds that have been telling of a bright to-morrow fade one by one away, and the night comes.

Then the prisoner breaks his bonds, and drawing his rude pallet beneath the window, tries to force the bars; but they resist all his efforts, so he takes to his file again. Through the soft, still air goes that harsh, grating noise, and a passer-by notes how loud the corncrakes cry that night. It is hard work; the iron is thick; but life is at stake, so he works with might and main. Through that short summer night he works and struggles with those pitiless bars; and as the time passes on, his hands grow less steady, and he almost wishes he had never begun. But he remembers at twelve o'clock of the day that is now dawning, he will be again brought before the magistrates, and transferred to another prison. What chance will he have then? This thought stirs him up to further exertion, and he works away. One bar yields, and now another. The dawn is creeping over the sky.

With trembling hands the prisoner fastens a rope round the bed, and lifting himself up to the window, squeezes himself through the narrow aperture, balancing himself for a moment on the sparrows'-ledge. The rope glides swiftly through his hand; he is nearly down, when the rope gives way, and with a dull splash he falls into the river. The current turns him over once or twice, and horrid thoughts of drowning flit across his mind; but he rises, and striking out manfully, he reaches the shore. He runs crouching along the bank till he comes opposite the Dun Cow, then plunging into the stream like an otter, he makes for the wharf at the back: ere many moments he is *tête-à-tête* with Richard Erlingham in a little room in the dull house. Half-an-hour afterwards he was making the best of his way to the back of the island, where friends were watching for him.

Another splash! another man is in the water. The current seizes him, and turns him over and over: he buffets with the stream, he tries to cry out; but the muddy, brackish water fills his mouth and takes away his breath. He buffets still more, and the stream, as if angered at his struggles, rushes over his head. Again he tries to cry out, but the water fills his mouth. He sinks; and then that cruel river, toying with its victim, bears him once more on its surface, but only that he may sink, never to rise a living man. The body floats past the wharves, and past dewy meadows, where cows are lowing; by pleasant cottage homes, whose inmates sleep the sleep of innocence; and past stately mansions and sloping lawns, ever onwards towards the sea. The sea refuses the hideous burden, and rejects the body of the self-murderer, which floats back up the river with the tide.

The gaoler's wife sits in the little parlour and waits. Her husband left the house hours ago, and he does not return. The day breaks, and the sun comes pouring into the room. The clock strikes ten; but still she sits there waiting to hear her doom. Eleven! They will be here presently to take away the prisoner. There is a summons at the door; she rises, moaning, "Husband, you might have taken me with you: I have stood by you ever; now you have left me alone." The gaol door stands open, but where is the gaoler?

Down among the reeds and rushes that grow rank and high, down by the river bank.

"Where is the gaoler?" they ask.

The wretched wife cannot answer.

Men crowd into the prison and speak rudely to her, but she heeds them not: sitting by the window, she looks out into the road, waiting. The men seize the keys, and go to take the murderer to justice. The empty cell and the rope hanging from the window tell their own story.

The whole town is in an uproar. Men are scouring the country in every direction, but to no purpose; for before the search began, the object of it was safe outside the Needles, in a swift-sailing craft that gave the king's cutter a wide berth.[14]

Alas! for that poor woman who sits at the window watching! A procession comes along the road, and the crowd standing around the gaol fall back awe-struck. On it comes, that sad company and their sad burden. The woman starts up and rushes to meet them. One look, one shriek, and she falls senseless at the feet of them who carry the body of the self-drowned husband.

There is a burial by night—not in hallowed ground: in the public thoroughfare that grave is made, and one broken-hearted woman weeps over the suicide's last resting place. Yet hardly his last, for her affection prompts her to steal the body and bury it in the shady corner of a village churchyard: kindly hearts who think, "This woman's case might have been mine," connive at her deed and even help her. But they know not the thoughts of her heart, nor the bitterness of her spirit, as she kneels beside that unmarked grave, and swears to be revenged! Then she rises and goes her way into the world.

And the cause of this misery, where is he? Plotting further mischief, with a smooth face and deceitful smile; weaving schemes for destroying his own relations—weaving schemes for amassing wealth; striking first one and then another from his path, as they stand in the way of his advancement, relentless, cruel; and the world looks on, and admires him for a clever man who will make his way. Those against whom he is plotting, go quietly on their way unknowing of their enemy.

---

14 The Needles are a row of tall rocks perched at the westernmost end of the Isle of Wight.

CHAPTER XV

THERE IS DANGER!

THERE is great trampling of horses in Harscourt courtyard, calling here and hurrying there. Mr. Dawson is going over to Merscombe to draw the great pool for salmon peel, and the stream for trout, much to Tye's disgust, for she prefers fly-fishing. Still she is going; a day's outing and a good ride are things not to be despised: besides, she knows, or guesses, that Edward, who is rather a favourite with Mr. Dawson on such occasions, may be there.

But stop! who comes here? Another troop of horsemen; but strangers, not invited guests. A young man rides at their head. Behind him Will's quick eyes discover a man to whom he owes a lasting grudge—the excise officer from Haven. People do say he was somehow the cause of Will's journey to Exeter: which may or may not be the case.

"Is Mr. Dawson in?" inquired the stranger, in a haughty tone.

Will touched his hat by way of reply, and leading the stranger's horse to the great door, assisted him to dismount, while he called to his master, who was busy at a table in the hall arranging some nets and fishing-tackle, that he was wanted. However rough and surly Mr. Dawson chose to be to his children and dependants, he knew how to behave to a gentleman; and such, in a moment, he judged the stranger to be, and therefore received him courteously enough.

"You are a magistrate, I believe, Mr. Dawson?"

"I have that honour."

"May I speak with you alone?" inquired Mr. Erlingham, casting a suspicious glance at Tye; who, ready equipped for her ride, stood with her great eyes fixed on the stranger, as if she would read his very thoughts.

Tye took the hint and left the hall. Mr. Dawson, on pretence of closing some door, followed her, and whispered—

"Go to Cross like lightning, and say, 'Danger!' "

Tye nodded, and her father returned to his conference with his visitor.

"As a magistrate, sir, I presume I may confide in your honour?" said Erlingham, bowing to Mr. Dawson.

Mr. Dawson bit his lip, and replied in an offended tone—

"I should presume so, sir."

"No offence, I hope: I am a stranger to you, and you to me. My name is Erlingham; I am in an office under government—the Customs, in fact—and I was staying with my friend Lord Crawford, when I received a letter—a very extraordinary letter—in consequence of which I thought it my duty, considering the position I hold under government, to come and see whether the letter was an imposition, or whether there was really any truth in it."

Such was Mr. Erlingham's honest account of how he became possessed of the information he had extracted from Tunny at the Dun Cow in Newport.

"May I inquire the purport of the letter?" inquired Mr. Dawson, paling before his own evil conscience.

"Oh, a smuggling transaction! By-the-by, you seem to have a good deal of that sort of thing down here?"

Mr. Dawson looked somewhat relieved, and answered in an offhand manner—

"Nothing very much, I believe: a keg or two now and then in a homeward-bound vessel, but nothing more."

"Indeed! you surprise me! I have had it reported to me that

gentlemen of some consequence are apt to make ventures in what they call the 'fair-trade.' "

"*I* know nothing of it, if it is so," said the virtuous magistrate, shrugging his shoulders, and elevating his eyebrows.

"Does not a Mr. Martin live near here?" inquired the official.

"Martin? Oh, yes! there are several of that name about here," was the reply.

"But Mr. Martin of Cross," resumed Mr. Erlingham, referring to his note-book.

"Martin of Cross, to be sure! he's my very next neighbour. You don't mean to say *he* is accused of anything?"

"I am afraid he is the head and chief of the offenders."

"Impossible!" cried Mr. Dawson, starting to his feet, in virtuous indignation. "They will accuse me next!—perfectly ridiculous!"

"Unless I'm misinformed, such, however, is the case," replied Erlingham, coolly; "but of course it remains to be proved. Hasn't this Mr. Martin a son, John Martin."

"Assuredly."

"And there is another mentioned particularly; let's see, I forget the name. Ah, here it is—Edward Mountjoy—isn't he rather notorious?"

"Edward Mountjoy! Why, he's but a lad; *he* can't be culpable at any rate: it's simply ridiculous," exclaimed Mr. Dawson, in real astonishment. Nor was he really culpable, any further than sailing in ships of questionable character, and enjoying the wild life of a smuggler; but he was culpable in standing in Erlingham's way, and Tunny owed him a grudge for being cognizant of his evil deed.

We must now turn to Tye, and see how she had been employed during the foregoing conversation. She knew better than her father the danger which really threatened, for, during the last few months, she had been let into more than one secret by Mountjoy; and, prompted as she was by her father's hint, she determined, if possible, to avert the blow that was about to fall, or at least break its force.

Her first impulse was to mount and be off to Cross; but one glance at the stable-yard showed her that this was impossible, for the men who had accompanied Mr. Erlingham were lounging about with their horses. She must get rid of them first.

"You must be tired after your long ride from Haven," she said in a bland tone to the obnoxious excisemen. "Do come in and have a glass of Harscourt ale. Here, Will! Robert! take these gentlemen's horses and give them a feed of corn; you can put the ponies in the shed behind. Do what I tell you, mind!" she muttered to Will as she passed him.

A glass of Harscourt ale after a ten-mile ride was not to be despised, and one by one the men dropped into the great kitchen, where by Tye's orders they were plentifully regaled.

"Now I must manage to keep their chief employed," thought Tye, and in a few minutes a tray bearing a large meat pie, with sundry other good things, to say nothing of ale and wine in abundance, was deposited before the official.

"That girl will be too late with all her nonsense," thought Mr. Dawson, scowling at Tye from behind Mr. Erlingham's back; "but there, I don't suppose anything would save Martin. What a fool he is to keep risking his property and liberty in this way!"

"Your horses and men will be ready when you are," said Tye, nodding to the officer of the customs, as she left the hall. She passed into the lesser hall, and going swiftly through the garden room, she reached unperceived the sheds at the back of the stables. Will had obeyed he; her pony was there: not a creature was to be seen, and in a moment the girl was in the saddle, galloping across the fields to Mr. Martin's house.

"Poor Edward!" muttered the girl. "I heard him mention your name; but they shan't catch you if I can help it: you shall get off, you shall!" and striking her horse sharper than he deserved, she dashed along like the wind.

She rode more leisurely as she neared Cross, and avoiding the village, made at once for the side-door, and looping the reins through a ring at the door, entered unushered into the usual sitting-room of the family. Mr. and Mrs. Martin were there alone, and high words were passing, as Tye unceremoniously opened the door and walked in.

"Mr. Martin," said the girl, gravely, laying her hand on his arm, "there is danger! and you have no time to lose. Where is your son?"

Mrs. Martin began to cry and moan.

"Command yourself," said Tye, gently, "and be ready, if any one comes, to receive them with a calm countenance: you may gain time by it, if you gain nothing else."

"John is at the cove, or Merscombe," said Mr. Martin, in a low voice. "We heard early this morning that some excisemen had been seen dodging about the lanes, and so they are gone to the mill to run the kegs the schooner brought the other night."

"They are in great danger," replied Tye, anxiously, "for there is an officer and a troop of men at Harscourt."

Mr. Martin stamped his foot impatiently on the floor, which sounded dull and hollow beneath his tread.

"Gratiana," he exclaimed, suddenly, "you are a brave girl and a good rider; you can be of great service to us if you dare."

"Dare! I am afraid of nothing, Mr. Martin!"

"Well, then, go into the stable, take that brown horse you rode one day, and ride as fast as he can carry you to Merscombe, and warn the men of what may happen. For myself, I must remain here: now lose not a moment."

Tye required no second bidding, and ere long she was galloping towards the cove on the "Brown Beauty."

Had it not been for her anxiety, she would thoroughly have enjoyed her ride; but as it was, she sat back in her saddle and urged her horse to his full speed, with many a foreboding thought as to the success of her mission.

Now she must draw rein, for a deep gully crosses the road. Gently there! Miss Dawson, take care of your horse! Now she fords the stream, the water up to her horse's hocks; for there has been a fresh, and the waters are high. Now up the narrow path, not more than two feet wide, steep and stony, and up the hill-side. The horse treads surely, and his rider sits firmly, little thinking that she is travelling a road which would excite surprise in many a one who has climbed the Alps. She glances down the gorge; not a soul is in sight. Now she is on the greensward again, and again the gallant animal goes bounding along.[15]

As Gratiana entered Merscombe, a number of men were loitering about the open space in front of the church (which stands in the midst of the village), whom she recognized as being engaged in smuggling.

"What's up" asked Tye, approaching the party.

"What's up, Miss Tye, that you are coursing over the country on Mr. Martin's best horse?"

"There's danger!" said the girl, bending down and speaking low. "The rock-riders are at Harscourt."[16]

---

15 Greensward: grass-covered ground.

16 Rock-rider: a ride officer, an excise officer.

"We knew there was mischief brewing," replied one of the men; "there have been two or three suspicious looking men wandering about the moor this day or two past. Have you seen Mr. Martin?"

"Yes; and he sent me on here. Where are Jack Martin and Edward Mountjoy?"

"Jack Martin was hopelessly drunk an hour ago; you can't warn him: the less he knows the better; but Mountjoy is down at the mill, helping to run the kegs. We are expecting them up every moment."

Tye was off again like a shot, but was soon obliged to moderate her pace and go slowly and cautiously, for the road was narrow, stony, and tremendously steep.

She reached the mill, which stood at the junction of two streams, overshadowed by a few fine trees—almost the only ones in the valley, for it was open to the west wind; and there, sure enough, were the smugglers, busily employed in binding the kegs to the rude panniers slung on either side of the horses, who were fastened together in a string with halters. Many of the animals were in fine condition, and more than one the girl recognized as Mr. Martin's; the fiery-eyed roan and fidgety chestnut among the number. There were ten or a dozen men settling the loads and talking vociferously, and in the middle stood Mountjoy, the youngest of the party, yet evidently for the time the mainspring and mover of all.

"Gratiana!" exclaimed Edward, as he caught sight of the girl, "what on earth has brought you here!"

"Mr. Martin sent me," replied Tye. "The rock-riders were at Harscourt when I left, especially for you: your name was particularly mentioned by the commissioner, or whatever he is."

The young man laughed bitterly.

"Some *friend*, no doubt," he muttered, "has done me this good turn."

In a few words the men were made acquainted with the state of affairs; and in five minutes the team was clattering and kicking up the glen that led to a lone farm on the moors: it was in the opposite direction to Merscombe, where they had intended going, as they were not particularly anxious to come face to face with the excisemen.

"Now, Tye, your horse must carry double, if he will; Captain Hockin's skiff is at the Quay—I must see if he will give me a berth for a few days."

Tye makes no objections, and up the steep furzy hill they wind; Mountjoy walking where speed is impossible, and sheltering himself as much as may be behind the horse.[17] It is a weary, long ascent, but looking back they see no one in pursuit, or any sign of danger. At last they reach the top of the cliff, and are out on the open downs, where the turf is smooth and short. The sailor springs up behind Tye, and off they go.

On—on—on! not a rut nor a stone to stop them! On—on—on! the wild goats fly before them. On—on—on! past brake, and bush, and furze, and heather; not a human being in sight, only the seagulls screaming above.

On, on; but hush! see! they are not alone on the cliffs! There is another rider! He is nearer the sea than they; he notes their headlong course, and the doubly burdened horse, and he calls on them to stop. Hi dress, his sword, and the pistols peeping from his holsters proclaim him an enemy.

Not a word do they speak. The horse seems to enter into its riders' wishes and tears along; but he is fagged, he has been going at a tremendous pace. Their pursuer gains on them; nearer and nearer

---

[17] Furzy: covered with furze, gorse.

echo his horse's hoofs. The "brown beauty" lays back his ears to listen, and strains every nerve. The moments seem like hours. Nearer and nearer!

"Sit steady, Tye!" whispers Edward.

There is the click of a pistol lock, a flash, a report! With a sudden bound, and a wild scream, the pursuing horse falls dead upon the sward.[18]

The wild shriek of the dying animal seemed to madden "the brown," for he dashed away with redoubled energy. Away from the downs, through narrow lanes, across brooks, down steep glen-sides, they continue their headlong course, till, fairly exhausted, they paused in a deep hollow near Quay.

The perspiration ran in streams from the weary horse, and Tye flung herself on the turf beside him, while her companion went to reconnoitre.

"Bah!" said Edward, shrugging his shoulders, "I made sure of Captain Hockin, and there isn't even a cockle-shell in the Quay: all cleared out, no doubt, last tide: smelt the excisemen, I suppose. Come, poor fellow! you must carry us a little further. You'll have a light load home, if that's any comfort to you."

"Where do you mean to go?"

"To Branscombe; they can hide goods; perhaps they'll hide me for a day or two."

And so they continued their weary way, taking the most unfrequented roads, till they came to the head of Branscombe valley. What a view lay stretched before them! In the foreground, rich oak woods fringing the cliffs to the water's edge. Then the broad blue bay bordered with an edge of gleaming sand, and in the distance,

[18] Sward: an expanse of short grass.

fantastic-shaped hills and grey moorlands. So different to their own bare cliffs!

"You must go no farther, Tye," said the sailor, as he slid off the horse. "I don't want you to be mixed up in this business publicly. I'm all right now; if they won't take me in at Branscombe, I shall be all right in the woods for a day or two. Now good-by: you have no time to lose. Let my poor mother know as soon as you can; and if I can't come back just yet, comfort her, and be a daughter to her, Tye, for old acquaintance sake, if for nothing else."

His voice trembled, and his eye was dimmed; while as for poor Tye, her head was bent to her knee, and bitter tears flowed fast down her cheeks. But there was no time to lose for either, and with a hurried farewell they separated reluctantly. Slowly Tye turns homeward. He heart is heavy, and her steed weary; and with measured steps they track their way over dreary moorlands, through deep black peat, and iron-coloured streams, covered with glistening bluish slime, where dingy-coloured snails crawl in and out among the decaying peat moss.

The shades of a September evening creep o'er the dreary waste, and hang around ere she reaches home. Leaving her horse in the care of a trusty farmer some little distance from Harscourt, she walks the rest of the way; stealing in through the garden-room, up to her own chamber. Then locking the door, and falling beside her bed, she weeps bitter—bitter tears.

Poor Tye!

CHAPTER XVI
A SUCCESSFUL FORAY

"WE ride as if we were going to cover—hardly like men in chase of culprits," said Mr. Erlingham, as Mr. Dawson led the way to Cross, rather too leisurely to suit the young official's wishes.

"Ah!" said the squire, "let's jog on; the road is none of the best, but the turf at the side will be soft for our horses' feet."

As they neared Cross there was nothing to indicate that they were expected; the children were playing in the middle of the road as usual, the pigs disporting themselves in the gutters, and the clothes were hanging to dry on Cross Gate, which stood open for any one to enter at their will.

The knocker was rather out of repair, and some time passed before a rosy-cheeked country maiden made her appearance, and, without listening to the stranger's inquiries, but incessantly curtsying, held open the door of the drawing-room.

The room was deserted, the blinds were down, and no giggling girls were there.

"I must see Mr. Martin immediately on business," said the official, casting a rapid glance at the room, and maintaining his position in the passage.

The maid continued curtsying and begging that the gentlemen would walk in, and she would see if the master was at home.

"You need not trouble Mr. Martin. Unless I am mistaken, he has a private room at the back; perhaps he is there."

"Master will be here in a minute, I daresay," replied the maid, still opposing her broad and comely person to any further entry into the house.

"I must see him instantly," said Mr. Erlingham, impatiently. "If he is in, stand back!"

The maid drew a little on one side, and at the same moment Mr. Martin made his appearance from the offices

"I am sorry I have detained you, gentlemen. Dawson, how do ye do? Pray walk in." And Mr. Martin pushed by the servant, and entered the drawing-room.

"Excuse me; have you not a room behind this?"

"Certainly—my private room."

"I would rather go there, if you please; be so good as to lead the way."

"On what authority, may I ask, do you enter my house and demand admittance in this domineering tone? I have not the honour of your acquaintance, sir, and do not understand your language."

"The king's warrant is my authority," answered Mr. Erlingham, drawing form his pocket a mysterious-looking document. "This is a warrant to search this house."

"On what grounds?"

"Contraband trading."

"I am innocent," replied Mr. Martin, but in rather a low voice.

"Possibly," rejoined Mr. Erlingham; "and if what you say is correct, of course it cannot matter our searching. Be so good as to show me your private room."

Mr. Martin moved unwillingly along the passage, and opened a door to the right.

"I will follow you, sir," said the official, as Mr. Martin hung back, and Mr. Martin was obliged to enter first.

"Hawkins, I want you," said Mr. Erlingham, to the exciseman who stood in the hall.

The door was closed, and Mr. Dawson, Mr. Erlingham,

Martin, and the exciseman stood in the room which Tye had so lately quitted.

"I am sorry to act in this way," said the official, apologetically, "but duty compels me. Hawkins, remove the hearthrug."

Mr. Martin turned deadly pale, and leant against the table.

"Life the carpet."

Hawkins obeyed.

Mr. Erlingham stooped down and felt along the boards. The perspiration stood on Mr. Martin's face, and his hands were clenched convulsively.

"There's a spring somewhere, Hawkins; try that side."

Suddenly there was a click; they had touched the spring. A plank readily yielded, and then another, when large bales of goods, cases of wines, &c., were revealed to the searchers.

"My information so far is wonderfully accurate, I see," said the official, delighted at the large amount of property he had discovered. "You must consider yourself in custody, Mr. Martin. Hawkins, leave some of the men here. Mr. Dawson and I will proceed at once; there is a good deal more work before us."

Mr. Dawson was thunderstruck. Much as he knew and suspected of Mr. Martin's proceedings, he was in no way mixed up in them, or aware in how systematic a manner things were carried on.

"Where do you want to go next?" inquired Mr. Dawson, as they remounted their horses.

"Is there not a place called 'the Mouth' near here, and Merscombe? I must go there, too. Which is nearest?"

" 'The Mouth' lies a little to our left on the Merscombe road, so we can go there on our way," was the reply.

They rode on, not at quite so violent a pace as Tye had gone along the same road an hour before; but Mr. Erlingham allowed no dawdling: his heart was in his work, and his appetite whetted by the goods he had discovered at Cross.

"The Mouth" was no other than the entrance to the glen, where years before Grace and the lads had fallen on the smuggling party; and down to the very rock where young Martin was then feasting, the searching party descended. It was a strikingly beautiful spot: the glen was so tortuous that no sign of the sea became visible till you passed through a narrow cleft in the cliffs, and stepped upon the beach of a sheltered cove; where, at most states of tide and wind, a skiff might lie snugly enough, when for miles on either hand was not the shadow of a landing-place.

Erlingham stopped and dismounted just at the last turn of the valley, before reaching the shore. He climbed and scrambled up the low cliff that bordered the stream, pushing aside the veil of ivy and briars that hung down a considerable distance in graceful festoons; but he evidently did not find what he sought.

"It is strange that I should be at fault here," muttered Erlingham; "the directions are so very minute."

"If you would condescend to say what you are looking for, doubtless some of the men who are idling about would assist you," said Mr. Dawson, snappishly! for he did not like his employment, following in the train of a man who confided none of his plans to him.

"These rascals are said to have a hiding-place, somewhere near here," replied Erlingham.

"They must be moles if they have," was the magistrate's polite rejoinder.

Hawkins, however, was more alive to the possibility of the truth of Erlingham's assertion, and clambering up the low, ivy-covered cliff, began pacing up and down the smooth level space of turf on the summit, striking his foot on the ground with some force at every step.

Suddenly he gave a shout.

"All right! I have found it! Come up here—quick!"

Mr. Erlingham hastened to obey the summons, but in no very amiable mood; he preferred making discoveries himself to having them made for him. The space on which Hawkins stood was about eight feet in circumference, perfectly level, and surrounded on all sides by steep, grassy mounds; which, in spite of its elevation, quite protected it from view on the land side. It was probably the remains of some old entrenchment.

It seemed as if children had lately been at play there, for there was more than one square marked on the turf by white pebbles from the beach, in the way children delight to place them, imagining them cities, houses, or fields.

Hawkins, however, suspected that the innocent-looking stones had been placed there for some less childish purpose, and he proved to be correct. Minutely examining the turf near the lines of stones, a feint mark was visible, as if the turf had been cut through.

"It is a cunning trick," said Hawkins, "and one I accidentally learned from an old hand at these things. Here lads, help me to lift the sod: unless I am mistaken, we shall find it yield easily; but you must be careful, for we stand at the edge of a pitfall, of the depth and contents of which we are quite ignorant."

The turf had been so artistically laid and pressed down, that it was not till after repeated attempts that the mass began to rise; when a hurdle about five feet square, covered with grass firmly planted on it, was lifted up.

A rope and light were speedily procured, and Hawkins claimed the right of descending first; he was followed immediately by Erlingham.

The first thing was to find if there was any other outlet, or if any men were concealed! but by the glimmering light of the lantern, nothing was to be seen but bales and kegs in great quantities. The only communication with the external air was by a long narrow chink in the rock, hidden by the trailing ivy.

Those employed in the capture were in great glee at their luck. It seldom fell to the lot of either chief or underling to make two such discoveries in one day, and Mr. Erlingham, as being the person who had led them to such good fortune, became at once an immense favourite among the men.

When Erlingham had satisfied himself that he had seen all that was to be seen, he started off again for Merscombe, which lay just on the other side of the hills.

The village, when they reached it, was as silent as death; not a human being was to be seen in the open space where Grace had warned the men. The invading party rode up to the public-house, intending to have some refreshment after all their fatigues; but the only people there were an old crone, muttering over the dying embers on one side of the hearth, and on the other, stretched at full length on the settle, Mr. Jack Martin, who in the general terror had been left to take care of himself. Finding the house thus deserted, the party proceeded to help themselves to what they could find, with very little scruple; on the ground that in all probability the spirits, of which they found an abundant store, had never paid the king's dues.

Poor Mr. Jack was not quite so lonely when they left as when they entered, for a sturdy fellow was left to keep watch and ward over the miserable prisoner, while the rest proceeded to Merscombe Mill, situated on the banks of a lovely stream just below the church.

The mill looked as innocent as mill could look; the old wheel slowly toiling on its endless round, and the water splashing and falling in miniature cascades, every now and then lighted by a gleam of the sun.

The miller and the miller's wife stood in the doorway, looking as calm and innocent as if smuggling were a thing never heard of in that sweet valley.

"How are you off for brandy, Mr. Miller?" inquired Erlingham, in a would-be jocose tone, as he splashed through the stream, and drew rein at the low gate of the miller's garden.

"Brandy, your worship! What should a poor man like me do with brandy?"

"Smuggle it, for aught I know," was the reply.

"Ah! your worship's laughing," said the wily miller, in a canting tone. "I leave that sort of thing to others; I have enough to do, to look after my mill and my two or three bits of fields, without going a meddling in the fair trade."

"I am glad to hear you are such a steady character," said the official; "but you must have enemies, for such information has reached government, that I and these gentlemen are sent down to see what you and others have been about; and I am sorry to inform you, you must consider yourself in custody for the present."

"You have a pretty cottage, Mrs. Miller," continued he, in the same tone to the woman, who kept fidgeting about her doorway; "with your leave, I will walk in."

The miller's wife would at this moment gladly have avoided the visit, but she could not decline the proffered honour. The miller was very brave.

"Pray search the house; look anywhere, do anything you like, and then you will see how wrongfully I am suspected."

The men took him at his word, and began tossing and turning over his effects in a very unceremonious manner.

"What a very queer smell there is in this house!" suggested Erlingham; and first one, and then another remarked, "What an extraordinary smell!" And so indeed there was: indeed, it increased and became so disagreeable, that several of the searchers were fain to seek a purer atmosphere outside the cottage.

The facts of the case were these: the miller, when he heard of the rock-riders, felt pretty secure as soon as the team Grace had seen had departed; having despatched all his "items," as he called his goods, on the back of one of Mr. Martin's horses.

But the miller's wife was not so much at ease. She had been doing a little business on her own account, and when the cry of danger spread through the country, she had four or five pieces of rich silk, destined to adorn some of the proudest dames in the country, lying in her box in an upstairs room. She trembled! She took out her treasures, and thought now of this hiding-place, now of that; but none pleased her; none seemed sufficiently secure; and it was not till the invaders had been telegraphed as being at Merscombe Church, that she had decided where to stow her precious stuffs. The place she selected was the oven; and knowing this, it is not difficult to imagine what caused the smell that so offended the official and his followers.

Great was the amusement of all present, except the Miller's wife, when the cause was discovered, and the once splendid silks were dragged forth, charred and utterly ruined.

"Not a bad joke, really," said Erlingham. "It will make a capital after-dinner story to tell when I get back to London."

By this time, evening was closing in, and, forgetting Edward Mountjoy for a time, in the satisfaction he felt at his day's success, Mr. Erlingham turned back towards Harscourt.

CHAPTER XVII

WHERE HAVE YOU BEEN, MISS TYE?

THERE was a gentle tap, and then another, at Tye's door. The girl started, and her heart beat violently; she was half afraid lest her part in Edward's escape might be made public, and bring down her father's wrath on her, and she feared to open the door.

"Tye, are you in?" inquired some one in a low voice; which, low as it was, was immediately recognized as that of mother Agnes.

The door was quietly opened, and as quietly shut, and mother Agnes sank into a chair by Tye's side.

"Oh, child! this is too dreadful! have they taken him?"

"No, mother, he is safe for the present—he is at Branscombe; they will be sure to take care of him there."

"How do you know? have you seen him?"

"Yes, mother;" and Tye related how her day had been employed.

"Bless you, child, and keep you from such sorrows as I have known. But hush! there is a step on the stairs; surely it is Mr. Dawson. I would rather not see him just now."

"He shan't come here: never fear, sit still: he is only come up with the stranger, perhaps."

"Is he going to stay here, then?"

"I presume so, there being nowhere else for him to go."

The heavy footstep came along the gallery, and the handle of the lock turned.

"Are you there, Tye?" asked Mr. Dawson, on the other side. "I want to speak to you."

"I'm very sorry," said Tye, "but you can't come in. What is it you want?" Tye very well knew what "speaking to" meant, and thought it best to keep the door between herself and her father.

"Open the door, Gratiana."

"I really can't: it's quite impossible. You'd better go and get ready for supper; it's quite ready, and you must be very tired: I'll be down in a minute."

Mr. Dawson turned away defeated, not choosing to have a scene before Mr. Erlingham, whose door was within two of his daughter's. As he went away he called out in a loud voice, "Make haste, Miss Dawson: Mr. Erlingham is our guest to-night."

Agnes Mountjoy turned paler than ever. "What name did he say?" she gasped, clutching the girl's arm.

"Erlingham: that must be the man who is chief of these fellows," said Tye.

"Erlingham!" muttered Agnes.

"Do you know the name, mother?"

"It was mine once, child. Thank Heaven, he did not catch Edward. He may call himself what he likes, and say he came here to break up the smuggling trade; but take my word for it, his object was to catch Edward."

"Why? what reason could he have?"

"Edward may one day stand between him and immense wealth: his object is to get rid of him. You have saved my son's life, Tye; for if this man is like what his father was, he would stop at nothing that could bring him wealth. Beware of him, and be cautious with him."

Damaris here in her turn attacked the door with the information that supper was ready, and Mr. Dawson is *such* a way.

Tye was simply but becomingly dressed, and her chain was her only ornament. The stranger bowed low as she entered the hall where the supper was spread, and regarded her with an unmistakable look of admiration. Tye blushed and passed to her seat, keeping as far from Mr. Dawson as possible.

"You deserted us this morning, Miss Dawson; you were ready for a ride when we arrived; you should have joined us in our hunt."

"Smuggler-hunting is hardly a sport for ladies, I should imagine," said Tye, contemptuously, "whatever it may be for gentlemen;" and she laid a stress on the last word."

Mr. Dawson scowled, and Mr. Erlingham bit his lip.

"We had rather a good day of it," said the official, as he held up a glass of claret to the light, admired its colour, and swallowed it; "but it's a bore that fellow Mountjoy has escaped: and yet he can't be far off, I should think."

Tye's face was crimson, and so was her neck, and then she grew very pale and cold. The official's eye was on her, and she felt it.

"I can't understand about Edward at all," said the magistrate. "No doubt he has been sailing in smugglers or privateers these six years; but he is such a lad, he can't have done anything to have called down so much suspicion on himself. I don't make it out: I believe it's someone who has a spite against him. Was your letter anonymous, or did you know the writer?"

"My information was well authenticated. The fact is, he seems above those with whom he associates; and though the vessels may belong to others, he is the manager and mainspring of everything doing about here."

"You said this morning, that Mr. Martin was the head and chief; you are not consistent."

At this moment the hall door was rudely thrown open, and two men entered.

"What do you want, Thomson? What's the matter man?"

"Matter enough! I've had my horse shot under me: plague to them that did it!"

"Your horse shot! why, how did you manage that?"

"I didn't do it. I was watching out on the cliffs, when I saw flying along like mad a horse with a lady on it, and a man riding up behind her. I saw they were up to mischief, so I put spurs to my horse, and should have overtaken them; but the fellow turned back and shot my poor beast, and I saw it was Edward Mountjoy."

"And has he escaped?" exclaimed Erlingham, in a loud voice.

"I expect so; for they made towards Quay, and no doubt, if there was no boat there, he will get away where there is one."

"Are you sure it was Mountjoy?"

"Certain: I have seen him many times at Haven."

A bitter oath escaped from the official, and he strode up and down the hall with a heavy, hurried tread

"Who do you suppose the woman was who aided him in his escape?"

"I have not the remotest idea; but she was beautifully mounted, and rode very well."

Suddenly Erlingham stopped in his walk before Tye, who was trembling in every limb.

"Miss Dawson, where have you been all day?" he asked, in an authoritative tone.

"What business is that of yours, sir? you have no right to inquire into my actions."

"You were dressed for riding when I arrived this morning, and then you disappeared. I cannot help connecting you with this villain's escape."

"When I associate with villains, it is not from my own choice, but by accident, Mr. Erlingham," and Tye looked as much to say, that is my case at present.

Mr. Dawson looked uneasily at his daughter.

"I should like to see your horses, Mr. Dawson," said Erlingham, turning to his host.

"Certainly: at once. If the horse is discovered, it will not be hard to identify the rider."

They adjourned to the stable, but the man was unable to identify either one in the stable as the one he had chased.

Mr. Erlingham tried to pass off what he had said, and suggested that it might have been some farmer's daughter or other; but he fully believed in his own mind that it was Tye, and no other, who had helped his unconscious enemy to elude his grasp.

When they returned, Tye had vanished. Mr. Dawson had his suspicions, too, and when he found his daughter fled, he followed her; and this time, Erlingham not being quite so close, demanded and obtained admission.

His daughter trembled when she saw him; he had on his black look.

"What have you been about all day?" he whispered, griping her shoulder in his left hand.[19]

No answer; no movement. The gripe tightened.

"Speak: I say, where have you been?"

Not a word. Tighter still the gripe, and the right hand is lifted.

"Have you seen Mountjoy to-day?"

No answer; but a moan from the pain that tight gripe gives. The right hand descends in full force upon that beautiful, proud face, and those clear eyes looking out into the night. A sharp cry, but never a word.

---

[19] Griping: gripping.

"You need not speak; I know it all. You have helped this fellow to escape: you have been much together of late. Now hear me; if you ever meet or speak to that man again, I'll blow his brains out, and I'll murder you, that I will!" And again the heavy hand came down, striking the girl from her seat, and laying her senseless on the floor. Mr. Dawson took out the key, and locked her in.

Erlingham remained a week or more at Harscourt, during which time Tye never made her appearance. He had enough to do; scarcely a house in Merscombe escaped without being searched; and the greater number of the people were exchequered, some for large, some for smaller sums.[20] Many were imprisoned through inability to pay the fines, and piteous are the tales you may hear to this day of the misery caused; but most found the means, though they mortgaged their land, and beggared themselves, to do it. The Martins were placed in a terrible position: their estates had to be mortgaged to the full extent of their value; their plate, horses, everything, in fact, of any value, had to be sold; and even then the elder must have languished in prison, had not Mr. Dawson, for certain pressing reasons, advanced him a very large sum of money to complete the required amount. Such were some of the delights of "the fair trade:" enriching some, and beggaring others, lowering the ideas of right and wrong, debasing those engaged in it, and all who came in contact with it.

If now, even after the lapse of fifty years, one looks at the houses where such scenes as we have been describing were acted, there seems a shade, a cloud over them, and the wind comes sobbing round them as if it were moaning over the deeds which

[20] Exchequered: prosecuted in the Court of Exchequer for tax evasion.

have been there committed. And where are the actors? Where are their descendants?

You may, with one or two exceptions, ask in vain. You see in the churches handsome monuments, chronicling good birth and noble deeds, and you ask who now bears these good old names?

A poor labouring man here, a public-house keeper yonder, will be pointed out to you as their last representative; and in most cases this degeneracy may be traced to the crimes and ignorance of those that have gone before them, who, forgetting that gentle blood should beget gentle deeds, have sunk instead of rising, by keeping company and following practices that every true gentleman should shun. They have relied too much on their position, and have forgotten those two great necessities—good character and good education. Their degraded and fallen posterity, their ruined homes and barren lands, are the consequence.

But to return to poor Tye. Her face perfectly horrified Damaris when she was permitted by her master to release his daughter on the following morning; and it was days, or rather weeks, ere she recovered the effects of the blows she had received. Her father himself was alarmed when he first saw her; but he spoke never a kindly word to the motherless girl, and her heart hardened within her. She never spoke to him for months after, and had a strange, proud, scornful look whenever he came near her. And not even, when, finding that Mountjoy was safe beyond the sea, for a time, at any rate, he softened a little towards her—giving her the brown horse she had so admired, of Mr. Martin's, which he had bought—did she change in her demeanour towards him, but steadily kept her own course; and Mr. Dawson found that, unless he chose to use violence, his only plan was to leave her undisturbed.

CHAPTER XVIII
LES SOLITAIRES

SOME few months after Mountjoy's flight, a new turn was given to Grace's thoughts, and a new interest opened to her.

Two or three miles from Harscourt, along the cliffs, stood an ancient manor-house, which had for years been untenanted. Just at this time it was taken by a stranger of the name of Horton, who came to reside there with an only daughter, about the same age as Grace Dawson. Who he was, or where he came from, no one knew; he seemed to have plenty of money at command, and was evidently a man of education and refinement: but he shunned all association with his neighbours, and in all probability no intimacy would have arisen with the Dawsons but for the circumstance of his being a tenant of the master of Harscourt; Durnscombe House being, in fact, the old residence of the family.

The poor girl, left entirely without any companionship except her brother's, and forbidden to see mother Agnes, greeted Mary Horton's arrival with delight, as affording some brightness to her dull life; and, despite Mr. Horton's very decided way of keeping every one at a distance, Grace resolved on losing no time in making herself at home at Durnscombe.

The sitting-room at Durnscombe was a delicious apartment, long and lofty, terminating in a bay-window, the width of the room. The walls were covered with carved panelling of dark oak, and the immense fireplace was ornamented with carved figures about two feet high, representing a boar hunt. The old furniture, suited to the style of the room, had been left, as too cumbrous and uncomfortable to be worth moving; but was now arranged with taste and many handsome articles of more recent date were intermixed with it. A thick carpet covered the centre of the room; a few valuable pictures hung against the walls, and heavy curtains of a rich crimson shaded the room from the full southern sun that poured in at the bay-window.

Tye paused a moment at the door in utter astonishment at the change that had been wrought in the old room; and seeing no one but Mr. Horton there, meditated an immediate retreat; but Mr. Horton's courteous greeting made her advance, though there was something in his tone which made the girl fancy he did not address her as an equal, and the colour burnt brightly on her cheek. She was so impulsive and friendly herself, that she felt uncomfortable and vexed. It was more agreeable when Mary Horton made her appearance; for she spoke gently, in a low voice, and though what she said were mere everyday trifles, they were so kindly spoken that the ruffled feelings of poor Tye were soothed.

Mary Horton was a striking-looking person. Though scarcely a year older than Grace, she had the appearance and manners of a woman of five-and-twenty; being quiet and reserved. She was tall and slight, with a profusion of light golden hair, a forehead almost too high for perfect beauty, and an exquisitely white skin. Her eyes were grey, with dark lashes, which shrouded and softened them. Her dress was very simple, but there was a certain something about her difficult to describe, which showed that she had either lived habitually in polished society, or that a naturally refined and highly cultivated mind reigned within her: and it was also evident that she did not think attention to her dress beneath her.

A little talk with Mary soon set Grace quite at her ease, and she began expatiating on the beauties of the country, the excellence of her pet horse, and the sagacity of her dogs. Mary smiled and listened, while Mr. Horton took up a book, and began to read; yet, somehow, as she proceeded, he listened to her in spite of himself; there was such freshness in her description, such revelling in the beauties of nature, as had seldom come under his notice.

"You ought to be a poet, Miss Dawson," he said, laying down his book and fixing his eyes on the now silent girl. "Are you fond of poetry?"

"I like 'Chevy Chase,' and some of the ballads," stammered Tye.

"Ah! that is your style of poetry: very good of its kind. Are you anything of a singer?"

Grace, at that moment, with those clear, clever eyes of his looking through and through her, felt as if she were nothing but a wretched heap of rags. She only shook her head by way of answer.

"Mary, go and sing," said Mr. Horton; and as his daughter rose and approached the magnificent instrument to do his bidding, he again took up his book, holding it so as to conceal his face.

The girl had often heard singing before, of course, and sang herself in a manner; but she was utterly unprepared for the flood of melody that came flowing out, filling the room, as Mary Horton sang Handel's most exquisite song, "Angels ever bright and fair."

The masterly alternations of expression, the marvellous control over the voice, now causing it to float in the far distance, now bringing it near in low yet distinct notes, and again allowing it to burst forth to its full power, would have delighted any one even well-acquainted with music; but to that wild child of nature, this new-found sense of melody was as light to a blind man when he recovers his sight—as hearing to the deaf.

"More! more!" cried Grace, as Mary paused; and again the glorious voice swelled out in "Oh! thou that tellest glad tidings!"

Grace was spell-bound, and without enquiring the why or the

wherefore, she mentally acknowledged that the people she was with were of a superior order to herself; and from that day the Mary Horton of that hour was to her the impersonation of all that is most charming and pleasing in woman.

"You are not accustomed to such music as that, Miss Dawson," said Mr. Horton, who had noticed Grace's tearful delight.

"I have dreamt of such music sometimes, when listening to the waves; they sing now and then when they are in the mood, but what they say is indistinct and dreamlike."

"Have you many companions?" he asked, abruptly.

"Only my brother."

"But you know the Martins and their set, and associate with them?"

"Very rarely; my father does not care that I should have many acquaintances, and I do not like the Martins."

"If that is the case, we shall be glad to see you here sometimes, and you must give Mary some riding lessons; for I have heard you are rather celebrated as a rider, and that pretty little horse you rode here seems as if you took a delight in such matters. But pray, Miss Dawson," he continued, "do your best to prevent people calling on us; we don't want company, do we, Mary?"

His daughter made him no direct answer, but going behind his chair, twined her arms round his neck and kissed him.

This simple action surprised Grace almost as much as the music, and it struck a sad chord in her breast. She had no mother, and she was worse than fatherless.

"I think Mary must try and teach you to sing," said Mr. Horton, kindly, as he held out his hand at parting.

Grace shook her head, and again that wretched feeling of inferiority and awkwardness overwhelmed her, nor did she recover her usual free and easy feelings till she and her horse had by mutual consent galloped a mile or two from Durnscombe.

From that day a new life began for Grace, a softening process commenced, and while she loved her old friends with a deep and true love, the new ones had a large share of her affections.

Reginald had left school and was loitering about at home, determined to follow no profession but the sea; to which his father utterly refused to consent. By degrees, he became as friendly with the Hortons as Grace was, and as the brother and sister grew less shy, they both learnt to join in Mary's songs; and often did their sweet rich voices join with the more cultivated one of their friend, and people passing by at eventide, hearing those young voices pouring out their melodies on the still night air, would pause and whisper, "'Tis the angels singing."

Those were happy days. Grace saw and felt Mary's superiority in many ways; and admiring, not envying, she set herself to work, to see if she could improve, knowing how Edward and mother Agnes would have approved her efforts. At Durnscombe, too, she was free from the persecutions of Jack Martin, who ever since the Merscombe affair had followed her like a shadow, much to her annoyance; his openly expressed admiration had more than once angered Grace almost beyond endurance.

From her father she met no opposition; he was well pleased that she should be with people in the Hortons' position, as he thought it might wean her from mother Agnes, of whom he stood a little in awe, for some reason.

These, indeed, as we have said, were happy days—perhaps some of the happiest days in her rough, stormy life. She was young and strong, free from affectation and sentimentality, fully believing that some day things would come all right, and Edward come back again; but living more in the present than in the future.

CHAPTER XIX
A LION IN THE DISTANCE

THE constant association of the Hortons and younger Dawsons could not fail to remove the *mauvaise honte* which the latter had felt when they first met.[21]

Few ways of meeting tend more to intimate acquaintanceship than riding parties. The necessity of breaking into small sets, the invigorating exercise, and the little courtesies which people are constantly called upon to render to one another, make them better acquainted in a week, than they would be in months, meeting in a more formal way.

Grace not only lost all fear of Mr. Horton, but began to feel that, without any effort on her part, she had gained a certain power over him, which, like a true woman, she soon found a great pleasure in exercising in little matters; Mr. Horton rather encouraging her petty tyranny than resenting it, and often choosing subjects for conversation, which he knew would excite her, for the mere pleasure of seeing her indignant and animated. He had somehow gleaned many facts as to her former adventures: of her predilection for sailors and the sea she made no secret, and many a lively discussion did she and Mr. Horton have on the merits and demerits of smugglers and smuggling.

One beautiful still autumn day, Mr. Horton, his daughter, and Grace set out for a long riding expedition. Reginald had preceded them, and was to join them at a valley they were bent on visiting.

They followed the very track she had taken on the day when she

---

[21] *Mauvaise honte*: false modesty, bashfulness, shyness.

aided Mountjoy's escape a couple of years before: every step was graven on her memory; but her spirits were light, and the clear blue sea without a ripple, lazily breaking with a gentle splash on the beach far below, the soft balmy air, the echoing turf beneath her horse's feet, made her forget she had ever cause for being sorrowful.

Mary Horton, in spite of Grace's lessons and example, was not a very bold horsewoman, and they rode leisurely along.

"Is that not the smuggler's mill?" inquired Mr. Horton, as they passed along the road at the bottom of Merscombe, and turned up toward the cliffs.

Grace answered in the affirmative, and anticipated one of the usual attacks on smuggling.

"By-the-by," he continued, "I heard such a strange story when I was in London the other day." (He had only just returned.) "It was curious to go such a distance to hear a story of this place; but it seems Mr. Erlingham knows this country well: some of your friends have given him trouble before now—eh, Miss Dawson?"

The bright colour rose to the girl's face, and her heart swelled within her; but she made no answer.

"He stayed at your father's house while he was on his searching expedition, did he not, Miss Dawson?"

Grace only nodded her head in assent, for the remembrance of that man caused her too much annoyance to permit her to trust herself to speak; and she began fretting her horse, till the Brown Beauty pranced and curveted in a way that alarmed Mary, and for a time stopped Mr. Horton.

A few kind words and caresses soon reduced the animal to his usual temper, and Mr. Horton again began his story, seemingly bent on tormenting Grace.

"I must tell my story to Mary; no doubt, Miss Dawson knows

it well already," said he, glancing at Tye, from under his deep brow; and then he proceeded to relate Tye's escapade with Edward and the Brown Beauty, adding sundry facts and incidents of which Grace knew as little as his daughter.

"It is really quite a romance," said Mary, quietly, as her father finished. "And did the smuggler really escape?"

"Yes, he managed to elude justice," replied Mr. Horton, looking into Tye's face; "he bore a very bad character, and it would have been a good thing for the country if he could have been made an example of."

Tye's great eyes dilated, her whole form trembled, and she gave Mr. Horton such a fierce look that he instinctively shrank back.

"You speak falsely," she muttered. "Mr. Erlingham is the bad man; he has his own reasons for misrepresenting facts." And she raised her hand, seeming to hesitate for a moment whether her riding-whip should not descend on the shoulders of Mountjoy's slanderer; but she forbore, and her horse received such a cut that he bounded away like a mad thing; nor did she rejoin her companions till they had ridden a good mile, when the cloud had cleared from her brow. Mr. Horton seemed contented with the storm he had raised, and for the rest of their ride left her in peace.

The unfortunate subject of dispute, however, was not destined to slumber for that day. Reginald had joined them at the end of the valley which was the object of their excursion, and dismounting from their horses, they seated themselves on the brow of the cliff, enjoying the splendid view that lay stretched before them. Immediately to the left, the stream in which Reginald had been fishing flung itself over the precipice in a lofty cascade; at their feet extended a wide bay, and to the right a peculiar semi-conical hill shut in the beach.

As they sat watching the waveless sea, unbroken by a single sail, a long low lugger-rigged vessel slowly rounded the left-hand extremity of the bay, and by dint of continual tacks, after some difficulty reached the opposite end, and disappeared round the rocks.[22]

Her movements attracted a great deal of attention, and there was something mysterious and dark-looking in her appearance which made Mr. Horton almost involuntarily exclaim, "Well, at any rate, there's a smuggler, Miss Dawson!"

Grace turned one of her fierce looks on the speaker; but before she had time to answer, Reginald had begun to explain, in a dreamy, careless sort of manner, that the vessel they saw was no smuggler, but one of Mr. Fowler of Torford's traders: "and all the world knows he is a good honest man," added Reginald.

Mr. Horton took the liberty of doubting that fact, for he had a decided prejudice against people employed in the coasting trade; but knowing the friendship that existed between the Dawsons and Lily Fowler, he held his peace.

It was curious that while Grace was noted all the country round as one of the best riders to be seen anywhere, Reginald, with the same training and opportunities, was, without exception, one of the worst horsemen in the neighbourhood, and he was constantly meeting with accidents, and getting into scrapes in consequence.

It happened that, on the day of which we are now writing, he had, to Will's intense disgust, insisted on taking a very handsome young horse, not yet thoroughly broken. Will was furious, but Reginald was determined, and away he went over the rough road, full tear, stooping till his head nearly touched his horse's neck,

---

[22] Lugger-rigged vessels were used extensively by smugglers due to their ability to outrun Revenue vessels during a long chase.

and standing a chance of losing his seat, at every long, irregular stride the horse took.

The horse and rider arrived safely at the valley, though they had more than one chance of a roll together, for the animal's joints were unknit, nor was he yet way-wise.

On the way home he kept the whole party in a fidget, for they fully expected he would meet with an accident at every step. The horse, not accustomed to the road, and fagged by his unwonted exercise, made two or three bad stumbles, and but for Reginald's strong arm would have been on his knees a dozen times over.

"Do, Reginald, get off, and lead him down this hill," petitioned Tye, as they neared Merscombe.

"Nonsense," was the rejoinder; "it's only his stupidity. Hold up, sir, I say!" giving the poor animal a tremendous blow, as he again tripped. The horse, terrified and confused at this treatment, made a bound forward, put his foot on a rolling stone, and down he went, throwing his rider some feet in advance, and cutting his own knees, shoulder, and head severely.

"What a bore!" said the lad, as he got up and shook himself. "I hope the horse is not hurt."

Alas! the poor beast stood with outstretched legs, trembling in every limb, the blood streaming from his knees and head.

Grace was too frightened to speak, she dreaded the tempest which she knew the accident would raise. Reginald also stood silent, looking at the horse, and thinking of the future.

Everybody was annoyed; it was an unpleasant ending to a pleasant day. The Hortons were very kind, but their attempts at consolation fell on deaf ears; for the bother and sister alone knew what was before them.

"I don't know what we shall do," said Tye, in a trembling voice.

"I daren't go home, and that is the long and short of it," added Reginald, thrusting his hands into his pockets, and staring at the poor dejected-looking horse.

"Nonsense!" cried Mr. Horton, "what should make you afraid of going home? Go straight to your father, and tell him the whole truth, and take the consequences of your fault, if you have committed any, on yourself."

"You don't know!" said Tye, in a low voice.

"You afraid too, Miss Dawson! Why, I thought you were afraid of nothing."

"You are mistaken," replied Tye, in the same voice: "you don't know. It is not for myself; I'm past caring; but Reginald, what will become of him?"

"If I could be of any possible use, Miss Dawson, only just speak the word; I would do anything for you."

Mr. Horton spoke in a tone which, in spite of her agitation, startled Grace, and when she looked up hastily in her companion's face she was still more surprised to note the look with which he regarded her.

"I thank you, Mr. Horton," replied the girl; and her voice shook, for he had spoken to her in that gentle tone which women love; "but no one can be of any use to us; we must brave the storm alone. Come, Regie, let us go on; we shall not mend matters by delaying. We must face our lion alone," she added, aside to her brother; but Mr. Horton caught the words, and feared that Grace anticipated some scene of violence: not from anything either of the Dawsons had ever said of their father—for they never mentioned any of his ways—but from the general character he bore among his neighbours.

"You pass Durnscombe on your way home, Miss Dawson.

Let me leave Mary there, and go on to Harscourt with you. I might possibly be of some service," persisted Mr. Horton.

"We are obliged," answered Grace, bending her head almost to her horse's mane, "but we prefer going to Harscourt alone."

"Tye, I can't go to Harscourt to-night," remonstrated Reginald, in a whisper.

"Brother, shame on you! You must come, be the result what it may."

"But, Tye——"

"Would you let people say you are afraid of your own father? Would you expose him? No, brother, you have brought this on yourself, and you must abide the consequences."

Reginald offered no further resistance, but walked by Mary Horton, lazily holding by her pommel' and as she talked quietly and gently to him, he forgot what awaited him.

Mr. Horton rode by Grace's side, and he, too, tried to divert his companion. "You are brave, Miss Dawson," he began, by way of compliment.

"You are mistaken; I am only obstinate."

"Obstinate! hardly that: you only have opinions of your own."

"I tell you, I am obstinate."

"A little obstinacy gives decision to a character."

"You are mistaken: obstinacy is a characteristic of the most undecided characters," and the girl glanced back at her brother: "but I don't understand arguments," said Tye.

"Few women do," replied Mr. Horton, in a sarcastic tone, which contrasted with his kindly manner of a minute before, and angered the girl.

"Women do not understand arguing, but they understand acting, which is more to the purpose."

"Few women know how to act, or have the power."

"You despise women."

"You are mistaken; I only despise weak women."

"All women are weak when their turn comes."

"What do you mean?"

"Every woman has her master; and when she meets him, she is weak."

"Have you met your master?"

"Possibly," was the reply.

In spite of her anxiety for Reginald, she could not help turning a merry, mischievous look on Mr. Horton, while her thoughts flew away to her sailor-lover, whom she was content to consider her master.

Again she met that kind yet commanding look, but this time something made her resent it: perhaps the thought of Mountjoy had come to her to warn her, and she turned away her head in silence.

"If ever I can be of service to you, only speak, and I shall be but too glad of an opportunity of showing how much I feel for and esteem you."

"You are kind," replied Grace, coldly, "but there is little chance of my troubling you."

"I am glad to hear it; but if report speaks truly, Mr. Dawson is not always the fit companion and protector of——"

"Sir!"

"I speak but of what I hear."

"You forget! Mr. Dawson is my father, sir."

"Yes, but still——"

"Hush, sir! Do not make me cease to respect you."

"But, Miss Dawson, hear me."

"Never, sir! Never from my lips shall come one word against

my father, nor will I admit one word in his disparagement from a stranger."

Mr. Horton drew back as she uttered the last word, and they proceeded in silence. No further offer to accompany the brother and sister was made when they reached Durnscombe, and they proceeded on their way alone.

CHAPTER XX

THE ENCOUNTER, AND WHAT CAME OF IT

FOR some time past there had been a constant interchange of visits between Mr. Dawson and Mr. Martin the elder. Had Grace been more at home, in all probability her suspicions would have been aroused, that all was not right; but she was so much of her time away, that it was not till Damaris told her of the constant conferences between the two friends, that she was aware of them: and even then she did not connect them in any way with herself, but considered that they had reference to that mysterious "business" which Mr. Martin and Mr. Dawson were supposed to transact together.

She certainly noticed that her father became daily more irritable, but she avoided any collision with him, and took refuge at Durnscombe.

The greater part of that lovely autumn day which she had spent on the cliffs with her friends, unsuspicious of any evil, her father and Mr. Martin had spent in plotting against her liberty. Mr. Martin was determined to make the most of his knowledge of a secret and to wrest every shilling he could from the unhappy man whom accident had placed in his power.

Both Reginald and Grace were possessed of what, in those days, were considered large fortunes, independent of their father; and Mr. Martin, who daily became more impoverished in spite of the large sums he managed to extract from Mr. Dawson, cast covetous glances at Grace's thousands, while his son imagined that he should like to make the girl his wife.

To do Mr. Dawson justice, he had tried every way to avoid sacrificing his daughter, but all to no avail; Mr. Martin was determined that he would have Grace and her fortune placed at his disposal without further delay.

The influence which Mr. Martin was known to exercise at Harscourt was a mystery to those who knew the parties well, but it is now time that it should be revealed. It has been already said that Mrs. Dawson died suddenly: it so happened that Mr. Martin was present at the time, and he alone, besides Mr. Dawson, knew how she died; and in that knowledge lay the secret of his influence. Instead of denouncing his friend as a man capable of striking down a defenceless woman in a burst of unprovoked passion, he turned the crime of his companion to his own advantage, and from that day forward Mr. Martin had more control over Harscourt than its nominal master.

When Mr. Martin was exchequered for his illegal trading, every one anticipated that he would be obliged to fly the country, as it was not thought possible for him to raise the amount of the fine imposed; but to every one's astonishment, the money was forthcoming to a day, and it was whispered about that Mr. Dawson supplied the means, though he had to mortgage part of his estates to raise the required sum. Not content with this sacrifice, he now coveted poor Tye.

"What do you want now?" inquired Mr. Dawson, surlily, as his quondam friend once more invaded Harscourt.

"I want you to settle that little family matter you and I have talked of several times. Jack gets impatient, and the young lady manages to keep so entirely out of the way, that we had better settle it at once, without consulting her."

"I have no intention of letting my daughter marry your son," was the reply. "I have told you many times I have not the least intention of giving in to your wishes."

"You speak unadvisedly, Dawson. I have no wish to threaten; but if you don't give in, I shall be obliged to enforce my demand; but let things be done in a friendly spirit. Let the wedding be this day six months, and I'll cease to trouble you from that day forward."

"I say my daughter shall not marry your son."

"And I, on the contrary, say she shall," rejoined Mr. Martin angrily. "It is my will, and I should think, by this time, you must have discovered that my will is law in this house."

"You have been well paid already; *this* is too much."

"You value your life, sir!" continued the tormentor, in a whisper.

Mr. Dawson answered with a groan.

"Well, sir, you have your choice; your daughter marries my son this day six months, or——" and the visitor bent a dark, threatening look on his luckless host, in lieu of finishing the sentence.

A gun lay on the table, and Mr. Dawson's hand stole towards it.

"Don't!" exclaimed Mr. Martin, nervously. "You might have an accident before you were aware of it."

Mr. Dawson continued to finger the weapon, and Martin slowly retreated towards the door, keeping his eye on his companion.

"You are afraid, are you?" murmured Dawson. "It's good for people to know what fear is sometimes; but make your mind easy, I am not going to shoot you to-day, whatever I may be tempted to do at some future time."

"For Heaven's sake, Dawson, don't talk in that way; we have had too much of that sort of thing here already." And Mr. Martin, without waiting to see the effect of his speech, having reached the door, rushed like a mad-man into the stable-yard, flung himself on his horse, and dashed away like the wind.

"He goes as if the old gentleman himself were after him!" said one of the men in the yard.

"I don't believe he is a hundred miles off, for the matter of that," replied Will; "but generalwise it is the old gentleman who seems shy of Mr. Martin: they have turned the tables to-day."

"Look sharp, Will," answered the man; "here he comes!"

True enough, Mr. Dawson stalked into the yard, looking as black as a thunder-cloud.

"Bless me!" muttered poor Will, "and Master Regie has been and taken the colt."

The amiable country gentleman rowed all the men, tormented the horses in their stalls, baited the chained dogs till their eyes glared with fury, and finally, discovering that the colt was missing, attacked Will with such a torrent of abuse, that the worthy individual considered it his duty to give warning there and then, though he had no intention of going, or his master of parting with him.

Such was the time that Reginald had chosen to add fuel to the flame.

As he and his sister entered the stable-yard, the first person they espied was Mr. Dawson walking up and down in no very placid mood.

"Why are you walking, sir?" he exclaimed, going up to his son. "What business had you to take the colt? where is he?"

"Reginald has had an accident, father," replied Grace, interposing.

"I did not ask you," he replied, angrily, laying his arm on his son's shoulder. "Reginald is old enough to answer for himself."

Reginald, annoyed at being bullied before the men who were in the yard, shook him off, and pushing his hair back from his face, stood before his father with a defiant air.

"What has happened, sir? do you hear when I speak? answer me at once! The colt has fallen down and broken his knees, I'll bet twenty pounds," said Mr. Dawson, with an awful oath.

"Exactly!" replied Reginald, still looking his father full in the face.

"Insolent dog!" exclaimed the enraged man: "I'll make you pay for this! I'll turn you out of doors, and no farthing of mine shall you ever see!"

"Better luck for me," muttered Reginald; "I shall be free."

Tye looked imploringly at her brother, but he took no heed.

His father looked at him for a moment, and then springing at him like a wild animal, struck him several blows in rapid succession on his head. Reginald was unprepared for this outburst, for his father of late had not attacked him personally, and for a second or two he stood confounded; but suddenly springing back, he cried, in a voice hoarse with indignation, "If you were not my father, I would strike you in return!"

The lad spoke with such energy, and with such flashing eyes, that even Mr. Dawson was startled, but only for a moment, and then he made another spring at his son, who this time avoided the blows aimed at him.

"You are a coward!" shrieked the enraged man.

"Not I, but you," rejoined the boy. "You know I cannot, shall not, attack you in return, and so you venture to strike me!"

"Father," said Grace, calm and pale from terror, laying her hand on his arm, "is it worth quarrelling with your only son, merely because a horse is hurt?"

"None of your preaching; go into the house and mind your own affairs; you will soon find you have enough concerning yourself to think about."

"I will not go unless you promise not to strike Reginald again. Go into the house, brother."

Mr. Dawson pushed the girl from him and lifted up his hand to strike her.

Tye's face flushed crimson at the insult, for many men were standing by.

"Sir! Mr. Dawson! you would not dare," she exclaimed. "Remember, we have had enough of that here!"

Mr. Dawson shrank back abashed; there was something in the words his daughter used, and which Mr. Martin years before had told her always to use when her father was in one of his violent moods, that awed the bully, though the speaker was ignorant of their real meaning; and Will whispered, as the pair turned towards the house, "Did you hear her say 'dare' to him? Bless us, what a spirit she has!"

Reginald had retreated to his own room, and there Tye followed him. She found him busily employed turning over his drawers, and putting aside a few necessary articles of clothing.

"What are you going to do?" she inquired, as she saw how he was employed, and half guessed his intentions.

"I'll not sleep another night in this house, I can tell you, after what has happened."

"But where can you go? what can you do? you have no money."

"I'm going to sea: you know how hard I tried to get his consent long ago, and he would not give it; and here I've been kicking my heels all this while, doing nothing: how can one help getting into scrapes? Now I shall start without waiting for his consent."

Grace saw by his manner that he was fully bent on going, and rather glad of the opportunity; and that in his present mood it would be no good attempting to thwart him. The least said, perhaps, the better: if left to himself, it was as likely as not that he would turn back before he had gone twenty miles.

She brought him what money she had, to add to his little purse, and also some rings and trinkets, which had been their mother's.

He took the money without hesitation, but would not touch the trinkets, with the exception of one ring, which Grace insisted not only on his taking, but on his wearing. It was a quaint signet-ring of gold, with a gold shield bearing an enamel cross on it: it was one which Mrs. Dawson had always worn, and had been taken from her finger after her death by mother Agnes, who had given it to Grace, telling her it was a charm.

"Now, Grace," said Reginald, as, having finished his preparations, he prepared to go, "I trust to you to prevent my father chasing me, if he should chance to take that fancy into his head; gain me half-an-hour's start, and I think I shall manage to get clear off: and keep a cheery heart, old girl—perhaps when next we meet I may be as gay a sailor as your friend Edward." And the lad set off with a smile on his handsome face, and a certain degree of delight in his heart. Poor Grace, left alone, sat down on his bed and wept as she had done the first time they were parted.

Little time, however, was allowed her to indulge in vain regrets; she was hastily summoned to supper; and dreading to give any further ground for altercation by causing any delay, she went down in her riding-dress.

"Where is Reginald?" inquired Mr. Dawson, as they sat down at the supper-table.

"He will not sup with us to-night," was the reply; and to Grace's great relief, her father continued his supper in silence, without making any further mention of his son.

The truth was, though Grace little guessed it, he was too much occupied with her future to think much of Reginald; but though vexed and annoyed at Mr. Martin's conduct, it was more because it trammelled and cramped him, and kept in his memory a time he would willingly have forgotten, than from any tenderness for the girl.

He had an ambition that she should marry well, and, as he fancied, raise the family above the position which they now occupied; for he was fully conscious that the glory of the Dawsons was sadly dimmed, and he had no great faith in Reginald.

Grace was different: even he could see that she was capable of taking a stand among the highest in the land, if she once had the opportunity; and now to think of her being sacrificed to a man in every way beneath her! But as if she were to blame for all this vexation, and not himself, he told her of Mr. Martin's proposal without one softening word. He told her that Mr. Martin had demanded her in marriage for his son, that he should give his consent, and that she must be prepared to marry Jack Martin that day six months.

Grace could not comprehend what her father said, she was so totally unprepared for anything of the kind. She had wit enough to know that young Martin fancied he liked her; but that her father should sanction his pretensions, seemed simply preposterous, and she thought it was merely the ravings of intoxication, or that it was only said to annoy her; but he hastened to undeceive her, again repeating what he had said.

Grace turned deadly pale and cold, for on his reiterated assertions, she could not but see he was in earnest.

"Never! never!" she cried, in agony, clasping her hands over her forehead. "I would rather kill myself than be his wife. I loathe him—I detest him!"

"I will have my way in this matter. I must!" replied Mr. Dawson, fiercely.

Tye shuddered at the ferocious look her father gave her; but she was as determined, now she was roused, as he could be, and turning boldly to him, she cried, in a defiant tone,—

"I will never be his wife—never! You shall tear me limb from limb sooner!"

"Maybe you have a more favoured lover," said Mr. Dawson, with a sneer.

Grace flushed rosy red as she answered,—

"Be that as it may, I will not marry the one favoured by you!"

"It is perchance the handsome stranger whose company you so much admire, that all the country is speaking of it?" continued her persecutor.

Poor Grace! It had never occurred to her to look on Mr. Horton as a lover; though she was conscious that he admired her to a certain degree, and could not help acknowledging that she liked being in his company; but to hear her father thus broadly allude to him, turned her thoughts to him, and thinking of his kind words and gentle looks in contrast to her father's violence, overwrought and excited as she was, she burst into an agony of tears.

Mr. Dawson laughed a bitter laugh.

"You are too savage, too cruel!" exclaimed the unhappy girl. "Mr. Horton is nothing to me; but why am I to be sacrificed to that wretched young Martin?"

"Because it is my will! Ah, madam, at last you will have to succumb: ever since you were the height of the table, you and I have been struggling which should be master, and now I have conquered."

"Not yet! not yet!" relied Grace: "six months may work wonders. You have not triumphed yet: you have boasted too soon, I understand you now, and shall act accordingly. You have unmasked yourself, and now it is time I should take means for protecting myself."

CHAPTER XXI

THE SORROWS OF GRACE DAWSON

POOR Grace! how she shuddered at the prospect before her! Her very skin crept with horror as she lay that night on her bed thinking of her impending fate.

"Marry Jack Martin!" she groaned again, in an agony of abhorrence at the mere thought of such a thing.

"Never, ever, never!" she cried, starting up in her bed, and clasping her hands. Through the room went the sad, soft sighing sound so often heard there—the sound Grace attributed to her dead mother's presence: it was the room in which she had rested after her death, and which popular superstition still considered she frequented.

The girl's last thought as she fell asleep. her first when she awoke, was of Mr. Horton. He was a person, as she thought, capable of coping with those at whose mercy and disposal she was. He was the only friend she had to turn to; so, as soon as it was possible, she made her escape from Harscourt, and hurrying through the fields as though all her enemies were in pursuit, she reached Durnscombe long before her usual hour.

"Not Miss Mary," she said, in a hurried tone, to the maid who answered her summons; "I want Mr. Horton; where is he?"

"He is in the study," was the reply.

Mr. Horton's study was a room which no one entered without his special leave; but Grace had neither time nor inclination to stand on ceremony, and without hesitation she crossed the threshold of the sanctum unbidden.

"Ah! Miss Dawson," said Mr. Horton, rising to meet his visitor, "I am afraid you had more on your hands last night than you could manage, and are come to seek my assistance: I shall regret nothing that will give me an opportunity of rendering you any service."

Grace had sunk breathless on the first seat that presented, fairly exhausted with her rapid walk and the agitation she felt: she did not speak, but held our both her hands to Mr. Horton, and with tears in her eyes seemed to appeal to him for protection without breaking silence.

"Only tell me what your trouble is, and how I can give you assistance, and it shall be done," said Mr. Horton.

"I am to be married this day—no, yesterday—six months," replied the girl, speaking her words slowly and distinctly.

"Married! to whom?"

"To Jack Martin."

"With your own consent?—but I need hardly ask that," said Mr. Horton. "Such a thing could not be."

"With my consent! no: I loathe, I detest him! but such is my father's will."

"Impossible! it is merely some momentary insanity; he cannot really mean to sanction anything so outrageous."

"Alas for me! I fear he is in right good earnest; and though I can withstand him in little things, I know not how to act now. Oh! help me if you have any pity."

Mr. Horton did not answer; he stood gazing into nothingness and meditating: he was not altogether sorry that fate had brought Grace to sue for his assistance. A fact had gradually dawned on Mr. Horton's mind, that Grace Dawson was a very charming person, and would make (so he thought) a very charming wife. He often caught himself wishing that he was a little younger, or that his daughter was not so nearly the same age as Grace, and that very morning he had half determined, in spite of his years and his daughter, to ask Grace to be his wife. He was not so very old after all, and he knew that he was still a decidedly handsome man; and now here Grace came and threw herself at his feet: was ever man more lucky?

Grace still gazed in his face, and tried to read his thoughts and see if there was any chance of aid.

"Have you any money, any fortune of your own? I think I heard something of the kind one day."

"I have 12,000*l*., which will be at my disposal when I come of age."[23]

"Ah! I see, these needy Martins want your money: make that over to them and you are safe."

Mr. Horton, still thinking of making Grace his wife, thought it would be no injury to her, if she got rid of her fortune: he would give her double; she would be more dependent on him too: he disliked women with money, at least he fancied so.

"Will you go to Cross with me, and tell them they shall have all my money if they will let me be free?" inquired Grace, rising and adjusting her hair, which in her hurried walk had escaped from its bands, and hung in picturesque confusion over her shoulders. "Do not let us waste time; this matter must be settled at once."

"You had better go by yourself, Miss Dawson; it would be better for me not to appear in the matter; at any rate just at present. It seems the best thing to be done at first; but if you find any difficulty, come back again to me."

She took his advice, and walked rapidly over the fields towards Cross.

Grace trembled as she pushed back the heavy iron gates, and

23 *L.*: *libra*, meaning pound.

paced alone along the drive to the house. Her heart beat quick, and she felt a choking in her throat.

Oh! you happy girls, who are sheltered from every bitter blast, and know only the sunny side of life, pity this poor Grace, who had only her own boldness and spirit to rely on. Do not chide her for forwardness, or, to use a more favourite expression, do not think her conduct unladylike. Few young ladies are now-a-days forced into marrying; they are manœuvred into that happy state, and nine times out of ten are willing victims, however much they may in after-life blame their parents for their unhappiness.

But Grace was motherless, friendless; and from a little girl she had been obliged in self defence to think and act for herself, as well as to guide Reginald. She did not moralize about things; she did not "analyse her feelings," after the manner of modern young ladies; she simply tried to see what was best to be done at the moment, and did it with right good will, not troubling herself about motives and principles; at least not in name. She knew right from wrong, and though she secretly strove to do the former, she did not theorize about the matter.

And as to principles, perhaps she had higher ones than those who make a parade of theirs. She had not *learned* to be high-principled, she was naturally noble-minded. She hated a lie, and had an innate perception of duty; though had you questioned her as to "why" she did this or acted thus, she would in all probability have answered you with a merry laugh: "Why? how could I do otherwise? it is the only thing to be done; at least, it seems so to me."

Now we by no means wish to infer that Grace was perfect: we have fairly told of her violent temper, in spite of the love we bore her, but any one who loved her, and who managed to gain her love—no very difficult thing, for she was wondrously affectionate—

might have ruled her with a look. Her outbursts of temper, too, were few in number, in comparison with the many times she suffered wrongfully from her father's injustice and tyranny. Let those who may carp at her conduct, just consider how they would have acted under similar circumstances, then let them give a fair judgment, not favouring themselves, but giving Grace the advantage, considering how few privileges she possessed.

Grace knew little of Mr. Martin: she had sifted his character as little as her own; but she had always considered him a kind man, for he had more than once interfered in her behalf with her father, and had taught her those talismanic words which often helped her when in trouble. That he had any object in so doing beyond natural kindness, she had never imagined.

We have just confessed that our heroine had one fault; now we must acknowledge to another: at least, we must record that she had a feeling which many people would consider as a sin.

In short, knowing that she would some day or other be possessed of a clear four hundred a year, she rather prided herself on her fortune, and often calculated what she would do with what appeared to her such boundless wealth. Unkind people would accuse her of being fond of money; but if the thoughts of her heart could have been made public, they would have seen that in her dreams more was given to others than reserved for herself.

She certainly intended to have a first-rate saddle for herself; but then came such visions as red cloaks for the old women, and smart ribbons for the young ones!

Last, not least, it was the great wish of her heart to have it in her power to help "poor cousin Frank." She was determined that his ardent desire to go to college should be gratified, that she should have the means of raising himself above his present position, and that hers should be the hand to help him.

Frank Dawson did not appear to advantage, as far as externals went, when in company with two such handsome lads as Reginald and Edward, but Grace had wit enough to perceive that he had something in him which Reginald lacked, and which, at any rate, was not yet developed in Edward, if it were there:—a force and power of will which she herself possessed in no ordinary degree for a woman.

Now she was suddenly called on to give up the means by which her secret objects could be obtained; and as she saw her fairy visions fading fast away, and stern reality coming in their place, the tears gathered in her eyes, and the landscape seemed to look more exact, more defined, real, than it had ever done before.

"I suppose this is what people call growing old," she said to herself, staring to see if the things she saw were really the same she had passed so many times, so altered did they appear.

The girl fancied she had spoken aloud, but it was just mental speaking; only her own innermost soul had heard her.

Still she started and turned pale, as she nearly ran against her cousin Frank Dawson, who was making a short cut across the fields on his way to the cottage at Combe; being the bearer of a letter from his friend Edward to the widow.

"Cousin Grace! I suppose you have forgotten me, it is so long since we have met!"

"Forgotten him! poor Grace; when he had but a moment before occupied all her thoughts.

She was too surprised to answer him, and Frank Dawson—ever rather sensitive—considering her silence to arise from pride, pushed hastily past her, and would have disappeared without another word, had not his cousin caught hold of his arm, like a drowning person to a straw, exclaiming,—"Frank, please don't go, I want you—I want somebody, I am in trouble!"

Frank Dawson at this period was about twenty, scarcely less awkward-looking than when first introduced to our readers, very tall and thin, with a marvellous mass of rich chestnut hair, that hung over his forehead like the mane of an untended horse. His clothes were all too small and too short, exhibiting long wrists and long ankles, altogether presenting a very odd appearance. But somehow, when Grace looked up in his face, she didn't laugh at him, but craved his protection, and felt he had both power and will to afford what she craved.

CHAPTER XXII

A MYSTERY WORTH KNOWING

"BUT, cousin, what can *I* do?" said Frank Dawson, for a moment seeming conscious of his awkward appearance; the colour rushing to his forehead, and the veins of his brow and neck beginning to swell.

"Come into the copse, Frank, and I will tell you all," and linking her plump arm in his, she drew him towards the plantation, which shielded them from observation. "You must help me, Frank," she repeated.

"I do not yet know in what you require my aid."

Ah! no. Only think, cousin, they want me to marry Mr. Martin's son."

"And why shouldn't you?" inquired the young man, in a bitter tone, fixing his clear, grey eyes on his companion.

"Frank!" exclaimed the girl, "how can you dream of such a thing?"

"He is not worse than many of your usual associates," replied her cousin, in the same tone.

"You are unkind, Frank," cried Grace, the tears gathering in her eyes. "I know I have no right to expect other treatment from you, our fathers being enemies; but I was in hopes that, after the happy days we have spent together at Combe, you would have been more friendly towards me. Indeed, I want a friend, and if you could look into my heart, Frank, you would see that what most vexes me in losing all my money is, that I shall never be able to help you to go to Oxford, as I have always hoped to do."

This reference to his most cherished wish rather mollified

Frank, whose temper that day happened to be none of the best, from some cause; but suddenly something appeared to flash across his mind, and turning fiercely upon poor Grace, he demanded in an angry voice,—

"Who has dared to touch your money?—no one had a right to a single farthing of it till you are of age."

Grace, who knew no cause for Frank's vehemence, drew herself up and answered haughtily,—

"I mean to touch it."

"You have no power," returned her cousin, "till you are of age; and if you die before that" (he shuddered while he spoke), "it will be mine."

"Yours! How is that? I thought my brother would have it."

"You are mistaken; our uncle's will says plainly, that if either of you die before you come of age, the money is to come to me. But what is it you are going to do with this money? You have no right to spend it."

"You must help me, Frank, or I shall be lost: it is all this money that has got me into difficulty."

"You have not yet told me in what I am to help you; explain yourself, and if I can be of any service to you, I will."

The girl hastily detailed the conversations with her father and Mr. Horton.

"Mr. Horton's advice is bad," said Frank, shaking his head, "his remedy is almost as desperate as the disease: other measures must be tried first. To part with such a sum of money is to part with the means to life: it must not be lightly done. But courage, Grace" (Frank never called her Tye, as her brother and Edward did), "I will go with you to Mr. Martin, and perhaps I may be able to be of greater service to you than many a one who is more strong and mighty than I am." And rising from the bank on which they had been seated, the cousins took their way to Cross.

"When I begin to speak, you be silent; that is all," said the young man, in reply to a question from Grace, as to what she was to do. "Just be natural, and say what comes first: try to get off the engagement; but say not a word about the money, unless absolutely obliged."

"I want Mr. Martin," said Grace, as the front door slowly opened. "Where shall I find him?"

"Missis and the young ladies are in the parlour," said the maid, laying her hand on the handle of the door.

"Not there, not there," said Tye, in a low, impatient voice. "It is Mr. Martin I want. Where is he?"

The maid, who since Mr. Erlingham's visit, had been particularly shy of visitors, was horrified, as Tye, putting her on one side, walked straight into Mr. Martin's private room, followed by her squire.

Mr. Martin started as they entered, and hastily collecting some letters and papers that lay on the table, thrust them in a mass into a drawer.

"Miss Dawson, your visit is an unexpected pleasure!" he exclaimed, coming across the room, and offering the girl both hands; but she took neither. "And your companion, too. To what am I indebted for a visit from Mr. Frank Dawson, and in your company Ah me! wonders will never cease. I thought you were not on speaking terms."

"I met my cousin accidentally on my way here, and craved his protection."

"I should have thought you hardly required protection here, Miss Dawson."

"So I thought till yesterday," replied Tye; "but affairs wear a different aspect now. I know I require a protector here more than anywhere."

"Ah! has your father communicated our conversation of yesterday to you?"

"Every particular."

"Hardly," replied Mr. Martin, with a cunning glance at his visitors.

Tye heeded not, but Frank's quick eye saw that there was something hidden.

"At any rate, sir," rejoined Tye, "he informed me that three men, that is, Mr. Dawson, Mr. Martin, and his son—these three men, mind you, calling themselves 'gentlemen,'—had determined that on a certain day one of this trio should marry a young lady who utterly loathes and detests this forced suitor."

"You speak severely, Miss Dawson."

"You act severely."

"Not at all: every girl likes to be married sooner or later; it is natural; and though you give yourself a few heirs now, you will settle down quietly enough after a bit. Your father is a bad manager; he should have left the matter to me and Jack, we should soon have persuaded you."

"I tell you," cried Grace, vehemently, "I hate you son, and never will I be his wife!"

"You speak ignorantly," said Mr. Martin, in a low voice. "You shall marry my son, and your father knows you must."

"You cannot make me marry him. I would denounce you all, even if you dragged me into the very church! I would kill you all rather than be married to him."

"You may be as violent as you like," said Mr. Martin, in the same low voice; "but at the time appointed you become Jack's wife, or——" and he cast a menacing look at Tye.

"You want this girl's money," said Frank, rising and leaning one hand on the table, gazing earnestly in Mr. Martin's face.

"Really, sir, I don't know what business you have in this matter," said Mr. Martin, contemptuously.

"More than you imagine," was the reply. "But answer me: you want this girl's money, is it not so?"

"Really——" began Mr. Martin.

"Hush, sir!" interrupted Frank. "I see why you want my cousin as your daughter-in-law; but cease to trouble her; she is not the prize you think."

"You will be punished for your insolence, beggar that you are!" hissed Mr. Martin between his teeth.

Frank winced at the word beggar, but he kept firm control over his temper.

"Poor I am, beggar I am not; but for your own sake hear me: if anything happens to my cousin before she is one-and-twenty, though she were married ten times over, her husband would be none the better for her fortune, for by the will of our uncle, it would be mine."

Mr. Martin staggered; he had no wish to be burdened with a daughter-in-law unpossessed of a certain independence, and it flashed across him whether he might not have been a little premature in demanding the hand of the presumed heiress.

"Of course, I am free, after what you have been told?" asked Grace.

Mr. Martin paused; Frank might be deceiving him; he must examine further into the matter, so he tried to temporize. But Grace would brook no delay in knowing his decision; she declared if he did not set her free from all engagement to his son, she would run away or commit suicide, and never mind what extravagance she committed; it would all be on his head.

Still Mr. Martin hesitated; he cared nothing for Tye's tirade, and was determined to finger her fortune, if possible.

Grace became more and more impatient at Mr. Martin's wavering, and forgetting Frank's warning, she said, "If you will let me be free, you shall have all my fortune; only don't make me marry that wretched fellow! I must—I will be my own mistress."

Frank frowned and bit his lip, while Mr. Martin, rejoicing at Tye's unguarded proposal, looked considerably more amiable.

"I tell you, Grace, you have no power over this money," rejoined Frank, fixing his eye on her; as if by its force alone he could have compelled her to do his bidding.

"I really wish, sir, you would be good enough to hold your tongue," replied Mr. Martin. "What is it you wished to say, Miss Dawson?" continued the worthy gentleman, turning towards the girl with a very different look to that with which he had favoured Frank.

"I say, sir, you may have the money if you will only let me be free," cried Tye, eagerly.

"But if Mr. Frank's account of this affair is correct, it may one day be his, not yours."

"I tell you, I will never marry Jack; but I will promise that if you will leave me alone, the day I am one-and-twenty, you shall have my money; will that satisfy you?"

"Grace, you are too rash! This man will make you keep your word, and long ere you come of age, you will deeply repent having made this promise."

"I'm sure I don't want to take any undue advantage of Miss Dawson," said Mr. Martin in a meek voice. "I think, on consideration, it would be better for her not to marry immediately; she is, when one thinks of it, young and inexperienced; but——" and Mr. Martin paused and fixed his eye on Grace. "I think I should like

Miss Dawson to promise that if she lives to come of age, she will marry Jack, and if she does not like to marry him, why she then can give him this money instead, which will then be entirely her own. Perhaps it would be better for her to sign a paper to that effect," and Mr. Martin looked from one to the other.

"You seem to forget, Mr. Martin, that any document she signed now would be of no use, she being a minor."

"True," said Mr. Martin, in a careless tone. "I forgot that; but Miss Dawson will make me a solemn promise to the same effect, and, unless I am much mistaken, I think she will keep her promise."

"Don't promise, cousin, I implore you," exclaimed Frank, placing himself between his cousin and Mr. Martin. "You will bitterly repent it: and this bad man is only threatening: he cannot really harm you. Stand firm, cousin, and don't be imposed upon!"

Before Frank was aware of his intention, Mr. Martin had seized him by the collar, and hastily opening the door, hurled his unwelcome visitor into the passage, closed the door, and double-bolted it.

It was all done in a moment, and, almost before Tye could rise from her seat, Mr. Martin seized her arm, and hurriedly whispered something in her ear. What it was we cannot tell; but Tye offered no resistance, and sank like a log on the chair from which she had risen.

Frank, as soon as he could regain his footing, battered most mercilessly at the door, and ere many minutes, Mr. Martin condescended to open it. The young man was prepared with a volley of abuse against his assailant; but one glance at his cousin put other thoughts out of his mind. She looked like death, her hands hanging listlessly by her side, her head drooping, and her whole figure the picture of despair.

"It's no use, Frank, saying any more. I must promise, and I have promised; only I needn't do anything: I needn't marry, till I'm one-and-twenty, because they don't want me without the money."

The girl slowly rose, and taking Frank's arm, drew him from the room, carefully avoiding touching Mr. Martin. Frank went less quietly, for as he passed out he shook his fist at Tye's tormentor, and swore vengeance on him some day.

"I think you're very foolish for giving in, cousin," said the youth, as they left Cross.

"Hush, Frank, you know nothing about the matter, and never shall. One thing, do not doubt me: nothing shall be done to your prejudice; I would rather die than they should cheat you. Alas! I have them in my power now; but I have dearly paid for my knowledge."

They walked on some distance in silence, till they came to the turning to Harscourt, when Frank paused, and was going to take leave of his companion.

"No, Frank! I want you to come with me; I want to see if it is really true."

"What's really true?" inquired Frank.

"Oh, never mind, only something I heard; I won't be kept in suspense; come and take care of me. You need not be afraid; my father won't *kill you.*"

The young man looked at his cousin with surprise, but she took no heed; and when they reached Harscourt, she took him in the garden way, and leaving him in the garden room, went in search of her father.

Mr. Dawson was in one of the front parlours, which was seldom used, except when he had business and money affairs to transact. He was seated, when his daughter entered, at an old-fashioned bureau, furnished with numerous minute drawers, looking over some dingy-looking papers.

"Father," said Tye, in a loud voice, as she shut the door, "I want a hundred pounds."

Mr. Dawson turned round and smiled a grim smile.

"I say I want a hundred pounds; I want it this minute; it is for my cousin Frank, and he is in the other room waiting."

"Frank here! How do you dare! How does he dare!" and Mr. Dawson sprang from his seat, and glowered ominously at his daughter.

"I've been at Cross and talking to Mr. Martin," replied Tye, coolly; "and I want a hundred pounds; and please to give it to me."

"The girl's mad," exclaimed Mr. Dawson.

"Far from it! I almost wish I was," said Tye, shuddering; and nearing her father, she whispered something in his ear. What it was, is not for us to say; but before long, she handed a hundred pounds to "poor cousin Frank," bidding him lose no time in going to college, and promising when that was expended more should be forthcoming.

Meanwhile, Mr. Dawson sat with his head leaning on the bureau, the perspiration standing in large drops on his forehead, his whole frame quivering.

"Villain!" he muttered: "villain! to tell even my own child!—to tell her that secret to get her in his power: and I—I have no power to protect her!"

CHAPTER XXIII
MOTHER AGNES

I THINK it well in this place to give some account of the antecedents of mother Agnes, who, as my readers may remember, had once borne the name of Erlingham. There was a gentleman of this name, a wealthy planter in one of the West Indian islands, who had an only daughter, the belle of the island. She was a sprightly, merry girl, with the smallest of feet, and the neatest of ankles, tall and graceful, with as sweet and noble a face as eyes e'er looked on; and many a man, young and old, rich and poor, looked with longing eyes on beautiful Agnes Erlingham, the heiress.

But Agnes was obdurate to all her lovers, at least to those of her own land: a stranger was destined to carry off the belle of the island.

One day there came sailing into the beautiful little harbour, not far from her father's house, a stately ship: not one of the lumbering old giants that used in those palmy days to bring home precious cargoes from those western isles, taking six months to do what now-a-days is done in as many weeks; but a fast-sailing schooner, looking like a living thing, as she glided between the graceful tropical trees, and cast anchor not far from the wharf from which Mr. Erlingham despatched his treasures.

No one was overjoyed to see that vessel, graceful as she was, in such close neighbourhood. She had, in spite of her beauty, a rakish, mischievous look, and folks whispered the word "pirate," and looked wisely at one another.

Yet somehow, after a few days, both the men and officers on board her had made acquaintances and friends with many.

The captain himself was a special favourite, a dashing, handsome fellow, who threw jokes and money about right and left; and as he abused both French and Americans, he was considered "all right:" though the good people of Harmony Town never for a moment believed that he was what he said he was, a gentleman sailing in his own yacht for pleasure only.

His second in command was a perfect giant, a first-rate seamen, and as kindly-hearted a being as the world held.

He acknowledged his captain as his superior, but for all that he kept watch and ward over him, as though he had been a child. He admired the young man, and he loved his vessel; and that was pretty much all that Long Jack, as he was familiarly termed, troubled his head about. Sometimes he was rich, sometimes poor (after the manner of sailors); but he cared little as long as he felt secure of his berth in the *Ocean Wave*.

Mr. Erlingham never concerned himself about his daughter's marrying; he was well content to have a pleasant voice to greet him when he came home, for his wife was dead; and he was too fully occupied in making sugar and making money to trouble himself about her proceedings.

"He supposed she would marry one of these days; girls generally married." And there the matter would have rested for him.

Now no sooner did Agnes Erlingham come into contact with the captain of the mysterious schooner (which she did in her father's house, he having taken a great fancy to the gay lad and his gigantic friend), than she decided in her own mind that he was the very handsomest, the most decidedly charming person she had ever beheld.

Nor did three weeks' constant intercourse at all dispel the pleasant illusion; far from it. By the end of that time Agnes had pledged her troth to Captain Mountjoy, of the *Ocean Wave*, and was determined that nothing this side of the grave should part them.

She had certain misgivings as to whether her father would approve her decision; but she was resolved to hold by her choice, let the consequences be what they might.

Her dream of happiness was of short duration; ugly names were whispered about against some of the crew, who had been recognized; and but for a friendly warning, the *Ocean Wave*, her captain and his companions, would have been captured by a frigate which had been for some time in search of the pirate (for such in truth was the graceful vessel), but who never dreamt of looking for her in a little harbour on the coast of a British possession.

Away flew the *Ocean Wave*, carrying with her the heart of Agnes Erlingham. It was a perilous time for the pirate, for she was closely chased; but she managed to escape, through the superior knowledge possessed by her commander of the various narrow channels among the islands.

The pirate captain's fancy for Agnes was a real one, and she was not a prize to be given up merely because a frigate hove in sight; so while his Majesty's ship *Terpsichore* was chasing imaginary pirates where they were not, the *Ocean Wave* was put about, and taken straight back to the place from whence she had come: not exactly into the harbour, but no very great distance from it.

The ship was recognized; and those who, not a fortnight before, had only been too delighted to entertain her commander, now called him all the worst names they could think of, much to Agnes' wrath, who thought Captain Mountjoy equally charming, whether he was a pirate or no.

So it fell out that one morning Agnes Erlingham was missing, and the *Ocean Wave* was seen no more.

Months passed, and no tidings were heard of the pirate or the lady. That she had fled with him, or been carried off by him, there was no doubt; as Ailsey, and English girl who had been brought up with her, acknowledged to having seen Mountjoy at Harmony the night before Agnes' disappearance.

Mr. Erlingham was more distressed at the event than people gave him credit for; and privately he tried to trace his daughter, but he could gain no tidings of her from any quarter.

Far away over the sea sits Agnes, with a baby on her lap; the wind howls, and the waves beat on the shore, as she listens and watches for her husband. It is the first time they have been separated, and he is only gone a short cruise; but she knows the danger he runs—his is a desperate trade,—and she rocks her baby to and fro, and listens to the storm.

Hark! over the water, louder than the storm, comes the booming sound of a gun, and Agnes lays her baby closer to her bosom. Again comes the sound; and the sailor's wife, opening her cottage door, looks out into the night. Then a dreadful thought strikes her:—can it be her husband's ship in distress, the bright *Ocean Wave*? and wrapping the baby up, she staggers against the storm on to the beach. Others are there before her,—wreckers, fiends in human shape. Alas, for the vessel! alas, for the crew! on she comes bounding upon the breakers, till with one last spring, one last struggle, she is on the shore. Oh! that cry of agony that goes up to heaven,—not the faint wail of women and children, but the cry of strong men battling for life!

Through the mist and through the darkness the woman looks, trying to pierce the gloom, and she sobs,—"Edward, my husband, where are you?" But no answer comes but the roaring surf, and the shouts of the wreckers.

Then she sees the inhuman wretches rifling the mangled bodies of the luckless crew; intent on plunder, not on mercy; and she creeps up to the ghastly corpses, and peers into the face of each, till with a wild shriek of sorrow she falls lifeless on the inanimate form of her husband.

So ended Agnes Mountjoy's happiness: so died her husband in the springtide of his youth and strength, and she was left with her boy to battle her way through life. She was poor, possessing little save the cottage and plot of ground in the valley of Combe; but she found friends who felt for her sorrow, and who cared for her kindly: foremost of all was the kind-hearted giant, who had loved her husband so well, and who had escaped from the wreck of the *Ocean Wave* by little short of a miracle; and secondly, Mrs. Dawson of Harscourt, who learnt to love and trust her as a sister.

When her trouble fell on her, her thoughts turned back to the home of her youth, and more than once she wrote to her father, imploring his forgiveness, but no answer came from him to her most urgent entreaties. Once indeed she heard through a nephew, whom he had taken into his confidence, to the effect that she was never to look to him for assistance, as he was resolute not to acknowledge her again as his daughter. Need we say that her letters had never reached him, and that he never sanctioned the cruel letter poor Agnes received.

This nephew of Agnes Mountjoy's father had been brought out from England by his uncle: he had married in the island, and had an only son, much the age of his young cousin Agnes. But he had disappointed his uncle much, having neglected all the opportunity given him for raising himself.

However, on the loss of Agnes, he was taken into favour again, and soon began to reckon on one day possessing the fortune of the rich West Indian. He filled his son, the Richard Erlingham already introduced to our readers, with the same hopes; and dying before his uncle, left behind him, in that son, one who was not likely to abandon the rich prospects that were before him.

In the case Agnes was not found, all the property of his great-uncle would naturally belong to Richard Erlingham, and so he determined the daughter should not be found.

He had been now for some years resident in England, having obtained a lucrative post under government, through his uncle's interest.

As long as the father lived, the elder Mr. Erlingham had no opportunity of reaching Europe. If ever he proposed the voyage to his nephew, some plea was found to divert him from his purpose, and for a year or two from that nephew's death his worthy son managed to keep the old man quiet with false reports. But at last, weary of repeated failures, he determined to come to England, whither, for some reason of his own, he felt sure his daughter had fled, and investigate for himself.

Nothing could exceed Richard Erlingham's dismay when his uncle, most unexpectedly, made his appearance. He knew not which way to turn to escape from his dilemma, for he was well aware that if Mr. Erlingham once consulted English lawyers and his English friends, steps would be taken which would, in a few weeks at most, inform Agnes of her true position, and for ever destroy his hopes of being his uncle's heir.

There was no time to be lost; he must act at once; so, begging his uncle to make his lodgings his home, he prepared to take the most prompt and vigorous steps to secure his coveted wealth.

The old man fell into the snare. Before morning dawned he was seriously ill, and in that state he continued for weeks. His case baffled the efforts of the physicians: if he was better for a day or two, he was sure to have a relapse more weakening than the first attack; but still it never occurred to them to attribute the attack to anything but the effects of a long sea voyage on an aged frame. At last, wearied of prescribing remedies which took no effect, it was decided that the old man should be removed to a purer air, and for that purpose a house at Chelsea was selected by his nephew.

CHAPTER XXIV
TRACKING THE DESTROYER

HOW strangely does the great city of London alter every year! One can remember, when a little child, pleasant country walks under walnut trees and between meadows and gardens, where now flaunting gin-palaces and gaudy shops meet one at every turn.

Many a time have we heard tales of how ladies in the olden time took off their jewels and secreted them, when they passed through the Five Fields and Bloody Bridge, now called Eaton Square, on their way home to their country villas at Chelsea and Fulham.

London still creeps westward, and now from St. Paul's to Putney Bridge is an almost uninterrupted street. Fifty years ago it was a pleasant country drive.

Fifty years ago, one summer afternoon, a young man left his cosy respectable lodgings, not far from Pall Mall, and turning down Parliament Street, walked leisurely along, now and then lifting his hat as a carriage drove by, or nodding familiarly as some more intimate acquaintance passed him, till he reached Westminster Bridge, where, calling a boatman, he bade him row towards Chelsea.

There seemed a hush even in the great city, as if the very noise was paralyzed by the heat. Heavy clouds hung in the heavens, and now and then a low mutter of distant thunder told of a coming storm.

But Richard Erlingham, for it was none other, bent on some fresh plot, or the accomplishment of some old one, heeded not the warning, and, seating himself in a wherry, rowed slowly up the river.[24]

---

[24] A light rowing boat used in inland waters.

Just as his boat shoved off, a woman, habited in black, glided down the broad stone steps to the river-side, and looked about as if searching for something.

"Hilloa, missus! what are you wanting?" cried one of the watermen, who were lounging about the steps in hopes of a fare.

"I want a boat, but I am not rich," she answered, in a low voice; "yet I must go at once. Will you row me after the boat that has just started?"

The men laughed among themselves for a moment, and then one stood up and offered to take her; she looked so wan and worn, that a gleam of pity shot through his heart, for he looked on her as some unfortunate creature who wished to follow the evil-eyed man who had just set off for Chelsea.

"Keep him in sight, but don't let him think we are following," said the woman, as they shot under Westminster Bridge. "I want to see where he goes, without being seen."

The widow of the self-murdered man was on the track of his destroyer. She was watching for an opportunity of taking that revenge she had sworn on his grave to have; and, like a shadow, Ailsey Phillips followed Richard Erlingham.

The boats floated on, past grey Lambeth Palace, past the stately pile of poor Nell Gwynne's Chelsea Hospital, past the great cedar-trees in the Physic Garden, to pleasant Cheyne Walk, with its fine old elms dipping towards the river, till the foremost boat grounded gently at the landing-place, opposite Don Saltero's coffee-house, once frequented by the wits of the day.

Erlingham took his way along the river bank, with elm-trees on one hand, and picturesque gabled houses on the other, and as he walked he jostled against the passers-by, and showed his great white teeth, till people pointed at him, and he, turning round to resent their remarks, nearly discovered Ailsey, who was close upon him, but she shrank back into a doorway and avoided him.

Now he leaves the river-side, and turning round by the old red church, with its square brick tower and quaint monuments, passes by more than one curious abode of the olden days, and under lime-trees that hang over garden walls, till he emerges into the King's Road, just opposite the Rose and Crown, a little old-fashioned wayside inn, built at four cross-ways.

There is a rack before the door, with hay, and a bucket near by, to tempt the weary horses, and through the pretty latticed windows, gay with flowers, comes the sound of pleasant laughter to tempt the weary traveller.

"It is very hot," said Erlingham, as he put down a tankard he had emptied at a draught.

"That's no news," returned the landlady, laughing. "Why, the very flies have known that all day, and the cat has known it too, as he has lain sleeping in the sun, and now he is telling that rain is coming: look how he is lying on his back! Puss, puss, you rogue!" she cried, laying her fat white hand on a gigantic tabby, "what business have you to be prophesying rain? Get up, you lazy cat!"

The cat altered his position, and gave an affectionate purr as he heard his mistress's voice, and stretching out his sleek velvet paws, just showed his claws a time or two, and then turned over on his back again, and insisted it was going to rain.

Somehow Erlingham's presence checked even the merry jokes of the blooming landlady of the Rose and Crown; and when he took his departure, it seemed as if a dark cloud had passed away, and they were once more blithe and lively.

"I wonder what brings that fellow down here so often?" said the landlady, as her unwelcome guest took his way up the King's

Road: "no good, I warrant."

"Is the old gentleman who lives in the Field Cottage his father?" inquired one of the customers.

"No one knows who either of them are," replied the woman; "but if there is money depending on his life, I'd rather not be the old man; for the young one looks to me as if he would not be very particular as to what he did."

"Hush, Mary, woman! don't take away a man's character that way," said the landlord, taking his pipe from his mouth and knocking off the ashes.

"Well now, Jim, don't you talk—you don't admire him any more than I do; and I know when a man has got those small, forward eyes poking out of his head, he never comes to any good—mark my words!" and she turned to the door, looking up and down the road, and watched the heavy clouds that hung over the sky in the east like a curtain; and speculated if there were any wayfarers likely to take refuge at the Rose and Crown during the storm that was rapidly approaching.

The only person in sight was the poor feeble woman in black, who slowly ascended the street from the river. Just as she reached the public house, she saw Erlingham, who had distanced her, turn up a lane to the left, and she lost sight of him.

The heat and heavy thunder air had taken away the poor creature's strength, and she sank, half fainting, on a bench that encircled an oak-tree, which grew before the inn-door, on which the eyes of Charles II may often have rested as he passed down the King's private road to Mistress Nell Gwynne's, down in Fulham Fields.

"Poor thing!" said the kindly landlady, emerging from her house; "come inside, you are weary and ill."

"Yes, I am very weary," replied Ailsey, "but I have no time to rest. Where does that road lead, there, to the left, where that gentleman just turned?"

"Only into the fields," was the reply.

"I must go on, I shall miss him," replied the woman, anxiously, as she rose to go; but her feet refused to carry her, and she sank once more on the bench.

"If you want to speak to that gentleman, if you wait here a bit you are sure to see him, for he always comes in for a glass of ale or spirits after he has paid his visit."

"I don't want to speak to him," said Ailsey. "I only want to know where he goes, and who he goes to see."

"I don't know who the old gentleman might be," replied the landlady; "but he has been living in the Field Cottage yonder for some months past; they say he is crazy, but I know nothing about him, though he lives so near, for no one is allowed to go in or out but the gentleman you have just seen."

"Is it possible that I have found him at last?" muttered Ailsey to herself; "can I really be so near?" and she looked across the fields to the long, low house the landlady pointed out to her, with eager eyes.

As she looked, a loud clap of thunder echoed through the air, and a few large drops of rain fell heavily on the dusty leaves of the oak-tree.

"You must come inside," said the landlady. "We are going to have a tremendous storm."

Ailsey rose and entered a quiet little parlour, fragrant with flowers. Hardly were the two women seated, when an awful peal of thunder suddenly burst over the house, which shook and trembled again beneath the reverberation; while at the same moment a vivid flash of lightning blazed through the sky, and hung about the windows of the inn. Ailsey fell on her knees, and lifting up her hands, exclaimed, "At last the judgment of heaven!" while her companion cried aloud, "A bolt has surely fallen."

One, two, three hours pass, and the rain still pours down, and Ailsey remains at the inn.

CHAPTER XXV

THE COTTAGE IN THE FIELDS

WHILE Ailsey rested at the Rose and Crown, Richard Erlingham had pursued his way, and as the good people at the inn surmised, had gone to the cottage in the fields. It stood not more than four hundred yards from the King's Road, but was so low and so surrounded by tall trees that it was scarcely visible.

Erlingham pulled twice at the jingling bell before he received any answer to his summons, and he could hear a deliberate step on the gravel, long ere the sliding cover of the small grating in the gate was pushed back by the custodian of the place to see who the visitor might be. One glance seemed sufficient, the slide was rapidly replaced, bolt and bar withdrawn, and Mr. Erlingham entered without speaking.

The house consisted of a single row of rooms, opening one into the other, a broad verandah in front being the only passage of the house. Low as the whole building was, it stood a little raised above the garden which sloped away from it, and was bordered by tall trees and thick shrubberies of lilac and laburnum.

The place looked more like a pleasure-house than a residence fitted for the English climate. Facing the north, it was dull and cheerless, the walls damp and green, the grass rank and high, the shrubs and flowers uncared for. In the centre of the lawn was a small pond, and a broken fountain, which had long ceased to throw its sparkling jet into the summer air; and now, as the sky lowered, and the thunder muttered, it seemed as if some peculiar curse lay on the place, and that the thunder, the lightning, and the storm were sent there especially.

In the verandah sat an old man, his eyes turned to the sky. He seemed at first unaware of any one's approach, but as soon as he caught sight of his visitor he strove to rise, but his strength failed him.

"Any news, Richard, any news?" he asked hurriedly.

His visitor shook his head.

The old man sank back in his chair, and tears rose to his eyes. "Oh Agnes! my own Agnes! what would I not give to see you once again! Are you sure, Richard, that you use all diligence to find her out? I feel so sure she is in England. I wish I could get stronger, but these constant attacks leave me so prostrate, I can do nothing. I have written to my old friend Horton, and to Laings, the merchant, but I have received no answer, which seems very strange. I want money, Richard; I wish you would go yourself to Laings, and tell him I wish particularly to see him; he really must come; it is of great importance. And Horton, too,—you see him, I know, sometimes. Pray, beg him to come to me."

Richard Erlingham stood by his uncle's side, paying little attention to what he said, for he was counting the hours that would elapse before the old man must die, and thinking if any of his friends would discover his retreat before that event *must* happen.

It was known among the old man's friends, that he was in England, and that very day Richard Erlingham had had to parry many questions concerning him as best he might. He had represented that his uncle was labouring under an attack of insanity, but this did not prevent his old friends from wishing to see the unhappy sufferer; and Erlingham could urge no very good reason for refusing to accede to their wishes: so he decided to put the finishing stroke to his villainies at once, and determined that the old man's fate should be no longer delayed.

As he stood watching, with evil eyes, his unfortunate victim, the peal of thunder that had so startled the two women burst, and the lightning struck a large elm not twenty yards from the verandah, splitting and shivering it into a hundred pieces, one of which struck Richard Erlingham sharply on the forehead. Even he, hardened as he was, was moved by the incident, and for a moment he looked relentingly towards the old man. But the thunder ceased, and as the fright passed away, the demon came back again.

He helped his uncle into the house, placed him in an easy chair in a small room surrounded by glass bookcases, and then busied himself in setting a small table, on which some fruit was placed, at the man's side, who looked up at him and thanked him for his kindness.

"Let me see," said Richard Erlingham. "You have no sugar; you should be careful not to eat our English fruit without sugar; it is so much more acid than what you are accustomed to." And the careful nephew went towards a side-table, on which, among other things, stood a small sugar-basin, covered with silver filigree.

The old man's back was towards his nephew, so that he could not see what he did; but there are eyes on you Richard Erlingham, that you wot not of: eyes eager to see any wrong deed of yours. Beware!—beware!

But the plotter thinks that his victim is the only living being near; and without thought of discovery he sprinkles the sugar with a white powder, which he takes from his pocket, before handing it to his uncle. Again the old man thanked him, and pressed him to sit down; but Richard Erlingham had done his work, and the storm, which, though severe, had lasted but a short time, having ceased, he took his leave; after refreshing himself at the Rose and Crown once more, he turned his face towards the great city.

CHAPTER XXVI
SUGARED PEACHES

AILSEY took up her abode at the Rose and Crown, under the protection of the kindly landlady, in preference to returning to London, where she was but a poor waif and stray, without home, without friends.

While she was sipping her tea with her new friend, the old man sat in silence and in solitude as the evening passed away. Only once did he move from the seat to which his dutiful nephew had led him when they had entered the house to take refuge from the storm, and that was to draw the table and the fruit on it nearer to him. His step was feeble, and his hand shook, so as to render him almost incapable of helping himself; but he selected a tempting peach and ate it, grumbling in the meantime that the servant had been so careless as to spill the sugar over the fruit: more than once his trembling hand let the peach fall into his plate, so that when he had finished hardly any sugar remained.

"How curiously that fruit tastes," said he, as he finished; and pushing the little table hastily from him, upset the fruit plates and the sugar basin on the floor.

The old man muttered a peevish exclamation, and laying his hand on the bell, rang violently.

Some moments elapsed, and no one answered the summons; again he rang, and again, but with like success. What a difference from what he had all his life been accustomed to!—the ready, cheerful obedience of attached servants and grateful slaves, who would have done his will without a second's hesitation.

At last, just as the old man had got half across his narrow

room, the door opened, and in stalked a tall gaunt woman little under six feet high.

"What are you making all this row about?" she exclaimed, shaking her head ominously at Mr. Erlingham.

"I've upset the table, and the peaches will be spoilt; pick them up at once—at once, I say," he repeated, seeing she had very little intention of doing his bidding.

"Pick 'em up yourself," she replied. "Don't suppose I'm going to be bidden hither and thither at a madman's will. Sit down and be quiet, and don't go a interrupting me at my tea again."

Mr. Erlingham looked up in mute amazement. Since his residence in the cottage this woman had been his constant and only attendant, for her husband, who lived in the house, was invisible all day, and only crept out with the bats in the evening. Hitherto, though not so regularly attended to as he could wish, a fact he had represented to his nephew, begging him to procure him better servants, he had never had cause to complain of the woman personally; but now, weak and ill as he felt, he summoned strength and courage to order her to leave the room that instant. He would willingly have ordered her out of the house, but the remembrance of his utter inability to do anything for himself restrained him; and, considering her drunk, reiterated his commands that she would take herself off, and not make her appearance again before she was more fit. Her only answer was a scornful laugh.

The old man shook with rage as well as weakness, and passed, as quickly as his feeble limbs would allow him, through the French window, along the verandah, and to the gates that led into the road. He had not walked so far since his first arrival there. Hastily he drew back the bolt, and tried to open the gate, but it was too tightly fastened; and as he turned round he saw the tall woman at his side, with a grin of fiendish triumph on her face. Then he knew that he was a prisoner, and quietly and sadly he crept back to the house.

The inhabitants of the Rose and Crown were just retiring for the night, when a violent battering at the door caused the landlord to rush downstairs, and the landlady to put her head and nightcap out of the window.

"Come down, for the love of heaven!" exclaimed the man who was the cause of all this tumult. "I can't and won't stand it! It's enough to drive a man mad."

"It seems to have took that effect upon you already, that's pretty sure, whatever it may be," returned the landlady. "What on earth makes you come here kicking up such a row at this time of night?"

"Do come down, there's a dear good woman, and let me in; it's too horrid!"

"The man's mad and no mistake," said the landlady, as accompanied by Ailsey, who had been aroused by the noise, she followed her husband downstairs.

In the passage stood a rough-looking man dressed like a sailor.

"Why, Mr. Thomson, it's you is it?" cried the rosy landlady. "Bless me, how scared you look! I always thought sailors were fearless folk; but maybe you have seen something or somebody you'd rather not have come across."

"True for you, Mrs. Bunce; I've seen a chap in a ranting, raving, mad fit, biting and tearing like a wild beast; and let me tell you, that's a sight that few would look at willingly. Strike a man down in fair fight; that's not so bad; but to see a poor unhappy chap writhing about and tearing himself to pieces, it's what I can't and won't stand," and Tunny (for Thomson was none other than the smuggler in disguise) let his hand fall with such a thump on the table that the glasses jingled again.

"Well, but, man, what is it you can't stand? Why can't you speak intelligible like?"

"Why, it's the old gentleman; and be whipped if I don't think some one's been cooking his goose for him: I never saw a man die natural that way."

"Is the old gentleman very bad, then?" inquired Mrs. Bunce.

"Cruel bad; I don't think he'll last out the night; but I'm not going to stay there listening to them screeches."

"Is your wife alone with him there?" asked the landlady.

"Oh, she don't care! She likes horrid sights; it just suits her."

"And have you locked her in, or has she locked you out? Eh?"

"Bless your heart, I didn't stop to lock the door, I made off double quick march."

The landlady gave Ailsey a quick look, and Ailsey, slipping out of the inn, made her way to the villa.

The door stood open as Tunny had left it, and she readily gained admittance to the house. On a sofa lay, or rather struggled, Mr. Erlingham.

Jane Tunny started as the stranger crossed the threshold, but she was so thoroughly awed at being alone with the dying man, that she never questioned Ailsey's right of entering there.

"Your husband came to the inn and said how ill your master was, and as I'm accustomed to sickness, I thought I might be of use."

Ailsey's appearance convinced Jane, who was a shrewd woman in her way, that she came with no evil intent; and in truth, strong-minded and able-bodied as she was, she was only too thankful to have a companion in that awful chamber.

The old man lay for a while quiescent, and then the paroxysm returned, and he rolled and fought and struggled so, that the two women could scarcely hold him.

Poor Ailsey, at no time one of the strongest, trembled from head to foot as she recognized her old master and saw his frightful sufferings.

"He looks as if he had been poisoned," she whispered to Jane.

"Poisoned!" cried Jane, looking at her suspiciously; "what should make you think so? He is mad, and suffers from fits; this is the worst, thought, he has ever had."

"In the West Indies I've seen people just as he is now, and they said it was some poison that the negroes know."

"West Indies!—well, that's queer, too; this gentleman comes from there; at least, he's always talking of foreign parts."

The woman had spoken in hurried whispers, and gradually the sufferer became more quiet, and looked inquiringly at them, but remained far too weak to speak. His eyes wandered restlessly about, as if searching for something. They offered him first one thing then another, but nothing appeared to satisfy him, and closing his eyes, he appeared to slumber.

"He has been like this before, you say?" inquired Ailsey.

"Oh, yes! many times! And he's always raving, too, about a daughter; and his nephew says his daughter has been dead these many years; so that shows he's mad."

"Poor man!" said Ailsey, compassionately.

"I do think he is to be pitied, though he is mad—at least his nephew says he is," said Jane, getting communicative, and showing that she had some doubt of the fact she had just before asserted.

The two women kept watch beside the prisoner all night; his sufferings gradually ceased, and he fell into a deep slumber.

Jane, who every now and then took a little comfort from a bottle which stood beside her, gradually dropped into an uneasy slumber, snoring tremendously, and every now and then starting up of a sudden, and making such a nose that the poor invalid moaned and shuddered in his sleep. Ailsey at last persuaded her to go and rest herself, promising to keep watch till morning.

Morning came. First one bird and then another began to chirp and chatter, and long gleams of sunshine crossed the damp garden—at first sickly, faint, and yellow; then, as the sun rose higher, shining full and strong between the shrubs.

And Ailsey sat and watched by her old master, and thought of the island far away in the western sea, and of the mango-trees, and the golden canes, and the soft rippling water, and then of all her sorrows; and bending her head over the old man, she muttered again the word she had muttered over her husband's grave, "Revenge!" "If only I knew where to find Miss Agnes, then I would bring that fellow to my feet speedily; but I must wait, must manœuvre. Have patience, Ailsey. Patience, and you shall triumph."

Thanks to Jane's libations, the sun was high in the heavens before she awoke, and Ailsey counted the moments, hoping that Mr. Erlingham might awake before his keeper, and thus give her an opportunity of discovering herself to him. Nor was she disappointed; long before the effects of the brandy had left the gaoler, the prisoner was wide awake. He quickly discovered the change in his attendant, and hastily inquired who she was.

"A friend," replied Ailsey, in a gentle voice.

"Friends are rare," said the old man, sadly; "but who are you, and how came you here?"

"I am your old servant, Ailsey," said the woman; "and last night, when you were ill, I was accidentally in the neighbourhood, and came to help your servant take care of you."

"Ailsey?" said the sick man, in an inquiring tone, as if striving to recollect something. "Ah! yes, now I remember—you were Agnes' maid. Poor Aggy! poor Aggy! they say she is dead and gone; but I don't believe them—I don't believe them."

"Nor I either; but you must keep quiet and not speak; and when your servant comes in, don't seem to know me, and I will stay with you and see if we can find Miss Aggy."

When Jane made her appearance, and found her charge so far recovered, she began to consider that she had better get rid of her self-invited visitor; and not being in the habit of mincing matters, told her as much as they sat at breakfast. But Ailsey had no intention of moving off so quickly.

"I want to stay in Chelsea a day or two; and as you seem to have plenty of room here, I should be very glad to pay you for my lodging; I could make myself of use, too," she continued, nodding her head towards the room where the sick man lay. "I don't believe he's through the wood yet."

"I can't let you stay. My master doesn't care to have more than me about here; and I should get a precious scolding if he knew any one had been here; but for the matter o' that, I'm not going to tell him."

"But if I pay you for letting me stay?"

"It's not likely you could make it worth my while; you don't look over rich," replied Jane, eying her companion.

"If you will let me stay, you shall have money."

"Well, but how much? My master pays me well, and I shall be faithful to him unless some one pays me better," she added, in a lower voice.

"Let me stay here and you shall be well paid; but you must not let Mr. Richard know I am here."

"You know Mr. Erlingham, then?"

"Mr. Erlingham is in the other room; Mr. Richard Erlingham is his nephew."

"For my part, I know nothing about either of them; a friend got me the place to look after the old man, and the young one comes now and then to see him."

"I'll tell you this much," said Ailsey, laying her hand on the woman's arm, "the old gentleman is as rich as a king; and if you help me to serve him, he will pay you like a king. Only you must keep our secret, and let no one know I am here."

Richard Erlingham was a gentleman, and Jane Tunny was only a sailor's wife; but they had one passion in common, and that was money. Nor did either scruple as to the means they used for obtaining it.

Jane had spoken truly when she said she was faithful to those who paid her highest, and Ailsey, seeing her ruling passion, determined that she should not be long before she fingered some of her promised reward, and in the meantime busied herself in making her master more comfortable.

Ailsey was not, however, destined to be successful in her endeavours to bring father and daughter together, or to prevent Richard Erlingham from gaining possession of his uncle's wealth. The old man's days were numbered, and Ailsey's only comfort was, when, scarcely a week after she had gained admission to the cottage, he breathed his last, that he had had one friend by his side to soothe his last hours.

His nephew visited him several times during those last few days; and it was immediately after one of his visits that the old man was seized with a fit from which he never recovered.

Ailsey of course had kept out of Richard Erlingham's sight; and Tunny also disappeared from the villa, for one glance at Ailsey was sufficient to show him, that she was the widow of his gaoler at Newport.

Erlingham, in selecting the person he did as his uncle's attendant, had merely chosen her because he believed her to be harsh and unscrupulous; and, unconscious of her relationship to Tunny, was little aware of the danger he ran, as the sailor might at any moment have revealed his schemes to his uncle, and discovered to him his daughter's place of retreat. But it was not to be.

Again, had Tunny not had his own reasons for avoiding Ailsey, she might possibly have obtained some clew to Agnes' whereabouts, and so have defeated Erlingham by producing the rightful heir. But it was not to be; Richard Erlingham took undisputed possession of his uncle's property.

A day or two before his death, Mr. Erlingham gave Ailsey a packet which he told her contained his will; but she was to make no use of it, unless she should find his daughter; "for," he said, "if she be not living, Richard is my heir; there is no occasion for making a will in his favour. Oh! that I could have seen my poor child once again! Seek her, for me, through the world, and tell her how I loved and forgave her. Oh! if she had only trusted me!"

Richard Erlingham was not a man to trust to chance inheritance. He produced a will in which everything was left to him: there was no flaw, no inaccuracy in the document, and he was congratulated on all sides on his marvellous good fortune.

Ailsey disappeared before the funeral, bearing with her the precious packet, and having a strong conviction that the old man had died from the effects of poison, administered by no other hand but that of his grateful nephew.

Jane Tunny, handsomely rewarded, retired to a secure hiding-place for her husband; and Erlingham, unknowing of the risk he had run in employing her, promised to recommend her to a trustworthy person when he had the opportunity; but somehow he found it more prudent to forget her, and though he often had occasion to employ Tunny, he never saw Jane again.

CHAPTER XIX
A SCHEMING BENEDICT

THE happiness and comfort which Grace derived from her association with the Hortons were not destined to last long. About a year after the incidents recorded in our last chapter, a dark shadow intervened between her and her friends.

Mr. Horton had known Mr. Erlingham's relations in the far west; accident had thrown them together in London, and it struck Mr. Erlingham that it might not be a disadvantageous thing for him, if he could persuade the graceful Mary Horton to become his wife, now that he was likely to be the undisputed possessor of his uncle's fortune.

How much of what poets and authors call "love" there was in the affair, far be it from me to say; but he certainly set about the matter in a very business-like way. First he ascertained the amount of her father's property, and that she would have no sharer in his almost princely fortune; and then, having occasion to be in the south of Ireland, on some one of his multifarious schemes, he thought proper to take the west country on his way home, and called unasked at Durnscombe.

It was an unwelcome and unexpected meeting between Grace and the stranger: she shrank from him as from a viper; and her dislike communicated itself in a degree, and for a time, to the Hortons, both father and daughter.

But after a while this feeling wore off, and even Tye could hardly withstand the charm of his manners and conversation.

Like many other men black and vile, Erlingham, when he chose, could turn himself from a hungry, greedy wolf to a gentle and unwontedly amusing lamb. And just now he did choose to make himself agreeable as agreeable could be.

He charmed Mr. Dawson by his judgment in horse-flesh and his seat on horseback, and even made friends with Mr. Martin of Cross, assuring him that he deeply regretted the part he had been compelled to take with regard to "that unfortunate affair." "But public men, you know, Mr. Martin, must pay a penalty for being public men: things are forced upon them in their public capacity that they would shrink from in their private position."

Mr. Martin bowed and was civil, thinking, perhaps, it was just as well to have a friend at court.

He paid a visit to the mill at Merscombe, and joked the miller's wife about her baked silks, and promised this one, and the other, to see if he could not get their penalties mitigated.

But there was one house he never entered, and that was the cottage in the Combe.

Whenever he looked at the place from a distance, whenever the place came to him in his thoughts, a ghastly spectre warned him back: an aged man, weeping for his only child—a murdered man struggling with his murderer—stood before him; and his blood froze, and the cold perspiration stood on his bloodless face!

And poor mother Agnes! Down in her cottage in the Combe she heard how near her enemy was; and she cowered beside her lonely hearth, and thought of the sailor far away on the sea.

She took some little comfort from the fact that, Erlingham, having possessed himself of everything his uncle had to leave, would cease to persecute her son.

Shortly after his uncle's death, to avoid all fuss, and any claims upon the property he had after so many years of manœuvring obtained, Richard Erlingham thought fit to send an intimation to his cousin that he had been constituted his uncle's legal heir, and that, hearing she was poor, he had desired his banker to pay her a hundred pounds on application.

This offer, as may be supposed, was scornfully declined; nor (knowing the sort of man she had to deal with) did she place much faith in his assertion concerning the elder Erlingham's will. She had always looked forward to the day when Edward would inherit this fortune, and be in a position to claim Grace openly and honestly. It was too much to give up without a struggle: so for the first time since her husband's death she left the Combe, and travelled up to far-off London.

But she found no comfort there. It was too true; she was disinherited and her son only a sailor lad. But though, as she thought, so hardly used, she turned with yearning to the old man's last home. She sought out the long low villa in the Chelsea fields where he had breathed his last agonized breath. The broken fountain, the moss-grown sun-dial, the riven tree, the desolate and overgrown garden—what a contrast to the old sunny home, under the mango-trees, by the cove in the far-off western isle!

And she sought the grave in the tiny graveyard by the old red church, round which the elm-trees waved, and the river flowed rippling by.

"Lift up your head, Agnes Mountjoy, a friend is near at hand."

"Lift up your head, Ailsey: the one you seek is by your side."

But the two stricken women pass by one another, touch one another, but neither head is lifted, and the stream of the great city parts them. How often do such things happen in life: a look, a turn, may change the whole current of one's destiny!

So Agnes went back to her cottage in the Combe, so lonely always, so doubly lonely now: for she hardly ever saw Grace, and felt utterly separated from her. She was jealous, too, that Grace—*her* Grace—should meet that man familiarly, and be so much with *his friends*, as she now designated the Hortons. Had she known all—had she but guessed Mr. Horton's admiration for Grace, she would have been still more annoyed and alarmed.

The few days for which Richard Erlingham first came to Durnscombe grew into weeks, and still he stayed. Mary gradually drew away from Grace, and Grace from Mary. Mary had found new interests, and Grace experienced a feeling of resentment with her for so doing, as if she had committed a sin against her.

But still Grace went to Durnscombe; she could not break off the habit she had formed, of turning her horse's head in that direction; and though, during the first few days of Erlingham's stay she had omitted her daily visits, they were resumed at Mr. Horton's urgent request, when he accompanied Mr. Erlingham on a visit to Harscourt.

The stranger's admiration of Mary was most undisguised; and as neither she nor her father seemed in any way to resent it, it soon became a recognized fact; and on any expedition Grace found herself left entirely to Mr. Horton's guidance and companionship. To say that she disliked this arrangement would be untrue. Grace was no longer a mere wild child of the cliffs; she was a very beautiful, and a very clever woman. We do not pretend to say she was accomplished, in the general acceptation of the word; her singing was her only accomplishment; but she had a clear quick mind, that could see and grasp anything worthy of being thought about, and in Mr. Horton she had had such a teacher as few women ever find.

Her beauty and her romance had first attracted him, the polished man of the world; but he soon found she possessed much greater and deeper charms, and he strove to arouse her dormant faculties and cultivate them for himself.

That any obstacle could arise, he never pictured to himself. When he had once formed the scheme, he worked steadily for the end, and now he thought he might put forth his hand, and gather the fruit of his many labours.

But all his calculations were doomed to be frustrated. As weeks wore on, and Mary was formally engaged to Erlingham, and the wedding-day fixed, Mr. Horton told his tale of love to Grace.

Ah! that flashing eye—that proud resentful cry!

"Never! never! never!"

Mr. Horton, unprepared for such an outburst, and yet undismayed, tried to appease and argue at once, but all to no purpose: "never! never!" was his only answer.

Poor girl! she saw now to what all those pleasant talks, those soft looks led; she should have seen before, some may say; but she was not one of those who think that every man who looks at them is in love, and she unwillingly fell into the snare.

But now she was alive, and away she sped to Harscourt more quickly than was her wont.

Mr. Horton had no intention of resigning her without another struggle, and he determined this time to try his luck with Mr. Dawson, but with as little success.

"I know not what encouragement my daughter may have given you, sir," said the worthy father "but my daughter is already engaged, with my consent, to Mr. Martin, and no other proposal can be entertained." And no argument Mr. Horton could use had the least effect in changing Mr. Dawson's decision; though when he was gone Mr. Dawson ground his teeth with rage, and with many a bitter oath against the Martins, lamented the impossibility of his daughter forming such an alliance, never considering whether she would have consented or no.

They met but once after that day. Grace felt guilty and uneasy, Mr. Horton hurt and disappointed. But Grace was to be Mary's bridesmaid: and so once more she went to Durnscombe, and for the last time they stood together in the old church on the cliffs.

And there that snowy cloud was merged into that black, stormy nature; and before the altar Mary promised, as many others have done before and since, to love, honour, and cherish, in sickness and health, for better, for worse.

Remember those words in years to come, Mary! Remember! for better, for worse!

After the wedding, Grace, who is tearful and humble, begs Mr. Horton's forgiveness for the wrong she has done him, but does not mend matters by saying she shall always think of him with affection, as Mary does.

CHAPTER XXVIII

A Conflict

IT was with slow steps and a heavy heart that Grace turned her face towards Combe, a few days after the Hortons' departure.

She could not keep all that had happened to herself: she wanted comfort and counsel. She had of late rather neglected mother Agnes, for after her father's first burst of anger and suspicion about Edward was over, she was free to go where she chose. He took little heed of her goings out and comings in, while he was sure that Mountjoy was out of reach, and his own comforts were sufficiently tended to. But now, in her grief and solitude, she turned towards her oldest and kindest friend. She chooses the path along the cliff—ay, what a path!—only just room for that light figure, those small, steady feet. The sea beats against the base of the cliffs; in places there is no beach, even at the lowest tides, but sombre black rocks sink deep among the waves: it seems as if the lightest puff of wind would send her down the giddy precipice. But with the eye and foot of a trained mountaineer, she winds along the track, pausing and steadying herself with her hands as she passes two or three pinnacles of rock, that dispute the right of man to pass that way. At last she turns suddenly from the sea, and follows a narrow terraced walk along the grassy slopes of Combe, down to the little cottage in the bottom.

There is a kindly welcome for her: Agnes hardly likes to chide her, but the tears are in her eyes.

"Mother, I have been doing wrong, and I have been punished for it." And in a trembling voice, and with burning cheeks, Grace tells of Mr. Horton's proposal

"It would have been well, my child," said mother Agnes, "if you had accepted it. It would have been an easy way of ridding yourself of Mr. Martin. It was such a marriage as your father would doubtless have approved."

Mother Agnes jerked out her words in an unwontedly abrupt manner. Grace looked up at her with amazement.

"You are angry with me, mother; but please—please forgive me for Edward's sake. I am but a child. Don't be angry—don't mother dear!"

"Hush—hush! you must not call me mother any more, or speak of Edward. You must forget it all."

The poor girl was utterly abashed at these words, and a thought darted through her mind, that Agnes was too hard upon her.

"It is no fault of yours, dear, I say this," continued Mrs. Mountjoy, divining what was passing in Grace's thoughts. "I have acted wrongly by you these many years; I must try my best to alter things before it is too late. I tell you, Grace, plainly, you must never think of Edward any more."

A deep flush came over the girl's face: a throbbing, beating of the heart, a choking in the throat. She dropped to her knees before her companion, and in a husky voice inquired if she had lately heard from Edward;—"because if you have," she continued, "and he loves some one else, tell me so and that will end the matter."

Mother Agnes was in a scrape; she felt bound to tell the girl that she knew nothing of the sort; but then, if she could break through the tie, what a right and proper thing she would have done.

She hesitated.

"Answer me, mother, I implore. Does Edward care for me no longer? Has he told you so?"

This time Agnes was forced to answer, "No."

"Ah! why do you torture me in this way, mother? what have I done? Can *I* help these men fancying that they should like to marry me? Is it my fault?"

And springing to her feet, she paced hurriedly up and down the cottage, her head thrown back, her eyes flashing.

"One says I am handsome and clever, and persecutes me on that account; the other says I am rich, and persecutes me for that! And now even you turn on me, as if I had not troubles and sorrows enough before!"

And Grace for a moment really believed herself overwhelmed with sorrows and annoyances; though to tell the truth, whatever she might have on her mind to vex her, she generally carried a cheerful countenance with her.

Mother Agnes was already penitent, and being little used to Grace's violence, was rather awed; still, in spite of it all, she was determined, having begun the matter, to ease her conscience, and be done with it; so, nerving herself for a new conflict, she began, in a humble tone, to try and soothe the girl.

"It is not you, Grace, who are to blame; or Edward, bless him: it is my fault, all of it."

"All of what?" cried Grace, pausing for a moment in her walk, and stamping her foot on the hard floor.

"I ought never to have let you be so much together; I might have foreseen what would come of it; but now it must all end. No good ever came of a clandestine marriage; I know it to my cost."

"I have no wish for a clandestine marriage," answered the girl, proudly. "When I marry Edward I will marry him before the world."

"Hush, child! you are too confident. It is all changed; it is all over now."

"How? why?" exclaimed Grace, impatiently.

"You terrify me, Grace. Be gentle, be yourself, and I will tell you."

"I am never gentle; I am wild and fierce," cried the girl. But she stopped by Agnes Mountjoy's side, and bade her speak on.

"Grace, I always thought, when you three played together at my knee, that one day Edward would be ten times as rich as your father, and be able to take his place in the rank from which my disobedience banished him: though his father was but a sailor, I am descended from as old a family as yours."

Grace moved away in disdain.

"What is all this to me?"

"You must listen, Grace, for it is much to me. I was young and wilful as you are now, and disobeyed my father, and he never forgave me—never!" repeated the poor woman bitterly. "Till lately I always hoped that in the eleventh hour he might have pity, but he died without one thought of me, and left all that wealth I so sincerely hoped might one day be my son's, to a cousin—none other, Grace, than your friend, Mr. Erlingham."

"My friend! You do well to twit me with my friends: I have so many and they are so kind!"[25] And again Grace tramped up and down the low-roofed room.

"You see, if he had had his rights, and been able to go openly to your father, it might all have been well; but now it is impossible, and only trouble will come, if it is not stopped."

"Trouble comes any way—every way," replied Grace more gently, clasping her hands. "There is no help anywhere. If I lose Edward, I shall lose my only hope and comfort. He promised to defend me, and he will, I know he will. Oh, where is he! why am I never to see him?"

[25] Twit: to taunt or reproach.

"You know why neither I nor you can see him, Grace; and it is well; your fancy will wear off in time."

"Hush! It is no mere fancy, mother. If it had been, do you think I should have resented Mr. Horton's conduct so? No; when he spoke of love, it jarred and grated like a rusty hinge. I know that I love Edward and he loves me."

She was quite soft and gentle now, like a little child. "Mother," she said, "forgive me; I have been violent; speak gently to me and forgive me."

Mother Agnes, put your arms round her neck, and draw her beautiful face to your bosom, and forgive her. Remember, it is your fault; you let her love; you never spoke a word of warning, or a word of blame.

But some evil spirit hovers near mother Agnes to-day. Never very wise of clear-headed, to-day she is cruel, and she shrinks from the prostrate girl.

"I have nothing to forgive, Grace; but for my sake you must mind what I say, and try and forget Edward."

Now all this while, though Agnes believed she was acting from the highest motives (and so she was to a certain extent), she was also, unconsciously to herself, actuated by a certain amount of jealousy and pique at Grace for having had any one to love, or to love her, except herself.

Grace sprang up again, and Agnes, unmindful of the fierce look that again lowered on her companion's face, went on in a complaining voice: "You had better do as your father wishes, and make the best of young Martin: after all, he may not be as bad as he seems."

Poor Grace! The Dawson blood was fairly up now, and a bitter, blasting storm swept over that young face, robbing it of its beauty.

"Woman," muttered Grace, "hold! If you were not his mother, I could strike you down at my feet. As to that miserable wretch that you speak of, I would murder him, or kill myself, rather than be his wife."

"Oh, Grace, Grace! what have I done?" exclaimed mother Agnes, seeing too late the evil spirit she had roused. "I implore you, forget what I said, and put away that awful look, and hush those frightful words. Child, you are as bad as your father!"

The tempest swept by, and the girl stood pale and awe-struck.

"Nearly as bad," she murmured in an undertone. "He did it in a passion, and I have spoken of, and even felt, a desire to do the same deed."

Mother Agnes said not another word, neither then nor afterwards; and she and the girl, after many mutual self-accusations and petitions for pardon, parted as lovingly as if no angry words had passed. They were the first, the last, the only cruel words that ever passed between them; and from that day forward Grace tended Agnes Mountjoy with a gentle, tender bearing, as if to make amends for that one wild outburst. Agnes, on her part, avoided all conversation concerning Edward, though she did not hesitate to give his letters into the girl's hands, or object to her adding to her own letters.

That fit of temper taught Grace to have a little more patience and forbearance with her father; for it showed her that she had the same spirit, and that, if indulged, it might lead to the same results.

VOLUME II

CHAPTER I

MINISTERING ANGELS

SWEET Lily! How every one loved her and blessed her! So very fair, so gentle, so good, how could they help loving her? She flitted about the old town like an angel. Was there sickness or sorrow, who so tender a nurse, so kind a friend, as "the Lily?"

The old looked to her for comfort, the young for kindly words and sweet smiles; and Lily's smiles were worth having, they were so overflowing with affectionate sympathy. She brought light and sunshine wherever she trod.

Many a letter did she write to rough sailors, and many a one did she read to the poor lone ones at home, who when they received the long-wished-for and precious packet, were unable to make out a line without her aid.

Many a little child did she teach and train to be as good and gentle as herself: and perhaps in the whole neighbourhood, no one exercised so good and extensive an influence as the little fairy daughter of the shipbuilder at Torford.

Her greatest sympathy was shown to the sailors and their families: she took but little interest, however kind she might be to them, in the lands-people; but from the dirtiest little urchin who paddled in the river, or danced upon the floating logs outside the shipyard, to the grey-headed old veteran who sat in the sun before his door, she took them under her special care and guardianship. And they paid back her kindness in their own rough way: whenever she appeared, there was a nod of recognition, a "bright day to you," or a murmured blessing.

"I tell you what it is," said one of the roughest men in Torford, as she and Grace passed by: "I tell you what: it isn't much such as I know about the angels; but it's my belief she is, or will be one some day. There's that about her as different from any one else as ever can be. I can't tell just what it is, I can't explain, but when she goes by it's as if something good passed; she's like a pleasant dream or the sight of home after a long voyage."

Grace and Lily were friends now. Since Reginald had been at sea, and the Hortons gone, they saw a great deal of each other.

There was no more than a couple of years' difference in their ages; but while Grace looked and acted as a woman, the Lily was still in appearance a little child, and Reginald was a strong bond of union between them, though they differed much in their opinion of him. Lily believed him perfect; Grace, though few sisters ever loved a brother better than she did Reginald, was anxious about him, and uneasy if he displayed the slightest changeableness or vacillation.

"If he falls into good hands," she would say, "he will do very well; but I am so afraid: he is so easily led and worked upon, in spite of his obstinacy."

"I don't think he is obstinate, dear Tye," the Lily would answer. "He is so dear and kind, you should not doubt him so."

It was a pleasant sight to see the two girls together, they both were so fresh and beautiful. Old folks will tell how, after their rides, they would come into the cottages in their riding habits, and how handsome they used to look in their hats, with their long hair falling over their shoulders.

"Bless you, 'twas a sight worth seeing, the two dear young ladies. They used to come like that, because they knew we liked to see them dressed out like; and sometimes, if they had pretty new dresses, they'd come by to show them to us. Miss Dawson—handsome Miss Dawson, as they used to call her—most times wore a blue dress.

There was a great painter in Torford once, who made a beautiful painting of her dressed in her blue dress, and she got the name of the blue lady after that. They used to say she was proud; but I never saw it, poor dear. I've seen her on her knees yonder, on my poor hearth, lighting up a bit of fire while I was ill, and Miss Lily tidying the room, bless them. Well, they are dead and gone. I wonder if there are any such young ladies now-a-days?"

I hope there are; for such visits as Lily and Grace paid among the poor did more to soften and humanize them than ten thousand ordinary district visitors would effect in a twelve-month.

It is utterly disgusting to see ladies, often very young ladies, invading the cottages of their poorer sisters, giving their advice and dictating to women old enough to be their mothers, and many a time wise enough to teach them many a thing of which they are utterly ignorant.

A woman's business among the poor—more especially a young woman's—is kindness. She is not called on to teach and preach; neither is she to be a mere substitute for a relieving officer. A little "present," quietly and unostentatiously given, is far more valued by the better class of poor (we are not speaking of beggars) than a large donation given as "charity."

However pleasant it may be to give, it is not always necessary. Cottagers like to be "visited," just as we like to be "visited' by pleasant people. They like kindly words and pleasant smiles, they like their children to be admired, and their household goods admired, and their absent ones inquired after, just as much as others; and the small acts of thoughtfulness and kindness which we accept and appreciate are accepted and appreciated by them.

As I write, I call to mind two girls who went much among the poor. They gave nothing, for they had nothing to give. They are gone and passed away. One is up among the angels; but if you go among those whom they once visited, you would hear their names mentioned with praise and blessings. "They were good ladies, bless 'em; it always did one good to see them; and you know, 'twasn't for what they gave, because they had nothing; but poor dear Miss May, bless her, before she went away, she said she must give me and Kitty a present, so she took her winter shawl and cut it in half, and gave half to each: there it is on my bed now! Poor dear, she's up among the angels!"

But we are wandering far away from Grace and Lily, who lived in days when "district visitors" were not.

To Grace, with all the load of secret anxiety she had upon her, this friendship was indeed a godsend; and without reasoning or inquiring why, she yielded herself for a time to Lily's influence and guidance: who could resist her?

Reginald meanwhile sailed to many different parts of the world, making his appearance now and then in Torford when least expected; but he was always sure of a welcome at the shipbuilder's; and as soon as he arrived a messenger was straightway despatched to Tye to come and join the kindly people of Torford.

Reginald made no advance towards a reconciliation with his father, nor did Mr. Dawson seem in any way to desire his presence at Harscourt; so that but for the visits to Torford, the brother and sister would have seen but little of one another.

The young man, devoted to the profession he had chosen, still kept to his boyish opinion that to be a real sailor, and thoroughly happy, he must have a ship of his own, that he might do with her as he listed, and sail when and where his fancy led him.

"Why not have a ship of your own, Regie, if you wish it so much? Have one built, and you can pay for it when you come of age," suggested Grace. And Reginald took the hint, and the keel of the new vessel was laid down in Captain Fowler's shipyard with much ceremony.

"She shall be launched the day I am one-and-twenty," said Reginald.

"And her name?" inquired the sister.

"Oh, never you think about the name! Lily and I will find one," was the reply.

What interest the two girls took in that vessel! They knew every plank and bolt in her; Lily looking on in superstitious awe, Grace exulting in her growth, and thinking with pride of the day that should see her breasting the waves with Reginald for her commander.

How often do we watch with eager heart the completion of some scheme on which our whole happiness seems to depend, and which, when completed, brings us only misery!

CHAPTER II
THE LAUNCH

THE new ship is finished, and the day come when she is first to try her strength upon the waters. Early in the morning all those interested in her fate are astir. It is a general holiday in the town; for the young owner is of this day of age, and instead of keeping the anniversary at the old house on the cliff, he chooses to call around him his shipmates and companions to join with him in rejoicing over the new ship, nameless as yet, but to be named when the tide, that is now at its lowest, shall have reached the level of the quay.

Cloudless is the sky above, blue the water, as silently it steals along over the broad sands without a ripple, creeping stealthily up the ditches that intersect the salt marshes; and as the day wears on, and the tide rises higher and higher, overflowing the salt marshes themselves.

From the country on all sides people are pouring in, on horseback and on foot. And up the river sails many a boat and skiff, while from the grand Old Court comes the greatest gentleman of the country, in his barge of state, rowed by twelve servingmen in livery, all to look at and admire "the great ship," that has so long been an object of wonder to all the country-side. To-day the largest ship ever built in the yards of Torford is to be launched.

But besides this attraction, there are others. Reginald Dawson has sent word far and wide that all shall be welcome, that all must come to the feast he means to give in honour of his birthday, and the name-day of his vessel; and old folk tell how one hundred bright golden guineas have been laid down, that all the poor of Torford may be feasted on that day, and about the long tables that are to be spread in the great covered rope-walk, the pride and boast of the people of Torford.

They tell, too, about the handsome, free-handed lad (for he is little more), who has won all hearts, and of his very beautiful sister, whom the young men in the country worship, though she scorns them all.

Inch by inch the tide has risen till it is even with the quay. The time draws near. The crowds throng the bridge, the quay, the shore; numberless boats stud the now broad river, and the acres of wood that float on the eddying tide are covered with hundreds of eager gazers, too intent on the sight to heed the danger of so unstable a stand.

Ye old giants of another world, how little did ye think, as ye waved in your primeval forest, the prop of numberless creepers, the home of multitudes of birds, that, lying mere inanimate logs on that ebbing river, ye should see so gay a throng—a throng gathered to honour the near relations of one o'er whose American home ye once waved—a noble Englishwoman, who, seeing her sons cut down by the Indians on her very threshold, obtained mercy for herself and her daughters by holding aloft—what think you, friends?—the copy of her marriage register from yon tiny English church. The Indians thought it was some charm—nor were they far wrong—and retreated.

Along the quay walks Gratiana Dawson, no degenerative relative of that noble Lady of Wyoming, so erect she walks, so firm she plants her foot, so open, so self-confident her look, yet not a shadow of boldness, only happiness and power stamped in every movement. And that beautiful girl by her side? Ah! sweet Lily Fowler, just as lovely, just as childlike as when, years ago, you sang to Reginald on the old oak staircase. How lovely are those two girls, yet how different! Gratiana, with her dusky hair and great dark eyes; and Lily, with her gleamy chestnut hair and eyes of starry blue: one so powerful and self-possessed; the other so drooping, blushing, humble.

They walked along, now greeting this one, now that, the observed of all observers; Lily in her favourite white, Gratiana in the floating blue gauzy dress, that had more than once gained her the name of "the blue lady of Harscourt." As they pass along towards the ship yard, the crowd falls back on either hand, to let them pass. Behind the girls follow Reginald Dawson and his friend, a mysterious foreigner, who comes from no one knows where, and who is the subject of many conjectures among the good folks of Torford. But the three seem quite satisfied with him and familiar, and every now and then Gratiana turns her handsome beaming face towards him, and speaks to him in that soft foreign tongue that she learnt as a child in mother Agnes' cottage down in the Combe.

See those four standing together on the ship's deck, while round are the *élite* of the company: people note how the greatest gentleman in the country, the old man familiar with court and camp, bows before the stately Gratiana, and is proud to be recognized as an acquaintance; and even Lily, their own Lily, whom they have known from her childhood, comes in for some of his admiration.

Now a bottle of rare old red wine is handed to the shrinking, trembling Lily, who, turning towards Reginald, inquires in her soft voice, so clear, so low, "What is the name I am to give her?"

And he answers loudly and distinctly, "Gratiana Dawson."

So Lily names the vessel, pouring out the blood-red wine upon the planks. Ah, Lily, Lily, beware! It is not wine, but your heart's blood, that is flowing there.

Those near by catch up the name, and group after group re-echo it: "Gratiana Dawson! Gratiana Dawson!" and shout after shout goes up to the pure blue sky, and down the broad valley, so that afterwards people fancied they had heard the shouting miles away.

And Tye stands there and hears her name resounding through the air, and her lips quiver just a very little, and her eyes are for a moment dim; but she is as erect, as self-possessed as ever, while down Lily's cheeks the tears are falling in showers, and down many a rugged, weather-beaten face as well.

This has been a secret between Lily and Reginald—this name. People are taken by surprise; none more so than Tye herself; and she feels more deeply than she cares to show this token of her brother's love—that elder brother over whom she watched with the protecting love of a mother.

The shouts die away, and the handsome stranger gives the chisel and mallet into Gratiana's hand: it is she who is first to set her namesake in motion.

She bares her white rounded arm, pushes back the blue ribbons that flutter against her cheek, and, adjusting the chisel in the already half-cut cable, whilst the other supports are knocked away by the workmen, with one blow she severs it.

"May my namesake be fortunate," she cries; and as the vessel slowly slips from her place, the cry is taken up, and "May she be fortunate," resounds through the air.

The bells strike out a merry peal, guns are fired, and cheer after cheer rings, now from the old bridge, now from the quay, now from the timber-rafts and boats upon the river.

The ship, no longer a nameless log, floats to her moorings a little way down the river, and the crowds turn towards the great green rope-walk, and wander about or sit in groups on the short, fragrant turf, waiting till the Dawsons and their friends shall come to take their seats at the head of the table. As they wait, they talk over the event of the morning, and the striking beauty of the four principal actors of the day, beautiful amid the beautiful: for Torford, and the country around, is famous for its stalwart men and lovely women. The stranger too—who is he? They speak in whispers, and wonder if it can be *he*; for it is said *he* was always brought up with the Dawsons; but then, surely, with that reward offered for his apprehension, he would hardly dare——. No name is mentioned but people understand that it is the young man who was employed in the great smuggling affair at Merscombe.

But who would have guessed, as the young stranger, with Gratiana by his side, walked slowly through the rope-yard, with a joyous smile and pleasant word for every one, that one word might send him to a felon's cell? He knew the people he was among, he knew their honest hearts, and was well assured that not for ten times the sum offered would one of that vast multitude have injured a hair on his head. As they pass by the Fowlers—who, however glad to see their Lily in the place of honour, have sufficient good sense and self-respect not to intrude upon the great folks of the neighbourhood who throng around the Dawsons—good-natured little Mrs. Fowler whispers to Tye, "How can *he* dare? ain't you afraid?"

Gratiana answers, with a scornful laugh:—

"I'll shake hands with the exciseman if he looks at him, and then, of course, he will be safe."

The exciseman is close beside her, and hears her words, and mutters as she passes him,—

"Any friend of Miss Dawson is safe to-day.: He lays a stress on the last word, as a warning, and Gratiana with a quick nod shows him that she understands his meaning.

Lily's sisters gather round her to see that no fold is out of place in the dress of their darling, and as she moves away they follow the beautiful figure with their loving eyes. "Sure in all the world," they say, "no one is so pretty as our Lily, except Miss Dawson."

The brother and sister and their principal guests, even the greatest gentleman of the neighbourhood, take their seats at the upper end of the immense table, and the people range themselves in parties, each set by itself. The large wooden shutters are all removed, and the walls decorated with flags and wreaths of flowers. They heed not the smell of the ropes, the majority of those assembled are well used to it, and in truth are all too busy and too happy to notice anything disagreeable, and take the pushing, crowding, noise, and clatter as part of the entertainment.

As evening comes, the crowd are once more in the open air. The band strikes up a merry tune, and soon the young ones of the party are dancing gayly on the short turf, while the elder sit and chat around.

The evening wears away. The great man floats down the river in his barge of state; as he takes his leave, the exciseman, who has been taking care of himself, whispers to the Dawsons' foreign friend—

"A fine old country gentleman; best wine in the county; don't believe one drop of it ever paid the king's duty."

"Likely enough not, for the Court lies close by the water, and there is a convenient landing-place."

The man for whose apprehension the reward is offered turns away with a bitter smile.

"The great may do anything,—but I! Well, I have dared to come here to-day; it was worth while, but I must be off again. The law makes me what I am!"

The sun has sunk on the sea, the full moon rises above the

distant woods, and the tide, now nearly again at its height, ripples and shimmers in the silvery light. The people are all dispersed. Up and down the quay pace the four friends, wearied with the day's excitement, enjoying the moonlight and the cool night air.

Now they separate; parting words are spoken, the last embrace given, and a boat glides gently down the stream, bearing the friend far away. Gratiana watches the boat and the dusky figures in it till it is lost in the darkness. As she turns her face, the pale moonbeams show how the tears are standing in those proud dark eyes, and Gratiana clings to the gentle, trembling Lily for support, as this morning the Lily clung to her.

"When shall we meet again?" murmured Grace.

CHAPTER III
KEEPING VIGIL

GRACE became a great lady in her more immediate neighbourhood. One by one the girls who had looked down on her in her rough girlish days, acknowledged that somehow she was their superior, not merely in her beauty, but in her attainments, and in that strange power of command and direction she seemed to have, without being in the least dictatorial or overbearing. It was more that they acknowledged her as their superior, than she asserted it.

The active, energetic spirit that in childhood had led her into pursuits hardly suitable to her sex and station, now turned into a more legitimate channel; and, in spite of Mr. Dawson, in all the country round there was no better ordered household or well-arranged table than that at Harscourt.

In all she did, however, there was a certain running away from self, a constant struggle to forget the past, and not to see the future, which gave her an older and more possessed air than of right belonged to her years. There were times when the weight on her became overpowering; and then, mounting her favourite horse, the two, as if by mutual consent, would tear along over the wild grassy downs, with the broad shiny sea on one hand, and the bleak moors and bogs of Tor on the other.

Of admirers she had no lack;—a handsome girl with a good fortune is not often left to herself; but let them have ever such great pretensions, Grace treated them all with indifference. Her entanglement (for engagement it could hardly be called) with Jack Martin got whispered about; but from Grace herself the most arrant gossip could learn nothing, for she was not a person any one would venture to cross-question on so delicate a subject.

As years and months passed by, and that dreaded birthday drew nearer, it became more and more evident that Jack Martin had no intention of being satisfied with her fortune alone. He was, or fancied himself, very much in love; and often did a burning blush rise on the poor girl's face at his coarse compliments and too openly avowed admiration. He beset and waylaid her on every opportunity, and often provoked her into one of her old outbursts of passion, which generally had the effect of ridding her of his attentions for a time.

There was one peculiarity in her, referred to here before more than once—the quaint fashion of her dress. Some say she took it from an old picture, others, that it was a fancy of her own: whichever may be the fact, it was a most becoming attire, consisting of a kind of hood or veil, which she could at pleasure draw round her face or throw back on her shoulders. It was just a thing that others were afraid to imitate, lest they should appear singular, though they all agreed in thinking it wonderfully becoming on the blue lady of Harscourt.

Mr. Dawson, meanwhile, went on much in his accustomed way, every day indulging more freely in his most beloved vice, and at times rendered perfectly frantic by intemperance and a tortured conscience. Strange that so degraded a being should have found any associates among men of his own class, but he was a man of money and position, and drunkenness then was not condemned as drunkenness is now.

As far as he knew, his daughter had neither seen nor heard of Edward Mountjoy since his flight from Merscombe Mill, and he flattered himself that in that quarter he had nothing to fear. Grace had obtained a great ascendancy over him, and as long as she left him undisturbed she was pretty free to go where she would. Many an evening did she pass down in the Combe with mother Agnes. Many a night did she spend on those wild cliffs, buffeting with the wind, and peering through the darkness for drifting vessels, with as eager eyes as the fearful wreckers that frequented the coast. Her heart was far away over the sea; how could she rest when the winds were roaring and the waves rolling in, mountains high? The people had a superstition about her, that she was not like other folks, that she saw and heard more than others; and she did nothing to alter their belief, but rather encouraged it; so that she was trusted, and her advice taken, in many private and rather questionable transactions. She fostered this fancy about herself, for her own purposes: their superstition enabled her to wander at will at any hour of the day or night, without fear of molestation.

"No one would raise a finger to hurt me," she would often answer, when warned that she ran great risks; "they know me too well and I have too many friends for any to venture to harm me."

These nightly rambles of the Lady of Harscourt became more frequent as time passed, and the days of her liberty drew towards their close. She had looked (perhaps without entirely allowing it even to herself) to Edward Mountjoy as her means of deliverance; but months passed, and neither she nor mother Agnes heard a word of him. Vague rumours sometimes reached them, but anything decided or satisfactory they could not glean; so night after night did the two watch, and wait, and listen for the one they loved best on earth. Reginald, too, was away, nor had she heard of him for some time. When last heard of, he had been in the West Indies, and it was supposed he was trading there.

Her namesake had proved a brave ship, and her young

commander had been prosperous. He was not content with the petty dangers of the coasting-trade, but, in spite of the risks which in those days attended foreign voyages, regarding his vessel with the same spirit and confidence with which a fine gentleman would regard his yacht, he ventured large sums on valuable cargoes, and dared to try his speed and strength even against the French privateers, hitherto with success and profit.

CHAPTER IV

A SPY

THE western breeze was blowing in fresh from the sea, sighing and moaning through the old oak woods by the Combe; now and then a snowy flake of foam came driving up the valley, telling of mighty waves that roared hard by, and reaching the little cottage that stood across the vale by the side of a brawling stream.

Near the flickering turf fire sat mother Agnes; you can see her through the lattice window; she moves to and fro uneasily on the low stool, and her face is covered with her hands. Look towards the sea, and along the path by the edge of the cliff you can see a form creeping on. The wind is high, and it is with evident difficulty the person is able to keep her footing. Now the figure approaches the cottage, and taps at the door.

The woman by the fire raises her head. The face is one to be remembered, so ashy pale, so wild, yet so beautiful: the high, clear forehead, the exquisite arched brow, the full blue eyes, the small aquiline nose, the bow-shaped mouth, the finely chiselled chin, are all so lovely. Yet look at those lines round the eyes and by the corners of the mouth, which tell of anxiety, longing, watching. But the sum and substance of most women's lives, you will say? True: she was a sailor's wife, and she is a sailor's mother, and she lives by the sea, and thinks that every blast she hears must reach her boy, though he may be in the Indian Ocean instead of on his native coast, and that every breaker which breaks upon the shore must do him damage though he be a hundred miles away.

"Is that you, Grace dear?" exclaimed the woman as she turned, and Gratiana entered. "Oh, such a night! What has brought you so far from home?"

"You, mother dear," replied the girl, taking one of the thin white hands of Widow Mountjoy between her plump ones, and pressing it to her boom. "But why have you no blind or shutter up, mother? it looks so dreary." I always fancy faces are looking in, and are pressed against the panes; it frightens me!"

"I left the window open," replied the mother: "I thought if he came——"

"Hush, mother! other faces might look in than his." And the younger woman went and carefully adjusted a check curtain against the window, and closed the shutters.

The elder sighed.

"Suppose he were to come, Gracie?"

"He will not come," was the rejoinder.

"Ah!" sighed the mother, "have you had news?"

No—none."

Another sigh, and the rocking resumed.

"Which way did you come, Gracie?"

"By the cliffs."

"How can you come that way, child? Why did you come that way?"

"To see what the sea was like. Just as you go to look at it so often."

"I don't go on the cliffs, child; but what did the sea look like? what did it say?"

"The sea was like a sea of light: every wave flashing and crested."

"But there is no moon now?"

"No; it was the sea's own light, that tells of storms; and there was a dark bank in the west, with bloody edges!"

A sob escaped from the woman, who sat rocking to and fro;

and the young one, who was seated opposite her, leaned on her hand and gazed into the embers.

"Gracie dear, don't go home by the cliffs, it frightens me so. Oh! those cliffs will be the death of you some day, I know they will—I feel it."

A creeping feeling went over Gratiana's body as her companion spoke, and she looked up to the window, expecting to see one of her dreaded faces peering in on her; but her own exertions had blocked out all visible intruders, and yet she felt some one was looking at her."

"What's that in the fire, Gracie? Look!"

"I see nothing, mother."

"Look again! don't you see there, in the corner! It is a winding-sheet! It is Edward's winding-sheet!"

"Hush! hush!" exclaimed the girl, "you shall not talk so! You are fancying all sorts of evils just because the wind is high."

But the colour had fled from Gratiana's rosy cheeks, and she was looking earnestly towards that part of the fire to which Agnes Mountjoy had pointed. The dreaded bit of firing swelled and hissed, then burst; and the winding-sheet fell at Grace's feet.

The elder woman began to moan—"The cliffs! the cliffs!"

"Hush, mother, hush! Listen! There was a whistle like the call of a wild bird."

"It is a plover, child."

"Plovers live in the highlands, not in the vales."

"It is a snipe calling to its mate, Grace."

"The snipes are gone long ago."

The two women bent their heads and listened.

Again it came, that curious whistle, as Grace had said, like the call of a wild bird."

"It's Edward's call!" murmured Agnes.

"Tut! mother—peace. Listen! there it is again! There is some one treading outside. I'll see who it is."

"Not for the world, Grace: sit still! there are those come here sometimes whom you know nothing of, and whom it wouldn't do for you to meet. Sit still—I'll see."

Agnes rose, and opening the door peered out into the night. The wind came rushing into the cottage, and sent the sparks from the smouldering embers flying up the wide open chimney.

Gratiana's face was turned inquiringly towards the door, and her foot patted the lime-ash floor impatiently, now and then changing its employment by pettishly poking a stray piece of wood back into its place.

"You are not alone, Agnes," said a man, emerging from the shadow of an adjoining shed. "Who is your company?"

"What's that to you, Tunny? What brings you here?" was the rejoinder, spoken in no very cordial tone.

"What's that to you Missis Agnes?" If you can't speak civil, I'll just go where I came from, and say I couldn't deliver his message, because you wouldn't let a man speak."

"A message!"

There was but one, that fond woman thought, who could send her a message. Her heart beat high, but she did not speak.

"Who's your company, friend? Surely you can trust an honest seafaring man with a secret, though he has had a little to do with the fair trade in his day. It isn't Miss Tye, is it?" he added, after a pause, during which not a muscle of that proud face had moved.

The woman started.

"Ah! I knew it was Miss Tye; I saw her creeping round the cliff, and guessed that none but her would be there such weather.

Come, let me in; my message is as much to her as you." And the sailor pushed by into the cottage.

Tye had caught the last words, and her face flushed rosy crimson.

"Well, Mis Tye, so that's you, is it? no more than I guessed when I saw a woman creeping like a spirit round the point. It's uncommon kind of you to come and keep a poor lone soul like Aggy company; more especially when her son's away:" and Tunny gave a knowing leer at the blushing girl.

"But the message, man—the message? What word did he send?" demanded Aggy.

"Who?—what message do you mean?"

"Why, the message you said Edward sent."

"I never said *he* sent any."

"It's too bad, trifling with her feelings in this way," said Tye indignantly. "You know she hasn't heard a word of her son for months. Why can't you tell her? Is he dead or alive—well or ill?"

"One for her and two for yourself. Eh? Miss Tye?"

The foot patted the floor again harder and quicker than it had done before, and the small head jerked backwards and forwards defiantly.

"Well, he's alive, that's certain; leastways he was the last time I saw him."

"Where is he?" asked the mother.

"That's more than I can say. One thing I know, he isn't where you two ladies would like him to be, that's here; and I don't consider you'll see him here for a precious long while either."

"Where did you see him last?" inquired Tye, in no very soft voice.

"Well, let's see; he was running a cargo on the Hampshire coast, down there below Lymington, and somehow it didn't succeed; the tubs were seized, and he and his craft got into trouble down by Swanage, and so he's had to disappear, and where he is I really don't know. I thought, perhaps, you might know."

"Why, you said you had a message, and led us to believe it was from him. What is it about? Quick!" the foot came down so hard this time that it tingled again.

"Well, it's just this, then, if you must have it. Says he, 'When you *see them*', that's you and his mother, 'just tell *her*', that's you, 'that I'm going to be married.' He talked about breaking it gently, and a lot o' stuff I don't understand. I'm only a plain sailor who tells the plain truth."

Tunny expected a burst of weeping and indignation from Gratiana; he was mistaken.

"How came you to meet Edward Mountjoy?" she asked. "You have not sailed with him this long while, not since Jack Martin was exchequered."

"True, young lady, but folks do meet in the world without sailing together. I had a little business down in that part of the world, and we happened to stumble on one another. I saw the young lady—as handsome a one as you see in a long day's march."

A tear trembled on Agnes Mountjoy's long eyelashes, and her lips were tightly compressed as she watched Gratiana's countenance.

"I am very glad to hear he is going to be married. It will be a good thing for him if the lady he has chosen manages him properly," said Gratiana, in her natural tone, keeping her eye fixed steadfastly on Tunny. "If you happen to meet him again, tell him an old friend was glad to hear of his good fortune, and tell him not to forget that he has a mother. Good night Agnes, I must be going now," she continued, drawing her hood over her head. "Mind you ain't late to-morrow. I shall have so much on my hands, I shan't be able to manage if you are not there to help."

"It's likely she came down here this time of night alone, just to ask Agnes to come up to help," muttered Tunny, but Agnes caught the girl's meaning, and promised Gratiana to be in time on the morrow.

"I don't believe one word of it; not one," said Gratiana to herself, as she hurriedly pursued her homeward way up a grassy dell; for at Agnes' request she had not taken the cliff path. Thoughts pressed quickly on her mind—memories of bygone days, promises made long ago, words half spoken, half remembered; and she did not—could not—believe that Edward had left her for another.

She walked so swiftly up the steep path, her agitated thoughts giving wings to her steps, that after a quarter of a mile she was glad to pause and rest on the broad stone placed edgeways, which served as a stile. The wind came whistling and sighing along the stunted hedge, which formed the barrier between the lands of Harscourt and the wild common; and as it eddied round her, it seemed laden with spirits and memories striving to make themselves known to her, to come back to her. She shuddered, and looked fearfully around; there was nothing to be seen, but the clouds flying over the face of heaven before the wild west wind, and the ghost-like form of the leafless bushes.

"I don't believe one word of it; not one!" exclaimed Gratiana aloud. Her own voice startled her, and she was alarmed in no small degree, when crossing the stile she found herself face to face with a man, who stood directly in her way. She tried to avoid him, but without success.

"What is it you don't believe, Miss Dawson?" asked the man, in a voice by which Grace immediately recognized him as the younger Martin.

"Nothing to you, Mr. Martin. Allow me to pass."

"You are very imprudent to be out alone at this hour; there are bad characters abroad."

"I am well aware of that, Mr. Martin. Allow me to pass."

"Where have you been, Miss Dawson?" inquired the man, still retaining a hold on her arm.

"By what right do you ask that"

"Might is right."

"Perhaps so, among your friends—such lawless wretches as you and your companions; but if you don't unhand me this moment, I will make every honourable gentleman in the country shun you!"

"You speak boldly, madam," said her assailant, tightening his hold on her arm.

Fortunately, her right hand was free, and in an instant she dealt Mr. Martin such a blow between his eyes, that from astonishment, more perhaps than from the weight of the blow, he let go his hold, and staggered back a pace or two, where he fell ignominiously into the ditch, owing to the moist, slippery bank. Tye, lithe and fleet as ever, bounded away on the instant; and though after a while, finding that she was not pursued, she somewhat slackened her pace, it was, nevertheless, with hurried footsteps that she entered the garden-room at Harscourt.

Jack Martin lifted himself out of the mud, in no very gentle temper. "Ah! you'll repent this some fine day, my lady," he muttered between his teeth, as he shook his clenched fist in the direction he guessed Tye must have taken. "I'll make you rue it, my fine bird, when you're captured; I'll break your spirit for you nicely."

"What are you growling about there, Martin? what's happened?" asked Tunny, who at this moment leaped over the stile.

"Enough's the matter: hang that girl, I do believe she is possessed sometimes."

"Oh—oh, master! so you and she have been at loggerheads, have you?"

"Hold your tongue! What did you find out yonder?"

"Now, master Martin, you bid me hold my tongue, and then you bid me speak: which command am I to obey?"

"Bother you; did you find out anything or nothing?"

"If you bother me that way, master, I shan't know how to get along; but I didn't learn much, that's certain, except that neither of them know where he is. I could see that at a glance; so we may be sure he isn't in this part of the world."

"I wish he was at the bottom of the red sea—I do. If I could get rid of him, I think somehow I should manage her."

"I told her he was going to be married," said Tunny, "but she took no more notice of it than if I'd told her I was going to be married. She did take it uncommon cool, I must say."

"Just because she did not believe you."

"How did you find out that, then?"

"I heard her say so. You'll not take her in in a minute. But I wonder how he managed to get out of our way?"

"I can't imagine," replied Tunny; "the train couldn't have been better laid—lots of men, and all to seize him and his; and then only to get a few paltry kegs."

"I wonder if he was drowned when the vessel went on shore?"

"I don't fancy it somehow. You see everything was cleared out of her,—nothing suspicious,—and she didn't look a bit like a wrecked vessel either. My belief is he got tired of her, and took some craft more to his fancy, and let the old one go her ways. Oh no! if he had been drowned, some of the others would have turned up somewhere."

"But here we are close by Harscourt; do you mean to go in and wish your handsome a good-night?"

"Thank you, I've had enough of her for the present." And the two worthies continued their way towards Cross, where Tunny entered the little public house, and young Martin turned into the ruinous gateway of Cross House.

CHAPTER V

THE UNEXPECTED INTERVIEW

GRACE avoided all chance of another meeting with her unwelcome lover, by confining herself almost entirely to the house or its immediate neighbourhood for some days after her rencontre with Tunny and her persecutor, not even venturing down to Combe.[26] But one stormy evening the wandering spirit came strongly on her, and wrapping her cloak round her, she took her way along the cliffs.

From earliest childhood the cliffs, during a storm, had been Grace's most beloved haunt. Often and often as a child, too weak to stand against the blast, had she crawled on all fours to the most dangerous parts, to revel in the wild scene below, and watch the foam-snow eddy up the gullies, or lie in quivering drifts in sheltered nooks. She had lost none of her love for that wild driving west wind. It came like an old friend to her, and she turned her face fearlessly towards it, till her long bright hair, escaping from its fastenings, streamed over her shoulders like a veil.

Who shall tell the thoughts that flitted through that busy brain? Thoughts of the past, hopes for the future, came and went in rapid succession. The present,—when she thought of that, she knew how near the edge of a frightful precipice she was.

No sign of deliverance appeared on her stormy horizon—no hope of escape.

"Will he ever come back—shall I ever see him again? Edward! Edward! where are you?" she cried.

---

26 Rencontre: meeting, encounter.

Over stony brakes she glided like a spirit, down one glen side, up another, with that remarkable sureness of foot which intimate knowledge of the path, and familiarity with the different objects at all hours of the day or night, gave her, till she reached a little nook in an open part of the down, well known as the "smugglers' look-out;" there she seated herself, and by the aid of the moon's fitful beams peered over the wild waste of foamy waters.

Suddenly she started—a strange thrill ran through her frame, as if some one were near her; she turned hastily round, but nothing but a few dark trunks of dwarf gorse could be descried in the darkness.

Her dreams had fled, and though she kept her seat a few moments, a sense of danger, and a terror rarely felt, made her wish herself in a less lonely or exposed situation.

At last she summoned courage to rise, and with hurried steps retraced her path towards Harscourt. Still that wretched feeling at times experienced in the dark—of some one or something we cannot see being near us—followed her, and more than one rapid glance did she cast around as she hurried on.

And soon she became certain that it was no mere fancy that had startled her: a black mass, which she had at first taken for a rather tall furze-bush, or old thorn-tree, advanced as rapidly as she did. If she paused, "it" paused, and as surely as she looked back, "it" was to be seen where no bush had been before.

Her way now led her over two wide enclosures, occasionally cultivated, and then over a stile into a deep glen, with a brawling stream, crossed by a single plank. She could by this time distinguish footsteps on the path behind her, and she resolved, as she felt she was being followed for some purpose—whether good or bad was hard to say—to take advantage of a tangled brake of gorse, briar, and fern, that bordered the side of the stream, and hide till her pursuer or unwelcome attendant had passed by. She flew down the slope, and regardless of the shower that rained on her from every mist-laden spray, crouched down beneath their dripping cover.

Swift as had been her movements, they had not escaped the observation of the person who followed her, who had arrived at the stile in time to see that she had not crossed the bridge. His eye had followed her to the bottom, but nothing had passed the bridge, or hid for a moment the plank that glittered from moisture in the uncertain light.

The man who had caused Grace all this terror paused at the edge of the stream, not many moments after the girl had hid herself; and as she heard the heavy footstep stop within a few feet of her hiding-place, she shook in every limb, fancying that this might be some further outrage or annoyance on the part of young Martin. Her heart beat audibly, and thankful was she to the gurgling stream for drowning the sound of her panting breath.

Hush, stream! stay thy babbling. Listen to the voice that comes so soft, yet clear, through the night air to the girl crouching among the brambles.

"Grace! Grace Dawson!"

So low, yet so distinct, there is but one voice on earth that sounds the same to Grace. She holds her breath, she clasps her hands, and listens.

"Grace, are you near? do you hear my voice? do you know me?"

She knows full well, but she has no power to move; she only crouches lower and lower, as though every portion of her frame that voice thrills like electricity.

"I must have missed her, I must have been mistaken," sighed the man, as he turned to continue his way; yet once again he calls on Grace.

Up, girl, quick! suppose he passes on, and you never meet again!

Grace springs to her feet as she fancies he turns away, and is at his side as he once more pronounces her name—

"Grace!"

"Edward!"

They say no more; words would only mar what they both feel; and so they stand by the slippery plank in the glen bottom on that wild, stormy night, and know that, though long years and broad seas have parted them, they are the same to one another as in the days when love was first spoken of between them.

There are passages in the life of every one who has ever loved, that it would be profanation to record. Those who have drunk most deeply of the joys of love—real love—will be the last to publish their knowledge, but guard it with a jealous secrecy; while those who can only imagine such happiness had best refrain from attempting to paint a land whose riches and beauteousness none can fitly describe.

Poor Grace! for one brief hour she was happy; and forgetting her troubles in her present joy, was ready to say with Thekla, "I have lived and loved."[27]

"Oh, Edward, when shall I find rest and peace?" exclaimed poor Grace, as she parted from her lover within a short distance of Harscourt.

"When you are my wife, Grace dear,—when we are far away from this dreary place,—away in the soft southern seas."

Grace made no answer, but shook her head despondingly.

---

[27] Thekla: from the *Wallenstein* trilogy of dramas by Friedrich Schiller. Thekla's song, translated from the German by Samuel Taylor Coleridge: 'I have lived and loved, and that was to-day——Make ready my grave-clothes to-morrow!"

"Those days will never come," she murmured to herself. "There is no escape."

"I've a new vessel waiting for us, Grace—a vessel that has never done a wrong thing, or taken an unlawful cargo. We abandoned the old one off the Hampshire coast, she was getting too well known, and the authorities were determined to have us; so we disappeared in a miraculous manner, as the wiseacres imagined, and I determined before we set out on a long cruise, just to come and see if a certain lady had quite forgotten me. I have tried to keep away, indeed I have, Grace; I have tried to forget you, because I know well enough I'm only a poor sailor, and you a rich lady; but I have loved you Grace, since you were a little girl, and I couldn't bear to think of you married to that fellow Martin; I couldn't stand that; I should kill him, I believe; and so I ventured back to the old place to see after you. You must come with me, Grace, and be queen of the new ship, and we will take my poor old mother back to her own land, and if she has lost one home we will make her another, and find peace, Grace—peace!"

But Grace only shook her head mournfully, and hurried into the house.

Edward Mountjoy had calculated that, so many years having elapsed since the affair at Merscombe, he might venture back without and great danger of being arrested; for in those days so many new things were constantly arising to occupy men's minds, that the old soon passed away and were forgotten.

But he could not calculate on the inveterate hate of a personal enemy, of whose existence even he was unaware.

Though Mountjoy had managed to elude Erlingham so far, more by accident than design, the plotter had not less diligently continued his endeavours to rid himself of him for ever. For this purpose he kept up a constant communication with Tunny, whom he protected from justice on the plea of the great service he could render the government by the betrayal of secrets.

It was to discover the young sailor, of whom, as we have seen, he had lost sight on the southern coast, that he ventured back to his old home, not without many misgivings as to the reception that awaited him, for his evil deeds, if not fully known, were more than guessed at. Whatever his equals might have thought of him, the Martins, for their own reasons, took him by the hand, and kept him in a sort of semi-incognito; from them he learned the position in which Grace stood to young Martin, while in his turn he informed them of the relation which had subsisted between that young lady and the smuggler captain, and of which he was aware.

Martin's rage knew no bounds when he discovered, or fancied he had discovered, the reason why Grace had so long resisted all his endeavours to make her his wife, and he swore to be revenged on Mountjoy. But a little reflection showed that both he and Tunny must act warily, as at one time they had been joined with Edward in certain transactions; and that, in fact, they were the men who had first initiated him into the mysteries of smuggling.

Grace and Mountjoy, unmindful of their enemies, met often, but in secret; no one but Agnes, Grace, and the farmer in whose house he was secreted, saw him, or knew he was in the country.

Grace's nightly rambles excited no more notice than any other young lady's daily walk would have done, for it had been her habit for years.

So the two talked and talked, and proposed this plan and the other; but at the end of a fortnight Mountjoy had in no way succeeded in getting Grace to consent to leave her home clandestinely. Unfortunately for them, these meetings were at last discovered by the very people most interested in preventing them. Prowling about Harscourt one night, unsuspected by the lovers, Jack Martin had seen enough to convince him that Mountjoy was in the neighbourhood, and immediately communicated the fact to Tunny, who managed to ferret out where Mountjoy concealed himself by day.

No time was to be lost, and they considered that the surest way to attain their end without committing themselves, was to give Mr. Dawson a hint of what was going on.

Alas! poor Grace. Though Mr. Dawson disliked the idea of his daughter's marriage to Martin nearly as much as she did, he was furious to think that her acquaintance with Mountjoy still continued. After the young man's flight, so little had been said of him, or known of his proceedings, that he had taken it for granted the fancy had passed.

In truth, he was fearful lest any breach with the Martins might be the means of bringing out facts he would willingly have kept secret from every living soul.

One word, one hint, was sufficient for him. Once set upon their track, he determined to leave no stone unturned till he had punished both.

CHAPTER VI
"OVER THE CLIFFS"

THERE are times in most people's lives when they are conscious of standing on the brink of a moral precipice; when they feel impelled onward they know not where, while an inward shrinking tells them there is danger ahead; and the voice of conscience or the instinct of self-preservation calls on them to pause and look well around them ere they move.

Some heed the mysterious warning and turn aside, never perhaps to know the danger they have escaped. Others retreat, and live to see the miseries from which they have been saved.

Others, again, go wilfully on, and only wake to find there is no return, no hope of escape from the troubles their own blindness has brought on them.

Gratiana Dawson felt this foreboding weighing on her when Edward urged her to fly with him, as the only way of escape open to save her from her father's tyranny and the Martins' designs.

She was fully sensible of the difficulties and dangers that beset her path, but how to alter matters was beyond her skill. To break with her affianced husband was utterly out of the question; ever to gain her father's consent, utterly hopeless; and the thought of a clandestine marriage most distasteful and galling.

Edward, when they last parted, had spoken harshly to her for not acting more promptly, and for keeping him waiting day after day when she knew the danger he ran in being there at all; and he had insisted that she must say ay or nay without further delay.

All day she wandered restlessly about the house, as if she was going to leave it for ever, and wished to stamp every nook and corner on her memory.

The curious ebony cabinet which stood in the garden-room and contained her girlish treasures, was opened and arranged, and the beautiful Indian chain which Mountjoy had given her before his flight, and which she had nearly ever since had to conceal from her father's jealous eyes, was for the hundredth time examined and admired.

The favourite horse and faithful dogs all came in for a share of her notice, and the servants told afterwards that they had remarked how gentle and friendly she was that day.

Mr. Dawson was more than usually silent and morose; he was longing for the night to come that he might convict and punish his daughter.

Night came at last, and Grace betook herself to her room, but not to rest. She soon glided noiselessly down the stairs and into the garden-room. The door creaked as she shut it, and she stood some moments motionless, to listen if the noise had disturbed her father.

There was no sound to be heard but the ticking of the great clock on the stairs. She approached the window, which she had purposely left open, but some slight noise caused her to pause, and round her seemed to float a heavy sigh, while an owl, starting from the ivy, hooted mournfully as he sailed past.

The girl started; it seemed an evil omen, and she could hardly summon courage to proceed.

Across the flower-garden she went, treading gently lest the crackling gravel should betray her; then hurriedly across the home fields, through the gate at the head of the glen. Every bush, every sound called on her to stop—to turn back: she heeded not: fate called her onward.

With unsteady steps she descends the narrow path down the cliff, steadying herself now by seizing a bunch of the sea-pink, now saving herself from falling by throwing all her weight against the rock, while the stones rattle and fall from under her feet. She feels giddy, and her legs give way beneath her, but she reaches the shore at last.

There are two stout arms open to receive her, and a true, honest heart to lean on; but Grace sinks on the shore and weeps;—strong, sturdy, defiant no longer; only a weak, loving woman, with nothing to rely on in herself—only in him whom she has loved and trusted so long.

"You shall come with me, Tye! I told you all along there is nothing to hope for from any one but ourselves; and if you do not come with me at once, he will discover that I am in the neighbourhood; you will only bring ruin and misery on yourself and me, and in the end you will be forced to marry Martin."

"Never, Edward! never!"

"Then come with me. My mother will go with us, and we will sail for America, and make a happy home far away."

Grace only answered by sobs.

"Dear Tye, we must act; we have no time to lose. I do not want to frighten you, but I heard to-day that if I stay here any longer, I run great risk of being arrested for the old affair. Your father knows I am not far off, and you can readily imagine he will despatch me if possible.

The girl roused herself. It was a new motive, or rather excuse, for doing what her heart half inclined her to do, to accede to her lover's wishes. She could brave danger herself, but she shrank from keeping Mountjoy in danger; but for her he might have been a thousand miles away.

"You will come, Tye dear; see, there is the boat just round the rocks; come now at once, Tye."

She hesitated, she longed to be at peace, but still she hesitated to cross the bound whence there was no return.

"Come, Tye," whispered the sailor, as he put his arm round her, and tried to draw her towards his boat.

Grace yielded for a moment, and advanced several paces towards the sea.

"That's right!" said Edward. "Be your own bold self, Tye—all will go well."

But she had already repented, and suddenly disengaging herself from Mountjoy, pushed him from her and stood looking towards the cliff.

"I must go home to-night, Edward, or mischief will happen. I feel as if death were near!"

"Don't trifle with me so, I implore you, Grace; this time to-morrow I may be on my road to gaol; my men are impatient; pray act, and act at once! Have I no influence over you? Have you lost your affection for me?"

Grace's tears fell fast. "Oh, Edward!" she exclaimed, "how can you be so cruel?"

"It is you who are cruel," rejoined Edward, walking up and down a narrow strip of sand between the rocks.

"I promise you," said Tye, gently laying her hand on the young man's arm—"I promise you I will go to-morrow—only not to-night. It is too dreadful; I cannot, will not, go now! To-morrow evening, if you think me worth coming for, I will be here—" and Tye sped away up the steep path, once or twice pausing and looking back at the dark figure she could see below, pacing backwards and forwards on that narrow strip of sand.

More than once she was half tempted to turn back to him, her heart yearned so for his love and kindness, but still she whispered to herself, "Only not to-night—to-morrow I will go."

With stealthy steps did the tyrant of Harscourt pursue his daughter. He followed her down the steep gully side as she wound her way to the beach where Mr. Dawson had been told she met her lover. He did not venture down the entire descent, as at one corner the moon shone full upon the path, and would in a moment have revealed him. So he concealed himself behind an angle of the rock and bided his time.

Just as he reached this spot, a small boat glided over the glossy sea, across the glittering moonlight, and the smuggler captain leapt on shore. So Mr. Dawson waited.

Hush! hear how the stones rattle! and now, that heavy breathing! the hill is steep, and Tye, breathless and trembling in every limb, pauses at the fatal angle.

She is face to face with her father.

Neither speaks, but Mr. Dawson seizes his daughter's arm as in a vice, and demands where she has been.

"On the shore," she replies faintly.

"Whom did you meet there?"

Grace makes no answer: what good will it do? she cares little what becomes of her.

"Do you answer me?" asked the enraged man, grinding his teeth, and hissing out his words.

Tye trembles. Oh! that she had gone with Mountjoy, or that he were here.

Still she gives no answer.

"I told you long ago, that I would be the death of you, if you went with that fellow Mountjoy. In spite of my warning you have continued to encourage him. Now I will be as good as my word."

As he spoke, he raised a stout thorn stick, and aimed a murderous blow at his daughter.

Grace bent to avoid the blow, forgetting on what dangerous ground she stood. The turf gave way beneath her feet; she uttered a wild scream, and grasped the turf and plants, but they too gave way, and down she went—slipping, sliding, slipping; the loose stones and broken slate rustling and rattling round her. In vain she tried to stop her course, clutching the soil, and trying to call on Mountjoy. In vain she now repented having withstood his entreaties. Her eyes grew dim, darkness closed over. On she went her headlong course, and Tye was gone!

That bad man stood still, and heard her struggles and her cry, yet stirred not a finger to help her, but felt a savage joy as he heard her hurrying to her destruction.

Then there came a thought of the future—a thought of the consequences of that foul deed; for if his hand had failed in dealing the blow, he was no less guilty of the intention of murder.

Supposing Mountjoy to be still on the beach, might he not come up to ask assistance? And if he should meet him, might he not suspect?

So he turned and hurried swiftly homeward.

He waited and listened all that night, and all the next morning, wondering when they would come to tell him the body was found.

It was whispered about the house that Miss Dawson was missing, and the servants talked one with another, and debated when she had been seen last, till some one summoned courage to tell their master, and they remembered long afterwards how calmly he had taken the announcement; but though he believed her lying at the bottom of that rugged precipice, he ordered them to go to this house and that, to find out if she had been seen or heard of. But she was never found, and the rumour got abroad that she had fallen from the cliff and been washed away; but how the rumour originated none ever knew, though a small piece of a dress resembling the dress she had worn was afterwards found sticking to some brambles near the path, and it seemed to give colour to the surmise.

As the evening came on, the winds and waves rose, and that wretched man went and watched how close the sea came in, and how it dashed up against the cliffs; he hoped that they would wash away that mangled body which he fancied he could see down on the shingle; but not all the water in the universe could wash his conscience clean, or blot out that hideous crime.

The night Grace Dawson disappeared, she wanted just a fortnight of being of age, and consequently her fortune could not be claimed by the Martins.

CHAPTER VII
CAPTIVES

HALF the population of the town of Dieppe are out upon the *Plage*.[28] The men are vociferating, the women laughing and holding up their children to see the English prize that one of their own vessels, built and christened in their little port, is bringing in. Now the crowd turns to the right along the *Plage*, towards the mouth of the river, which forms the entrance of the harbour. On they come, those two vessels, like living creatures, in their pride and power, with all sails set. How skilfully they wind in and out among the sandbanks; how majestically they glide up the narrow channel, while the crowd goes on by their side, and the sailors shout, and the crowd shout and run, that they may reach the harbour as soon as the vessels! Now they float in the land-locked harbour, with broad quays on either hand, and tall picturesque houses, with balconies gay with flowers, and the towers of the great churches rising above all, from whose steeples peals the sound of bells, while the people shout, and the sailors shout, "We have conquered! we have gained a prize!" And children's faces up in the high windows beam with joy as they clap their hands, and shout, "We have taken a prize!"

And far away over the sea, in English cottage-homes, sit women with children round their knees, and the children ask, "Where is father? When will he come home?" And the village maidens look towards the sea for the ship they know so well, which they shall never see again. And the mothers say, "By and by he will come."

---

28 *Plage*: beach, shore.

But he never comes again, or not till years have blotted him out from the memories of those who loved him best.

On the quay stand waiting the mayor and the custom-house officers, while at a little distance are a company of soldiers, and the commandant of the castle that rises on the cliff overhanging the town.

Again a shout, "*La Belle Marie* is a brave ship; the sailors of *La Belle Marie* are brave men." Then the sails are furled—sails with many a hole in them from balls, for there has been hard fighting between the crews of these two vessels, and the decks are stained with blood, and yonder in a corner lie two or three pale bloody corpses with an old sail only partially hiding the hideous sight. They belong to the vanquished party; the conquerors, though many are severely wounded, have lost none.

And now the poor Englishmen are led on shore, handcuffed and chained two and two. The women press round them and pity them, for they are wounded and dispirited; and last of all walks their commander, apparently not more than two and twenty, tall and slight. The women point at him and draw back whispering. "He is handsome," they say. "Has *l'air noble*."[29] "Has magnificent eyes." "Looks like a hero." "Has so fine a mouth." And he walks on between the soldiers and the people who line the streets, with his chestnut hair floating in the breeze, and those large sleepy eyes looking inquiringly out from under the long dark curly lashes to see if any friend is at hand, or if there is any chance of escape before they reach that frowning old feudal castle that rises above the town; but he looks in vain. Through narrow streets, by stately churches, they go, till they begin to ascend the hill to the château, and

[29] L'air noble: a noble air.

leave the town behind them, except a few pleasant homes bowered among limes and acacia-trees, with arbours covered with the trailing vine. The approach to the castle was along what had once been a fosse, which being useless, from its position, since the introduction of fire-arms, had gradually been diverted from its original purpose, and was now covered with short green turf. There was still a ditch round the walls, over which a small drawbridge gave entrance to the narrow gate through which the captives passed, and then it closed with a heavy clang, and they were shut out from the outer world. They were taken to a room on the opposite side of the courtyard, and the commandant proceeded to register their names.

"And your name, sir?" he asked, turning to the young captain.

"Reginald Dawson," was the reply.

The officer was about fifty, scarred and seamed, with but one arm. He looked at Reginald with an inquiring glance, and his prisoner, thinking he had not understood his name, repeated it.

"I understand," said the commandant, and he wrote down the name.

"Put this gentleman into cell No. 20, solitary," he said, turning to one of the soldiers; and Reginald, in spite of his remonstrances, was separated from his companions, led across the courtyard again, and after passing through divers narrow passages, and up a winding stair, he found himself in a cell about eight feet square. There was a large window strongly barred and grated, looking toward the town, and the pleasant hills and woods beyond; and among the masts that rose from the harbour he thought he could distinguish those of his own *Gratiana*. The young sailor's heart sank, and bitter thoughts stole through his mind. He had fought manfully, but had been overpowered by superior numbers. It was but just noon when he had entered his prison, and the long shadows of evening were gradually fading away ere any step approached the door. Weary and faint, he lay on the hard floor and rested his head against the window-seat, which was the only resting-place in his miserable abode. Then a rough-looking man opened the door, and thrusting in a small flask of execrable wine and some coarse bread, departed without a word.

The night came, with the silver queen riding majestically through the cloudless heavens, and making the streets below look like scenes in fairyland, with their quaint, unearthly shadows.

Again there was a step upon the stair, and the door opened and the commandant stood before Reginald. He sat down on the seat beside him and peered into his face.

For a moment—but for a moment—a fiendish thought darted through the prisoner's mind: "I will kill this old man and escape!" but the uplifted arm fell, and the action passed unnoticed by his visitor.

"You are called Reginald Dawson," said the officer, in tolerable English. "What was your father's name?"

"The same."

"And your mother?" inquired the officer, peering still nearer into the young man's face.

"Angélique: she was a Frenchwoman."

The commandant's arms were round the prisoner's neck, and tears ran down his war-beaten face.

"You have fallen among friends, young man: I am your mother's elder brother."

Reginald's great eyes opened, and a ray of hope came to him; but he looked at his clanking irons and barred window, and his hope died away again.

"Your mother used to wear a curious ring, something like the one you wear. May I see it?"

Reginald showed him the ring.

"It is the same," said the officer, touching it. "Good-night; I must go my rounds now. You shall have some better provision than the gaoler brought you; but you must submit to your lodging, else I shall not be able to assist you."

Half-an-hour passed, and again came a step, light and gentle, up that dismal stair. The door swayed back on its hinges, and a young girl of sixteen made her appearance, carrying a basket with the promised supper. She was slightly made, with a dark complexion, and large, lustrous black eyes.

Reginald started from his recumbent position, and the girl, blushing deeply, seated herself on the window-seat, and spread forth her treasures by her side.

She signed to him to eat, and that she would wait. "I am to be your gaoler," she said, slowly, in English.

Reginald, delighted, began to talk rapidly in his own tongue, but he soon found his companion's knowledge of it confined to the few words she had spoken, but she gave him to understand she was the commandant's daughter, and his cousin. When he had finished, she carefully collected the least fragment, and taking the larger part of the coarse bread, which was his prison allowance, hid it in her basket, and retired.

Every night for some time she never failed, and by degrees the young folks made great progress in each other's language.

"I fancied from that captain's name, that he was a person of some importance; but from inquiries I've made, I feel satisfied I was mistaken. He may be put in the common-room with the other men," said the commandant, to the rough gaoler one day, after the sailors had been in the castle about a fortnight.

The gaoler looked cunningly at his superior officer, and walked away whistling. The same day Reginald was once more among his old companions, and to a certain extent at liberty, for, as there was no chance of escape, and a pretty strong garrison, they were allowed to range about the courtyard, and lie in the sun on the broad esplanade overlooking the sea. Their number was indeed diminished, for some had died of their neglected wounds, and some few had been drafted away with other captives to a more distant prison. The first time Reginald encountered the commandant's daughter, he sprang forward to address her, but a sign from her showed that she was unwilling to recognize him, and looking up he saw the eyes of the grim turnkey fastened on them.

Do you know what it is to be a prisoner? Few, who are not grievous sinners, know what the inside of an English prison is, unless curiosity or benevolence have induced some to penetrate behind those dull, blank walls, and enter through the massive portal.

But alas! few among us do not know, either in our own persons, or those most dear to us, the misery of a home-prison: the room of sickness—perhaps of death.

Oh! how the bright sun seems to twit us, as, chained to a couch of suffering, we see all else rejoicing in the open air, among fair scenes and flowers. How our heart yearns for one breath of the free, open air—for one hour to feel the power of unfettered action, to climb the green hillside, to join once more with our fellows! But the heavy weight of pain presses us down, the long, thin, white hand, that once was so firmly knit, the stumbling, tottering foot, that once was so steady, reminds us that we are no longer as others, that we are beyond the pale.

If the habitual invalid feels this, does not the prisoner in full strength and health suffer still more acutely?

"On all prisoners and captives have mercy"

CHAPTER VIII

AN IMPERIAL COMMANDANT

REGINALD'S love of carpentering and knowledge of ship-building, small as it was, was now to do him good service. France, at that time, had been drained, by incessant and disastrous wars, of the majority of her young and able men. This was severely felt in those trades where strength and ability were requisite; and in none more than in the dockyards and seaport towns: for while so many French vessels were captured by English cruisers and privateers, they could with difficulty get fresh ones built, or injured ones repaired, from the scarcity of ship-carpenters. In consequence of this difficulty, many English prisoners were employed, and two men, confined in the château with Reginald Dawson, were thus occupied in the harbour into which the luckless *Gratiana* had been brought. One of these men had sailed with young Dawson, and the other was a Torford man, who soon became a friend in captivity to the others. Most of their original companions had, as we have said before, been drafted off to other prisons, nor would these three have remained, had not there been some chance of turning them to account.

Reginald soon became an avowed favourite, not only with the old commandant and his dark-eyed daughter, but among the men and officers of the garrison, many of whom were hardly superior in rank to their men. The commandant was of nobler origin. Sprung from one of the best families of France, boasting the historical name of De Rohan, he had, in the wild frenzy of the French revolution, abandoned his little and distinctive "De," and joined himself heart and hand in deeds that lost him for ever his rich patrimony and ancestral home in sunny Dauphiné, and sent his father an exile to a foreign land. His son had thought the father dead for years, for no tidings had he ever heard of him; but he was mistaken, the little wizened dancing-master in the country town was Commandant Rohan's father, the Marquis de Rohan, whose greatest treasures were his fiddle, his snuff-box, and his reminiscences of *la vieille cour.*[30] Those who touch pitch must needs be defiled: and few would have guessed that the governor of the castle on the cliff was descended from such a stock as the De Rohans. He had served through most of the earlier campaigns of Napoleon Buonaparte: in the marshes of Italy, and under the scorching suns of Egypt, he had gradually lost the polish of the *garde de corps*, and acquired the roystering manners of a harassed trooper, not knowing where he should find his day's meal or his night's lodging.[31]

The passion, or rather the frenzy, for freedom, by which he and many others had been smitten in those evil days, had died out, after the bloody days of September;[32] but, little by little, a stronger and more absorbing passion had risen up in his mind, a passion shared by many, for *le petit caporal.*[33] Rohan had neither the abilities nor the luck to become a marshal of the empire, a prince, or a king; but the emperor remembered the enthusiasm he had seen him display, and rewarded him by appointing him commandant of one

---

30 *La vieille cour*: the old court.

31 *Garde de corps*: the king's bodyguard, which was exclusively aristocratic.

32 The September Massacres of 1792—the mass killing of prisoners and civilians, sometimes referred to as the 'First Terror' of the French Revolution.

33 *Le petit caporal*: the little corporal, the nickname of Napoleon Bonaparte.

of the imperial fortresses. Rohan felt that he was shelved rather than promoted, but he was a wise man, and kept his own counsel; and no one, to the day of his death, ever heard him speak a word in disparagement of the emperor.

But he was no longer a gentleman, nor had his marriage with a daughter of the people tended in any way to raise him. She, however, was dead and gone, and the only one belonging to him in existence, as far as he knew, was his daughter.

It was with no little emotion that he had recognised the ring which Reginald always wore—the ring poor Tye had given him the evening he had left Harscourt. It was, in fact, an heirloom in his family, and had been given to his sister on her marriage. But he did not dare to recognize his nephew openly, though he resolved, if possible, to give him his liberty, and Reginald's fancy for carpentering gave him an excuse.

However, Commandant Rohan was not a man to do anything without receiving something in return; and he imagined that it would be a very good thing for his daughter if he could arrange a marriage between her and her cousin. She possessed nothing, and Reginald, if he regained his liberty, would be in every point of view a most desirable husband for her.

There were times, even in those earlier days, when it struck the commandant, that, sooner or later, he might have to fly his native country, and a comfortable asylum secured in England was a thing not to be despised.

Reginald, accustomed to be made much of at Torford, and only too delighted to find that even in prison he received some sort of indulgence, readily fell into the snare laid for him, and forgetting the sweet, fair Lily, paid his court most assiduously to his dark-eyed cousin. It helped to wile away the tedium of captivity, and after a few weeks he found himself—he could scarcely tell how or why—formally betrothed to the commandant's daughter.

He was not a very ardent lover, but she was not very *exigeante*, so they got on very well, he profiting much by the many alleviations it was in her power to make of his privations, and enjoying many indulgences not accorded to the other prisoners.[34] He had no means of communicating with his friends in England, and they, hearing no tidings, concluded he was dead, for there was a faint rumour that the *Gratiana* had been seen in hot conflict with a large French vessel, not far from the French coast.

Grace was lost and gone before the rumour got about, and poor Lily almost sank beneath the blow. He was gone for ever! She would not be comforted—would admit of no hope. He was lost, never to be seen again.

Then, when she fully believed she should never look on that dear face again, she acknowledged to herself how she had loved him, how her very existence was bound up in him. "Perhaps," she murmured gently to herself, "if he had lived he would have loved me, but now I may love him as I will, without any wrong."

Poor child! she little guessed, while she poured out her heart in yearning misery, that in the Château at Dieppe was her lost friend, enjoying himself as far as possible, and raising up a barrier, not to be passed, between them—a barrier worse than death to her.

Dawson and his companions went regularly to work in the harbour, and as they proved themselves pretty trustworthy, though they were not on parole, the watch kept on their movements was not very strict. They formed acquaintances among the townspeople, and as they were always ready to give a helping hand in the fortress,

---

[34] *Exigeante*: hard to please, demanding.

they became favourites with both officers and men, and many a summer evening was spent in games and mirth on the esplanade of the château. But everything they did was done with one object, and that was escape—freedom.

Reginald had yielded to his uncle's manœuvres the more readily, as giving him a claim to any assistance in the commandant's power; and though that worthy never actually counselled Dawson to make the attempt, he showed him the possibility of it by constant hints and innuendoes.

Hortense, acting under her father's directions, was, when opportunity offered, more plain-spoken and the men at length determined to try their luck. Hortense was, of course, aware of their intentions, but they did not confide the time they had chosen, lest she should betray them involuntarily by showing any extra anxiety.

It was with anxious hearts that they went to their work, when they at last fixed on a day for an attempt. If they succeeded, all well and good; but they were in a strange land, where every man's hand was against them: and if they failed, a much more rigorous and severe imprisonment, if not death itself, awaited them.

CHAPTER IX
THE ESCAPE

THE evening was dark and stormy, but still the men worked on. Their guard, not finding the weather to his mind, nor the damp mud on which Reginald and his companions had to stand to finish their business of caulking, retired to a neighbouring dram-shop to refresh his inner man, never doubting that he should find his charge on his return. He was a careless, drunken fellow, and had for that reason been selected for his present charge by Commandant Rohan.

"Now or never," whispered Reginald, and in a few moments Reginald, Lovering, and Bowden were dodging in and out among the hulls of the vessels. They reached the drawbridge, which crossed the stream to the little fishing suburb, and hiding under its shadow, bided their time till a few straggling passengers had vanished, and then swiftly crossing the road got into the shade of a long avenue of trees, where they ran as fast as they could manage through the long dark grass. The weather favoured them, for a rolling mist came driving in from the sea, and would have effectually prevented their being discovered in their present locale.

After they had run nearly a mile, they paused to take breath and to consider what course they had better pursue.

Reginald remembered the place his uncle had so often mentioned—"Petite Abbeville to the West"—and also Hortense's advice. "To the west let us go, and Providence may chance to put a boat in our way." To the west they turned, having to swim the river, and wade through low marshy ground intersected with dykes, with alder-trees growing along their banks. But now the night closed in upon them, and the thick clouds and mist prevented their being able to catch a glimpse of a single star that might have served as a guide; and so they wandered on and on till they came to rising ground, and corn-fields, and apple-trees planted among the corn. As the deep bells of the churches tolled out their solemn evening chime, they found they were still quite close to the town, much closer than was pleasant, so they started forward again through the mist and darkness, to come once more upon the river they had left hours ago.

So they wandered about all night, cold and weary, and when morning began to dawn, saw, a mile from them, the castle towering upon the cliff.

Then they started off for their lives, and reached a high road, which they crossed in safety, and so on till they came to a deep glen, with trees and thick underwood, and there they hid themselves, having nothing to eat but some apples they had picked up as they came along.

The soldier was not a little astonished when he returned from his companions in the dram-shop, and found that his prisoners had disappeared; but as the eddying tide was rising fast, and was already some inches deep round the vessel on which they had been at work, he concluded that, like good people, they had returned to the château, as they had done on a previous occasion when he happened to miss them, and so, returning to the dram-shop, he took an extra glass to sustain him under the castigation he was likely to receive, and, after flirting slightly with a pretty girl, who lived in the square, betook himself leisurely enough to the château.

The trio, strange to say, had not arrived. The soldier and a companion were sent in quest of them; doubtless, they had lost their way. It was with a quaking heart that Joseph returned for a second time without his charge, and was assailed the moment he crossed the threshold by the commandant apparently in a most furious rage.

"What has become of these men?" thundered the ancient warrior, in a tremendous voice.

"Ain't they come home?" inquired Joseph, meekly, trying to look round the commandant, as if he thought they were hid behind him.

"Come home!" roared the governor. "You know they are not. Where are they, sir?"

Joseph looked up in despair; close by stood the officers, some soldiers, and the grim turnkey, who always made his appearance when least wanted. Everybody's eyebrows were elevated, and every man's hands, in true French fashion, was in his pockets. Suddenly, a bright thought flashed through Joseph's rather bemuddled brain.

"Englishmen are all *diables*; I have heard Monsieur le Commandant say that with my own ears.[35] How can one Frenchman watch three *diables*?"

There was a general laugh, and even the commandant looked less like a thunder-cloud.

This sally produced a diversion in his favour, and Joseph gained courage.

"I was standing just so," quoth Joseph, putting himself in an attitude, "and all in a moment they disappeared."

"Why didn't you give the alarm, then, at once, and not go tramping about on a fool's errand? I don't believe one word you say," shouted M. Rohan—"not one;" and he flourished about, ordering the unfortunate Joseph into arrest, and commanding a party of soldiers to make ready immediately to accompany him on a searching expedition.

---

[35] Diables: devils.

The old soldier's face changed, as he shut the door of his parlour behind him, and was alone with Hortense, who had watched the scene from the door.

"You acted to perfection," whispered the girl, "but they are stupid, they have chosen such bad weather. What can they do such a night as this?"

"They are young and strong. I have done my part, now they must do theirs." And the old man sighed, and Hortense sighed—to keep him company.

It is painful to have to record a great man's failings, and M. Rohan, not having a valet, was a great man. Moreover, he was a member of "the great army," and therefore ought to have known better. M. Rohan went out with the full determination of *not* finding the three strangers, and if the truth must be told, led his men where he very well guessed they were not to be found. M. Rohan had a heart, as he was in the habit of informing people—a French heart—but still a true one. He loved his little sallow black-eyed daughter, though he had not loved her mother, and he loved the memory of a gentle sister, and it was his love of this memory that made him forget the principles on which his great leader acted, and on which, as a loyal subject, he should have acted, viz.—self.

Having said thus much, our readers will doubtless not be surprised when they hear that Monsieur Rohan returned to the château at a late hour of the night, decidedly wet and decidedly cross, *sacréing* in a most violent and vicious manner, and completely taking in the grim gaoler, who had had his eye on him this long while past.[36]

---

[36] *Sacréing*: cursing.

The three sailors sat crouching together in the underwood, wet and miserable. The pitiless rain and mist kept driving in clouds round them, while the wind sighed and whistled through the dead leaves that still hung on the trees, and in the distance they heard the roar of the ground sea. That sound was their only comfort, for they knew they were near the shore.

All day long they sat in the woods; towards evening the rain cleared off, and the mist curled up the hills and over the sea in fantastic forms, while every bush and every blade of grass was powdered with countless diamonds.

At last Lovering was sent to reconnoitre, and came back with some apples, and the intelligence that about a mile to the west was a small village in a valley, and on the shore lay several boats.

This was welcome news, and as it grew darker, they made their way to the beach, and cautiously approached the boats.

They held their breath for fear, and trembled as the large stones of which the beach was composed rolled beneath their feet, and made sufficient noise to reveal their whereabouts to any passer-by.

The village, fortunately for them, was three or four hundred yards from the beach, embowered in luxuriant orchards, so that, unless some one chanced to be on the beach, they were secure enough from detection. They crept towards one of the boats that lay nearest the sea, and, with one glance, seeing it had the requisites of sails and oars, speedily launched it, and were once more afloat! afloat, but not out of danger; far—far from it.

The wind was of little service, but, seizing the oars, they rowed out boldly towards the open sea. Half-an-hour passed: no one spoke. Life and death depended on their exertions, and they rowed manfully. But now, upon the shore, lights pass backwards and forwards. The villagers have discovered that one of their boats is missing, and from many causes they fancy that the runaway sailors must be the thieves: for was she not high and dry upon the beach, firmly chained to her moorings?

As they passed out of the bay they caught the wind, and hoisting sail, flew before the breeze, steering, as they guessed, away from land: and for a while, the lights, which now and then appeared, aided them in their calculations, but the sky was still too obscured for them to gain any knowledge from the stars. Compass they had none.

Morning found them on the waste of waters, out of sight of land. So far well, but whither were they steering? They had nothing to eat but the apples they had gathered, and all the drink they had between them was a very small quantity of brandy in a flask belonging to Reginald. On they drove all that day, and the wind rose till it became a tempest, and the billow rolled mountains high, and the last apple was eaten, and the last drop of brandy gone. And still the boat held out, but the men's strength was failing fast. Not a sail, not a speck of land, but clear blue mountains, crested with white, rising one above the other, as far as eye could see; sea and sky—sky and sea! And never a drop of water, and never a crust of bread. And so they went on three whole days and nights; and poor Bowden laid down in the bottom of the boat, and longed for death, and raved till his wild shrieks pierced through the air, and chilled the little life that was left in his companions.

On the fourth morning they saw behind them an island they must have passed in the night, and land looming ahead of them. They were too weak to shout, the words died on their lips; but on they sped towards the land, whether belonging to friend or foe they cared not, for they felt they were dying.

On they flew, the wind roaring, and the waves dashing over them, but they had—what they had not known for long—hope! The sun shone out, and the clouds careered over the bright blue sky, and the sands sparkled in the sunlight, and green fields gladdened their eyes, and they saw stately ships, and soldiers walking on the quays in the well-known English uniform, and Lovering whispered, hoarsely,—

"We are saved—it is Jersey!"

Under the bows of great ships they went, and the sailors pointed at them; they looked so strange and wild, with that wretched man shrieking and yelling in the bottom of the boat. Men shouted to them to stay, and asked who they were, and whence they came, but they had no strength to answer, and the boat drove on till she grounded gently on the shore.

Then soldiers and sailors, gentle and simple, crowded round them, and questioned them, but they answered nothing, only whispering, "We are dead men." Then out from the crowd stepped two English sailors, and they cried, "Captain Dawson, is it you? We thought you were gone long ago."

And when the young man heard a voice he knew calling him by his own name, he fell upon the shore in a swoon, and Lovering, striving to raise him, fell too. Then kindly friends rose up for those poor forlorn wanderers, and took them to their own homes, and cared kindly for them. But the poor maniac raved and raved till he had no strength left, and then he died, and his wife and children saw him no more.

CHAPTER X
REGINALD'S RETURN

THE winter day is drawing to a close, and the Lily brings her chair nearer to the window to catch the last rays of light for her work, and as she sits she sings low and sweetly to herself. She is alone, thinking on the days that are gone. But hark! there is a step in the quiet street, not the brisk short step of one coming back in youth and gladness, but a slow, lingering, uncertain footfall.

Lily lays down her work and listens, while a strange light flashes from her eyes, and the colour flushes to her forehead. The step comes nearer and nearer. She holds her breath; can she be mistaken? or is it really Reginald? Her hands are clasped over her heart to still, if possible, its wild beatings. A shadow falls upon the window; she knows now he is come, but she never moves, a dimness comes over her eyes. He enters the house unbidden—his steps sound through the old hall—and once more he and Lily are face to face.

But still the girl sat motionless, till the sailor, sinking at her feet, and unclasping her small white hands, buries his face in her dress, and bursts into a wild bitter agony of tears.

Women's tears come so readily that one thinks them but natural, however sorrowful they may be, but a man's tears are only wrung from him in some overwhelming grief, and are terrible.

"Poor Grace—poor Grace!" he muttered. "Gone! I shall never see her again! Oh! sister, why did you leave me. What shall I do without you?"

There came no tears to Lily's eyes. He was back again with her, yet his first thought was of the lost sister. Good and gentle as she was, she was but a woman, and a jealous pang shot through her at the idea that his first thought was for another. But it was but for a moment, and then she laid her hands caressingly on the bowed head, and smoothed the thick brown curls, and whispered softly,—

"Reginald, my poor friend! dear Reginald!"

As she spoke she trembled. Suppose he were to guess that in those dark days, when she believed him dead, she had confessed to herself her love for him? Oh, that must never be! she would rather die first. So she lifted up her face that had bent lovingly over him, though he did not see it, and drew her hands away from the thick curls, and laid them on his shoulder. And so she sat, he at her feet, his head on her knees.

"Lily," he said, at last, raising his head and looking full in her face, "you have always been a sister to me. Now you must be Grace and Lily in one—my only sister."

Lily looked down into his face, but she uttered never a word.

"I have always loved you as a sister, dearest, and always shall. You must be kind to me, Lily, and patient, for I am very sorrowful."

Still no answer, but one little hand is laid softly on the young man's forehead, and wanders lovingly over his hair.

"You will be my sister, Lily? Speak, dear, I want to hear your voice."

He has put his arms round the girl, and looks earnestly in her face.

She answers, "Yes, for ever," and shudders as she speaks.

He does not heed it, and goes on talking, now about Grace, now about his ship and his misfortunes, and at last he tells her all—yes, everything.

He tells of the old castle on the cliff, and his relation the commandant, and of his cousin his betrothed wife. The Lily sits and listens silently. The flush fades away from her face as he goes on, and her head is dizzy. Is it a dream, or is it really true, that Reginald—her Reginald—is to be married to another—a stranger?

Better that he had never come home, better that she had never seen him again, than this. Was this the answer to her earnest prayer that he might but come back again? Yes, her desire was fulfilled to the letter: yet what a bitter mockery of all her hopes was this. He was there, kneeling at her feet, holding her hands, but he was no longer her Reginald. A distance wider than the universe was between them—never to be passed.

She did not ask him if he loved his cousin, not a word did she utter in any way to upbraid or censure him for his conduct, she only accused herself.

"I was presumptuous. I fancied—and others told me—that he loved me; but I ought to have known better. If he had loved me, he would have asked me to be his wife long ago. No, he never loved me; I am unloved!"

Oh! the bitterness of a woman's heart when she feels the one she loves has passed her by—the misery of unrequited affection.

Such disappointment are the common lot of women. Some grow soured, peevish, and uncharitable to those more fortunate; others weep and mourn till their grief passes, and they become kind, gentle-hearted old maids, if they do not form a second attachment. Occasionally, such a disappointment utterly stuns and overwhelms. So it was with Lily. Her heart grew cold within her as Reginald talked on, but she neither wept nor complained.

The evening is come now, it is almost night. The panelled room is dark and dreary, only around Lily's pale face a light seems to linger.

Reginald has talked on till his tears are dried and he is cheerful again, so much so that his manner jars on Lily.

"It is cold," she said, at last, "very cold. Come into the other room, Mr. Dawson; they will be glad to see you."

She rose abruptly, shuddering. Reginald never noticed how she had called him Mr. Dawson, though it was the first time in their long acquaintance she had ever done so: he was thinking of other matters.

"Not to-night," he replied. "I only came to see you. To-day I am wearied, Lily dear. Good-bye."

"Good-bye, Mr. Dawson," said the Lily, folding her arms.

"Have I vexed you, have I angered you, Lily?" asked her companion, eagerly. "I cannot part with you so, my sister," and his strong arm was round her.

She did not repulse him, but let her head fall and nestle on his shoulder.

"What is it, Lily? What can I have said to vex you?"

Lily's arms are gently raised and encircle his neck; her soft, pale face is pressed against his. "Good-bye," she whispers, "good-bye, Reginald."

The arms are suddenly unclasped, and she is gone, Reginald standing bewildered by himself.

What does it mean? What is the matter with Lily? and, pondering, he leaves the house without seeing any of the rest of the family.

That evening, when Lily at last joined her family at supper, the first inquiries were as to what had become of Reginald. They had quite depended on him staying with them. It was unfair his running away, for they had left him undisturbed with Lily for hours.

"Was it so long?" she asked, as she seated herself on a low stool before the fire.

"I daresay the time didn't seem long to you, miss," said her father, laughing; "no doubt you had enough to say to one another: and how does he bear his poor sister's affair?"

"He will forget it soon; at least, the horror of it."

"And the wedding, Lily: when is the wedding to be?" inquired her brother.

A shudder was the only answer.

"Come, child, why don't you answer?" said her father, kindly. "You must not be shy; what day have you and Reginald fixed on? You must let us know in good time. Won't we have a jolly day, that's all!"

"Father dear," said Lily, dropping down by her father's knee; "you must not talk so, dear; it hurts me very much. Reginald never asked me to be his wife, nor ever means to. I am his sister now, as Grace was; nothing else."

The ship-builder elevated his shaggy brows and looked puzzled.

"Well, child, I must say I don't understand the matter; but I wouldn't vex you for the world; only, in my days, young men asked women to be their wives, not their sisters, when they were in love with them."

"But he isn't in love with me, dear father: he never was," said Lily, nearly breaking down.

"If he wasn't, he ought to have been, that's all I can say; and it doesn't say much for his taste, that's my opinion, whatever you may say."

"Hush, father! dear father! please don't say any more about it ever," and she laid her face against the great rough man, who looked down on her so lovingly and tenderly: Lily could not deceive him. He felt all was not right, but what could he do to comfort her?

The mother and he talked the matter over by themselves, but they could not make it out. They had always imagined that Reginald and Lily were made for one another, and had always considered the match as settled. Perhaps even now it would all come right.

CHAPTER XI
WOMAN'S HONOUR

LILY bore herself bravely under her trial. She went as regularly about the light household duties that fell to her share, as if nothing was weighing her heart to the earth. She was as kindly and friendly as ever, but those who loved her most, and watched every look and turn of their darling, noticed the pale cheek, the lagging step, but they mentioned not these things to her. "It may be only a lover's quarrel," they said to each other; "no doubt it will all come right at last."

They knew nothing of Reginald's engagement, for he had charged Lily to keep it a secret; and they looked anxiously for his return to Torford (which he had suddenly quitted for Harscourt, the very night of his return), thinking that then there might be a reconciliation between the two.

Days passed by, but no Reginald made his appearance, and it was not till the end of a fortnight that he once more paid the Fowlers a visit. This time Lily did not see him alone, she had to meet him before many persons; but she was calm and quiet as if nothing were amiss, seated in the window with her work.

Reginald never addressed her particularly during his visit, but talked and chatted with her brother and sisters, as if she was not there. To tell the truth, something began to whisper to the young man that he had not acted kindly by the girl; but how he had erred, he did not care to think.

Men and women differ most materially on the subject of those they love. A woman naturally becomes attached to those she constantly associates with; but men seem generally to prefer those of whom they know but little, or, at any rate, not those they know most intimately.

Thus while year by year the Lily's love had grown for Reginald, till it was part of her being; he had never thought of her but as a sort of sister, a creature sometimes to pet, sometimes to use as a friend and confidant, but as a lover he had never thought of her. Yet somehow he had pondered over the reception she had given him on the night of his return, the way she had put her arms round his neck, the way she had wished him good-bye, and he felt she loved him. Grace had never spoken or acted so to him: he had never seen Lily act so to her own brother. It was not as a brother she regarded him.

His vanity was pleased at the idea, but then there was Hortense, and as he mused he half wished he was not hampered.

Though apparently he took little heed of Lily, he watched her narrowly, and her keeping aloof from him, still further persuaded him that she loved him. "She is afraid of showing it," he said to himself, nor was he far wrong. "I wonder if she really does love me; I should like to find out." And he set to work to find out, and every day found him at the Fowlers.

Poor Lily! At first she tried to struggle with her love, and cast it out, but it was a task beyond her strength. When he was alone in the dark, silent night, she would struggle and argue with herself, and form all sorts of good resolutions; but when the day and Reginald came, what could she do? "No one will suffer but myself," she thought; "no one will be miserable but me. I must, I may love him on, and no one need know."

But she was mistaken; the person most nearly interested saw it all now, and the knowledge made him discover fresh charms in the sweet Lily every time they met.

He had promised to marry Hortense Rohan, but he now loved Lily Fowler. And those who loved her looked on and said, "It will all come right in the end."

Suddenly did she awake from her pleasant dream to find herself standing on the edge of a precipice. The love she so coveted was within her grasp—nay, was hers; but not of right, not lawfully.

He spoke out,—

"I love you, Lily; when will you be my wife?"

She did not twine her arms round his neck, or nestle her head on his shoulder, but with a sharp cry she sprang from him. She stood staring vacantly before her, her small hands clenched on her breast; heaving words refused to come; but thoughts, ah! how busily did they fly through her head!

"This is what I am come to; I have stolen the love that belonged to another; I have come between those that should be one." She felt utterly degraded in her own estimation.

"Lily, speak; you look so wild—what is the matter? Do you not love me after all"

Yes, after all she loved him, but she was not going to tell him so.

"You forget Hortense," she answered, hoarsely.

"I can't think of her now; I love you! I have always loved you! I see it now."

"Hush! how can I believe you? you told her you loved her?"

"I don't think I ever did. I was persuaded into promising to marry, and I had nothing else to do."

"Yes; but you promised, and but for that promise you would not now have been here."

"I tell you," he exclaimed, passionately, "she is nothing to me; how could I be such a fool as ever to look at her, knowing you! No, Lily, you must not trifle; come and sit down and be reasonable."

But all his efforts were fruitless. The girl utterly refused to be a party to the breach of his promise. His temper rose at what he called her wilfulness, and she, frightened at the storm she had raised, knelt at his feet and sued for pardon, and took all the blame to herself; but in spite of his persuasions she would not give him one word of encouragement, nor even confess she returned his love.

"I should never know a moment's happiness or peace, Reginald, if I married you. You must keep your promise, and I will be your sister as you asked me only a little while ago."

Reginald was nearly beside himself with passion—angry with the gentle creature he really loved, for thwarting him—angry with himself for having yielded to Rohan.

"I see it all!" he exclaimed, fiercely, in his rage, "you do not love me; if you did, so paltry a reason as this promise would not separate us!"

She did not answer him—she did not dare—it would only encourage him if she told the truth; and her love, however wrong, she could not deny.

"You do not love me—you never did!" he exclaimed again.

Still she would not speak; and with fearful, bitter words he left her.

He was gone! Should she call him back and tell him how he misjudged her? When she saw him no longer, it seemed more than she could bear—she must speak to him just once again; but as she hesitated, his quick angry step in the street grew fainter and fainter, and she was alone.

Poor little Mrs. Fowler had been anxiously listening to Reginald's loud tones, and when he suddenly rushed by her and out of the house, she saw something was very much amiss, and hastened into the room, to find Lily standing where the young man had left her.

"My child, my darling, what is the matter? Oh, do tell your poor old mother, my little Lily!"

"I have got you still—you, my own kind mother," said the girl; "you will always love me, mother, and never doubt my love."

"Who could doubt you, dearest?—you, the best——"

"Hush, mother; I am not good; I have done very wrong, mother; but I am punished bitterly."

The mother was puzzled, and looked anxiously at her daughter.

"Have you and he quarrelled, Lily?" she asked, in a low timid voice, as if fearful of intruding on the girl's thoughts.

"Mr. Dawson asked me to marry him and I refused, mother, and he is vexed."

"No wonder, child!" cried Mrs. Fowler, feeling in her little way quite indignant; "why on earth don't you marry him? You have been telling him as plainly as acts could do, this month past, that you loved him: then, why not marry him? I don't understand it."

Others then had noticed her: she had betrayed herself to all.

"I know it, mother," she replied; "I have acted very wrongly; I feel humbled to the dust; but, mother, dear, don't be vexed with me, and don't blame poor Reginald."

"But dear, do think over it, and let me tell him you didn't mean what you said."

"But I do mean it, mother; I can never marry him."

"But you love him, child?"

The only answer was a burst of tears, and the girl bent down by her mother's side as she would have done when a little child.

"Mother, don't let any one talk to me about this; I couldn't bear it. Tell them he asked me to be his wife, and I refused him; then they can't say he dealt unjustly by me."

"But is it the truth?"

"The very truth, mother."

"Ay, Lily, the truth, but not all the truth. He will come again, darling, and all will be right," said Mrs. Fowler.

"No, mother; he will not come back again; and if he did, I would not alter."

Lily was right, he did not come back again. His pride was wounded, he was piqued at Lily's obstinate refusal; yet for all, he did not cease to love her, though he tried to seem indifferent.

It was only by accident she heard of him; only once in the course of many weeks did she see him, and then the sight haunted her to her dying day: Reginald, her Reginald, surrounded by a troop of the wildest and worst characters in Torford, shouting and roystering along the quays, far from sober, and causing all quiet passengers to retreat before them.

CHAPTER XII

FLIGHT OF COLONEL ROHAN

MY readers may remember a certain gaoler at Dieppe, who, during the incarceration of the English captives, Reginald and his companions, and the manœuvres of Colonel Rohan to effect their liberation, ever kept a watchful eye on his superior, and manifestly suspected his conduct. When the prisoners were gone, although the matter had been so well managed, that no shadow of proof could be brought of the complicity of the commandant, yet the gaoler would not give up his suspicions, and by-and-by he began to talk. Possibly he thought, that by making a display of fidelity to the Government, he should be promoted to a higher office than his present one of assistant-gaoler at Dieppe, and obtain what he much desired—a more ample provision for the large family with which he was encumbered. But, whatever was the reason—whether moved by the love of lucre, or the spirit of envy against his superior—certain it is that he had taken occasion, at the drinking-house that he frequented, to let drop some hints that all was not right about the prisoners. As soon as the disappearance of the Englishmen was known to the Government, an investigation was instituted. At that time the gaoler seems to have been uncertain how to act, and to have kept his suspicions to himself. Nothing, therefore, came of that inquiry, except a general warning to the officials to be more careful for the future. But after the investigation was over, and the commission had left Dieppe, the gaoler was heard to say, that if people had told all they knew, the inquiry would have ended differently; and that a certain gentleman had been very kind to the prisoners—a precious deal kinder, indeed, than he had ever been to a Frenchman in his life. What did it all mean?—sending them meat and wine and delicacies, and letting them go about very loosely guarded; for his part, he did not understand it.

These conversations of the gaoler, repeated in the little circle at Dieppe, gradually spread a cloud of suspicion round the head of the commandant, and, although they had not yet gone further or reached the ears of the authorities, Colonel Rohan was very much afraid that they would do so, and bring down upon him a second court of inquiry, whose sentence, his heart told him, would not be so favourable as that of the first.

Nay, very soon the now dreaded gaoler began to assume an air and manner towards his superior, which made that superior feel that he would not long content himself with breathing suspicions; and that he himself was in danger of speedy arrest and punishment. Having once come to this conclusion, he determined to seek safety in flight, and, like so many refugees of that period who sought the shores of Albion—Bourbonists, Republicans, Bonapartists in turn—he also looked towards the white cliffs for preservation.

Hortense, independently of the risk they ran in delaying, was anxious, on her own account, to forward her father's plan. Though less rapturously in love, perhaps, than some young ladies, yet she had become accustomed to the society of Reginald. She felt his absence much. Time, which had been so pleasantly passed, now hung heavy on her hands; the kind words, the pleasant smile, the assisting arm, were a terrible loss. Besides which, what hope was there of her seeing Reginald again for many a year, or even at all, as she sometimes confessed to herself, whilst that cruel depth of ocean rolled between them? But now she would behold him in a few days. He would not have time to forget her; or, after the manner of treacherous men, lose the thought of the old love in a new.

Thus reasoned Hortense, and her preparations were steadily made. The commandant and his daughter fled to England, and turned their faces, in the first place, to the great wilderness of London.

What more melancholy than to be a stranger alone in a great city! And what city so great as London! What loneliness so intense as the loneliness of a labyrinth of dismal streets and dull spiritless houses, from whose windows not one friendly face looks on the wanderer!

Traversing those streets without a friend, what a strange agony of longing comes over one! a longing for faces long since turned to dust—for pleasant fields and breezy hillsides we may never tread again—a longing for the days of our youth that have passed for ever.

One seems amid the din to hear the pleasant rippling of some well-known brook, the cool splash of the summer waves, the sighing of the wind amid the trees; one looks up, and the fairy-land vanishes. Crowds of busy, hurrying people, eagerly strive after things we know not of, each living in a world of his own of which we are ignorant, and the houses seem to grow more sharp and defined, and the noise louder and more jarring, and we feel how utterly we are alone.

Side by side wandered the commandant and his daughter, each buried in their own thoughts; he looking back—she looking forward. He calling to remembrance the old château in sunny Dieppe—she thinking she was in the same land as Reginald.

Poor and friendless, they wander from street to street, from house to house, in search of a home suited to their slender means.

Oh, the intense wretchedness of a poor London home! Forced aside, as the poor are, into narrow by-streets and dilapidated houses, still now and then they crowd up to the very gates of our palaces.

See that lonesome widow and her little hungry children. They live over the stables of yon rich man's horses, and would, in their want and misery, fain eat the corn that the horses leave. From their close and reeking room they can see into the rich man's house, see gay faces and little forms at the windows that seem, in their brightness, to mock the misery of the poor.

Weary and footsore—weary and heavy-hearted—did those two tread the streets of London, ere they found a lodging in a dirty back street in St. Giles's. A low eating-house was the only shelter that the heir of the De Rohan and his only child could afford.

Colonel Rohan's head drooped more and more, his step grew more unsteady, his temper more morose, as day after day he sat in his dark room, and saw his little hoard of money gradually lessening. Was the punishment of his unfaithfulness to his king to be starvation in a strange land? Was he to die the death to which he and his party had condemned so many innocent ones—the death of an exile?

Then began that struggling for existence, that anxiety and toiling for a morsel of bread, that too many know from bitter experience. Hortense was the first to see the necessity of action. A new strength and life seemed to awake within her. Yet what could she do? To what employment could she turn her hand? Her slender stock of accomplishments were soon reviewed. Fine embroidery, velvet painting, and dancing, these were all she knew. The numbers of poor French ladies who, in those days, with the same accomplishments, were endeavouring to gain a livelihood, had overstocked the market; and, friendless and unknown, she had but little chance of succeeding. Fortunately for her, her landlady, the keeper of the eating-house, was ambitious of having her daughters brought up above their station; and considering velvet painting and dancing as two very telling accomplishments, was glad to give her lodgers their rooms rent free on condition of Hortense undertaking their education. Humble as was this introduction, it was something; and by degrees, Hortense found ample employment, and, removing from the eating-house, opened a dancing-school with her father's assistance; and he who had paced the painted galleries of Versailles, and been present at the gaiety of the court of Marie Antoinette, was, to gain a morsel of bread, content to teach the rising generation of St. Giles's to walk straight, and hold up their heads. What must not people submit to, when they come to that hand-to-hand struggle for life!

But with all her struggling, Hortense seemed no nearer Reginald and Torford, than she had been at Dieppe. So she toiled, and worked, and stinted herself of the very necessities of life, that she might get together a sufficient sum to carry her into the west.

It was a weary life. Day after day did she crawl down those dirty narrow stairs, and wait for and watch the postman, in hope of a letter; day after day did she return to her dismal room empty-handed and disappointed.

Mechanically, she went through the duties required of her with a heavy heart and absent mind; and some of her elder pupils speculated whether or no mademoiselle were in love. Perhaps she might be: but who would ever fall in love with her, a little ugly brown thing?

Their present lodging, though a step above the eating-house, was no very choice abode—a tall narrow house in a by-street in Bloomsbury, every room boasting a separate establishment.

The commandant and his daughter occupied the ground floor, the front room serving by day as the dancing school, by night as the commandant's bed-chamber. Behind was a smaller room, looking into a narrow, filthy courtyard, common to all the lodgers, and which room belonged more especially to Hortense. There she manufactured such dishes as their slender means could afford; and there, at night, on a wretched sofa, she laid her aching head, and pondered in the darkness on the past life—the present and the future.

What a change from the old castle on the cliff, with the great sea and the free air—to that close, smoky room, from which not a square yard of sky was visible! Poor girl! she worked bravely on, but she had a hard task; yet as long as she had employment, she never murmured; and though her pupils belonged neither to the highest or richest in the community, their number made up for their other deficiencies; and more than one kind friend did the little dark Frenchwoman make among her humble associates, for she had a kindly heart, and was ever ready to render such little services as lay in her power, towards those among whom it was her lot to dwell; and kindness rarely fails to beget kindness.

So she plodded on her way, waiting for letters that never came, listening for a footstep which was never to cross her threshold, believing in a heart that was no longer hers.

"I will seek him! I will! I will!" she would exclaim to herself, in the dark night. "I will work and starve till I have the means: and then I will go and seek him."

You must have patience, Hortense, patience! Many a weary month, many a weary year must you work and wait before your object is attained.

But she cannot see into the future, and hope is strong within her; and so she adds week by week, if it is but a few pence, to a hoard that she keeps unknown to her father, hid away in a secure place.

Thus the commandant and his daughter live on their monotonous life, and his head sinks more and more on his breast, and his step day by day grows more and more feeble.

CHAPTER XIII
THE OLD MARQUIS

THE quiet life of the refugees was destined to be disturbed from a quarter that neither for a moment suspected.

One day Hortense's little back-room was invaded rather unceremoniously by her landlady, who also introduced a counterpart of herself in untidiness and dirt.

"You mustn't be offended, miss, at my coming in all of a hurry like, but my friend here's in trouble about a lodger of hers, and she came to ask my advice; but when she told me all about it, I said it's beyond me, I don't understand foreign tongues more than you do. I can't help you. Then she said to me, 'Haven't you a young lady lives with you who speaks foreign? One of the French Revolution folks?' 'So I have, to be sure,' said I; so without more to do I brought her up here, for I know you'll do a kindness if you can."

Hortense's knowledge of England was not very extensive, but she made out enough to interest her; so, quieting the resentment she had felt at the entrance of her uninvited company, she proceeded to question her visitors as to what they wanted of her.

"Well, you see, miss, the long and short of it is, there's an old gentleman has been lodging with my friend some months past, and he's been taken with a kind of fever, or something, and he's off his head; and though he could speak English well enough when he was well, now he seems to have forgotten it altogether, and he keeps talking away in a language my friend here can't make out a bit. I hear you and the old gentleman, your papa, sometimes talking together what I don't understand; so, maybe you'll be able to make out what my friend's lodger means."

The girl hastily dressed herself and accompanied the two women as they wished. The house was at no great distance, and of much the same calibre as the one they had inhabited: but if anything, it was still more dirty and wretched. At the door, some filthy, half-dressed children were playing on the steps. The floor of the entrance was of wood, but so coated with mud, from the constant passing to and fro, that it differed little in appearance from the road outside; the walls were smeared and stained, with here and there a large hole in the plastering, while the corners of the stairs were the receptacles of every species of abomination. It was with difficulty that Hortense made her way up the narrow winding staircase, and found herself in the room of the sick man.

It was a small back-room, commanding, in consequence of being more elevated, a wider view than Hortense's; a wider, but not a more cheerful one. Close by was a tiny court of houses, built in what had, in days gone by, been a garden. From house to house lines were stretched, on which hung the rags of some of the inhabitants. Over the low outhouses and buildings two lean cats were scrambling; an imprisoned lark thrilled out its song from a neighbouring house; and here and there was a broken pot with a sickly plant, or two or three scarlet-runners—trained on strings along the side of a window by some poor wretch who remembered the country and the green fields, and whose soul was longing for liberty, like the poor caged lark.[37]

So much for the exterior. Now turn to the interior. A grate choked with ashes, but no fire; a single chair, a small valise, and on the ground a thing they called a bed, a mere heap of shavings, and a solitary quilt. Stretched on this miserable resting-place lay a

---

[37] Scarlet-runners: a type of runner bean (*Phaseolus coccineus*).

withered old man, who, as they entered, was jabbering to himself in French. His voice was weak and low, and the girl had to stoop down by his side to catch what he was saying.

"Make haste, make haste," he said, turning to his visitor, "bring me my court dress, my sword, and hat: his Majesty is waiting for me—he will be displeased. Sire, I come; your Majesty remembers me! Yes, I am the well-known Maquis de Rohan. Yes, sire, I have lived in poverty and exile these many years. Your Majesty will not overlook the merits of an old servant of the throne of France. I am sorry, madam," he continued, altering his tone and manner, "that I can no longer attend your daughters; but my King summons me, I must obey the call. A peer of France must not be absent when a long-exiled monarch regains his throne. Farewell, madame! Should chance ever lead you to visit my country, count on me. I am your servant, and the château of the Marquis de Rohan shall be yours."

Suddenly the pitiful reality of his position seemed to force itself on his wandering mind.

"Sacré," he hissed between his teeth: "the villain, the cochon, the bête, the diable![38] Emperor indeed! Set him above the head of kings—kings with centuries of noble blood! Stand back, mademoiselle, I am no poor miserable citizen: I am Jean Baptiste Marquis de Rohan, Pair de France."

Little did the daughter of Commandant Rohan know of courts, kings, or nobles. Of her father's antecedents she was totally ignorant, and it never occurred to her to connect the poor sufferer, who proclaimed himself Marquis de Rohan, with herself, in spite of the similarity of names.

Like most girls she had had her day-dreams, and had pictured

---

[38] *Sacré*, Damn; *cochon*, pig; *bête*, brute; *diable*, devil.

to herself what princes and nobles should be like, but she never imagined that such as herself had anything to do with these far off divinities, neither had she ever imagined a noble in the position of the forlorn man before her. But her woman's heart was roused at the sight of the lonely old man, and she spoke some soothing words to comfort him.

"Hush," he whispered, placing his trembling finger to his lips, "am I in France? Am I at home? Some one speaks my own tongue; who are you, mademoiselle?"

"I am a poor exile like yourself," replied Hortense.

"Are you for the king?" he inquired, laying hold of her dress, and peering into her face.

"I am for him who rules in France now," she replied, evading the question.

"Who rules? Who governs France—beautiful France?" he muttered to himself. "Ah! the Bourbons are on the throne once more! Thy lawful sovereign is restored to the seat of his ancestors. The usurper Napoleon has fled; I go to claim my rights. Who rules in France? in beautiful France?"

The old man's head dropped back on the bundle that formed his pillow, and he tossed and moaned in anguish of mind and body.

"He's quite beside himself," said the landlady; "he talks of kings and dukes, as if such as he have anything to do with such folk; not but what he calls himself a marquis; a precious poor one, I should fancy, if he is. See, that queer 'malle,' as he calls it, is all the goods he has, except a grand snuffbox he makes a great parade of. I don't know what to do with him one bit;[39] I can't afford to keep him, and he doesn't appear to have much money, for when he was

---

[39] Malle: trunk.

well, green stuff and bread were the chief of his food."

"I've nothing to give—I can't afford it." What common expressions—yet how often heard from those who, an hour after, will squander ten times the required sum on some trumpery indulgence! It is the poor who are really generous, for they give of their little, they deny themselves for others; this is real giving, real generosity.

Hortense could find a use for every farthing she earned, and she had that strong feeling that most women have when they can and do earn money—that it is their very own, to use a very favourite phrase of childhood: she thought she might use it as she chose, and hoard it to gratify her own wishes; for a moment she thought, "What have I to do with this man? He is a stranger, he is nothing to me." But the blood rushed to her cheeks for shame at the unuttered thought, and she felt she must aid and relieve the poor creature so accidentally brought to her notice, even if she were obliged to trench on her beloved hoard.

"He is a compatriot of mine," she said, at length, rising from the floor where she had been kneeling beside the old emigré. "I will come again presently. If you will take care of him, I will give you what I can; but we are very poor, as you know."

"But honest," put in her landlady; "never an hour after time with their rent, though they go without their dinner for it; not that their dinner can cost much," she added, aside to her friend, "for most times it's as you say of him yonder—green stuff and bread and something, some weak broth they call potage."

They turned and left the old man to himself, and Hortense hurried home to see what could be spared from their slender store for their still more necessitous countryman.

There lay the little dancing-master of the English country town, the somewhile Marquis de Rohan; the man who had for years been the delight of the coterie of Broad Street; the brave defender of ladies who needed no defence.

Well for him had he been content with his modest conquests and snug lodgings; but, like many others, he forsook the substance for the shadow, and, in striving after what he had, at no time of his life, been really fitted for—political importance—he had lost all.

More than once, during the early period of Napoleon's power, rumours arose, from time to time, of political changes in France, and of Bourbon restoration. One of these rumours, uttered with greater confidence than usual, had brought De Rohan to London. There he hoped to have the news confirmed, to cross to France, and regain his rank and wealth. We need scarcely say he was disappointed, and the disappointment was greater than his weakened frame could bear. He fell ill, spent all the money in his possession, and was quite incapable, even had he desired it, of returning to his home in Broad Street. Sad and outcast condition of a peer of France!

CHAPTER XIV
THE EXILE

HORTENSE kept her adventure a secret from her father. He had become day by day more dull and low-spirited, and she was unwilling to give him any cause of anxiety. He had managed to get introductions to two or three schools, where he taught fencing and drill, and so added a few shillings to the common stock; but though active and energetic whilst actually employed, as soon as the necessity for exertion was withdrawn, he would slink into a corner and remain for hours without speaking or noticing anything.

Day after day his daughter stole a few moments from her other duties for her old protégé, and many a sigh did she heave at the inroads she felt bound to make on her hoard.

The poor old man was gradually sinking under age, infirmities, and misery; half his time he did not recognize his kind attendant, at other times he would promise her the most extravagant rewards for her kindness, or implore her piteously to give her charity to a poor old exile.

At length the commandant, dull and listless as he appeared, began to take note of her frequent absences, and with the feeling so common to minds naturally weak, or rendered so by illness or age, suspected that, as he was not trusted with her secret, she must have some bad motive for concealing it, and determined to discover it without her guessing his intention. He therefore commenced a system of espionage to unravel what one simple question would have made plain to him.

He was not long in discovering all that was to be discovered;

but, persuaded that something more than mere charity prompted his daughter's constant attentions to an old man, he resolved on paying a visit to the mysterious friend himself.

It was one of the old Marquis's good days; he was brighter and more alive than usual, and was half sitting up on his bed, rendered much more comfortable by the kindness and thoughtfulness of Hortense; and, when the uninvited visitor entered, was engaged in turning over some papers, yellow and musty from age, the valise open by his side.

"Pardon, monsieur," said the intruder.

"Pardon, monsieur," said the old man, bowing.

"We are compatriots, I perceive," continued M. Rohan.

"Truly," was the answer, with another bow. "Be seated," he continued, after a moment's pause, during which he surveyed his visitor with a scrutinizing gaze. "To what am I indebted for your amiable attentions?"

Telling the truth not always being polite, M. Rohan stammered out some excuse about his daughter.

"Ah!" exclaimed the marquis, "you are the father of my amiable young friend! I am charmed! Excuse my rising, I am an invalid. Allow me to offer you a pinch of snuff."

As he spoke, he held out the gold snuffbox, which more than anything else had proved to the good old ladies at Newport that the dancing-master was a real marquis. It was of peculiar form and richly chased, while on a small medallion on the lid were the interlaced initials of its owner, surmounted by a coronet.

M. Rohan started as he took it in his hand. After a few moments' examination, he felt sure he had seen it before, and the initials confirmed him in his opinion. They were his own.

"May I ask where you obtained this box?" he inquired, abruptly.

"It is mine! It has been mine for years," replied the old man, in some anxiety.

A tremor passed over the younger man.

"Your name, sir! Quick!"

"I am Jean Baptiste Marquis de Rohan."

M. Rohan uttered a sharp cry, and fixed his eyes intently on the speaker.

"Do you know the name? But of course you do; every Frenchman knows the De Rohans."

"Father!"

The Marquis started and seemed searching his memory, as the word brought back the old life, the olden times.

"Father!"

It was a piteous sight to see the old man bowing down before one still more aged, imploring him but to speak one word—to pardon him."

He looked at him in wonder, and the poor weak mind began again to wander.

"I had a son," he said. "He was a lieutenant in the body-guard of his Majesty. You are an old man, as old as I am. When mademoiselle comes back, she will explain matters to you—I am Marquis de Rohan—Marquis de Rohan!" and murmuring to himself, the old man laid down his head and closed his eyes.

Some hours after, Hortense entered the room, bringing in her hand some little delicacy for the sick man. Poor girl! she came lightly up the stairs, and entered unbidden into the now familiar room. How still, how unearthly it seems! The evening is drawing in, and the room is close and dark; but she sees, she feels something different, something wrong. No sound, no movement. Two prostrate figures! Who is the stranger? She creeps on; she stoops down by the bed.

Oh! for a sound—for the slightest breath, to break this awful death stillness! Shuddering, she puts her hand on the thin hand that lies on the coverlet. It is cold—icy cold! She puts her hand on the forehead of the man who lies by the bedside. He is warm, but he neither moves nor speaks. She peers into the face and sees—her father!

Poor girl! poor, lonely, desolate girl!

It was slowly, very slowly, that M. Rohan recovered from the shock of his unexpected meeting with his father; but he was never himself again. He had no power to exert himself; he resigned himself more entirely than ever into his daughter's guidance, and looked to her in the very smallest trifle. She was perplexed and heavy-hearted. Little by little their connection with the poor old exile was revealed to her; and, in spite of all her troubles and sorrows, her heart swelled within her as she thought—I am of noble birth.

They followed the old man to his last resting-place in that close, crowded London graveyard. One cannot call so horrible a place by the beautiful, peaceful word, "churchyard:" a word with which one connects remembrances of waving trees, and rows of crimson-cupped yews, and peaceful country Sundays, with the old bells sounding over the meadows. No: in the reeking graveyard of a London parish the Marquis de Rohan rests.

And while he lies there, the old ladies of Newport lament over the ingratitude and forgetfulness of their friend.

"Now," so they say to one another, "that he has regained his position in society, he has forgotten his old friends."

"He was a first-rate écarté player," says another.[40]

---

[40] Écarté: an old French card game for two players.

So they speak of the old man, little dreaming where he is.

It was impossible for the two exiles to resume their former mode of life. One was sinking rapidly into premature old age; the other found the constant attention of which her father stood in need, and the many duties of their small household, as much as she had strength to manage; her pupils also began to diminish in number, and she saw but too clearly that further trials were in store for them. Her hoard was not quite exhausted; she would, so she thought to herself, make one last effort to find her cousin, one desperate struggle to reach the west, and the only relations she had ever heard of. The loneliness was beyond endurance. The close air and narrow streets of London suffocated her; she must change, she must escape.

Her father, since the old man's funeral, had never left the house; he sat, hour after hour, moping and moaning to himself, taking heed of nothing.

Hortense was desperate; she saw no time was to be lost, if she were ever to carry out her project of finding her way to Harscourt; so, one evening, she abruptly asked her father if he would like to change his home.

Home! What a mockery to call such a place as that Home!

To her surprise he gladly seized the idea. He would start there and then: not a day, not an hour must be lost; they must go at once.

He took a childish and active delight in the smallest detail in their arrangements, and ere many days were past, their few affairs were arranged, and they were once more on their travels.

We will not follow them step by step on that weary journey. M. Rohan gradually lost all pleasure in the change, and at every step became more and more feeble, and, at length, quite childish. It was a weary time: sometimes, driven by bitter poverty to ask charity, they were repulsed with haughty words and stinging sneers; but still they struggled onward, westward—ever westward.

There is a churchyard in a pretty village in sweet, soft Devon. Many lovely, peaceful churchyards there are in our beautiful country, but few more lovely than that of Morton. Tall elms surround it, and an evergreen hedge divides it from the parsonage garden. The quaint old latticed windows look out from amid a bower of rare shrubs; and creepers, myrtles, and fuchsias climb to the eaves; thick-clustered, climbing roses fling their long shoots over the mossy roof; and in among the flower beds, gay with a hundred colours, little laughing children are chasing one another.

The sun shines full on the church, and its beautifully kept churchyard; on many of the graves, especially those of little children, sweet-scented flowers bloom, while here and there a delicate rose or choice evergreen gives an air of cheerfulness and hope, without in any way marring the solemnity of the place. But even at pleasant Morton is a damp, sunless spot, where the roses bloom not, and the evergreens droop: "the north side," where self-murderers, evil livers, and strangers, lie buried in unmarked graves.

One tombstone there is, and only one, a cold-looking blue slate. Read the inscription—

"JEAN BAPTISTE DE ROHAN,
Lieutenant in the Corps Royale under his Majesty
Louis XVI.
R. I. P."

There is no mention of the Revolution, no mention of Napoleon, no mention of the commandant of the Château of Dieppe—all is buried in oblivion. Hortense wishes only to remember that he was once one of the regiment composed of the flower of the old French nobility—that he was a "De Rohan."

CHAPTER XV
THE MUSKETS

LILY Fowler—gentle, quiet, loving Lily—you have done more mischief—thus you reason in your self-condemning humility—than a whole life can undo. Better have kept him as a brother, and seen him another woman's husband: better have had your heart wither within you and have seen him safe: that to watch him sinking lower and lower at every step, your heart bursting with misery, your conscience upbraiding you as the cause of this sad change!

No one was more fully alive to the evil she had, as she thought, produced, than this gentle girl, and often, through the still hours of the night, her head was bowed in bitter repentance and self-accusation.

She had changed sadly; her step was on the old staircase, and echoed through the hall, but it was slow and uncertain, and her sweet voice never challenged the birds outside. The poetry of her life was gone.

Reginald and young Fowler had never associated much; their habits and tastes differed in many ways, and Lily never encouraged any intimacy between them. She knew enough of her brother to be assured he was no very good companion for one of Reginald's temper, since his friends were among the lowest and most suspicious class in Torford.

The ship-builder was also alive to his son's demerits, but thought, "Time will change him; and when he marries, he will settle down."

Unfortunately, as it turned out, Fowler happened to be at home just at the time of the rupture between Lily and Reginald, and, the check of Lily's influence removed, he seemed to take a fiendish delight in degrading and lowering the young man as far as lay in his power. He introduced him to his own boon companions, and finally persuaded him to join him in the ownership of a vessel he had long desired to possess. Reginald's funds were getting low, and he was no longer able or perhaps cared to have a vessel of his own. The freshness of his youth was passing rapidly away before the storm of passion, self-indulgence, and debauchery. In a few months his very countenance was altered. The sleepy brown eyes flashed viciously, the handsome mouth was swollen and distorted with drink; and the sailor's dress, that used to be so neat and becoming, was now soiled and slatternly. The upright gait, the quick, manly step, was exchanged for a slouching, shambling walk.

The friends of better days drew back from him, and many a one recalled to mind the rejoicings on his one-and-twentieth birthday, and the launch of the *Gratiana*, and wondered if he were the same man. And Lily saw him pass, and shrank away, shuddering, and murmuring to herself, "This is my work."

Not altogether: Grace had seen deeper into Reginald's character than ever Lily had done. The germ of this falling off had ever been there, though held in check for awhile by the two women who loved him so.

Now he was going headlong to destruction. Sometimes he would pause and look back with regret, but then an evil spirit would whisper, "It is her fault; it is her heartless conduct that has brought you to this; go on—let her see what she has done."

We will not follow the luckless young man step by step in his downward career—it is no pleasing task; in our story the result of his declension is what we have to look to.

A year passed by—the young men sailing and trading together; sometimes one commanding for a cruise, sometimes the other. Steady folks shook their heads, and looked suspiciously on the venture, nor could any very clear account be obtained of their voyage. Their crew consisted of a rough set, picked up at various ports—not Torford men—and often changed.

More and more did Fowler gain the ascendancy over Reginald, till he became but a tool in his hands.

"It is your turn, Dawson, this time," said Fowler, as the two men sat in the parlour of a low public-house at the mouth of the river; a wild, lonely spot, far away from any other house, and known as the resort of lawless characters.

"Well, where am I to go? what villainy are you up to now?" answered the other, sullenly. "I wish you'd do the dirty work yourself, or leave it undone."

"Nonsense, my good fellow," replied Fowler; "there's no dirty work. You just take the *Spite* quietly over the bar—I daresay you know where you can pick up a few kegs; it's a pity she should go empty—and make your way to Liverpool. There's a cargo of fire-arms, or something of that kind, waiting there for a trusty hand; ship them—" The speaker paused and looked round, drew closer to his companion, and lowered his voice to a whisper.

"Speak out, man," said Reginald, roughly: "I want no secrets."

"Hush, fool!" hissed the other; "I would not trust you, if I understood their vile lingo."

"Well, where am I to take these things to?"

"Sail to the south of Ireland."

"What port?"

"No port, stupid! sail away well to the south, and if you fall in with a Frenchman, perhaps it will hardly be worth your while to show fight—you had better make the best bargain you can with him. Perhaps, in consideration of your cargo, he'll let you off with your ship: for, you see, they say they are badly off for arms on the other side of the Channel."

Reginald started up, and, for a moment, a look of his old self came over him; his eyes flashed, his lips quivered.

"You mean, villain," he said, hoarsely—"you mean that I am to take these fire-arms and deliver them over to the enemy!"

"Don't call me a villain, and don't make such a row, man. I never asked you to deliver over the cargo to the enemy; I only advised you how to act, should you be placed in a certain position."

For a moment a thought of Lily stayed the young man from acceding to Fowler's proposal, but the evil spirit turned even the thought of her to mischief.

"What is she to me?" exclaimed Reginald, bitterly: "what care I what she thinks of me?? Let her see the work of her own deeds. It is she who has driven me to this!"

Fowler laughed a mocking laugh. It mattered little to him from what motive Reginald granted his request, so long as his object was attained.

"Well, then," he said, after a pause, "I suppose I may count on you. It's rather a ticklish affair, but it will pay well, and I know you like a spice of danger."

It was convenient for Fowler to put his business off on his friend, on the plea of his understanding the French language; but Fowler understood quite enough of French to make all his arrangements without consulting his partner; and as it afterwards turned out, he had not hesitated to use Reginald's name in the negotiations he had had with the French merchant, who had prompted the whole affair.

But of this Reginald knew nothing; though occasionally obstinate, he was by nature easily led, and of late his passions and his desperation had thrown him entirely into the hands of Fowler; he could not, he had not the courage or the desire to act independently; he must do as he was bid.

Accordingly, two days after the conversation just related, the *Spite*—a good and honest trader as she was supposed, and of late certainly a successful one—was slipping down the river, on the ebb tide, under the command of Reginald. As her ropes were loosed from their holdings on the quay, and her sails were unfurled and shaken out, and the cries of her men at the capstan were listened to,—"There," it was remarked, "goes the luckiest trader in town. That fellow Fowler is getting as rich as a Jew."

"How long will it last?" some one answered. The *Spite* was already suspected.

Meanwhile, along by the green fields, and the pleasant cottages, which, on either side, edged the banks of the river; across the ever restless, foaming bar—rough and tumultuous at all times, but in storms the witness and the cause of wrecks and death—swiftly as with the wings of a bird, the *Spite* follows on her watery path;—now she is in the open channel, and now away—away towards the broader sea.

A week—ten days have passed. It is deep night: there is no moon: and a light streak or two in the western sky alone breaks the pall which hangs above the moving waters, midway between England and France. The light masts of a small vessel rise and fall on the waves, and exhibit their outline against the grey western streaks. There is scarce a breath of wind, scarce a ripple on the water; and though way is kept on the vessel, it is so slight that she seems almost motionless. Two men alone are on deck—the captain and his mate.

The men pace the deck of the vessel for some time in silence;

every now and then they pause, and gaze earnestly into the darkness, apparently in vain. That which they seem to be expecting does not meet their sight; they again turn and resume their walk. After some time, as if by mutual consent, they again pause.

"I wonder, Pauley," said the captain, "whether that fellow will keep his appointment. Surely this should be the place, and the time is up."

"Don't be afraid, captain," answered Pauley; "he's safe enough to come. I dare say he's not very far off; but it's so precious dark, one can't see an inch forward; and he's careful and shy, and won't give the sign too soon."

"Hang his shyness!" said the captain. "I wish he would come at once, and get the job over. I don't like it at all, I assure you; and others begin to think we are not quite as honest as we seem. Did you see that King's cutter this afternoon—how she made a tack in our wake, as if she had her suspicions, and was resolved to have a look at us? I was half afraid she would search us, and uncommonly glad I was when she seemed to alter her mind, and took another course."

"And so was I," rejoined the mate. "I was thinking it was over with us. Here in the open channel, with so fast a vessel as that at our heels, and so many on all points of the compass to second her, we should have but a poor chance."

"We must have been taken, or been drowned," said the captain. "However, we have escaped that danger; and if we can get rid of our cargo to-night, we can meet her again to-morrow with safety."

"I wish we might meet her," replied the mate; "it would be a capital trick, captain. I wish she would search us and find nothing aboard; we should then leave with a good character, and perhaps be safer for the future."

"But it is time our friend should be here; if he is not quick, morning will come upon us, and then it will not be pleasant to meet one of the King's ships."

As the man spoke, a pale green light exhibited itself at about the distance of a quarter of a mile.

"There she is!" exclaimed the captain. "Show the light, Pauley."

A light of a similar colour was shown over the ship's side. The sails were turned more to the wind, and the two vessels gradually approached each other.

"Give me the trumpet, Pauley. What ship is that?"

"*L'Italie*," was the reply, which came softened across the water.

"All right!" said the captain, as he gave *Morengo* in return.

Meanwhile a boat was sent over the side of the new comer; her crew descended; the dip of oars was heard; she came alongside the vessel which had been so long awaiting her, and a single individual, no other than her captain, mounted the deck. The two commanders went down into the cabin, and remained for some time closeted together. And now a busy scene took place on deck. All hands were turned up; heavy packages were brought from the hold of one, and transferred to that of the other; and rosy clouds, heralds of the sun, appeared in the sky before the work was finished.

"And now," said the strange captain, "this day two months in the same place."

"I don't know," said the other.

"Yes—I say, yes. I tell you, Mr. Fowler has engaged that I shall have a similar quantity in two months, and he must keep to his bargain."

"I never promise," was the answer; "I know nothing about it. It is a dangerous business: I run all the risk, and he ought not to have made any engagement without me."

"I can't help that," was the rejoinder; "but a bargain's a bargain, and must be kept."

There was no reply, and the two captains parted, and the two vessels went their ways, one to the shores of France, and one to the coasts of England.

Meanwhile a rumour spread at Torford that something unfortunate had happened to the *Spite*. If her owners were not considered the brightest of characters, she was regarded as a *bonâ fide* trading vessel; and certain it was that young Fowler had made some very successful ventures. No surprise was therefore felt when it was first announced that she was gone to Liverpool, under the command of Reginald, to ship a valuable cargo for the south of Ireland; and very general was the sympathy felt when a few weeks after it was reported that she had been seized by French pirates, while beating about against adverse winds off the coast of Ireland.

A great deal was said about the gallant resistance the English ship had offered, and how she had only yielded to overpowering numbers. The enemy, it was said, had possessed themselves of the cargo, which was not mentioned, but had allowed the crew not only to escape, but to bring their vessel with them.

The *Spite* was not brought back again to Torford, but people heard how she was refreighted, and trading about the north coast, as was said, to keep out of danger.

Young Fowler remained quietly at Torford, assisting his father, and apparently leaving all the direction of the vessel to Reginald.

A year passed, and rumours began to be whispered at Torford that the Spite, though ostensibly trading in the north seas, had more than once, since her first capture, fallen in with French cruisers, and that, as in the first instance, they had contented themselves with taking only the cargo.

Suspicion was aroused; even the sleepy government began to look about and inquire. The *Spite* was not the only vessel that had met with similar treatment, and, strangely enough, in almost every instance the cargo seized happened to be fire-arms!

It was soon proved, beyond all doubt, that a large trade was carried on with France, by certain dishonest men, in supplying the munition of war. The vessels employed were regular traders, but commanded, as in the case of the *Spite*, by men whom circumstances had rendered desperate.

The illegal traffic, it was proved, had been carried on by men well acquainted with the French tongue, and Reginald Dawson's name was brought prominently forward, as the person most likely to have originated the whole scheme. The fact of his being half French was ferreted out. His long imprisonment, his almost miraculous escape, and the fact that his uncle held, or had held, a responsible appointment under the Emperor, all told, or seemed to tell, against him, and against him were the most decided measures pointed.

CHAPTER XVI
THE CHASE

ANY one acquainted with the northern coast of Cornwall and Devon will remember how inaccessible and dangerous it generally is; how black and rugged are its rocks—here uplifting themselves in sharp and rugged precipices, and there running in long lines with the sea, like the sharpened teeth of some huge monster, upon which the Atlantic waves fret and foam incessantly. And yet occasionally there are small nooks and bays, which a person well acquainted with the country may make use of in emergencies. Some, indeed, are so fearfully dangerous, that nothing but dire necessity could tempt a mariner into them; and unless both wind and tide are favourable, even with the most accurate knowledge of the locality, certain destruction must inevitably attend the attempt.

The King's officers, who had been some days on the look-out for the *Spite* and her commander, happened to fall in with her in the chops of the Bristol Channel. The vessel was recognized, and orders were given to chase.

Reginald, at the time, had the advantage of being some way ahead, which made the chase a lengthened one. Besides, he felt how serious was the occasion. Were he caught, there was no chance of pardon, for he had actually arms on board. He had been driven somewhat out of his way, but he had just shipped a new cargo, which he had undertaken to deliver, as he had done in many instances before. He must then escape, if possible; this was the first resource. Every sail was spread, every rope was strained—in vain. The King's ships—and there were two—gained upon him rapidly; then it was resolved to lighten his vessel of every needless incumbrance, by getting rid of her cargo—those contraband arms, which were the cause of his terror and guilt, and which now seemed to his frightened conscience to burden the vessel with their weight, and to act as a clog upon her speed. One by one the heavy chests of arms were brought up from the hold, and hauled into the water; and Reginald felt a sort of relief as each one in turn plunged into the depths, and the circling swirl of foam closed over them for ever.

Once more the ropes were tightened, and every effort made to add increased speed to the progress of the *Spite*; and, as if instinct with life, and understanding what was required of her, the little bark appeared to be struggling bravely through the water, and even to gain on her pursuers. The wind had fallen in a degree, and this gave the smaller vessel an advantage, and as Reginald looked over her side, and saw the speed at which she was going, and marked the recoiling waves and the seething train in her wake, the hopes of safety and freedom once more sprang up in his breast. Again he cast a quick and searching glance on every sail, on every spar, on every bit of cordage. He called his crew into a brief activity to adjust this and regulate that; and when nothing more could be done, all the men relapsed into a deep and watchful silence, and nothing was heard but the straining of the mast, the hoarse murmur of the wind in the ropes, or the hiss and splash of the leaping waves, as they yielded to the force of the vessel. Minutes and hours passed, and the crew of the *Spite* entertained high hopes. The little vessel was doing her work gallantly; she was apparently uninjured; everything held on, and of late she seemed to have kept her position in advance. Once more escape seemed possible, and Reginald inwardly vowed that he would never run such a risk again. But alas! their hopes were soon mingled with doubt. The wind gradually freshened, and the *Spite* laboured much in the heavier sea. The larger ships had now the advantage, and their hulls began to rise large and threatening on the sight.

There was a consultation on board the *Spite*. Reginald was desperate; it seemed hopeless to contend any longer; there was no refuge, no harbour; all along the coast, as far as eye could reach, nothing appeared but beetling cliffs, resting on their eternal foundations of serried rocks—sharp, dangerous, inhospitable; and in the open channel capture would be certain and speedy.

"What is to be done?" he said, turning to Pauley. "Is there a chance? I see none."

Pauley mused a little; he was an old, skilful seaman; he had spent his life in these waters. He knew, it was his boast, "every inch of the coast in the dark, and could put a boat wherever a fish could swim." The old man spoke—

"Yes; there is a chance—a small chance—and I think I can manage it. I have done the deed before. It is a difficult job in the dark; but there are generally some friends not far off, and perhaps we shall get help; and if we succeed, shan't we bamboozle those fellows behind us, that's all. But you must keep the boat on for an hour; we shall then reach the spot where I think I can lay her up snug and safe, and we shall be able to cut and run."

"Where do you propose going?" asked Reginald.

"You know Castle Lock?"

"No, I don't know it; I've heard of it, but I do not know it."

"I know it," said the mate; "for I was born and bred close to it, and many a time have I taken a boat into its blessed harbour; and I'll take the *Spite* there, I hope."

Meantime the *Spite* had been kept steadily on her course, and as steadily the King's ships has been following in her wake, and promised soon to overhaul her. Gradually the course of the *Spite* was somewhat altered. Before, her commander had no distinct purpose in his mind, excepting to escape capture. How he should do this he did not see, and his sole object was to drive his vessel down the Channel out of the way of her pursuers as fast as she would go; but now he had a definite object, and the *Spite* was gradually edged nearer and nearer towards the shore.

The King's ships perceived this, and were evidently puzzled. There was no harbour in sight, no convenient shore upon which the smuggler could be stranded. Were the men desperate? Were they mad? Were they resolved to wreck the vessel, and sacrifice their own lives recklessly and certainly, rather than be taken? for nothing was to be seen but a hopeless line of stone, and surging breakers ever advancing to the attack, and ever beaten from those iron shores. "Let us see if a ball will stop her."

The King's officers did not like the idea of losing their prize; they did not wish her to go on shore, and be knocked to pieces. Follow her in the direction she was now going, they could not; they were already sufficiently near the coast; there was risk to their own vessel.

Accordingly, a flash was seen from the bow of the larger vessel, then a wreath of smoke curled up into the sky, and the hollow boom of a gun sounded across the water; a slight splash here and there marked the course of the ball as it touched the crests of the waves, and it finally plunged, not to rise again, within a few yards of the *Spite's* side.

But the *Spite* till held on her way, bent, as it would seem, on certain destruction—bent upon dashing herself against that huge rock, which, projecting beyond others, rises like a mountain in the water. The evening has closed rapidly, and it is almost dark, but still there is light enough to show the now shadowy little vessel still rushing on against that black mass, as if to precipitate herself on its rugged bosom, and end all uncertainty at once.

The crews of the King's ships are suddenly startled. The *Spite* has disappeared; but how and where? Did that rock open to let her pass? Is there any known channel there?

In truth, the entrance of the little harbour in which the *Spite* has taken refuge is so narrow, that, but for certain landmarks, those knowing the coast most intimately could not determine where to find it, and to strangers it seemed little short of magic that any vessel could make its way through those gigantic cliffs.

There were those, however, on the coast who knew the *Spite* and her commander well, and she was recognized by some of those on the look-out on the cliffs. They saw how hotly she was chased, and when they beheld her head put landward, they guessed the intention of her master, and hurried to the cove to have things ready for her reception.

The entrance to the harbour is much in the form of the letter S, and so exceedingly narrow that, on entering the first angle, the ship, if of any size, is drawn into the second by ropes thrown from the cliff, and is then towed round the small quay which crosses the narrow basin. It is really an awful place at any time; and in a storm, one of the most striking and terrifying spots that can be found in the west of England; perhaps without rival anywhere.

The *Spite* passed the outer rock; and as she lost the wind in entering the fissure, her sails flapped idly against her masts; but the ropes are brought to bear, and, after a few moments, the draught of air that rushes down the side gully touches her stern and impels her forward to the second bend; then more ropes are thrown from the opposite side, and in ten minutes she is within the quay.

Her crew had run much too great a hazard to risk being captured in the narrow port they had chosen, nor was it in their plan to attempt to save the vessel.

It was doubtful if their pursuers, even if they knew the entrance of the harbour, would attempt to follow them immediately; yet without hesitation they abandoned the *Spite*, having first destroyed all papers and everything of value they could not carry with them, and in an hour or so from their entering the harbour, the place was deserted by every human being, save one old woman, who was too lame to join in the general fight, and too blind and deaf to be able to give any account of the fugitives. These, breaking up into small parties of two or three, made the best of their way, some to the great slate quarries on the hills, three or four miles off; some to the mines; and others to wild, desolate villages, away on the upland moors of the neighbourhood.

Dawson, in more imminent danger than the rest, secured the first horse he could find, and made his way towards Harscourt by unfrequented roads. Poor fellow! how wretched and tumultuous were his feelings! Miserable must be the forebodings and conscience of such a man, if he had any conscience, or consideration for conscience left, in such circumstances as this. And he had time to think, as in the dead of night he traversed the dreary uplands between Castle Lock and Harscourt. Where was he to go? What refuge would hide him? As the hunted beast flies to his lair, so his first impulse was leading him to the home of his boyhood—that boyhood which was comparatively fresh and innocent—that boyhood which, despite his father's tyranny, spent in the company of Grace and Edward, was happiness; and how great happiness, compared with his present shame and distress!—in the belief that it could come back to him, and that he could spend his time over again. Never would he take up with such a man as Fowler, never be the weak fool he now felt himself to have been, never be persuaded by others to violate his country's laws. Alas, Reginald! you know not your own instability. Thus it is people who do wrong always reason. Impending punishment makes them wise, and opportunity too often makes them repeat their folly.

The rain set in cold and drizzly as he made his way across the moorlands, and the wind swept by in gusts with a doleful sighing. All seemed against him. It was impossible to reach Harscourt that night, and he resolved to seek a temporary shelter in the house of a farmer residing near the road, and with whom he had transacted some business in past times.

The farmer, who was in bed, arose at the summons made at his door, and admitted Reginald into his house, not before he needed refreshment. The poor young man was quite worn out. The excitement of the day, during which it had so long remained in doubt whether he should escape the King's ships or no, and the fatigue and drenching rain which he had endured since, had nearly exhausted his strength. But the farmer was naturally of a kind heart, and stirred himself at once to make him comfortable. He provided Reginald with some dry clothes, made up a blazing wood fire, brought out some cold meat, not forgetting the bottle of spirits and the boiling water, and the young man's blood began again to circulate in his veins, and the prospect before him to appear less terrible than before.

The farmer did not seem to be in a hurry to interrupt him, and contented himself with eyeing Reginald with a curious speculative glance, whilst he was still at his meal; but when he had almost finished the provisions before him, and was evidently much strengthened, he ventured to ask, with a sort of understanding look,—

"And, master, what's in the wind now? Where have you come from at this hour of the night, and where are you going?"

Reginald knew this man, and felt that he could thoroughly trust him. Indeed, this might have been said of a large portion of the farmers of those parts, and in those days. There was scarcely an individual who looked upon smuggling and smugglers with other than friendly eyes, and did not supply himself with spirits by their assistance. It was not yet understood that the "fair trade," as it was called—the very name betokening the views held concerning it—was a disobedience to the King. It was generally held to be *fair* to buy in the cheapest market, that it was a hardship to be prevented from doing so, and that to evade the customs was only evading a tax which was unjustly levied. In the present day, when fair ladies stuff their petticoats with lace, or bury in the recesses of their travelling-box some forbidden indulgence from the Continent, they reason in the same way.

Accordingly, Reginald at once put the farmer in possession of the facts which we have lately recorded, and deeply interested was the man as he listened with fixed attention to all the details of the escape.

"And what will you do now?" was his inquiry, when Reginald had arrived at the end of his story.

"I hardly know," answered Reginald, "what is best to be done. The night was so bad, and I was so tired, that I knocked you up; but I was on my road to Harscourt, and I suppose I had better go on there."

"And what will you do at Harscourt?"

"Oh! hide somewhere or other. I must let Fowler know; he is in for it as much as I am, and he will help me to get out of the way."

"My dear man," said the farmer after a pause, "if you wish to escape you must not go to Harscourt. Why, of course, the officers will go to your father's house in the very first instance, and of course they will keep a look-out there for a very long time to come. No, you must not go to Harscourt."

"Where then can I go?"

"You must go to some very safe place indeed, for there will be a sharp search after you, I fancy: the cave—you know where I mean—what think you of the cave? It is not very far from this, and I'll see to the provision; and if you'll take my advice, you'll go this very night."

"It is hard," said Reginald; for he felt now so very comfortable, that he wished to believe the danger distant. He coveted a good rest; and his luxurious nature, even though life was in danger, did not like to leave the warm apartment and sheltering roof. "It is hard to be obliged to turn out like a dog; but I suppose I had better."

"You certainly had better; it will be dangerous to wait till to-morrow. Come, come along; I will go with you."

The farmer went into a closet and brought out some cold pork, some bread, and part of a cheese. He then opened a cupboard and extracted a black bottle.

"This will do for the present," he observed, "and there is more where this came from."

He then fastened up in a bundle an old horse-cloth and a few other things to make a bed, and when he had filled a basket with the provisions, the two men left the house.

The house of the farmer was about a couple of miles from the sea-coast, and, like so many of the farmhouses of the neighbourhood, stood on a hill, looking down on its own combe, which terminated in the sea. Rapidly the men passed down the little path, through the brushwood which shrouded the hillside, out upon the little flat valley at its foot, along by the tiny streamlet which gurgled ambitiously on the night air, now become still and calm, and at length the stones of the pebbly beach crunched beneath their feet. On they pressed, over the rolling slippery boulders, between sharp projecting points, through weedy pools, just described, by the hill, till at last they arrived at an aggregate of rocks, tossed about in labyrinthine confusion, which seemed to make all passage in that direction impossible. The farmer and Reginald knew better. They could find their way in the dark; but by daylight, and to an observant eye, one or two slight indentations, just large enough to rest the foot on, might be seen on a wall of perpendicular rock by which the men mounted; and then winding by a tortuous course among some rocks beyond, they found themselves opposite a small opening in the hill, just large enough for a man to creep through.

"Here we are," said Reginald.

"Yes, here we are," replied the farmer; "and the King's officers may look long enough, they won't put their hand upon you now. But come, go into your house."

Reginald crept into the hole, the farmer handed in the provisions and clothes, and then followed.

"You will be safe here," he said, "and comfortable enough for a few days," after he had struck a light and they had looked round the cavern.

It was, indeed, a spacious apartment. Once within the entrance, and the roof rose to a considerable elevation, so that a hundred persons might occupy it, and walk about with comfort.

"Well," said the farmer, after he had sat and talked for some time, "it is time that I should be going. Morning will be breaking, and it is well that I should get home before I am seen; not that there is any fear if I was; but it is as well there should be no talk.

Can I do anything more for you. I hate to see a good fellow like you in trouble, and I will do all I can."

"You are very kind," replied Reginald, "and I shall always remember it, if I get out of this scrape, as I hope I shall. But you'll be sure to bring me news?"

"Oh, yes; I'll be here again to-night."

"And you'll tell Fowler?"

"Yes, I'll tell him."

"Say, he must help me: he got me into this, and if he does not get me out, I'll expose him."

"You may depend upon me," said the farmer. "Good-night."

"Good-night," answered Reginald, and the two men parted.

CHAPTER XVII
CASTLE LOCK

THE pursuers were completely baffled; they could not for some time discover by what expedient their expected prize had disappeared.

At last, some prying lieutenant who had calculated on coming in for his share of the reward that had been offered by Government for the arrest of Dawson, suggested that, by the charts, they must be just opposite the little nook of Castle Lock, and no doubt, relying on the known difficulty of the entrance, the smugglers would there be found.

"Five pounds—ten pounds to any man who will guide us into the harbour!" shouted the captain, who guessed that the lieutenant had surmised rightly as to the place of refuge. But though the word was passed from mouth to mouth, no one responded to the invitation, and orders were given to steer for land.

Now there was one man on board who knew the entrance to the harbour as well, or rather better, than he knew his letters; but not five hundred pounds would have tempted him to reveal it, under existing circumstances.

This was no other than Long Jack the smuggler, who had joined his Majesty's navy, not from choice, but compulsion; and who sympathized much more with the pursued than the pursuers.

"I didn't nurse him and tend him when he floated starving into Jersey, to help to hang him at last. If they can't find their way without my help, they may go back to the place from whence they came empty-handed."

"They'll have the ship in bits before they know where they

are, if they keep on this tack," muttered Long Jack, to a companion. "If they get inside yonder headland," directing observation to the fine rock before mentioned, "not all the post-captains and admirals in the fleet will get her out again, with this wind."

This speech being reported, poor old Long Jack was called up to be questioned, for, as the captain sagely remarked, "If he knows the coast so well, he knows the way into Castle Lock harbour."

"I might try to take you there," said the seaman; "but I much doubt if you'd ever come back again. The great rough cliffs rise sheer out of the water, and the big blue waves, with this western wind, roll in like race-horses, and would soon knock the finest ship in his Majesty's navy into ten thousand bits. It's my advice, that we don't go too near."

"Well," was the reply, "we will keep the ship out of harm's way: but man the boats—we have still that resource."

The boats were manned, and after a hard pull they made the entrance, not without some difficulty. Not a soul, as we have before said, was to be seen; but there lay the vessel, her sail still and swelling in the breeze.

The *Spite* went safe into Castle Lock, but she never came out again, except in broken spars and planks washed by the waves.

The man-o-war's men, eager to have something to show, determined at all hazards to take their prize with them. With the ebbing tide they got her outside the quay, but just as they were rounding the last angle, the wind, that seemed to spring from the cliffs, caught and drove her back against the rocks! The man at the helm was knocked from his hold by the shock, the rudder became jammed in the rocks, and the vessel, swinging round, came with her side bang against the giant wall. All, in a moment, was confusion, for no one was capable of giving an order.

Long Jack, now that his friends were safe, lent a willing and powerful hand, and aided them by his knowledge of the place; but it was all of no avail. The *Spite* never came out of Castle Lock, and several of her captors perished with her. Had the sea been much disturbed, not a soul would have lived to tell the tale; and as it was, those who escaped were grievously knocked against the craggy rocks that start up on every hand.

Young Fowler, as part-owner of the *Spite*, was arrested, and every one at Torford fully believed that on the trial it would come out, that he was the person most nearly concerned; but it proved otherwise. Every communication, from the very first, had not only been in Reginald's name, but in his handwriting, as it appeared; and his having evaded the law made things look still worse for him. Where he was, or what had become of him, no one seemed to have a notion; but it was supposed, from the place in which he was last seen, that he was hiding in the mines.

Many suffered, but Fowler was entirely acquitted, while on the absent Reginald the severest sentence of the law was passed.

The whole matter was a bitter blow to the Fowlers. The trial lasted long, and there was a strong prejudice against Fowler, and some did not hesitate to assert openly that Reginald must in some way have been his dupe, and acting under his orders.

The joy at their son's escape from punishment was sorely damped by the heavy sentence passed on Reginald, who for so many years had been looked on as one of themselves, and who, in spite of all, still held a large place in their affections. It was the death-blow to one, the dearest of the family. Lily had gradually become more like the sweet flower whose name she bore—more fair, more gentle than she had been even as a child—more like an angel. The blue eyes grew sparkling, the step more light and noiseless, and the people whispered that her end was near. Most bitter to her was the disgrace of the man she loved, most torturing the silence which she felt bound to keep on all things relating to him; she bore her sorrow by herself.

From the day the sentence was passed, a still more visible change came over her, and she never stept over the threshold again.

People said, Reginald should have come boldly forward and defended himself, and stood the consequences of his conduct; and, as we have before said, many maintained (nor were they far wrong) that Fowler, though acquitted, was the real culprit.

In truth, it was he who kept Reginald a prisoner in the cavern we have mentioned, until his plans and schemes resulted in his own acquittal. It would not have suited him at all to have had Dawson placed at the bar with him, for he could have proved that most, if not all, the documents used as proofs against him were forgeries, and that in no single instance had he signed his name to, or been materially benefited by, the transactions.

Wily and deep as a serpent, while Reginald bore all the blame, Fowler got all the profit, and large sums of money stood in his name in various banks at a distance from Torford—where he tried to pass as a ruined and injured man, without, however, gaining much sympathy.

Meanwhile, Reginald subsisted on such fare as Fowler with the help of the farmer thought fit to convey to him, and was kept quiet by exaggerated accounts of his danger, and promises to provide means of escape as soon as it could be done with safety.

CHAPTER XVIII
THE LILY FADES

WHILE these scenes were being acted at Torford, Hortense and her father were slowly wending their way westward; and now De Rohan sleeps in the quiet churchyard at Moreton, and his daughter pursues her way alone.

It was some weeks after the acquittal of Fowler that Hortense reached Torford—not so very far, as she fancied, from the fulfilment of all her hopes. Her money was well nigh gone, and she wandered, forlorn and miserable, along the quay at Torford, where Reginald had so often paced in his better days, so handsome and admired. She walked slowly on, looking for some one whom she could venture to address, and from whom she could crave a night's lodging, and directions for reaching Harscourt, near which she knew she was.

A dark, sinister-looking man stood leaning against some bales of merchandise, and something in the stranger's appearance attracted his attention. After watching her for some time, he inquired if she were in search of anyone.

"Reginald Dawson," answered the girl, stopping by the dark-looking man's side.

"Hush, girl! that is a name not to be mentioned here!" exclaimed the man, testily, his brow contracting as he spoke. "He is an outlaw and a reprobate. And who are you? By your looks you are not English."

"I am his cousin," replied Hortense; and she rapidly explained her present position; how they had fled from France, how she and her father had wandered in search of their English relatives, how he had died, and how she now was pursuing her way in hopes of finding Reginald.

The man took her bundle from her, and bade her follow him. "It was no use," he said, "her thinking to find any kindness at Mr. Dawson's hands; he would take her to those who had always been Reginald's friends." And he led her up the broad quiet street, and into the house where Reginald had spent so many years.

There was silence there; no merry voices echoed through the hall, no fairy child or light-hearted girl sat singing on the stairs. In an upper room that looked over the long roof of the rope-house, down the pleasant river, Lily lay dying, and all the house was hushed. The sturdy merchant's jovial laugh was stilled; the mother's call to daughters and servants was not heard; and if any chanced to speak loudly, or shut a door roughly, a sorrowing shake of the head, and Lily's name uttered in a low voice, restored the mournful silence.

Fowler's heavy tread, as he entered the house, alarmed the watchers in the sick chamber, and one of his sisters rapidly descended the stairs with uplifted finger, to warn him to be quiet. Seeing a stranger, she gently opened the parlour door and beckoned them to enter, and looked with questioning eyes at Hortense.

"She is Reginald's cousin," muttered Fowler; "she has come to seek him; but mind what I say, Dorothy, keep her here and take care of her, and keep her quiet. I don't want him or his doings ripped up again."

In the small room that from her childhood had been her favourite haunt, lay Lily—so thin, so pale, so wan, with her small white hands crossed on her bosom, and her long chestnut hair streaming unconfined over the pillows. Her eyes were closed, but they were turned towards the open window, through which came sweet odours of rose, and eglantine, and fresh meadow grass, borne on the wings of the soft summer wind.

"Who came in?" she asked, as her sister softly re-entered the room.

"Our brother," was the reply.

"I heard two people—who was the second?"

"A stranger."

Lily sighed, but still she seemed bent on knowing who the stranger was.

"It was a French girl William met wandering on the quay."

A faint flush came over the wan face,—

"What is she called?" she asked eagerly. "Is it Hortense, Reginald's cousin, who helped him to escape?"

They answered "Yes," though they did not know so much of Reginald's story as Lily did.

"I should like to see her—I must see her. Mother, dearest," continued the girl, "I have something I must tell her."

Her mother besought her not to agitate herself; and for their sakes, if not for her own, to husband her fast-failing strength; but nothing would pacify her, and, at her urgent entreaties, she had a long solitary interview with the stranger.

A day and night passed, and still those kindly people sympathized with the poor lonely stranger, little guessing how much she had to do with their present affliction.

The last scene came.

Father, mother, sisters, and that one brother, who leaned against the wall, with his arms folded across his chest, and his dark brow knit, were there, and Hortense alone in a corner, sobbing and weeping for the grief she beheld, and for her own sorrow that lay heavy at her heart.

Lily, the spirit-child, the spirit-woman, lay on her bed, with her white hands folded and her thin lips gently moving, talking to the angels that hovered round, waiting to carry their sister spirit to a land where there is no more sorrow.

"Where is Reginald?" she asked, suddenly opening her eyes, and fixing them on her brother. "Where have you hid him? Brother! brother! with my dying breath, remember, I charge you to make him reparation. It is you who have brought him to the depths he is now in; you are spared. With my last breath I demand of you reparation! And you," she continued, turning to Hortense, "seek him out and save him, and tell him my last thought on earth was for him and his happiness." Then twining her arms round her mother's neck, her spirit floated away with the angels.

There is a funeral in a village churchyard, near relations mourning for the loss of their sunshine, friends weeping for the gentle friend, old and poor bewailing the kindly girl who so often had soothed their sorrows and ministered to their wants; and even the rough and sturdy seamen who had helped to bear her light body to its last resting-place, or had walked in long procession behind the sad burden, shed tears as they think of the little, graceful maiden, with her pleasant smile, who had so often greeted them at the end of their voyages, who had entered into their interests, their joys, and their sorrows; tending their wives and children, or aged parents, when they were far away.

When the last straggler has departed, and Night draws her dark curtain over all the land, a little boat floats silently up the river with the tide. No oar breaks the gurgling ripple, and the only voyager lies in the bottom, guiding his skiff by the rudder.

Presently he runs her ashore in a shady nook, and takes his way through narrow lanes, where the trees overarch his head, to the quiet country churchyard. There he finds the newly-made grave, round which so lately stood so large a crowd, but no truer mourner ever wept over that grave than the lonely man, who lies there with his head on the fresh turf. "She is gone, gone for ever. Oh! Lilly, not one last look, not one last word!" And the lonely mourner sheds bitter self-reproaching tears. Long he stays there, long it is ere he can tear himself away, and then he cautiously pursues his path across the fields to the town, to take one last look at the old house where Lily was once a happy, singing child, and he a happy boy; and then he walks back to his boat, and, as the tide turns, floats silently down the river till he reaches a small sloop moored just inside the bar. As he stands upon the deck the sails are set, and they go over the rough waves of the bar, and across the blue waters of the bay, and past the island, into the wide sea.

He is free once more.

Fowler's reason for taking Hortense so quickly under his protection as he had done, was the fear lest she might talk too openly of Reginald, whose existence, for many reasons, he wished forgotten, and not from any charitable feeling to the poor wanderer; but this refuge, once opened, was destined to prove a permanent home.

The Fowlers, when the first shock of their grief was over, tried to bring about a meeting between her and her uncle; but Mr. Dawson would have nothing to do with her, accused her of being, in some unexplained manner, the cause of his son's disgrace; and forbade her ever to attempt to intrude herself upon him.

CHAPTER XIX
A ROUGH WOOER

LILY was dead and gone, and a dull cloud settled on the Fowlers. Strange to say, the one bright, cheerful spot was the French stranger, who still lingered among them. A good, true heart had Hortense de Rohan; give her one kind word and she would repay you ten. The kindness the Fowlers showed her woke in her breast such devotion that she would willingly have laid down her life for them. She attended on Mr. Fowler, and seemed to know all his little ways by intuition, better than those who had lived with him all their lives. Sweet Lily had done this before her, but she was an angel.

Soon the little foreign woman became a necessity in the Fowlers' house; and if she spoke of going forth into the world and seeking her fortune, a grievous clamour was raised on all sides; and truthful assurance that she was regarded as a daughter, that she but took the place of their lost Lily, reassured her and ket her with them.

There is no more difficult position than that of a nurse. The kindest husband is apt to grow fractious with the most self-denying wives. The most loving parent sometimes is dictatorial to the child, who gives up everything to soothe his last hours. But Hortense never flagged. She gave in to Mr. Fowler's caprices, and humoured his wife's fancies, till they looked on her as the person, now dear Lily was gone, to keep peace and comfort in their house.

She devoted herself to Mr. Fowler, and was with him alone at his death. His daughters were married and happy in their own circles; honest-hearted, loving women they were, cherishing, as something sacred, the memory of the young sister who was gone from them;

always anxiously looking for some trait in the characters, or some feature in the faces, of their children that might resemble Lily. They had all received from their father, in his lifetime, what had been considered good portions for girls in their class of life: "I would rather give it you out and out in my life, than that there should be quarrels and heart-burnings when I am gone." The truth was, he suspected his son, and did not care to leave his daughters at his mercy.

These arrangements did not at all please the son, and he bitterly inveighed against his father, for, as he declared, leaving him without a shilling; but he was neither pitied nor believed; for not very long afterwards, he bought a very good estate in the neighbourhood, and almost immediately began to build a house on a wooded knoll overlooking the sea, on a scale that caused many comments, much surprise, and a great deal of suspicion, among the people of Torford.

"What did a man like William Fowler want with such a house? Surely, what had been good enough for his father ought to be good enough for him; any one would think he meant to turn gentleman instead of ship-builder."

But though the ship-building continued to be carried on in the name of Fowler, its owner troubled himself little in the actual business further than to see he was not cheated, and that he made, and did not lose, money by the concern. He called himself a merchant, took a counting-house in High Street, engaged a couple of clerks, and really set to work to make his fortune. Soon he infused more spirit and activity into the trade of Torford than it had ever known. Others, seeing how Fowler's speculations answered, followed his example and speculated themselves, or joined in some of his many ways of making money; and finding that he was generally successful, the town's-people grew less shy of him, and allowed his very questionable antecedents by degrees to sink into oblivion.

But the greatest change of opinion concerning him was wrought among the ladies of Torford. With women he had never been a favourite. He was too harsh and overbearing, too little skilled in the ways of the female world, to please. Perhaps, had he been better looking, he might have been tolerated; but his hard, ill-favoured face repulsed instead of attracting. This was in bygone days; now he possessed what the majority value above worth, or birth, or honesty. He was rich; and many a young woman, who, in other days, would have gathered her dress closer to her as he passed, as if his very touch would contaminate, now smiled sweetly on him, and would not have answered "no" had he offered to make her his wife and the mistress of the pretty house at Knoll.

He, however, had no intention of asking any Torford damsel to share his fortune, however handsome or charming she might be. He had an ambition beyond his money; he desired to rise in the social scale; yet, after all, the desire to rise would never have entered into his mind, but that he believed that it would give him more influence, and so enable him to amass more wealth. Rough as he was in some things, he had wit enough to see that a vulgar wife is a great impediment to a man; and as he had but small chance, as he thought, of wedding a daughter of any of the neighbouring gentry, he turned his thoughts to the foreign girl, who now tended his mother with the love and devotion of a daughter.

Mrs. Fowler and Hortense lived alone in the large house that had once been too small for its cheerful, happy inmates. William Fowler came almost every day, but he was an unwelcome visitor. His mother was always constrained and uneasy in his presence, for he was sure to have something disagreeable to tell her, or some complaint to make against his dead father—the husband she had loved so long and so truly—which pained the poor old lady deeply; and Hortense shrank from him as from a viper—but why, she could not say, for he always treated her civilly, and with more consideration than he did any other human being. Yet he seemed to exercise a power and authority over her, which she could not account for; she felt, as it were compelled to do what he suggested, in the veriest trifles, and she endeavoured to elude this influence by avoiding him as much as possible, and hardly speaking to him face to face.

When she had occasion to talk with him, she would turn her back upon him to avoid his piercing eyes, and close the conversation on the first opportunity.

When, however, William Fowler was out of the way, Hortense was happy enough, and having no personally sad memories connected with the house, would go singing about, wakening echoes that sounded mournful enough in Mrs. Fowler's ears; but she never checked her visitor.

"Poor thing!" she would say, "she has so little pleasure; 'tis but a dull life she leads here, and she has been kind to me and mine."

Often, too, did little feet patter through the hall and up the stairs, and the widow, as she heard them, thought of her own children who were women now, and of old life that had passed away, and of the child who was gone before and waiting for her—the lost child whose memory was more dear than all her living children. In the summer weather she would sit for hours in the sun in Lily's garden, amid Lily's flowers, seemingly watching her grandchildren as they chased each other and the butterflies among the tiny beds, but in reality only seeing the fairy form that had once sported there, as gay and bright as any of her grandchildren.

"I am sure, mother, you must be dull here in this great house, all alone," her daughter would say; "do come and live with us—you and Hortense; we should be so proud if you would."

"But, dear, if I came to you, Sarah would be vexed, because you know she tried hard to persuade me to live with her; but I can't, dear, indeed I can't. I couldn't leave the old house; it would break my heart! And the garden; and the flowers!—no, dear, thank you for your kindness, but I must end my days here, and Hortense will take care of me, won't you?" she continued, putting out her hand to the girl.

"Truly, yes, *ma mère*," answered Hortense. "You have been my mother; I am your daughter. The father, before he died, bade me never leave you, and I promised. But why should I talk of going? Whither could I go—I who am along in the world—who have nothing but you, *ma mère*?"

"You will be kind to her when I am gone, won't you?" said Mrs. Fowler to her daughter.

"Surely, mother, you may trust us," was the reply; "indeed, I expect Sarah and I should quarrel as much who was to have her, as we do now about you; you need not be at all afraid."

But there was another provision for her future, of which Hortense was as ignorant as a child, though she was not destined to remain very long in ignorance on the matter. Carefully as she avoided Fowler, she was not always successful; and one day, to her great annoyance, she found herself *tête-à-tête* with him. She made, as usual, an attempt at escape, but he insisted on her remaining, as he had something to say to her, to which she must listen. "Must" from him, in that stern, cold voice, she no more dared to disobey than a well-trained dog; and she nerved herself to hear something disagreeable, little dreaming what was coming.

She seated herself as he desired, but kept her face averted, while he, kneeling with one knee on a chair, and his arms crossed leaning on the back, confronted her.

"I want to marry you," he said, after a moment's pause.

"*O ciel!*" exclaimed Hortense, clasping her hands, and springing from her seat.[41]

"Sit down, if you please, and be quiet; I want you to listen, not to talk."

She obeyed mechanically.

"I don't understand what people mean by being in love; but I know I would rather, for many reasons, marry you than any woman I ever saw. You are quiet and self-possessed, not given to gadding about or gossiping, cheerful and active. I have watched you this long while; I like you, and I mean to marry you."

Hortense listened to this address in mute amazement. She had imagined that she must be as disagreeable to him as he was to her; and as to marrying him, she had no more thought of doing so than she had of marrying Napoleon Buonaparte.

"You understand me, I suppose?" he added, after a brief pause.

"I believe I do; but I do not wish to marry."

"We shall see! Perhaps I have been too abrupt; but you must not mind me; you know I am rough, and don't stand on ceremony; but I wish to make you my wife; and what is more, you must consent."

This was said in that commanding tone he so often used towards her, and Hortense felt, as usual, compelled to do his bidding; but she determined to resist his influence, and turned towards him to renew her refusal, and to plead her engagement to Reginald; but when she raised her eyes to his, her courage died within her; those

---

41 *O ciel!*: oh, heavens!

piercing eyes fascinated and conquered her, and she felt that he had her in some inconceivable manner under his control.

"I cannot leave your mother," she murmured.

Fowler saw he had conquered.

"Do not distress yourself; I can wait, or some arrangement can be made for her; besides, I don't wish to marry till Knoll is finished and habitable. Give me your hand, Hortense, and say it is a bargain."

He took her hand as it lay listlessly on her knee, and holding it a moment in both his, he turned and left her to herself.

"I won't marry him; nothing shall make me!" she cried; but though she was brave and bold enough when he was absent, she felt utterly powerless in his presence, and by degrees even found herself listening with interest to his plans, and dazzled with the wealth he promised her. She had heard enough of Reginald's story to know that it was most improbable that he would ever be enabled to return again to England, and his whereabouts was unknown to any human being in Torford.

Gradually it was whispered about that Fowler was going to marry the foreign girl. The sisters were delighted. It was a good marriage in their estimation, for they loved Hortense, and they were glad for her sake that she should be well and independently provided for. Old Mrs. Fowler was pleased, but begged her new daughter not to leave her: "She had not long to live."

On this one point Hortense stood her ground; but Fowler was not kept waiting long. The new house had not been finished many months, when the poor old lady went to her husband and her well-loved child. She said they had been looking for her a long time, and often reproached her for not coming; and she would repeat conversations which she alleges she had held with them.

It was a quiet, lonesome sort of wedding; for, his mother dead, Fowler insisted on Hortense keeping her word with him, and hardly a month elapsed between the funeral and the wedding. People shook their heads, and said it was sure to be unlucky; but Fowler did not care for their croakings, and went on with his schemes triumphantly.

CHAPTER XX
THE TYRANT'S END

LOOK at yonder house! look at the stunted trees, through whose leafless branches the mist is driving! Look at the broken windows, with here a piece of paper, there a bit of rag, to stop the eddying currents as they sweep round that mournful place, and penetrate through many a crack and cranny. See the overgrown garden, the weedy courtyard, the ruined stables, the empty stalls.

Harscourt is changed! poor old Harscourt! the sins and iniquities of thine owners seem visited on thee; and as the mist-laden wind rushes moaning on, the old house, too, seems to moan and lament on the days that are gone. No light young girlish form now flits across the windows; no snowy curtain, arranged by graceful hands, relieves the monotony of the great broad panes; but dull and blank they look out towards the sea, like the sightless eyes of a blind man.

There are no prancing horses, no busy grooms there now. The "Brown Beauty" lies buried under yonder hillock, and one or two aged dogs limping about, with drooping heads and lagging steps, are the only living things around.

Well may that house be deemed an accursed place; well may the country folk shun it, even in broad day. There are sights to be seen, and sounds to be heard there, enough to freeze one's life-blood.

In the gloomy house still lives Mr. Dawson, deserted by all save Damaris and Will, whose reasons for remaining would be hard to give. There is some mystery; and when questioned, Damaris has more than once answered, "I will know all; I will know what became of my young lady."

Tye has been lost and gone these many years, but the remembrance of her has not faded away. She was beautiful and unfortunate, and her end was mysterious. Gathered round the winter fire, and round the house-door in the summer gloaming, folks still relate her sad tale, her mysterious fate. Some maintain she is still alive—for, weeks after her disappearance, a bit of a blue dress, which every one knew she wore when last seen alive, was found hitched to a briar on the cliff; and though they fancied they could trace marks as if something had rolled down, no body was found or any other trace of the disaster.

As years pass on, strange things are whispered. People say that the girl is seen on moonlight nights wandering round the old house, dressed in the very blue gown she was last seen in. First one sees the spectre, and then another, till it is the common talk of the country. Even stalwart men declare how on stormy nights she rides through the lanes on the "Brown Beauty," brushing quite close to them. As the whispers grow, so Mr. Dawson hangs his head, and is seldom or ever seen, except by Mr. Martin, who haunts Harscourt like an evil spirit.

Money now seemed plentiful with Mr. Martin, while Mr. Dawson as evidently had less and less to share with him. Nothing was lost on Damaris; she treasured up every chance word, hoping it might give a clue to her mistress's fate. She had her suspicions, but all was dark and undecided, till a circumstance occurred which seemed to throw a glimmer of light into the murky darkness.

Mr. Martin was one day paying one of his long and apparently unwelcome visits. High words, as usual, passed between them, and Damaris overheard her master exclaim vehemently, "I did not do it, I say; I did not kill her."

There was a pause for a moment, and then came a frightful

shriek that rang and echoed through the house, and made Damaris, regardless of consequences, burst hurriedly into the room. To her dying day she never forgot what she saw and heard there. Mr. Dawson stood near the hearth—despair, terror, agony, indelibly stamped on his face; while opposite him sat Mr. Martin, looking scarcely less terrified than his companion.

"It is untrue!" exclaimed Mr. Dawson, looking toward the door that led to the garden-room, as if addressing some one standing there; "I did not murder you—you fell over!"

Damaris and Mr. Martin shuddered. Still the wretched man kept his eye fixed on the door, and again he exclaimed,—

"You fell over—I did not kill you!"

Suddenly he seemed to shrink together, and uttering another fearful shriek, cried,—

"Save me—save me! do not let her touch me! It is Grace; do you not see her? She is coming—she is coming!"

The wretched being sank on his knees before Mr. Martin, and clung to him like a child, trembling in every limb, while great drops of perspiration stood on his forehead.

"Guilty conscience needs no accuser," muttered Damaris, as she stood before her master. "It's what I've guessed all along; no wonder she haunts him, poor dear."

Mr. Dawson remained crouched on the floor, and it was a considerable time before he could gain sufficient courage to relax his grasp on Mr. Martin, or raise his head. When he did so, his first look was towards the garden-door. With a deep-drawn breath the look of alarm gradually passed away: whatever he had seen, or fancied he saw, was no longer there, and after awhile he tried to pass over the affair as if nothing had happened: but neither of his companions were to be deceived; they were fully satisfied now as to what had become of Grace, while Damaris called to mind how she had seen him peering over the cliff, days after the girl's disappearance.

From that day forward, Mr. Martin exercised more power than ever over the unfortunate man, and even Damaris ventured to do her own will. The paroxysm, however, was not a solitary attack. Constantly was the household roused by the screams of its wretched master, till one by one the servants left, glad to escape the frightful temper, and still more frightful terrors of the conscience-tortured man.

Soon it got about that Miss Dawson constantly walked about the hall and garden-room, and Damaris affirmed that though she never saw Miss Tye, many and many a time did she hear her in her own room sighing and moaning, just as she used to do when the master had been cruel to her as a child; but as to seeing her, she couldn't exactly say she ever did; but there, that was Miss Tye all over; she knew if she saw her, she would be just frightened to death, and so, remembering her friendship, she never came nigh her to horrify her, as she did some folks.

The miserable man lived on for years. His son he never saw, and gradually he sank into a dishonoured old age, uncared for and abhorred. Long before his death he was hardly accountable for his actions for days together: he was insensible from excessive drinking, and nothing could prevail on him to moderate his self-indulgence till he was literally on his death-bed; then face to face with death, he looked back and trembled; he looked forward and trembled: there was no hope in either direction.

How could he die with this load and weight on his conscience? what awaited him after? Then in bitter, abject misery he cried for help and comfort. But who could give him these?

Poor Damaris, who was as ignorant as she could well be, and had only some vague notions of right and wrong, picked up from her mistress in their girlish days, knew not how to deal with him; but she had a fancy—founded on she knew not what, for there were no schools in those parts, and the church was far away, and she had hardly been there six times in her life—that a clergyman might do him some good, as the doctor couldn't. So she sent for the vicar to come.

Strange as it may seem, Mr. Dawson was only too thankful to see him; he, like Damaris, fancied the vicar might do him some good and give him comfort.

But the young man stood awestruck beside the aged sinner. Gentle, kind, and loving, not one word of hope or consolation could he speak. We must draw a veil over that bad man's end. When all hope was past, when he knew he had but a few hours to live, he was seized with a passion, as it were, to defy all laws human and divine, to boast of his evil deeds, and to leave the world he had cursed with a curse on his lips.

There, on his death-bed, did he tell all his evil deeds to those around him, how he had murdered his young foreign wife in his rage and violence, how he had persecuted his children, and how he had followed his daughter with the full intention of murdering her; and that, but for her fall, he most certainly should have done it. He published his crimes, he revelled with fiendish delight in their horrors, while his terrified hearers shrank from him as from a leper. He told all the tale of poor Grace's wrongs. How Mr. Martin, having been a witness of his wife's murder, instead of denouncing him, had made it a means of extorting money from him. How he had got poor Tye into his meshes by threatening to divulge the horrid secret, if she did not consent to do his will. He told all, everything, and denounced his friend as a villain, greater in some things than himself, till that worthy slunk from the room humbled and crestfallen, to be from that day forward a pariah and an outcast from all men.

So Mr. Dawson died as he had lived, at enmity with all; and when he was named, people spoke of him in whispers, as of some evil thing.

No mourner had he. Will was the only one who followed him to his last resting-place; for his kinsman, Richard Dawson, now a prosperous lawyer, who came down on the news of his death to take possession in Reginald's absence, shrank from identifying himself with such a man.

He was not laid by the pretty, gentle wife on the sunny southern side, but away, in a dark dull corner, they made his nameless grave, as though his very bones were unworthy to lie among the quiet dead. A low mound, without holy cross or simple slab, is all that marks the grave of the "wicked Dawson of Harscourt."

And Damaris fancies she knows all.

Not yet, Damaris—not yet these many years—will you see the last of the Dawsons of Harscourt.

CHAPTER XXI

SAVED

NOW we must go back a few years in our story. Mr. Dawson being dead, and not able to do her an injury, we may as well confess, what possibly some have already guessed, that Tye was not dead. No; the dreadful fate which by many was supposed to have befallen her had been averted, and, as by a miracle, her life had been spared.

Mr. Dawson fully believed what he had revealed in his ravings, and confessed on his death-bed. He never doubted that he had caused his daughter's death, and, as he said in his last hours, he did it intentionally; it was no mere accident.

On that fearful night, when Grace had resisted all her lover's entreaties to fly with him, and had fled away up the path, unwitting of the danger that awaited her, Edward continued pacing up and down the beach, instead of, as was his usual custom after his stolen interviews with Grace, at once retiring to his hiding-place.

He had not been alone many minutes when he was startled by a shrill cry, and turning in the direction from which it proceeded, he saw, by the moonlight, a body rapidly descending a shelving part of the cliff.

"Grace has missed her footing," he muttered to himself, as he rushed towards the spot just in time to receive the inanimate form of the unfortunate girl in his arms.

A faint moan was all the sign of life she gave; but what might be the extent of the injuries she had received, Mountjoy could form no idea. Quickly and tenderly he lifted her in his arms, and carrying her to his boat, laid her gently in the bottom, seized the oars, and with quick, strong strokes, rowed out upon the sea.

It was no great distance to the mouth of Combe, and thither he turned his boat, not caring whether he was betrayed or not, and never thinking of the danger he ran in approaching his mother's cottage. Every moment seemed an hour; none but those who have watched beside those they love best on earth, expecting every breath to be the last, can form any idea of what that strong man felt, with that poor bruised, helpless woman lying at his feet. Love and terror nerved his arm, and the boat flew on like a living thing.

As the boat touched the shore at Combe, mother Agnes stood beside her son. She had been waiting for him; she was, as he told Grace, to be their companion.

"Where is Grace?" she asked, "would she not come with you?"

"Her body is there, mother," he answered, pointing to the heap in the bottom of the boat; "but come, mother, there is no time to lose: I must be back in the schooner. I would have risked another night on shore, mother, if she had lived; but she is dead, mother—dead! She fell from the cliff."

"Oh! the cliffs! the cliffs!" mutter mother Agnes, as she seated herself beside the luckless Grace. "I always said they would be the death of her!"

And there lay that beautiful woman, so mercilessly bruised and battered, that nought but the eye of love could have recognized her as she lay there—a mass of tangled hair and blood.

Not a word did the strong-armed oarsman speak; and mother Agnes, sat with her cloak lightly drawn around her, holding her breath as she would have done had a sleeping child been near, lest she should disturb her. Poor mother Agnes! this was her last, her worst blow! Her own darling daughter, as she fondly thought Grace; her only son's best loved one—gone!—gone for ever! Those full brown eyes never to look in hers more; that bright, cheery laugh never to sound again! And mother Agnes longed for tears, but even that comfort was denied her.

So they rowed on, Mountjoy now and then resting his oars; for even he, excited as he was, felt the length and exertion of that fearful voyage. The dawn was breaking, ere they reached the schooner's side, and sadly and silently he bore the inanimate form of Gratiana Dawson on to the deck of that vessel, of which his fondest hope had been to hail her queen.

"She lives still, thank heaven!" exclaimed Edward, as he laid his burden on a mattress that had been flung on the deck. "O Grace! Grace! speak to me, let me hear your voice!"

A piteous moan was all the answer, and the strong man bent his head over the woman he loved, and bitter tears, such as men only shed in some great agony, fell on the poor marred face.

There was no time for lingering; with all sails spread the beautiful vessel sped on her way—not to the distant land of America, where Mountjoy had meant to take his bride, but to a well-known harbour, where poor Grace might be safely landed, and where they might obtain some advice to mitigate the torments she endured.

During the two days and nights that elapsed ere they reached their destination, a fierce struggle had been going on in Mountjoy's mind. It was impossible to part with Grace now, equally impossible to take her with him. It was also impossible to keep his vessel hanging about the English coast, for though she was new, and had not as yet obtained a bad reputation, it would have been difficult to give a satisfactory account of her, and his crew did not care to idle about any longer. There was but one thing to be done, and that, however bitter it might be to him, he resolved on doing. He would give up his ship to his men, and take his chance for the future.

But when, after landing Grace, and seeing her properly attended to, he returned once more to his vessel, his heart sank within him. He had gathered round him a set of men who were good and honest in their relation to him as their commander. The ship was his own, and in possessing himself of her, so many dreams of Grace had been woven into everything that had been done to her, that it was hard to give her up. This was the colour Grace preferred; that seat had been invented purposely for her; and now she was lying hopelessly injured, so the doctor said. What, after all, was the ship to the woman he had loved so well?

His voice shook as he announced his intentions of resigning his command.

"I give my share in the ship up to you, Bellamy. Be her captain; take care of her and of your men; and spare the weak and succour the helpless."

The men received this address in silence; and Edward stood, without speaking further.

"Look here, captain," said Bellamy, at last, "this won't do; we can't spare you, and you can't spare us. We've worked together, and understand each other, and we can't part—'twould never answer. Now, don't you trouble yourself to speak; I know what you are going to say, how that you can't leave that poor lady, and no more you ought to do; and I doubt whether she'll be able to come afloat this long time, if ever; but you stay a bit and see how things turn out, and I'll take the ship and keep her employed, and out of harm's way, as well as may be, on the American coast. We've got an American flag, I believe, we can use if we want it; and this time six months, say, or it may be eight, I'll bring her back, if we are alive and well; and then, if things turn out fortunate, you can take your old post, and we shall be together again. Don't be afraid of trusting us, captain. I'm a rough sailor, but you nor no one else ever caught Lance Bellamy in a lie; did you now, captain; because if you ever did, speak it out and let me know?"

"Never!" replied Edward, holding out his hand to the man, whom he had known for years. "Bellamy, do as you will; take my vessel, and don't forget to come back for me; I shall watch for you."

He stayed on board some hours, arranging matters with his substitute; and then, taking a silent but heartfelt leave of his ship and crew, he landed, and stood on the beach watching her, as in the faint morning light she sailed forth upon the waters.

He never mentioned the compact with his crew to his mother, nor to Grace, even when she was able to listen to anything. Indeed, she spoke but little, and suffered so much both in body and mind, that all they could do was to nurse and tend her without a murmur or an impatient word, and keep her as quiet and tranquil as it was possible.

Once, indeed, Edward and mother Agnes ventured to question her as to the cause of her accident; but the agonized look of terror she cast on them, and her earnest entreaties that they should never mention what was past to her, or ever let any communication pass between her family and them, made them regard it as a subject never to be spoken of.

Not even to them would that brave girl breathe one word of the truth; and, whatever they might suspect, from her lips, to her dying day, they never heard the history of that night.

CHAPTER XXII
STOKE PETROCK

THE town to which Mountjoy took Grace, and where he dismissed his ships, was a small sea-port on the south coast of Devon; and there they remained until she was pronounced out of danger; and then he moved more inland, from the fear of any chance encounter with old associates. He also assumed his mother's name, as less likely to betray him than his own.

The little cottage which he made his residence, was situated in a small village, at the head of a splendid glen, close to the edge of the outskirts of Dartmoor. Two minutes' walk, and you were out on the wild, with one of the finest scenes in the county spread out before you. Immediately below was the rocky glen, gradually widening into a lovely wooded vale, while in front was the blue sea, with many a noble ship, and at a distance the town of Plymouth was plainly seen.

Though so near a great town, Stoke Petrock was a lonely place, with but little passing, except when a gang of French prisoners went by to Princetown, away in the centre of the moor. The village, however, possessed one of the handsomest churches in the neighbourhood, and its noble tower could be seen from far out at sea. There was the parsonage too, a comfortable, old-fashioned place; and there was a good-sized house, belonging to the owner of the greater part of the parish, a captain in the navy, of the name of Douglas.

The cottage itself was small, but pretty and convenient, a perfect bower of roses and myrtles; and poor Tye, worn out as she was, could not repress a cry of pleasure as she caught her first view of it.

Captain Douglas was absent with his ship; but before many days elapsed, Mrs. Douglas sent to inquire after the invalid, and ventured to send a present of some fruit.

The clergyman came too, and his kind, motherly old wife. They did not pry into the strangers' circumstances, but offered such assistance as Grace's state seemed to require. One sent her an easy chair; another a cushion, that was so soft, it ought in itself to have cured all aches and pains; while Mrs. Bolton, the clergyman's wife, who thought all the ailments in life might be cured by generous diet, was constantly stepping over with something nourishing, for the manufacture of which her cook was famous.

The devotion of Edward and mother Agnes was unbounded. They seemed only to live for Grace; and the doctor declared that nothing short of the tenderness and care with which they nursed her would have ever enabled her to rally from the fearful shock she had evidently sustained, mentally and bodily.

When questioned by the neighbours as to what was amiss with the strange lady, he would shake his head, look mysterious to excite attention, and whisper, looking cautiously around the while, "A fall; but pray don't mention it; don't say I said it; but why she has not every bone in her body broken, or why she is alive at all, I don't know."

As Grace got better, some of these kind people would come and sit by her; but of all her new acquaintance, it was Mrs. Douglas who pleased her most. In some things, Grace fancied she resembled Lily Fowler, but she was stronger and more self-dependent. She was many years her husband's junior, so the doctor told them, and was the daughter of one of the captain's friends, who had left his daughter to the guardianship of his only friend, a bachelor.

"What could he do but marry her?" asked the doctor, shrugging his shoulders; "and a very wise thing for both parties, that's my opinion. Never saw a more devoted couple in my life—that's my opinion. She's one of those gentle, loving mannered women that conquer everybody. Bless you, why, if she asked me to do anything, in ever such a quiet beseeching way, as if she were asking a favour, I'd no more dare refuse her than I dare fight that blackguard Nap single-handed! She's a nice woman is Mrs. Douglas, that's my opinion;" and the doctor would take pinch after pinch of snuff till he nearly choked everyone within half a mile of him.

If Grace liked Mrs. Dawson best, she was not insensible to the kind old doctor's merits; and she soon felt that many a kindness which she received from others, was in a measure due to him. It was he who, in answer to the clergyman's question as to whether the poor invalid was in want of anything, had answered, "She wants everything but love and money. They seem to have plenty of the latter; and if the former would cure her, she'd want no doctor. The man treats the woman, though, as a nurse; I never saw such skill and tenderness in all my days, and they are not a few now. Ah me!"

One day, as Mrs. Douglas sat by Grace's side, keeping watch, as she called it, while Edward was taking a ride across the moor to refresh himself, on a horse lent him by the doctor, Mrs. Douglas said something about Grace's "husband."

"I am not married yet," rejoined Grace, blushing rosy red. "As soon as I can get as far as the church, we are to be married; we have been engaged a long, long time—more than five years now, and we should have been married before this but for my accident. We were brought up together, and have loved each other from childhood," continued Tye, as if she wished to explain her relation to Edward, to her new friend.

"I hope you will get well soon," said Mrs. Dawson, kindly.

"I hope so, for his sake," answered Grace. "When I am well enough to go to church, will you come with me? You are, I fancy, like a dear friend I may never see again; and though you are married, and cannot be my bridesmaid, I should like to have you with me."

"I should be so glad," replied Mrs. Douglas, who for one little moment had felt surprised that Grace was not already married, but who felt perfectly reassured, as Grace looked her full in the face, and asked her to come to her wedding.

"And if I really do get better, and well enough to go to church, would you buy me my wedding gown? I have a special fancy about it: no doubt you would choose white, but I must have blue, the very palest you can find; and it must be made in a particular way, as I always used to wear it. At home, in old times, they used to call me the blue lady. Yes, I must be married in blue. I am sure he will like it for old associations' sake; but he must not know about it. Is it asking too much, after having known you so short a time?"

"No, indeed," answered the new friend. "It will be quite interesting to me; it will remind me of my own wedding; and when a woman loves her husband, she loves specially the remembrance of the day that made her really his."

"I hope I shall be better soon," repeated Grace. "I managed to get across the room yesterday with Edward's help, and when he comes in I shall get him to pilot me as far as the porch."

After being obliged to keep her sofa for many months, Grace began to get well all of a sudden; it seemed as if she had passed some crisis in her illness, and rapidly she regained her strength and power of walking—in the end, a slight limp being the only reminder of her fearful fall. Every one in the little circle at Stoke were delighted at her recovery; and to have seen the church on the day of the wedding, no one would have thought that Edward and Grace had come only a few months before utter strangers into the place.

Mrs. Douglas's school-girls, all dressed in their best, strewed flowers along the church path, she herself supporting Grace on one side, the doctor on the other—arrayed, as he took special pains to inform everybody, in his wedding-coat, which Mrs. Doctor had kept locked up for years, lest he should wear it out. "But on such an occasion as the present, of course, she could not object to my wearing it; but, dear me! there she is, looking at me from behind a tombstone!"

The tone in which this was spoken, suggested the possibility of him having possessed himself of the coat without his wife's knowledge.

There was the clergyman's wife in the church, busily arranging some cushions, so that the lame bride might kneel without inconvenience, while the parson himself was on the church tower, hoisting a large flag, at Mrs. Dawson's special request, she having a fancy that flags—at any rate, those belonging to her good husband—were sure to bring good luck, and were a necessary sign of rejoicing.

A lady's wedding—and a lady they all felt Grace to be—was a novelty to the villagers of Stoke, and the girls and women lined the church path, and all available seats in the church were occupied. Grace, in her quaint dress, made a most picturesque bride. She had not regained the roundness of form and features which had once distinguished her; her face too was pale, and her eyes looked larger than ever; but there was an expression of happiness and peace on her countenance, as she left the altar with her husband, such as had never rested there before.

It was on her wedding-day that Grace Dawson, for the last time, spoke of her father.

"Remember!" she said, "from this day I am only yours; my father believes me dead; Reginald will believe me dead; for all our sakes it is best so. Farewell, old life! may our new one be more peaceful and blessed."

Peaceful and happy their life proved. They had known each other too long and too intimately to find out anything to disappoint them. Edward continued just as kind and true as he had ever been, and Grace as loving and trusting; but as time passed by, Tye saw a dark cloud rising, and, like a true, brave woman as she was, instead of letting it overwhelm her, she determined, as far as might be, to prevent its bursting over her head.

It was hardly to be imagined that a man reared as Edward had been, could sit quietly down indoors, doing nothing. The easy life he led began to pall upon him, and often did he follow in fancy the fortunes of his departed ship. The period had passed which Bellamy had mentioned for his return, and at last thoughts began to find a place in Mountjoy's breast, that Bellamy intended to play him false.

Near the house was a lofty rock, from which could be seen a wide expanse of sea and land, and there Edward and Grace would sit for hours together, watching the vessels as they came in and out of Plymouth Sound.

Grace noticed how he got more and more silent, and how he would absent himself from home during long hours, and she divined the true cause of his restlessness and dulness. She, on her part, was not a woman to wish to see a man idle, and living a useless life; but was it for her to bid him go?"

She pondered and pondered, and at last determined, cost her what it might, to speak.

"Edward," she said, abruptly, one evening when they were alone together, "are you ever going to sea again?"

"How strange that you should speak; just at that moment I was trying to summon courage to tell you how I longed to be once more afloat."

And then he told her of the arrangement he had made with Bellamy, and how disappointed he was at the non-arrival of the ship.

"I hope she will never come back, Edward."

"My dear Tye! what do you mean?"

"I mean, Edward, that since I have been ill, I have thought of many things which I never thought of before, and that since I have known Mrs. Douglas a wish has sprung up in my heart, that you should not go to sea in the same capacity as you used to do. Why should you not some day be as much respected as Captain Douglas seems to be, by everyone who knows him?"

"You are ambitious, Tye."

"Yes, my husband, very ambitious for you. Mrs. Douglas knows you have been a sailor, and—don't be vexed with me, Edward—I ventured the other day to question her about the chances of your getting some appointment. I am sure she would do anything in her power for either of us, she is so truly kind; and her husband is coming home in a few days, and then you must see what can be done."

"You do not know the difficulties of what you propose. It is not likely that Captain Douglas would interest himself for me. I am afraid, Grace, I must seek some more easily obtained employment, and that you must learn to be less ambitious in your desires."

But Tye was not to be disheartened by a few dispiriting words; and when, on the next Sunday, she saw Captain Douglas for the first time in church, all her hopes revived as she looked into his good, honest, manly face, and saw with what a genial smile he greeted old and young, rich and poor.

The next day, Mrs. Douglas and her husband paid a visit to the cottage, but Edward was out wandering on the moor. The captain, who acknowledged that if he had a weakness, it was to look at a handsome face, was mightily smitten with Grace, and spoke out his admiration in such decided language, that Mrs. Douglas declared she should be quite jealous if he was not careful of his conduct, which rebuke was taken in earnest by the honest man, and he felt himself bound to make a thousand apologies to everybody.

"Make him come and ask himself," whispered Mrs. Douglas, as they took their leave. "I feel sure he will succeed, but he must be bold and honest."

Tye Triumphed: that evening, with some little persuasion, she induced her husband to seek an interview with Captain Douglas.

"I know it will all turn out well—I feel it will," exclaimed the sanguine Tye. "Oh! I wish it was to-morrow, and all settled! I am so impatient."

CHAPTER XXIII
CAPTAIN DOUGLAS

IT was impossible for Mountjoy not to feel anxious and excited when he found himself in Captain Douglas's dining-room. He could not now retreat; he must give some reason for his requesting the interview; and yet he must tell many things he would willingly have forgotten, or give up the hopes he had formed of following his profession in a more legitimate way than he had hitherto done.

He had, however, little time for resolutions or irresolutions; a short, quick step sounded through the hall, and Captain Douglas entered. He was a short, strongly-built man, about forty, a little bald, his hair beginning to show a few streaks of grey. He had a bright, cheery face, and greeted his visitor in a manner that set Mountjoy at his ease at once.

"Mrs. Dawson has quite interested me with her account of your wife; a handsome woman, sir, upon my word; one of the handsomest people I ever saw."

"Almost as handsome as Mrs. Douglas," rejoined Mountjoy, with a smile.

"Very good, sir; very well answered; I shall tell Mrs. Douglas your opinion of her. Well, she is handsome, sir, and good, too, and she has taken a great fancy to your wife and your mother—very striking-looking old lady—handsome once, too—very handsome. I hope you mean to stay in this part of the world, for I shall be off again soon, and I should be glad to think that Mrs. Douglas had neighbours she liked; she is not generally sociable, but she has taken an amazing fancy to your wife."

"I hope my wife and mother will continue at the cottage, and have the benefit of Mrs. Douglas's kindness and countenance; as to myself, my plans are very uncertain. I took the liberty of coming to you to see if you could in any way aid me. My earnest desire is to enter the navy."

"Rather late in life, isn't it, my good sir?" inquired Captain Douglas, scanning his visitor from under his shaggy brow, with a look that seemed to try and read his most secret thought.

"I have been at sea ever since I was fourteen."

"Humph! In what capacity, may I ask?"

"I have been owner and commander of late."

"Where is your vessel now?"

"I have none; I resigned my command; I gave her to my crew: indeed, she was as much theirs as mine, for we had worked together for years."

"And what made you abandon her?"

"My wife: she had a very fearful accident before we were married. She was thrown entirely on my mother and myself, and I gave up the ship rather than leave her."

"Quite right, and quite a romance! Rescue a young lady from a perilous situation, fall in love with her, marry her—all quite right. I shall tell Mrs. Douglas of it. Very lucky fellow to pick up such a very handsome woman. But to return to yourself; I presume, sir, you were the captain of a privateer?"

"I have no wish to deceive you, sir; I followed the calling my father had followed before me. I was a privateer, and a smuggler as well."

"I wish such fine-looking fellows as you are would join the service in the first place, and not go wasting your years and energies on an employment which of course I, as a naval man, look down upon. But still sometimes that adventurous life brings us fine materials in skilful seamen. I daresay now, you yourself know how to manage a vessel pretty tidily?"

"I wish you would try me!" answered Mountjoy, eagerly.

"Well, well, we must not be in too great a hurry; but I'll talk it over with Mrs. Douglas, and see what I can do; but you know, taking the circumstances into consideration, if you enter the navy, you cannot enter as an officer; you must be content to begin as a subordinate, whatever position you may ultimately reach."

"I do not care in what position I enter, so long as I can get a chance of rising; only find me employment, and that soon, and I shall be eternally obliged to you. This idle life destroys me."

"Well spoken, young man; but we cannot act in such a hurry as your wishes would suggest. I, you know, have a position, and it wouldn't do for me to risk it. You must confess that as yet we are strangers, and however much prepossessed in your favour, still I should like to think a little ere I made any decided promise to aid you."

Mountjoy sighed; he feared lest caution should prevent Captain Douglas from assisting him.

"There is one question I must ask you, and which you must answer me honestly. Something tells me you will be able to answer it as I could wish; but still I must hear what I want from your own lips," said Captain Douglas in a kind voice, hesitating, as if he feared to wound his visitor."

"What is it?" replied Mountjoy.

"Did you ever do a deed that compromised your honour as a gentleman? I am not afraid of using that last word, because I feel you will understand me."

"I have been a privateer and a smuggler, Captain Douglas."

"So you told me before; but one is permitted by government, and the other is supported by some to be sanctioned by the injustice of the laws. I did not mean in either of these capacities; but in your position as a man, have you ever done anything to disgrace yourself?"

"I have never wittingly done an injustice to man, woman or child. I have been true to my country, my mother, and to Grace."

"Ah, yes! that sweet lady; you have been true to her, too. Have you known her long, or was your marriage a mere romantic accident?"

"Grace and I have known and loved each other from childhood."

"A runaway match?"

"If she would have consented to have joined her fortunes unhesitatingly to mine, neither she nor I would have been in our present embarrassments; she would not have been crippled, nor I seeking employment; but this is a subject on which I must not speak. She would be annoyed if she imagined her name or actions were brought under discussion, and I honour and value her too deeply to vex her, even in thought."

"Don't fear me," answered Captain Douglas. "The assurance that your wife has known and trusted you for years, is no mean recommendation. A woman with such a noble pair of steady brown eyes as she has, is not likely to be taken in by a ne'er-do-weel. It is your soft, die-away ladies that are generally taken in by men; but bless me, I believe your wife would fire a broadside into an enemy's ship with more *sang-froid*, as the frogs say, than she would go to court."[42]

---

[42] *Sang-froid*: coolness of mind, the ability to remain calm in a difficult or dangerous situation.

"She has done things in her day that required from her more nerve than would be required of you in attacking an enemy. She is one of the bravest hearts that ever beat, and for her sake I would sacrifice much, could I find an opening to some honourable employment."

"Well, I must consider. I won't make any rash promises; but I will try what I can do. Your name, I believe, is Erlingham?"

"That is the name by which I wish to be known; it was my mother's name. But if you wish it, I have no objection to tell you my real name, as I believe you to be a man of honour, who will not use it to my hurt."

"You may trust in me implicitly; but I must know as much about you as you can tell me."

"My name is Edward Mountjoy."

"Mountjoy—Mountjoy? well, that is curious. The first time I was ever afloat, a callow little nestling, fresh from my mother's apron-string, I was in the *Terpsichore*, on the West Indian station, and a beautiful little vessel, the *Ocean Wave*, gave no end of trouble. The men declared she was bewitched, for, chase her where we would, she was sure to disappear, and she never was caught; and what became of her I know not; but her commander's name has never slipped my memory. It was the same as yours, and my terror for months; for the elder mids were always bullying me, and talking of how we should have to fight the pirate, if we came up to her; that we should assuredly be beaten, in which case the pirates always made a practice of feasting themselves on the youngest mid.[43]

Only the other day I met an old messmate, and he reminded

---

43 Mid: midshipman, a young gentleman who is in training at sea to become an officer in the navy.

me of my terrors, and asked me if I had heard Mountjoy was come to light again, and was busy at his old tricks on the English coast. I suppose now that was you?"

"I suppose so," answered Edward, unable to repress a smile at the fancy of his being a formidable pirate; "and your old enemy was my father. But I should not wish these things to get wind here. It might cause annoyance to my mother and wife."

"You may rely on my discretion. It won't harm my telling Mrs. Douglas, she never repeats anything, and she will be so amused at my coming face to face with the son of my former bugbear. Fancy what a thing it will be if I can turn such sea-blood as yours is into its legitimate channel. Who knows but some day I may see you a post-captain: there's no harm done by fancying such things might happen, is there?"[44]

"No, indeed!" rejoined Edward. "I trust myself in your hands, believing you will do for me what you can."

"You're a nice young lady," said Captain Douglas to his wife, as he joined her in the garden after Mountjoy's departure. "I thought you were so prudent about making acquaintance, and so careful whom you admitted into your society; and here you have been associating for months with a well-known pirate and his family!" And the captain drew his shaggy brows together, and looked unutterably fierce.

"Oh, dear! I am very sorry if I have done wrong," answered Mrs. Douglas, timidly.

"Think of his coming here to ask me to get him into the navy!"

Mrs. Douglas did not speak.

---

[44] Post-captain: any officer in command of a ship was addressed by the courtesy title of 'captain', regardless of his actual rank, but a post-captain had achieved that rank.

"I shouldn't at all wonder now, if you and that brown-eyed wife of his had been talking it over."

"Well, one day she said her husband was a sailor, and that he would like to get honourable employment, and I did say I thought perhaps you might be able to help him. You know, the other day Lord —— was complaining how short they were of experienced seamen. Do, my good husband, if you are able, exert your good offices in behalf of Mr. Erlingham.

"And what do you think Lord —— would say to me if I went to him and said, 'May it please you, my lord, Mrs. Douglas has got a pet pirate, and she begs you will make him a post-captain this week, an admiral next, and the week after give him the command of the Channel fleet?"

"He would laugh at you, as I do now," replied Mrs. Douglas; "but if you went and said, I know a man who has been a seaman for years; he is ambitious of rising in the world; he is willing to take any position where he will have a chance of getting on; I believe he has the stuff of a good officer in him;—he would take him directly if you would say that."

"Now I call that a pretty audacious speech for a timid woman! And you are not the least ashamed of his being a pirate, or anything else that's bad?"

"I don't believe he is the least bad; and you are not to tell Lord —— that he was a pirate, as you are pleased to call him. Lord —— may suspect what he likes, but you are not to tell him; and mind you add that his wife is a particular friend of mine. You can go over this afternoon to Plymouth; you will have plenty of time if you start at once."

"And this is the language of a timid woman to a post-captain in his Majesty's navy?"

"Yes; and very proper language too, for you are all such horrid tyrants on your ships, that it is a very wise regulation you should be sent home for a few months at a time to be kept a little in order, and know what it is to be under command."

"Well, I'll do your bidding in this matter, at any rate, little woman; only the next time you ask me to do anything, I won't, or you'll get spoilt."

"Don't you know sailors' wives always are spoilt," replied Mrs. Douglas, linking her arm through her husband's. "It's an old story, and I do not think you are the man to break into so good a custom."

"I'm afraid I'm a soft-hearted old chap," relied Captain Douglas; "but I must not stop here flirting with you, if I am to get to Plymouth to-day; so good-bye, little woman, for the present."

CHAPTER XXIV
ONCE MORE AFLOAT

GRACE was waiting at the garden-gate for her husband's return. She would have given much, had it been possible, to have been present at the interview with Captain Douglas, for now, the notion of Edward's going to sea having once entered her active mind, she was as eager for it as he could be.

"He gives me hopes, but promises nothing, Tye," was Edward's answer to the quick inquiries of his wife.

"Hope is a great thing gained, Edward; and I am quite sure Mrs. Douglas will use her interest for us. You must, you shall succeed."

"You are getting your old self again, Tye. It is pleasant to hear you speaking as vehemently as you would have done ten years ago. I declare I have proved myself a capital doctor."

"The best I could have, dearest. But come with me to our seat, and let us settle which ship you shall sail in." So the two took their way to the rock, and watched the vessels as they came in and out of the harbour.

"Do look at that man yonder, Tye; did you ever see such an infamous horseman? I declare it is Captain Douglas. Really, Tye, you must offer to give him some riding lessons!"

"See, Edward, he has turned down the Plymouth road. Dear good man, depend upon it he is gone to see if he can manage anything for you."

Tye was right. Captain Douglas liked doing a good-natured thing, and he liked pleasing his wife; and, as it happened, he was enabled to do both. It chanced on that very day, that a seaman, or, I believe, to speak more correctly, a petty officer, who held an important position in the Admiral's ship, had been suddenly disabled, and there was some difficulty in supplying his place. Captain Douglas managed to give such an account of Mountjoy, as induced those in authority to warrant his making an offer to him of filling the vacant post, if he proved himself capable of discharging his duties. Captain Douglas was more than satisfied at the success of his mission, and early the next morning he and his *protégé* took the road to Plymouth.

"Grace," said Mrs. Mountjoy, nervously, "why is Edward gone into the town with Captain Douglas? I don't like his going into Plymouth and about the port, it's not safe for him; he will be wanting to go to sea again, if you don't take care."

"He does want to go to sea, mother."

"But Grace, you will not let him? If you ask him to stay he will never go."

"But I shall not ask him to stay."

"You are in one of your old moods, Grace; you are cold and cruel."

"Neither one nor the other, mother; it would be cruelty to keep Edward here. He is gone to-day to see if he can find employment."

"This is too bad, Grace!" exclaimed mother Agnes, angrily, "to take such a step, and never say one word to me, never consult me, nor think of me!"

"We have acted as we have to spare you, mother. You must not be angry with me. Do you think it is nothing to me to part with Edward?" and Grace walked away to hide the tears she could not keep back.

It was with a slow and measured tread that Edward approached the cottage that evening. His wife was on the look-out for him, and as he caught sight of her he beckoned her to come to him, and without speaking led her toward the rock. The sun was just sinking towards the low Cornish hills, shooting upwards long streams of light, and tinting the grey granite-strewn moor with a warm rosy hue; and there, in that lovely bay, lay the fleet, each ship standing out distinctly in the clear air.

"You have been disappointed?" said Tye, sadly.

"No, dearest, no! Look at that ship, Grace—the largest of them all. I fancy you can see the admiral's flag flying even from here. That is my ship, Tye; it is the one you picked out this morning."

Grace nestled near to her husband, and laid her head on his shoulder.

"Are you sorry, Tye?"

"Glad for your sake, very glad! But you are so still, Edward; do you already repent?"

"No, I do not repent; but it is impossible to take a step so important as this may be, without feeling anxious and doubtful as to how it may answer."

"My husband, you must hope and have faith in yourself, as I have in you and for you. Bitter as it will be parting with you, I shall feel so proud in thinking you are in an honourable position, however humble it may be!"

There was but little time for preparation, and the hurry and bustle of getting things in order left but little leisure for the indulgence of grief; and within a week of that first visit to Plymouth, Grace sat alone on the rock, watching the last sail of the fleet disappear below the horizon.

Edward's position for the first few months was not a very enviable one. Some of the men tried to get up a cabal against him, being jealous of the appointment of a stranger to the post he held, and noticing that there were some of the details of his Majesty's

Navy of which he was ignorant or careless. But a man who can and will learn is not likely to remain long ignorant, and by degrees he mastered the whole business thoroughly, and by his constant quiet and consistent conduct won the respect both of men and officers. He had a way of attaching the former to him, while keeping them quite as much at a distance as did the superior officers themselves, and never permitting an undue familiarity, which attracted even the admiral's notice in time, and made him more than once remark what a good officer Mountjoy would make; and on many occasions the admiral expressed his approbation of Edward's conduct, and of the way in which he performed his duties.

We cannot follow Mountjoy in his present career; it is written in the pages of the history of those days. Enough for us that he had the good fortune to sail in the admiral's vessel on the day of a memorable engagement and a splendid victory, and in consequence of the skill he showed that day he was enrolled among the officers of his Majesty's navy. What rejoicings there were for that victory! how the great guns at Plymouth kept booming over the blue sea; how the bells rang out from every tower in England, none more cheerily than those of Stoke!

And Grace? With the news of the victory had come the names of those who had distinguished themselves, and who were recommended for promotion, and in the list she read her husband's name. Thanks to Captain Douglas, she got the news at the earliest moment, and it made her feel as if every gun that was fired, and every peal that struck out, was solely for Edward's honour and glorification; while mother Agnes ever after had a confused notion that her son had taken command of the admiral as well as the ship, and had won the engagement almost single-handed.

What wonderful nonsense sensible Grace talked to her boy,

a toddling fellow just a twelvemonth old, at the rock that evening! How she gravely assured him that the cannon were firing for father, the bells ringing for father, and how pretty it was to see the little chap clapping his hands, and repeating the one word she had taught him, "father," "father!"

The whole village of Stoke was beside itself at the news. It felt that it had in some way had a hand in the victory, and would have its own bells ring when all the other bells had stopped, and would not take the flag down from the church tower, and announced its intention of "doing something" when the gallant sailor should return.

Grace had become a great favourite among the simple villagers; her frank, easy manner won the hearts of those who, when she came among them an almost hopeless invalid and utter stranger, had from natural friendliness shown her many a little kindness. Her boy was the idol of the whole female population of the village, from Mrs. Douglas downwards; and he was pronounced on all hands to be the very handsomest and most wonderful child that ever was beheld. He was acknowledged, however, even by his best friends, to have a temper; but that was no harm in a boy.

It proved a long time before the good folk of Stoke had an opportunity of testifying their delight at Edward's success. Hi ship on her return to England was taken to Sheerness, and almost immediately he was transferred to another man-of-war in his new rank. Thanks to the friends he had raised up for himself, there was no delay, and he found himself in a position that a year ago he had thought utterly unattainable.

He had, however, no leisure to take a long journey down to Stoke, and it was only by hurrying up to Chatham by the speediest conveyance that existed in those days, that Grace caught even a few hours sight of her husband; and his son was obliged to remain a stranger to him for some years to come, which was the greatest grief Grace knew.

When he had sailed, she again returned to the cottage, and there her life passed tranquilly. Her boy gave her employment enough, if there had been nothing else to do than to keep him in order, and prevent his being spoilt,—a rather difficult task. There really seemed a conspiracy against poor Tye in her efforts to control her son, and make him what she called well-behaved.

Mother Agnes, of course, did her best to ruin him. Mrs. Douglas seconding all her efforts, and even Captain Douglas joining Tye's enemies, and throwing his weight into the scale against her Reginald; or, as the captain invariable called him, in spite of all remonstrance, "my young Pirate;" he was just the sort of boy to take the affections not only of women, but of men by storm; and Captain Douglas was as devoted to him as if he had been a child of his own; and when Grace would appeal to him with tears in her eyes, not to grant him some indulgence, which she thought he ought to be denied,—

"Bah! my dear madam, I defy any one to spoil that child. He always minds you, now doesn't he, ma'am, and obeys you when he's got the chance, that's to say, when he's alone with you? Well, what more do you want?"

"Why, I want him to learn to read before his father comes back"—this was when the youth was nearing the age of four years—"and how am I possibly to do it if one day you will have him go to Plymouth to see some show there, and another the doctor carries him off before him on horseback, for I don't know how many hours? and a few days ago nothing would satisfy Mr. Bolton but he must take him down to the river-side to teach him to fish:" and here a remembrance of her own early exploits in this particular branch brought a smile to her face.

"There, now, that looks more sensible," said Captain Douglas. "I ask you, my dear madam—not that I know anything of your former history, or have any desire to pry into it—but I take the liberty of asking, did you never, in your young days, like a little bit of indulgence? had you no taste for freedom? Can you conscientiously assert, that if there had been a doctor, which possibly there was not, in your part of the world, and that doctor had one fine day said to you, 'Miss Tye—I know that's what would have called you—Miss Tye, would you like a ride?' you would not have been as pleased to go as my young Pirate yonder? would you not just have stretched out your hand, and with a little assistance have placed your foot, and then with one little jump have taken your seat in front of the said doctor? And very pretty you would have looked under the circumstances."

Tye could only laugh at the picture which the captain drew, and he continued, getting quite excited as he proceeded,—

"Can you venture to assert, madam, that you never tumbled into the water? for that, I believe, was the real crime imputed to my dear young Pirate on the day Mr. Bolton is supposed to have kidnapped him."

"Often and often," replied Tye, most thoroughly amused.

"I knew you had," replied the captain, triumphantly; "it's written on your face, and no doubt you climbed over walls and tore your frocks, and helped yourself to apples—if there were any apples in the country you came from—and did all sorts of naughty things, and, in fact, were as bold and bad a girl as you want to make out my poor dear young Pirate is a boy."

"All true except the apples, my good friend," replied Grace;

"and perhaps I might have sinned in that particular also, had I chanced to like apples."

"You needn't assure me: I'm right—I know I am—it's all written in your face! But what I want to impress upon you, is this: don't fancy that boy is entirely yours; he isn't. He belongs to me and Mrs. Douglas, and the doctor, and the Boltons, and the whole village; and I won't see him put upon, I won't."

"Now, my dear captain, you know my only reason for acting as I do is, that his father should be pleased with him when he comes back; and if he isn't good, you know it will be my fault."

"Good madam! he's the best boy in the country, and you shan't abuse him! Pleased with him! why, the man would be mad if he wasn't as proud as Jupiter of him! You let him go free and happy, and grow up bold, and if he wants a little training and keeping in order, he'll soon get that when he's on board ships. Don't look at me in that way, madam; of course I mean him to be a sailor; and now if I hear any more of this nonsense about learning to read, and all that, well, I'll give him a pony his very next birthday, and then there will be a pretty kettle of fish! You'll have no chance then! Ah! there's the boy. Come here, my young Pirate."

The boy sprang to meet him, and lifted up his bright, beautiful face to his friend, who drew his brows together, and looked fiercely at the little fellow.

"I say, my small Pirate, are you a bad boy?"

"No, I ain't," replied the child, keeping his great eyes—the exact counterpart of his mother's—steadily fixed on the captain's.

"I say, young Pirate, if you ever disobey your mother, or vex her, I'll—never be Captain Daddy to you any more."

The boy looked at him a moment, and then at his mother, and a blush spread over his face, and his hands twitched nervously.

Twice he essayed to speak before he could quite make up his mind, and then, in his childish words, he tried to excuse himself.

"I'm sorry I vexed mamma, and tumbled into the water; but there was such a dear little fish, and I thought mamma would be so proud if I could catch it: so I stooped down and put my hands in the water, as she told me once she and father used to do when they were little, and the water was too deep, and I fell in, and when I got out again the dear little fish was gone, and I was so sorry."

"Convicted, madam, convicted by your own son! Don't tell me, madam; it's written in your face!" cried Captain Douglas, triumphantly. "The next thing I shall hear is that you were in the habit of riding across country."

"Guilty: I plead guilty," answered Grace, merrily; "but you will be making some more discoveries if I don't take care, so I shall wish you good-bye."

CHAPTER XXV
UNCERTAIN RICHES

FOWLER was not destined to be disappointed in the estimate he had formed of his wife: as in his other speculations, so he was successful also in that greatest of all speculations, marriage. Hortense managed her establishment, which was on an equal scale with those of the best families in the neighbourhood, as if from childhood she had been accustomed to the riches and luxury that now surrounded her. She dressed richly, but in exquisite taste. Her carriage was the prettiest in the neighbourhood, her dinners the most *recherché*: for Fowler gave dinners now; and soon, at his table, you might have seen men and women who would not have returned his bow during his father's lifetime.

He certainly possessed the art of making money, and of drawing people into his schemes in a manner which would have appeared perfectly wonderful, did one not so often see this power possessed by unscrupulous people. He would lend a man money one day, and on the next, draw it again from his pocket, by embarking him in some speculation, the proceeds of which generally fell to Fowler's share.

He almost monopolized the trade of the town. He traded in coals in the name of one tool. He was the real owner of large lime-kilns, which ostensibly belonged to another. The wine-merchant bought his stock with Fowler's money, and two or three of the principal mills in and near Torford were really the property of the speculating man.

Hortense had a large circle of acquaintances, but she had no friends. So her husband willed, and his will was law. She was forbidden any communication with his sisters, which both to her and to them was a grief; nor was she allowed to give any reason for her conduct, which indeed it would have been hard to find. People thought her proud and puffed up with her good fortune; but the truth was, it would have ill suited Fowler to have strangers coming in and out at all hours. Hortense's life was not entirely spent in dressing, or driving, or giving parties: she had to work, and work hard, for an exigeant taskmaster. He had, it is true, clerks whom he employed in such of his dealings as would have borne the investigation of any honest man; but there were other transactions which it would have been folly to trust to any second person, except indeed a wife so completely under control as Hortense. But whatever he did of an underhand nature was most carefully kept secret, and the most cautious were thus far obliged to acknowledge that Fowler had either never done the questionable deeds that had been laid to his charge, or that he had turned over an entirely new leaf.

Thus, at length, he became universally trusted; and many a widow blest him for putting her in the way of increasing her slender income, and many a weary old man thanked heaven that by the aid of Mr. Fowler he need work no longer.

But even when standing apparently on the highest pinnacle of fortune, Fowler trembled. He knew it was but a crumbling structure which he had raised: he knew how little stability there was in the showy fabric that so dazzled men; he was well aware that it was a mere lucky chance that kept his head above water: but with the recklessness of a thorough gambler, he kept venturing more and more.

His most desperate ventures were not made at Torford, but at a distance; and these, while he thought they would bring him in larger and quicker gains than what he called his plodding work at Torford, in the end got him into trouble.

His luck began to turn; one speculation and another failed, though unknown to those among whom he lived, from whose pockets he managed to extract funds to make good the deficiencies, without his dupes ever dreaming that he was ruining them.

All, however, went on apparently as flourishing as it had done for years. Those who had trusted him received the large interest he gave at the first moment it was due, and he was accounted the richest man in the district, and people even began to talk of him representing a neighbouring borough when an opportunity should occur.

Suddenly the news came that Fowler was not to be trusted. A ship with a valuable cargo, which had been lost a few months previously, was said to have been unfairly dealt by. Great had been the sympathy for the merchant at the time of his supposed loss, and there had been a talk of showing their feeling for him in some tangible manner, but Fowler had discouraged this, though he said her cargo was worth many thousand pounds, and was but inadequately insured.

The insurance company, however, would gladly have had it less than it proved; and though Fowler talked of his loss, it got whispered about that he had gained rather than been a loser in the matter; but the whole of Torford seemed shaken to its foundations, when, not long after, a deliberate charge of fraud was made against Fowler on account of this ship.

Necessarily in his many transactions at home and abroad, he had by degrees been obliged, spite of his desires to the contrary, to employ many agents, and in this matter, one whom he had trusted more than any man, betrayed him. Some difference with his employer as to the amount due to him in the transaction is supposed to have been the reason for his revelations.

This man informed those interested in the matter that he, with his own hand, had sunk the ship, after the whole of the cargo had been removed to smaller craft, which had conveyed the goods in different directions, and disposed of them for the benefit of the man, who, at the same time, claimed reparation for the misfortune he had experienced.

Up to the day this discovery was made, Fowler had been the most popular man in the town; now his name was anathematized by high and low, as they trembled to think how they had trusted him, and how deeply involved many of them were in the schemes of one capable of such a fraud. He had cheated one—might he not have cheated others?

Every hour that passed proved that he had done so; and when the officers tardily started for Knoll, to serve a warrant which they held against him, they were accompanied by numbers of people, who had trusted Fowler, and went with some ill-defined purpose of getting justice from him.

Hortense met the party on the flight of stone steps leading to the hall door. She stood there waiting for them, her dress gently fluttering in the wind. She was perfectly calm and quiet, and bade them welcome, as if she were the hostess receiving a party of friends.

"You seek Mr. Fowler, I presume, gentlemen," she said, in a voice as calm as her outward aspect, "but he is not at home. He left this last night for the north of England: he is gone on business."

"Pretty business, too," shouted the crowd, while the officers proceeded to enter and search the house, not putting much faith in Mrs. Fowler's assertions. But all their searchings were in vain.

Fowler having truly, as his wife had said, left Knoll on the first rumour of the discovery of his fraud.

Weeks passed, and while no tidings could be gained of the fugitive, things came hourly to light, which showed that from the time Fowler had settled at Knoll, and very probably long before, he had been carrying on a gigantic system of swindling, and many a household was reduced to utter penury and despair. His creditors, and they were many, seized on everything that could legally be called his, and anticipated a rich booty at Knoll. But when they attempted to take possession, Hortense claimed the land, the house, and everything it contained as hers, nor could they oust her from her position. The property was settled on her in such a way that it was impossible to dispossess her, and while many of her husband's victims were starving, she remained at Knoll surrounded by every luxury.

One alteration she made, and that was, to dismiss all her servants but a single old woman, and that to all appearance was the only sacrifice she intended to make to public opinion, and her name was soon as much execrated as that of her husband, but she seemed to trouble herself very little as to what people thought of her, and was never seen beyond the gates of Knoll.

Meanwhile, Fowler was supposed to have taken with him a large sum of money, and to have escaped to America; but one day the Torford world was once more put into a state of commotion by hearing that Fowler had been seen at Hull. This rumour was immediately followed up by action; but news in those days travelled slowly, and by the time the necessary authority to arrest him reached Hull, Fowler was beyond the reach of the law. He had been in Hull, it was reported, lodging in a low part of the town, and there he had died, and the landlady gave his clothes, some money, and a few papers up to those who sought him, which were all identified as having belonged to him, but he had been dead many days, and his body interred in the common grave of one of the large parishes, and all attempts at identification proved fruitless.

Not long after this, Mrs. Fowler suddenly dismissed the one servant she had retained, and from that day forward all the previsions required at Knoll were brought to Mrs. Fowler by a farm-servant, who lived at the lodge, and no human being ever passed the threshold of Knoll House.

People naturally thought all this mysterious, but strive as they would, they gained no enlightenment on the subject.

The old woman at the farm could tell them nothing; she knew nothing, she heard nothing. Her mistress, she said, unlocked the door, took the provisions, and locked the door again. It was very little she spoke, but she looked very sad and solemn. There Hortense lived apparently in solitude. The gates and doors of Knoll were closed against all comers, the road approaching the house became grass-grown, and the house itself, in the eyes of passers-by, had an uncomfortable look.

CHAPTER XXVI

HORTENSE IN SORROW

TWO years had passed by since Hortense had been seen or spoken to by any one in the neighbourhood, when, one morning, to the astonishment of the villagers of Knoll, they saw her walking with hurried steps down the street, and enter the parsonage garden.

The clergyman was as surprised to see her as his parishioners had been; and, as he looked at her, he shuddered, she was so strange and wild; and he noticed that her hair, which had been so black when he had last seen her, was as white as an old woman's.

"I have a confession to make," she said, hurriedly; "and you, as a priest, are bound to hear it. I have lived such a life of terror these past two years that I shall die if I do not speak."

"Calm yourself, my dear madam," replied the clergyman, in a kind voice. "You are trembling from head to foot."

"No wonder! no wonder!" exclaimed the unhappy woman. "Why I have not gone mad long ago, I know not! The dread of discovery! The shame I have felt at seeming to keep for my own advantage what did not of right belong to me! The curses of those poor robbed widows, those beggared children! Yet I am thankful now I have survived it all—lived to be free at last! Free!" she shrieked, "free! I am not mad, indeed I am not," she continued, as the clergyman looked at her suspiciously. "I will make reparation; I will give up everything; I will turn their cursings into blessings, as far as I am concerned; they shall know it was for no self-gratification that I kept possession of that accursed wealth!"

"You must absolve me," she continued, after a pause. "He

made me do it; and I dare not for my life disobey him, he would have killed me if I had not done his bidding. I never disobeyed my husband!"

"But Mr. Fowler has been dead more than two years. Why, if you intended to make reparation for some of his frauds, did you not make it sooner, and spare many an innocent soul two years of misery?"

Hortense laughed a wild, mocking laugh.

"Dead! William Fowler dead! This time yesterday, William Fowler was as strong and well as you are!"

The clergyman uttered an exclamation of surprise.

"Yes," she continued, "as well as you are! He was at Knoll, and I left him there."

Her listener was now fully persuaded she was insane, and thought that, having heard of the spectre, she, too, had fancied she had seen it.

"This is a delusion, my dear madam," he replied, "that you must strive to overcome."

"Delusion! Is it a delusion to have a man walking about the house all day, and sitting at the same fireside with you for two whole years?—a man whom the world supposed to be mouldering in his grave?—a man whom, if they had known him to be alive, they would have seized and hung, for having robbed, and cheated, and forged! Is it a delusion that I have undergone these two whole years, dreading every hour that the truth might be discovered; and that the supposed dead man might be dragged from his hiding-place by those he had wronged, and who hated him enough to tear him to pieces, before even justice could reach him? You doubt me still. Will you come to Knoll and see all that remains of William Fowler? It lies there on his own hearth-stone, where he bade me bury him. But I am free now, and will do his bidding no longer!"

"I will come with you, and we will call and ask the doctor to go with us," replied the clergyman, whom none of Hortense's assurances at all convinced of the truth of her story, but more than ever confirmed him in the idea of her insanity.

How desolate and uncared-for did the once trim approach to Knoll now look! The road, mossy and untrodden; the gardens choked with weeds, the creepers hanging neglected from the trellis; and the atmosphere of the house itself so damp and close! how different to what it used to be in those gay days, when the successful merchant entertained his friends with all that was costly and luxurious.

"He is there," she said, pointing to what had been their private sitting-room. "Don't you go if you are afraid of horrid sights; let the doctor go, he is more used to such things." But the two, little dreaming what was in store for them, went in together.

There, on the hearthstone, as Hortense had said, lay William Fowler, his hand still clasping the pistol with which he had destroyed his own life.

It is not difficult to imagine the astonishment of every one at this discovery, and the rage of those who found they had been outwitted. Hortense's part in the business soon came to light; for, her husband dead, and the power which he had so long exercised over her removed, she unhesitatingly told everything she knew relative to his affairs, and produced many missing papers and deeds, by which property supposed to have been lost for ever was restored to its owners.

She told how he had managed to conceal himself for some time at Hull while waiting for a chance of escape; how he discovered that he was recognized, and managed to exchange clothes with a dying stranger; who, from wearing linen marked with Fowler's name, caused the mistake about his death, whilst the delay in arresting him favoured the deception. After his escape from Hull, he wandered about till the money he had taken with him was well nigh spent, and then he ventured back to his old quarters. Hortense, who had never believed the rumour of his death, was by no means surprised to see him again, knowing that it was his intention to return there, should he fail in his intention of leaving England; and the power he had always exercised over her assured him that he was safe from betrayal.

It was in consequence of his return that she had dismissed her maid, and she had lived alone with him in one constant agony of apprehension, lest he should be discovered and brought to justice. The shifts she had been put to, to procure sufficient food without exciting suspicion, and the torments she endured from his excited and morose mind, were almost too much for her. His once beautiful home had been his gaol, and at last, in a fit of despair and horror at his condition, he had died by his own hand.

Hortense fulfilled what she had promised on the morning of her husband's death; no sooner was he buried—not in the place he had ordered her, in a vault under the hearthstone, on which he was found dead, and which, it was discovered, he had used as a place of concealment for any papers that might have led to his conviction, had they chanced to fall into other hands, but in the churchyard at Knoll—than she gave up everything of which she was possessed in right of William Fowler, retaining only a legacy to earn her daily bread.

It might at first be thought that Hortense had a resource in her sisters-in-law, and that, mindful of their promise in old days, they would have given her a home. But in truth, they were almost as much shocked as the rest of the world at the revelations about their brother, and were unwilling to be mixed up with him in any way. Moreover, as a sort of palliative for their brother, when talking about him to their husbands, and in the circle of their friends, they remarked, as a very odd coincidence, that all these infamous schemes for making money and cheating his fellow-men had been entered upon since his marriage with Hortense. When once the idea had been started, it speedily grew into absolute conviction, and poor Hortense, the plotting foreign wife, was made responsible for William Fowler's wickedness. She had been educated in these contrivances, had brought them with her from the Continent, and had suggested them to her husband. She was the inventor of them, and poor William had weakly yielded to her devices. The world in general knew otherwise; but the family (near relations do these things) persuaded itself that he was unfortunate rather than culpable. Hortense, therefore, had little chance of sympathy from her sisters, and was again obliged to sustain herself as she could.

CHAPTER XXVII
ADVANCEMENT

OCCUPIED as Grace was with her boy, and the little duties and interests that sprang up around her, there were times when she chafed against the long separation from her husband, and sometimes, in her passionate longing to see him, she felt as if she must fly away, leave all, and go into the world to seek him, if but to have one look. Many and many an hour did she sit on the rock, watching the Plymouth road, the way by which he had left Stoke, and thinking, "Will he ever come back?"

He came at last. She was at her usual post when her longing eyes caught sight of the well-known figure coming briskly towards her. With something of her old impetuosity and swiftness, she ran down the hill to meet him, and then sped away like a deer to the cottage.

"My boy, Reginald! mother Agnes! where are you all? My boy, where is he?"

But with all her energy she did not succeed in unearthing her torment, as she called him, till Edward stood at the garden gate.

"There," said Grace, pushing the boy towards his father—"there!"

"My own dear child!" was all the delighted man could say; but he folded the little fellow so lovingly in his arms, and looked so tenderly on the noble face turned inquiringly up to his, that Grace was fain to run indoors, and hide her tears of joy.

"Captain Daddy said you would love me and be proud of me," said the boy, nestling against his father, "for I know you are my father, and I'm so glad you are an officer like him; but where's your sword—I want to see your sword—and your cocked hat? Shall you wear your sword and cocked hat on Sunday, to frighten the boys, as Captain Daddy does?"

"I shall see how the boys behave first," answered Mountjoy, smiling; "but I must go and find mamma and grandma now, and we'll have a chat about those matters another time."

How much those two had to tell each other, and how many questions the enchanted mother Agnes had to ask! It seemed as if neither party ever could come to the end of all the news they had to impart, and often they sat in silence, as Tye said, "from really not knowing which end to begin at."

"There's one thing I can tell you, Grace, that Captain Douglas is one of the kindest and most disinterested of men. He is always saying a good word for me here, or recommending me to notice there; and between him and Lord —— I really am rising rapidly. It seems there is more in me than I ever thought, at least these kind friends say so. My old fancy for drawing is declared invaluable, and a smattering of languages is another thing that is of great service, and my powers of calculating are brought to use. And so you see, they say I am to get on in my profession, and my wife will be so conceited there will be no doing anything with her."

"I won't be prouder of you than you deserve," rejoined Tye; "but I always knew you would get on."

"Many a thing that comes of use to me now, Tye, I learned out of the books the vicar lent me years ago, when I was a boy in Carden harbour. I do believe that both he and Frank would be pleased to hear how I am succeeding; but we will never breathe a word of our existence till, to use an expression of Frank's, we are on the topmost round of the ladder."

"You ambitious creature!" laughed Grace.

"Who made me ambitious, madam? Why, no one but your

ambitious self. But here comes Captain, or I believe I may say Admiral Douglas, for he is to be promoted!"

"A pretty way to bring up children!" he exclaimed, in his would-be ferocious tone, which Tye had learned to disregard. "A hopeful young pirate, that son of yours, madam! What do you suppose is his last piece of impudence? Mrs. Douglas called him in from the lawn, where he was playing, to give him a bit of cake, and she said, in her quiet way, 'Reginald, the captain is made a rear-admiral, ain't you glad?' He knew from her voice he was expected to say 'yes,' so he said it, and then he and the cake disappeared out of the window. But now comes the villany of the thing. In a few minutes—when I suppose he had finished the cake—I heard a most awful row, evidently my lord imitating a snorting, whinnying horse: so I just stepped out to see what the noise was all about, when the young villain galloped up to me, mounted on a long pea-stick, and cried, 'Get out of the way! take care of yourself, my man! I'm riding Captain Daddy; and he's so vicious—he's a rearing animal;' and with that he tossed his head, and lifted his stick-horse up in front, and then flung up its tail behind, to make believe it was rearing and kicking; and then round the lawn he went, shouting at the top of his voice, 'I'm riding Captain Daddy, and he's a rearing animal!' and if you will believe me, there was Mrs. Douglas at the window in an actual fit of laughing! There, my good sir, you see the sort of education your lady gives your son in your absence!" And the good man, who in truth had invented part at any rate of his tirade, to hide in a sort of way the pleasure he felt at his promotion, flung himself into a chair, rubbed his bald head till it shone again, and then laid his handkerchief over it to keep off the flies.

Truly and heartily did they congratulate the friend to whom they owed so much, and to whom, as they afterwards found, they were to owe still more; and for many days the village was in an unwonted state of rejoicing. Mrs. Douglas hoisted her flag on the church tower, Mrs. Bolton had the bells rung, and the new admiral insisted on having a feast for all the poor people in the parish, while Mrs. Douglas entertained all the world and his wife.

But in this world partings soon follow on meetings, and the time drew near when both Admiral Douglas and Edward, who, to his great delight, was appointed to the same ship, must once more try their fortunes on the wide seas. Often during his stay at home, Edward had spoken of the vessel he had abandoned, and which in return seemed to have abandoned him. No tidings had he ever received of either crew or ship, and several times he had expressed fears to Grace, that some evil had overtaken her or Bellamy, as he could not otherwise explain his never having received tidings of them.

One evening, however, only a few nights before he was to leave, the mystery was solved. The husband and wife were sitting in the pretty honeysuckle porch, when, in the dusk, they saw a man pass and repass their gate. His movements attracted their attention, and at last Edward went to the gate and inquired if he was seeking any one.

"I am seeking you," replied the stranger, "for by your voice I know you are Captain Mountjoy, whatever they call you now."

"Bellamy! Is it possible that at last you are come back!" exclaimed Mountjoy, overpowered at the sudden appearance of his old messmate. "Come inside, man—come in and tell us your story! See, here is my wife, all strong and well; and yourself, man, how have you fared?"

"Bad enough, captain, or you'd have seen me many a year ago. Well for you the lady was too ill to go, you and she have been spared a time of misery. I've heard lately of your good fortune, and it rejoiced me more than I can well tell you, and I've thought many a time that the lady's accident was a bit of providence to keep you from harm."

"And the vessel?"

"Lost to us within a few months of your parting from her. We were taken prisoners, by as blackhearted a villain of a pirate as ever sailed the seas, and he made us serve with his crew, and help them in their wickedness. They were slavers, captain—men-stealers. Oh! the horrors I have seen! enough to chill one's blood, and make one's heart cease beating. 'Tis a long story, captain, and one I don't care to think about; but I escaped at last, and came into this country to try and find you out; but I have been obliged to be cautious, for fear of being pressed before I found you. I was so afraid you would think I hadn't acted honestly about the ship—that I hadn't kept my word: and the thought that you should doubt me, and think evil of me, hurt me cruel, sure enough. Now I've seen you and told you, I don't care how soon I go to sea, for I have no one to care for, or any one that cares for me."

"That's not quite the fact, old friend," replied Edward, kindly. "If you choose, you can get a berth in my ship, and we shall once more sail together."

"And you wouldn't mind my coming It wouldn't make you vexed to have me near you?"

"Most certainly not! I can say with truth of you, that we sailed together for years, and I never knew you tell a lie or break your word; and I'll tell you what, Bellamy, that's a character a duke might be proud of, and I'm proud to call any honest man my friend."

In the few days that Bellamy remained at Stoke he got regularly adopted into the little community, as if he had been known for years. It is a certain fact that the better and purer people are, the less they suspect others, and every one seemed to take Bellamy's sudden appearance and friendship for Mountjoy as a perfectly natural matter, in which there was nothing mysterious, and with which they had nothing to do.

Everybody tried to be very brave when the hour of parting came, but every one failed signally. Poor little Reginald was wild with grief at the loss of his father, for whom a most devoted love had been awakened during the happy weeks he had been at Stoke; and in the confusion and bustle that succeeded the departure of the admiral and his companions, the young gentleman managed to make his escape, and get a mile or two on the Plymouth road before he was recaptured. When questioned as to what had been his intentions, he assured every one that he was going to join his ship, the admiral having promised to make him first lieutenant, a name which, for many months after, he sturdily refused to give up; but at last settled back into his old position as "the young pirate."

Mrs. Douglas and Grace resumed again their quiet lives, counting the months that must elapse before they could see their husbands again;—listening to the wind when it came rushing up the glen, or sighing over the moor, and fancying every blast must reach those they loved. The war and the many dangers to which they were exposed, kept the absent ones constantly in their thoughts, and the common interest they both had, drew them nearer and nearer together, till they were sisters in all but name;—the kind old clergyman and his wife watching over them as if they had been their daughters.

Edward succeeded; year by year he made some step, some progress, till Grace declared she grew quite giddy at his elevation, and hardly knew how to make enough of him during his flying visits; while he, every time, as it were, he re-made her acquaintance, thanked heaven more and more for having given him so good and true a wife. Her second boy, Douglas, almost rivalled his elder brother in the affection of Mrs. Douglas, but "the young pirate" never lost his hold on the affections of "Captain Daddy," or of his father; whose greatest delight was, on his return, to fold the noble fellow in his arms, and say in his quiet, loving way, "My own dear boy!" that was his name for him, let others call him what they might, and his mother, noticing it, adopted the same name.

And now we must turn away to some others whom we knew, and Grace knew, in the old days, and see how they are all faring in the world.

CHAPTER XXVIII

MR. ERLINGHAM

THE lives of those of our actors who are left on the stage, go on, to all appearance, smoothly enough; at any rate, there are no startling incidents to relate. One at least is preposterous—more than preposterous—triumphant. He has reached his goal. The object his father had set before him as a little child—the object he had set before himself as a man—the object he had lied, forged, ay, murdered for, was obtained; and Richard Erlingham was one of the richest commoners in England.

Yet what did that avail him? The gold and silver that covered his table were no more pleasure to him than so much brass and lead. The costly viands were but ashes in his mouth. He had destroyed the power of enjoying wealth by the means he had taken to amass it. It was not exactly that he was afraid of detection; for he believed that he had acted too cautiously to arouse suspicion, even in those he had used as his tools in some of his worst transactions; but his conscience he could by no means quiet—there ever rose before him the memory of his evil deeds. His house was magnificent, his furniture superb, his equipage the handsomest that could be obtained; but he purchased all these things, not for any pleasure they gave him individually, but from the paltry motive of outshining others. His rooms were decorated with costly statues and pictures, which he had no taste to admire—his bookshelves were filled with rare and wise books he did not care to open. He spent hours wandering about his house examining his possessions, and his greatest pleasure was to gratify some want.

His beautiful wife was but one of his possessions. His fancy for her had subsided into cold indifference; and, but that she added to his importance by her beauty and her cleverness, he would in all probability have rid himself of her by some means.

She had besides some claim on his consideration on account of her wealth, which almost equalled his own; and her father, who lived with her, protected her from any slight or impertinence to which she might otherwise have been subjected.

Mary Horton's marriage had not proved happy. She and her husband never actually quarrelled, never disputed; but by degrees, though they inhabited the same house, no two people could have been more widely separated.

They had no interest in common; she had her pursuits, in which her father joined her, and he his employments, in which she had no share.

No little child came to be a link between them; and, finding soon after her marriage that she had made a great and irremediable mistake in the greatest event of a woman's life, she first felt coolly towards her husband, till at last a strong feeling of dislike and repugnance arose.

What had induced her in the first place to marry him was a mystery, but one which is often seen—a woman marrying a man decidedly her inferior in everything. She could not help feeling ashamed of him in those circles she and Mr. Horton most frequented; and every low-bred action, or exhibition of false taste, was like a dagger to the refined wife. But the world passed unheeded many a gaucherie that tortured Mary, for Richard Erlingham's wealth gilded all his actions and words. So much for Mr. Erlingham: he was, what the world calls, a successful man.

All this time Reginald is an outlaw; Hortense Fowler pursues her course at Torford; and Frank Dawson is a hard-working, rising man.

Mr. Erlingham's sense of security was, however, soon to be shaken.

CHAPTER XXIX
AN UNWELCOME VISITOR

CAPTAIN Tunny was not at this time in the best of circumstances. What he undertook had generally failed, and as time passed on he found himself extremely short of money. He had earned for himself so bad a name that owners of vessels hesitated to employ him; and it was only by doing odd jobs, of a rather questionable description, for such of his companions as had not utterly cast him off, that he managed to earn a scanty subsistence.

Oftentimes he thought of Erlingham, and the large fortune he now enjoyed; but, until driven by necessity, Captain Tunny did not care to bring himself under the notice of a man who, he knew, was not to be trusted, but was capable of any villany to rid himself of those who stood in his way.

At last a series of misfortunes and losses emboldened him, and he presented himself at the door of the rich man's house.

He had not much difficulty in gaining admission, though his appearance said but little in his favour, for the servants were accustomed to admit quite as questionable-looking personages to interviews, "on business," with their master.

It was some little time before Mr. Erlingham recognized his visitor, and when he did, his welcome was not very cordial, for he did not see at that moment what use Tunny could be to him.

Mr. Erlingham was considerably aged since we saw him last, and his hair as white as snow. He looked about him cautiously and spoke deliberately; yet strange to say, there was a quietness and repose about his manners which had been quite absent when a younger man. He had sinned on with impunity, and fancied himself secure in his triumph.

Tunny's appearance was displeasing to him; it brought back to his memory the fact of his cousin's existence, and also the fact that his cousin's son had entirely eluded his stratagems. He was well informed of the disappearance of both Agnes and Edward; but his satisfaction would have been more complete could he have been certain that neither survived. The thought would often occur to him—suppose they were to make their appearance? Yet what have I to fear?—the will is all right.

When he saw Tunny he was startled. Had he come to tell him any news of those he had so deeply injured, or was it to ask some mere trifling favour? Tunny soon set all doubt aside.

"Well, Mr. Erlingham, a nice house you have got, and plenty of servants, as it seems; no doubt plenty of money—you are a lucky man, sir."

His host, not knowing what to answer, merely bowed his head.

"Well, Mr. Erlingham, I've been unlucky; people call me a villain; do people ever call you that name, eh, sir?—but no! lucky people are seldom called villains; it's only those that fail who get their real names given them."

"Really, sir," said Mr. Erlingham, rising, and laying his hand on the bell——

"Hold hard! If *you* please," said Tunny, leaving the easy chair into which he had thrown himself on first entering the room. "I'm come here to have a chat with you on business, and you must hear me out."

"I cannot stand your insolent intrusion," replied Mr. Erlingham, haughtily. "I must insist that you leave my house immediately!"

"When I have finished my business, and not before," answered the sailor, reseating himself. "It will be best for you, Mr. Erlingham, to be quiet, and let me have my say, without interrupting me."

"You shall smart for your impudence, depend upon it," cried Mr. Erlingham.

"And you too, sir," rejoined Tunny, with a malicious grin. "How came you by your wealth—your silver and your gold, your grand house, your carriages and your horses? By villany, Mr. Erlingham—villany of the deepest dye! Folks say I'm a villain, and so no doubt I am, but I never did the tithe of the wickedness that you have done. I wronged the fatherless and the widow once, to gain my liberty; but you have wronged them, year after year, for the sake of gain."

At first Mr. Erlingham felt alarmed at the vehemence with which the man spoke, but, regaining his self-assurance, he inquired, with a sneer,—

"And to what does all this tirade tend?"

"I don't know what tirade means," said Tunny, sulkily, stopped in the middle of his harangue; "but the long and short of it is, I want money, and it must be forthcoming without delay."

Mr. Erlingham's answer was a scornful laugh.

"Beware," said Tunny, "how you provoke me too far; you are in my power."

"You overrate the worth of your knowledge," was the answer. "True, I used you once for my own purposes; but there was nothing criminal in what I did: you can prove nothing against me."

Tunny hesitated a moment. Mr. Erlingham was right; it was sometimes difficult to prove the most undoubted offences; still Tunny was determined to get something out of his quondam ally, so he tried a different tack.

"Well, I think any gentleman wouldn't hesitate to assist a poor fellow who was the means of putting so much in his pocket, as I was, Mr. Erlingham, in that Mountjoy business."

"You betrayed your own friends for your own benefit, and can in no way claim recompense from me. Indeed, nothing shall induce me to assist you in any way, after the language you have thought fit to use towards me; and if you do not instantly leave the house, I shall give you in charge for attempting to extort money;" and again Mr. Erlingham laid his hand on the bell-rope.

"At your peril!" exclaimed Tunny, in a loud voice, exasperated at the threat. "Unless you pay me down a hundred pounds before I leave this room, by midday to-morrow the whole town shall ring with your misdeeds! I know more of you, and your doings, than you think for."

"Possibly," said Mr. Erlingham, coolly. "There are many little incidents in a man's life that he cannot remember; but I can afford to despise you and your threats."

"If you won't pay me for holding my tongue, there are those who will pay me for speaking; and your bold-faced assurance has so put me up, that, hang me! if you'd pay me a thousand pounds down this moment, I'd have my say out, and let all the world know which of us two is the bigger rogue."

"Turn that fellow out," cried Mr. Erlingham; "and never let him cross my door again," he added, pompously.

"Never fear me," replied Tunny. "I should be sorry to keep company with such as you. I shall go and tell my tale to Frank Dawson; and perhaps when you stand before the judge," going close up to him, "charged with murder, Mr. Erlingham—ay, murder, I say—perhaps you will be sorry you weren't a little more civil to an old assistant." And Tunny left the house, muttering to himself, as he walked along, "I'll go to the old parson's son: maybe he'll remember me, and people say he's marvellously clever. He shall hear every word of the whole story; and if I can't get money, why I'll just be revenged on that fellow, who has got so much more than his right. Ah, well! perhaps if I had let Mountjoy alone, and not driven him out of the country, I might have had a friend to help me now, for he was always a good-hearted lad; and after all, it wasn't him who told upon me."

As Tunny pursued his way, bent on finding Frank Dawson, who was now a barrister of some eminence, Mr. Erlingham paced up and down his room in no very happy state of mind. Tunny's last words had raised up a phantom he would willingly have buried in oblivion; and though he could not in any way imagine how Tunny could have gained such knowledge of the cause of his uncle's death, yet he was not able to assure himself that his threats were mere idle words, spoken in an excitement of passion. He knew the accusation was too frightfully true, to be able to quiet his conscience; but it would have affected him less, had not Tunny avowed his intention of telling his tale to Frank Dawson—a man he knew well by reputation, and who, he fancied, would be only too glad of any incident which might serve to bring him into notoriety, and display the great powers he was said to possess of collecting and sifting evidence.

CHAPTER XXX

FRANK DAWSON AND HIS CLIENT

IT was late in the evening ere Tunny, by dint of numberless inquiries, found out the residence of the rising lawyer.

The house presented a curious contrast to that of Erlingham. Situated in a dull street near Russell Square, its exterior was not of a very cheerful character; but as you crossed the threshold, you left the dreariness outside, for it was a cosy English home; and as Tunny was ushered into Frank Dawson's presence, a lady, with a pleasant, bright face, rose from the seat she had occupied by the fireside, and taking a little child, who was seated at the lawyer's feet, by the hand, left the room, casting, as she passed, a curious look at her husband's tough visitor.

Tunny did not feel so much at his ease in Frank Dawson's presence as he had done in Erlingham's, whose iniquities he felt had placed him on his own level, if not below him; but he knew enough of the man in whose house he now was, to feel that he was entirely his superior.

"I took the liberty of coming to you, sir, on a little business," said he, at last, in a hesitating voice, and without venturing to take a chair; "because I knew you and yours long ago, and people say you are very clever in your way, and I want you to make it all clear. But perhaps you don't remember me, sir?"

It was a gift Frank Dawson possessed, and which aided him greatly in his profession, that he never forgot a face once seen, or failed in giving the right name to a person with whom he had once conversed.

"Surely," he said, after a moment's pause, "you are the Captain

Tunny, who years ago commanded the coaster with the queer name—the *Loupa Laddie* or some such thing—down at Carden?"

"The same, sir. I've led a rough life, and a bad one, since then, Mr. Dawson, and been in many an ugly scrape; but I'm not to blame in the business I'm come to tell you about now: at least, not much: perhaps I ought to have spoken sooner."

Every moment in Frank Dawson's day was worth a grain of gold to him, but he made no attempt to hurry his unpromising-looking client, as many in his position would have done, but left him to tell his story in his own time and way, suspecting that it might prove some romance of sea life, which, if not profitable, might be interesting and exciting; and, next to a good brief, Dawson liked a good story.

"Well, Mr. Dawson, you see, it's about a murder," said Tunny, at last, nervously; as if he had great difficulty in pronouncing the word.

"Bah! man, murder!" exclaimed Frank Dawson, with disgust; "I'd rather you went to any one but me to tell your story; the last case I had of that kind, I declared I would never take another."

"Hear me out, sir," exclaimed Tunny, eagerly, "and then you can decide. I only want you to tell me how I am to set to work, to bring the murderer to justice. You see he is a rich man, and people wouldn't believe me, likely enough; but if you took the matter up, folks would listen."

"Possibly; but I have no wish to be made an instrument of revenge, and it strikes me that that is your motive in revealing this murder. When did it take place?"

"Many years ago. You remember young Mountjoy, who used to sail with me?"

"Edward Mountjoy! to be sure! Poor fellow, I wonder what

has become of him; we were great friends once; and poor Grace too—dear me, how time flies, and how people are forgotten!"

Suddenly, Frank Dawson sprang up, and laying his hand heavily on Tunny's shoulder, demanded, in a husky voice, if it was Grace's murder he came to tell him of.

"I know nothing of how Miss Dawson came by her end," replied Tunny. "I may have my suspicions, but I know nothing."

Frank Dawson relaxed his grasp, and sank back in his chair. "I would give a great deal," he muttered to himself, "to know what became if her: I owe her everything I possess. I have always had a hope that in some way she escaped with Mountjoy. Have you ever seen him since then?"

"Never; maybe the hand that did for his grandfather may have overtaken him too; if it has, it's my fault, for I betrayed him. But it is not of them I want to speak," said the man, before Mr. Dawson had time to interrupt him. "It's about Mountjoy's grandfather, who, to my certain knowledge, came to his death by unfair means."

"That must be going back a good many years, is it not?" asked the lawyer.

"Not so many as you might fancy," rejoined Tunny; "and the murderer is a man you know well, by name Mr. Richard Erlingham."

"What on earth can he have to do with Mountjoy, or anyone belonging to him?"

"He is nearly related to them; and the large fortune he managed to get hold of, belonged of right to Edward Mountjoy. I say, sir, that Richard Erlingham murdered his uncle to obtain his wealth.

"Have you any proof?"

"None but my bare word."

"And has Mr. Erlingham any reason to suppose that you suspect him?"

"None, beyond what I told him myself this very day."

"You have seen him, then?"

"Yes; I was short of money, and I thought maybe he'd give me some, for years ago I did him a good turn; but he has grown proud, and now he may suffer for it."

There was something in the sailor's manner which, in spite of the vagueness and improbability of Tunny's accusation, impressed the lawyer with the idea that there must be some foundation for the story, and he proceeded to cross-examine Tunny till he had drawn from him a history of his previous connection with Erlingham; how years before he had known him as a lad in the West Indies; how he had known Agnes Mountjoy at Combe; how he had persuaded Edward to join his vessel against her earnest wish; and how in after years, believing that Mountjoy had informed against him, and been the cause of his incarceration, he had betrayed his existence, and his mother's place of retreat to Erlingham, to gain his assistance in getting free.

He told, too, how it chanced when the elder Mr. Erlingham unexpectedly arrived in England, and was seized with his last illness, the woman selected to wait on him by Erlingham was none other than Tunny's own wife, from whom he had been separated for some years, and of whose antecedents Mr. Erlingham knew nothing.

At that time he happened to be in trouble, and could think of no more secure hiding-place than the lone villa at Chelsea. There he had seen Richard Erlingham come to visit the old man; he described minutely the state of bondage in which he was kept; his frightful sufferings; and finally, his having seen Mr. Erlingham tampering with the sugar which a few moments afterwards he handed to his uncle.

"And why did you not make an effort to save the old man?"

inquired Frank Dawson, sternly, as his visitor finished his narration, to which he had listened with breathless attention, every moment more fully convinced that Tunny spoke the truth.

"The devil held me back: I wanted to get a hold of Erlingham."

"Yet you took no steps to denounce him."

"I was afraid. When the deed was done, I thought, if it comes to light, and it gets known I was in the house at the time, they will suspect me; and he is so clever, he would have managed to throw the suspicion on me; so I set off as quick as may be, and I have never been near the place since, nor near my wife, who I fancy must have known something of what was going on."

"You must be cautious," said the lawyer; "you have been too minute in your descriptions: the account you give of all the circumstances of the case are too clear for me to pass it over in silence; still you must wait awhile; and if we can possibly gain any clue to the whereabouts of Mrs. Mountjoy and her son, it would be of great importance in the matter; but even there we must proceed cautiously, for Mr. Erlingham's suspicion must not be roused until we have further proof than we at present possess;" and desiring Tunny to give him an address where he might find him, he dismissed him for the present, promising to let him know when he thought it advisable to move in the business.

"I never will believe she was killed," said the lawyer to himself, when he was once more alone. "How strange if after all I should find her! and if what this fellow says is true, and Mountjoy is heir to this wealth, I may be able in a measure to repay her old girlish kindness to me: I believe fully if we can find Mountjoy, Grace will not be far distant."

"Has that man been telling you anything about your cousin?" asked the lawyer's wife, who had glided back into the room when

Tunny had taken his departure, and who had overheard her husband's speech to himself.

"Not exactly; but he has told me a strange tale, Margaret, and one which, unless I am mistaken, will cause no little stir if it should all come to light; but it's a difficult business—very, and so complicated—very;" and finishing with this expression, for which he was often quizzed by his brother barristers, he took up his pen and went on with his work; and she placing herself near him, so that he could put out his hand to her every now and then to assure her than she was not quite forgotten in all his labours, took up her needle and went on with her sewing.

CHAPTER XXI
THE GALA NIGHT

IT is gala night at Lord A——'s. All the world is there; it is one of a series of entertainments he is giving to all his friends and acquaintances, in celebration of the peace, and —— House is full to overflowing. Princes and dukes, generals and great naval commanders, are there, all in full uniform, brilliant with orders. Women in rich attire, sparkling with jewels. The magnificent suite of apartments glitter with gilding, and are radiant with thousands of wax-lights and glistening chandeliers. Some of the greatest men the earth has ever seen were there—men whose names are written in the pages of history; and many were there who eagerly sought to catch a glimpse of those great ones with whose exploits Europe had rung for years.

Mr. Horton and his daughter, Mrs. Erlingham, were there; and, contrary to his usual custom, Mr. Erlingham had accompanied them. Since Tunny's visit he had been restless and anxious, and he eagerly seized on anything to distract his mind from the unpleasant remembrances that seemed to rise up around him like ghosts.

Frank Dawson and his wife were there too; he had taken advantage of the *entrée* he possessed to A——'s house to show her some of those she knew well by name. It was seldom that she left her quiet fireside; but this was a special occasion.

No sooner did Frank Dawson discover the Erlinghams, whom he knew only by sight, than he managed unperceived to get into their immediate neighbourhood; not a movement or word of Mr. Erlingham was lost to the acute lawyer, though constantly plied with questions by his inquisitive wife.

Suddenly there was a hush, and every one fell back to make a passage for the royal party, who were the lions of the evening, with their numerous suite.

In a quiet corner, just behind the place where Dawson and his wife had taken their stand, sat two ladies, whose quiet but elegant dress attracted little attention. As the royal party approached where they were sitting, they rose and joined the eager lookers-on, Frank Dawson making room for the younger lady of the two, who appeared a little lame—a courtesy which she acknowledged by a graceful bend of the head, without, however, moving her eyes from the approaching group.

The two ladies bent eagerly forward, but their attention seemed more directed to the suite than to the principal personages.

"There they are," said the elder lady; and as she spoke, Lord —— with a younger man at his side, passed close by and recognized the two ladies, with a bright smile; his companion also, one sleeve of whose coat hung empty at his side, nodded familiarly to one of the ladies.

"What a handsome man! Who is he, walking by Lord ——'s side? He has lost his arm—do find out who he is!" echoed on all sides.

The person who attracted so much attention was certainly a very striking-looking person, apparently still on the sunny side of forty. He wore a full-dress naval suit, and was decorated with more than one riband. Perhaps the bright, cheery glance he had given to the two simply dressed ladies might have had something to do with the attention bestowed on him at this point, for no one seemed to know who he was, so that there was no special reason for his being more noticed than many others by whom he was surrounded.

But the stranger's face had a curious attraction to Frank Dawson, he could not take his eyes off him.

"What is the matter? Whom are you looking at so eagerly?" inquired his wife. "My arm will be black and blue, you have pressed it so."

"If ever I saw Edward Mountjoy in this world I've seen him to-night," replied Dawson, in an excited tone. "Margey, girl, go and sit quietly in that corner till I come back; I must go and find out without delay who the handsome man with one arm may be;" and Dawson took his way through the crowd towards the inner apartments, but without remarking the effect his words had produced on one at least of the ladies who had been standing beside him.

Frank Dawson was well known to many who were sauntering about, and people readily made way for him, as with more energy and activity than is commonly displayed in such scenes, he searched about for some one to give him the information he desired.

At length he stumbled on the very person to satisfy his curiosity, a little man, whose sole business in life seemed to be knowing who everybody was. He was a walking peerage, and knew every one who was to be known, at least, by sight and reputation; and could tell the degrees of relationship in which "every one" stood to one another.

Mr. Ricks was a short stout man with a very bald shiny head, twinkling black eyes, and a queer hesitating way of speaking, so that half what he said was usually lost to his hearers. Frank Dawson generally avoided him, but just at this moment he haled him cordially, to the little man's intense delight, as it would enable him to say, "What my friend Dawson said to me at Lord A——'s," for the next month to come.

"Ricks," said the lawyer, eagerly, "who is that handsome

fellow with the one arm there, talking to the Duke of ——?"

"Oh! my dear fellow, don't you know? Why that's the man who so distinguished himself in America, took twenty ships in half-an-hour, and would have taken the President prisoner, only, you see, there wasn't time, because there was to be a ball somewhere, at the palace, I suppose; but I'm not sure."

"But his name?" inquired Dawson, with a smile, at Mr. Ricks's mistake, who never by any chance was correct in any of his information, unless it related to names.

"Erlingham, Captain Erlingham, K. C. B., Sir Edward Erlingham, I should have said," replied the little man pompously; "not that he's gazetted yet, but in a day or two that will be his title."

"It is a most curious coincidence," said Dawson. "Do you know anything more about him?"

"Nothing, only that he is a great favourite at the admiralty, and with Lord L——. By-the-by, do you think he can be any relative to the rich Mr. Erlingham, who lives more like a prince than a subject?"

"Can't say," replied Dawson, evasively; and he hastily left Mr. Ricks's side, having obtained all the information he wanted.

He turned on one side, and watched Captain Erlingham for awhile with eager interest. He had not forgotten the first time they had met, for he never for a moment doubted that the Edward Mountjoy of former days was the admired Captain Erlingham of that night, thought fit company for princes and peers. He thought of the sailor lad in Carden Harbour, he thought of his beautiful cousin Grace; and he said "To-morrow I will solve this mystery."

Suddenly he remembered that he had left his good wife Margey to shift for herself, in a scene she was little accustomed to, and with sundry misgivings of conscience, he hastened to rejoin her;

but he had not gone many steps, before a heavy hand was laid on his shoulder, and turning round he found himself face to face with Captain Erlingham.

"Surely I am not wrong in addressing you as Frank Dawson," said he in a pleasant open tone, extending his one hand to the lawyer.

"Nor I in believing you to be Edward Mountjoy," said Dawson, by way of answer.

"Right," replied the other; "but I have been called by my mother's name so many years, that my old name seems strange to me. But if you can spare the time, come to me to-morrow and I will introduce you to my wife; she is an old acquaintance of yours," and with another hearty shake of the hand, Captain Erlingham rejoined the illustrious party to which he was attached.

"O Frank! where have you been all this time?" exclaimed the tired Margey, as her husband once more rejoined her; "and I have wanted you so, something so very, very odd has happened. Those two ladies who were seated here when the prince came in, do you know, Frank, they knew you by name; but that perhaps," continued the little woman, proudly, "was not so strange; but I heard the younger one say you were her cousin; and Frank, she is so handsome, more beautiful than any one I ever saw, something like you."

"I know I'm very handsome in your eyes," said Dawson, laughing; "but where is this beautiful lady now?"

"She passed on with her companion; but I haven't told you all, Frank. Mr. Horton, and his daughter, Mrs. Erlingham, were standing near—you know I know them by sight—and they both exclaimed at once, 'What a wonderful likeness that lady bears to poor Grace Dawson!' Now, Frank, do tell me who can this lady be who says that you are her cousin, and who these people say, is so like your cousin Grace."

"Time will show, Margey; the plot thickens. Unless I'm mistaken, to-morrow you and I shall unravel the mystery; and now having shown you all the great people, and come across a decided adventure, I think you and I will betake ourselves to our own unfashionable home."

CHAPTER XXXII
CONSCIENCE

IN spite of all that there was to interest any one who wished to be interested and enjoy themselves at Lord A——'s, Mr. Erlingham was ill at ease, and found little to amuse him. He could not get away from himself, and the gay groups passed before him like phantoms in a dream, while his thoughts were occupied by deeds of bygone years, and the threatening face of Captain Tunny seemed ever before his eyes. A feeling of oppression and apprehension weighed him down, and a presentiment of coming evil made him fearful of being alone, and drove him to be more with his wife and her father than was his wont. In general he left them to go into society by themselves; but, as we have said, he thought proper to accompany them to Lord A——'s.

He was standing with them when the royal party passed, and heard his wife's exclamation of surprise at the likeness of the mysterious stranger to Grace Dawson.

The name went through him like a dagger. It was so strange; only a day or two before Tunny had sprung up as if from the dead, and now to hear Grace Dawson's name after so many years of silence, seemed to him as if more trouble was near. He staggered back to a seat, and tried to shut out the ghost his own troubled conscience had raised; for even if it were Grace Dawson, what harm could she do him?

"Suppose Mountjoy were to make his appearance," he muttered to himself. "But what nonsense it is being downcast; I can't think what is come to me; people will observe me if I don't take care;" and with a violent effort of self-control he once more joined in the gazing throng.

Mr. Ricks was by no means satisfied with the scanty information he gained from the lawyer, as to Captain Erlingham's relations, and he went buzzing about the rooms, and lighting now on one, now on another of his acquaintance, in hopes of finding some one to clear up the mystery. As fate willed, he after many ineffectual attempts, stumbled on the person best able to inform him, if he were so minded; none other than Mr. Erlingham himself.

Mr. Erlingham saw the little man approaching, and tried to avoid him, for he had on more than one occasion been sorely tried by his cross-examinations; but Mr. Ricks was too much in earnest to be balked of his desired gossip, and in spite of Mr. Erlingham's forbidding manner, he greeted him as if he were his dearest friend.

"My dear fellow," said Mr. Ricks, familiarly, "how are you this evening? enchanted to see you; glad you sometimes break through your rules, and join the gay world; 'tis a duty one owes to society, indeed it is, so much useful information to be gained. By-the-by, can you tell me anything of your namesake who passed up just now in the Prince's suite? Captain Erlingham, you know, who has distinguished himself so much? He is to be made a K. C. B. at once, and no doubt he'll get a baronetage, perhaps a peerage, if he goes on at this rate. What relation is he to you?"

"I have no relations of the name of Erlingham," replied Mr. Erlingham, snappishly.

"Are you quite sure?" insisted Mr. Ricks; "you see it is an uncommon name, and people say he is a West Indian like yourself; and some add—but this is quite between ourselves—that it is his mother's name which he has assumed; I overheard that by accident last night. Does that throw any light on the matter?"

Had a thunderbolt fallen at Mr. Erlingham's feet, it could not have affected him more than this apparently harmless speech. He had never to this moment thought it probable or possible that Edward Mountjoy, whom he only knew or thought of as a common sailor, could by any succession of events find himself in a position to associate with the greatest in the land; but he felt at once overwhelmed with a conviction that this distinguished officer was none other than his wronged cousin.

In an instant too, he felt that it was Grace Dawson and none other, that his wife had seen; and coupling this unexpected and unwelcome apparition with Tunny's visit, he felt how close he stood on the very edge of a volcano, ready at any moment to vomit forth its flames and devour him.

Suppose the sailor had fulfilled his threat, and told his story to Frank Dawson? He was lost—utterly hopelessly lost!

"My dear sir," said poor Mr. Ricks in great trouble, at getting no answer to his queries, "do pray tell me who this gentleman is; it is of great importance to me to know. Lady Montague charged me not to come near her till I had found out, and Mrs. Howard wished to know if he was married; she was really quite taken with him. But the handsome widow must find some other cavalier, for Captain Erlingham is married to one of the most beautiful women I ever saw; I know her Christian name, it is Grace, or Gratiana, I overheard that too; but I must discover her maiden name, it's of the greatest importance. But goodness me, Mr. Erlingham, what is the matter?—how deadly pale you look, and how you shake!—dear me, dear me, what shall I do?" and the little man flitted about in the greatest trouble.

"I tell you I know nothing of this man," said Erlingham, in a hoarse whisper; "begone, I want none of your gossip!"

Mr. Ricks needed no second bidding; he got out of Mr. Erlingham's way as quickly as possible, muttering to himself, "What shall I do? and Lady Montague told me to be sure and find out."

Poor little man, he needed not have troubled himself, he had enough to tell Lady Montague before many days were over.

Mr. Erlingham lost all control over himself, and, hastily leaving the gay apartments, rushed down the wide stairs, and through the great hall out into the street, pushing against ladies in his headlong course, and only escaping being stopped by astonished servants, through the quickness of his movements.

He rushed on along the streets at the same headlong pace, till the cool night air calmed him in a measure, and he began to consider whither he was wandering.

Anywhere, away from self,—but that was impossible. So he walked on, now gazing upward at the countless myriads of stars that looked down on him, as if they knew his deeds, and in their calm quietness rebuked him—now staring into the darkness, and seeing mocking demons, beckoning to him and deriding him.

He wandered about all that night. He went as far as Chelsea, and looked at the low house in the King's Road. It stood empty, the riven tree still rearing its shattered head, and the night wind sighing round it like voices from the dead.

He went down to the old wooden bridge, and watched the water as it eddied and gurgled round the piers, and thought, "Shall I plunge in there and end it all, and wash out my misery?" but he had not courage, and, with a shudder, he turned away.

Day was creeping over the sky as he let himself into his great house—the home fitted up with everything that luxury could imagine or money buy, and he thought to himself, "Shall I be able to keep all this, or will they take it from me?"

He sat down in his own room and wondered why Mountjoy and Frank Dawson did not come and charge him with the ill that he had done; he took it for granted they knew everything, and never made an effort, either to avert suspicion, or save himself from exposure. His own conscience pronounced his judgment, and he sat and awaited his doom.

CHAPTER XXXIII

SIR EDWARD

IT was a meeting to be remembered, that which took place on the morning succeeding Lord A.'s fête.

Frank Dawson's delight was unbounded, at once more seeing those he had so long looked on as dead and gone; and his amiable little wife, none other than the "Ocean Margaret" of other days, wept with delight, and embraced every one as if she had known them all her life.

There was Mrs. Mountjoy, or mother Agnes, as Grace still called her; now an aged lady, wondrously thin and fair, with a cloud of black lace shading her once beautiful face and enveloping her figure; and Grace, as noble a looking matron as eyes ere lighted on, and Sir Edward, with his fine open face, and Frank Dawson, as queer-looking and as odd as ever, and pretty Ocean Margaret, happy because her husband is happy.

"So you were not killed after all, cousin Grace. What a shame of you to keep us all in ignorance of your escape!" said Frank Dawson; "only a runaway match, instead of a murder; really it is quite a take in. What will the good folks in the West say, when they hear that the lady who fell over the cliffs a dozen years ago, and whose ghost has been walking about in a blue dress ever since, never fell over the cliffs, and never had a ghost?"

"You are mistaken, Frank; it is but too true that the accident which people supposed happened to me, really did; my marriage was no runaway match; but there is a mystery, if not a ghost, attached to my story, and we never speak of it," replied Lady Erlingham, in a tone which showed that Frank was treading on forbidden ground.

"Poor Reginald," he rejoined, after a moment's pause; "how glad he will be to hear you are still alive and well!"

"My poor brother!" answered Grace, "I have heard his story accidentally. Is he still an outlaw?"

"Alas, yes! but we must hope some day to see his sentence reversed. I believe him to have been more sinned against than sinning; but it is a sad subject, let us talk of something else."

"By-the-by, Sir Edward, I heard, a day or two ago, a romance concerning a relative of yours; and if what I heard prove true, you will come into a noble fortune! Really, some men seem ever in luck's way; here you are a distinguished man in your profession, and now, unless I am mistaken, you will find yourself a rich man, without any trouble on your part. I'll leave no stone unturned, I can assure you, in the endeavour to secure your inheritance."

"It is nothing more than I owe to this fair lady here," he continued, taking Grace's hand in his. "Do you remember, cousin, the hundred pounds you gave me once, at Harscourt? Cousin, without you, I should most likely at this moment have been grovelling in some country attorney's office; but, thanks to your generosity, I am a rising man, working steadily toward the goal I set before me as a lad—the chancellorship of England. Don't think me too ambitious; I am well aware I may never reach the coveted position, but aiming at it keeps me up to the mark. But now, honestly, I have no time to waste; I must speak to you Mountjoy (I must call you the old name), on important business. Let us leave the ladies to gossip, and you come and stroll with me towards my chambers, I will tell my tale as we go along. Madge, I'll come back for you by-and-by."

Frank Dawson never inquired if his arrangements were convenient or agreeable,—he was bent on doing business, and doing it his own way,—and, without more ado, took Sir Edward straight to an attorney, who, he had discovered, had once managed the elder Erlingham's affairs.

Frank Dawson's name procured them a cordial welcome from the old lawyer; but his surprise was boundless, when he heard the name of his other visitor. "I was not aware that there was any one of the name in England, except Mr. Richard Erlingham," said the old man; "are you related to him?"

Edward explained who he was; the old man constantly interrupting him with exclamations of surprise, as he gave in a few words the history of his life, and his mother's story.

"Ah!" said the attorney, as Sir Edward paused, "I always believed Richard Erlingham to be a villain. Why did he prevent my seeing my old friend, when he was ill and dying, but for some villany of his own?"

"He had very good reason for keeping every one out of his way," said Frank Dawson. "He is accused of having murdered him."

"My poor friend! my poor friend!" murmured the lawyer, "your fate shall be avenged. I, too, will bring an accusation against your murderer. Gentlemen, the will deposited in Doctors' Commons, as the will of the elder Erlingham's, is a forgery; I have examined it more than once, and am fully persuaded I am right. Moreover, there is, or ought to be, a will leaving everything unconditionally to his daughter; I drew it out myself: he would not sign it, he said, till on his deathbed, that it might be his *last* will."

"If we could find that, I expect Mr. Richard Erlingham would hardly care to contest the matter with us."

There was much to be discussed, much to be planned, and there was no time to be lost. Tunny was sent for and examined; but when Mrs. Mountjoy heard the accusation against her cousin, she implored, that if possible, this dreadful deed might not be made public, and Grace interceded for Mary Horton's sake.

"Well," said Sir Edward, "I dropped my father's name because he was a privateer and I am a smuggler; but it is less disgraced than the name of Erlingham. From this day I shall resume my old name: surely the many services I have rendered to my country have washed out any stain that rested on the name of Mountjoy."

CHAPTER XXXIV

AILSEY PHILLIPS

WE must now turn our thoughts to Ailsey Phillips, the gaoler's widow, of whom we have lost sight for some years.

She had formed a determination at the time of the elder Erlingham's death in some way to discover his daughter. Her plans were vague and indefinite, and it is not much to be wondered at all if all her attempts failed. Aimless, purposeless journeys from one end of England to the other, with no guide of any description, generally ended in her finding herself back in London penniless and broken both in mind and body.

The acquaintance she had so accidentally formed with the landlady of the Rose and Crown, was destined to prove a permanent friendship between the two women; and she usually betook herself to the little old-fashioned inn, where she was ever sure of a kindly welcome after her fruitless searchings.

Ailsey had never had many friends, and since the dismal end of her husband she had carefully avoided the few she had ever known. She did not care to have the past recalled, and therefore she felt most at her ease with those who knew nothing of what had been. She was possessed of a small annuity, which kept her above want, and prevented her being a burden on those who befriended her, whilst it gave her the means of attempting to find one whom she did not even know was alive.

"What gay times we live in!" said the rosy landlady, as she stood under the oak-tree in front of her house, watching the carriages as they drove down to a grand fête at Lord ——'s. "Anybody, to see the gay dresses and pleasant smiles, would never fancy that a single poor chap had lost his life in these great victories they make so much boast of. I wonder if those who look so cheerful think of the heavy-hearted creatures who have lost the ones they loved best in these horrid wars"

"Some have cause to be cheerful and look proud, though," said a man standing by: he was a servant belonging to one of the carriages that had not long before passed down the road. "What a sight it was at Lord A—'s the other night! and how those who had distinguished themselves were put forward and thought fit company for princes. Why, there was one man there that night, that I can mind in a very different position, nothing more or less than captain of a smuggler or some such thing; and there he was among the greatest of the land, and bless me if they haven't given him a title, and now he's Sir Edward Erlingham—not that that is his real name, but they say 'twas his mother's, so I suppose he has a right to call himself what he likes."

Ailsey, who had been standing by her friend, heard the man's remarks with breathless agitation.

"Erlingham?" said the landlady musingly; "why, Ailsey, that's surely the name of the old gentleman as died up in the low house, a day or two after you first came here; I wonder if he had anything to do with this Sir Edward; only fancy his having a title, and he a smuggler's son; well, these are wonderful days;" and the landlady lifted up her eyes and hands, and turned into her clean, cheerful bar to serve some of the many customers that the grand fête at Ashburnham House brought to her inn, in the persons of the coachmen and servants belonging to the guests.

"How strange, if after all my seeking I should find them by chance!" muttered Ailsey to herself. His name was Edward, and it would be no great wonder if his son should follow the same trade as his father.

Ailsey was one of those women who, often for months together low and despondent, and incapable of any exertion, suddenly, if anything occurs to interest or excite them, wake to new life, and seem capable of any amount of fatigue. This chance mention of the name of Erlingham roused Ailsey, and set her once more speculating on finding Agnes Mountjoy, but a less pure gratification seemed within her reach, one she had pined for for years—revenge on Richard Erlingham.

If Agnes or her son could be found, she had it in her power to bring her enemy, the destroyer of her husband, to the very dust.

She followed the man who had spoken, and subjected him to a most minute examination; and at last was fully satisfied that she had discovered those she sought.

Not an hour did she lose—she took her way at once to the house, where her informant had told her that not only Sir Edward, but his wife and mother, were to be found.

It was evening before she reached her destination, and some time elapsed ere she could gain admittance. The servant would willingly have refused her any access to those she sought, deeming her some impostor, but her vehemence attracted attention; and at last Edward Mountjoy himself made his appearance, and took her into a room where Frank Dawson was seated at a table examining some papers, with an elderly gentleman with whom he was in eager conversation as Ailsey entered—none other than the lawyer and friend of old Mr. Erlingham.

"What is your business, my good woman?" inquired Sir Edward, as he closed the door. "You seemed so determined to see me, that no doubt you have something to say; but pray make short work of it, for we are all engaged in matters of some importance."

Ailsey looked fixedly at him, and through the mists of thirty years and more, she seemed to see the pirate captain of the *Ocean Wave.*

"If you are, as I believe you to be, the son of a Captain Mountjoy who married Agnes Erlingham," replied Ailsey slowly, "I have something of great importance to tell you."

Sir Edward uttered an exclamation of surprise, and glanced towards his companions, who were as much interested as himself.

"You may not know that you are heir to a great fortune," continued the woman, looking up at Mountjoy.

"They say so," he rejoined; "but it seems difficult to prove; can you throw any light on the subject?"

"I was with Mr. Erlingham when he died," was the reply.

"But you are not Tunny's wife, surely?" cried Frank Dawson, starting up.

"I know no one of that name," said Ailsey. "Accident led me to the deathbed of my old master. I found him guarded by those whose object it was to separate him from all whom he knew or loved. He recognized and trusted me—I had been a companion of the daughter he had come to England to find—and the night before his murder—ah! gentlemen, you may well start, but I speak advisedly—the night before his murder he gave into my hand a paper, a will, he said, and charged me to keep it till I should find his daughter; or if she was dead, and had left children, I was to give it to them."

Edward Mountjoy walked up and down the room with hurried strides; but the two lawyers eagerly seized the document Ailsey held in her hand, and were soon busily employed examining its contents.

"Sir Edward!" exclaimed the elder man, after a few minutes' pause, "I congratulate you! this paper is nothing more or less than the lost will! But in the name of all that's wonderful, woman, why have you kept it to yourself all these years? Why didn't you bring it to me? I should have taken steps immediately to have put the matter right, and not have allowed that villain to triumph so long."

Poor Ailsey defended herself as best she could, and gave a detailed account of her many unbusinesslike attempts to find Mrs. Mountjoy.

"What was that you said about murder?" asked Frank Dawson, who had not hitherto spoken.

"The man who has possession of the money now is the murderer," replied Ailsey, with flashing eyes. "Expose him gentlemen; let all the world know what he is! I tell you, I will swear that he poisoned the old man with some herb that the negroes use; I have seen its effects in the West Indies, and I saw it act the same on him!"

"What a strange confirmation of that sailor's story!" whispered Frank Dawson. "We must move in the matter now it is thus confirmed; it would be impossible to come to any compromise."

CHAPTER XXXV
JUDGMENT

WHILE the lawyers are silently and swiftly hunting out fresh proofs of Richard Erlingham's crimes, he sits in his great house, waiting.

With every means of escape at his command, he took no advantage of the facilities his wealth afforded him, but sat in his chair as if chained by some invisible influence.

They come at last, not as he had pictured them, armed with all the terrors of the law; but when the three friends entered his room he knew they had come to accuse him, and that was enough.

He did not rise at their entrance, and only by a slight motion of his head and hand did he show that he was aware of their presence.

Frank Dawson was the spokesman, and he spoke out boldly and fearlessly, for he felt that every word of accusation he uttered was true. Not one word did Richard Erlingham utter as the lawyer detailed his deeds with a minuteness and exactness that seemed like magic. How he had tampered with the gaoler at Newport, how he had tried to get Mountjoy into his power, how for years he had followed him like an evil spirit, and then the scene in the house at Chelsea, and lastly the undoubted forgery of his uncle's will.

"And now," continued Frank Dawson, "we come to tell you that a warrant will be issued against you, but there is still time to escape. For the sake of your wife and for the sake of those unhappily connected with you, take advantage of the delay and get out of England as quickly as possible, and you will be safe from pursuit."

Richard Erlingham, though he sits there in his chair in his own drawing-room, is already safe from human pursuit; he is never to stand at an earthly bar, his conscience has judged, condemned, executed him: Richard Erlingham is dead!

There is an inquest in that grand house. Men walk with muffled tread over the thick carpets. One of the jurymen is an upholsterer who furnished the palace whose king lies there cold and still, and he whispers to his fellows how much this and that cost, and what a close-handed fellow the dead man was, in spire of all the magnificence they see.

And they give their verdict how "the rich man died of disease of the heart brought on by anxiety in money matters." That is what is said; but other things ooze out, and Mr. Ricks tells a fine story to his friends, how Sir Edward Erlingham Mountjoy was the real heir to Mr. Erlingham's fortune, and how the thought of parting with it was too much for him.

The world never knows all the truth, and soon it forgets the little it ever knew.

Mrs. Erlingham and her father know everything. Frank Dawson and Edward Mountjoy tried to palliate and hide the worst facts, but she would know all, and calmly and coldly she heard every incident in her late husband's life.

Restitution, full and ample was made, and mother Agnes in her old days was once more a rich woman; but when the affairs of the dead man were examined into, large sums were found that he had himself amassed. Mr. Horton and his daughter implored the Mountjoys to accept them, but not a shilling would they take excepting what was legally theirs; they would have no share in that ill-gotten wealth.

Mrs. Erlingham had similar scruples; not a shilling would she touch; and at last, by mutual consent, the riches that Erlingham had sold his soul to procure were given to the poor.

Little had he dreamt to what all his struggles had tended,—simply to enrich those he had despised on earth.

Lady Mountjoy went to Mrs. Erlingham, and prayed her, by the memory of their girlish friendship, to bear her no ill-will for the part she had unconsciously borne in her present trial. "It seems so strange," said Grace, "that you who were always so pure and good should be so grievously afflicted."

"I thought so too, Tye, at first," was Mary's reply, "but I see now I deserved it all. Pride has been my sin through life; I have always imagined myself superior to every one; pride has been my fault, and in my pride I am punished."

Mrs. Erlingham and her father did not remain in England, she could not face her former associates, and they sought in foreign lands the oblivion of the past that was denied them in their native land.

Some who wandered over the Continent during the first years that immediately followed the Peace, may call to mind a tall, pale woman with a singularly high forehead, who, accompanied by an elderly man, was constantly to be seen in every picture gallery from Dresden to Rome, whose presence was welcome in many an *atelier*, and whose liberality cheered the heart of more than one struggling artist. Those who chanced to meet her as well as those whom she succoured, never knew her by any other name than "Mr. Horton's daughter."

CHAPTER XXXVI

THE END

THERE is one more of out *dramatis personæ* whose tale must be told. We must chronicle the end of the bright-eyed boy who once played on the wild Atlantic cliffs, and won so many hearts as a lad—Reginald Dawson.

For years he had been living a wild, rough life in Mexico. It was but rarely any news was heard of him. When his father died, Frank Dawson had undertaken the management of the remainder of the Harscourt property, which being entailed, Mr. Dawson had been unable to part with, and occasional letters therefore passed between the cousins.

The knowledge of his sister's existence awoke a new life in him; the good spirit that had slumbered so long, the spirit of childhood and innocence, once more showed itself, and a longing to see his old home took possession of him—but alas! he was an outlaw.

Men who have once transgressed cannot regain their position by mere regrets and repentance, and so Reginald found.

It was not until many years of peace and security had made people forget the enormity of the crime he had at least shared in, that Frank Dawson, now vice-chancellor, and Edward Erlingham Mountjoy, now an admiral, ventured to try their influence to get his sentence reversed. Things had come to light, Fowler's villainies had been exposed, and his friends ventured to plead his cause. They were successful, and Reginald was once more permitted to return to his native land. But kind as they all were to him, he could not but feel that after the life he had led, he had little in common with them, that it would be better for all that he should live independently and alone at Harscourt; so thitherward he turned his steps. And he came back to Torford at last. The same man, yet so different, no longer walking erect, with flashing eyes and proud yet gentle mien. His head and heart bowed, his hair silvered, his face wrinkled, he slunk along the streets, dreading to be recognized.

Ah! who shall tell the pangs of remorse that that man felt as he stood once more on the old bridge at Torford, and saw the quays along which he had so often strolled when he was a boy, the red brick school-house, the ship-yard where the ill-fated *Gratiana* had been launched, the river where she had first floated, and the quiet street leading from the quay where he had spent so many happy hours. Oh, what deep, deep feelings of regret for the years, the life that had been wasted! for he felt and knew that he had thrown himself away, had sunk without a struggle to keep above water, and here he was come back to his old home, like a poor battered piece of wreck cast upon the shore.

Slowly he made his way along the quays, keeping his head down, lest he should be recognized, and trembling when he felt he attracted attention; but none knew him; though he passed many an old acquaintance, none guessed that that bent man was the once handsome and gay Reginald Dawson.

He felt like a man in a dream as he once more trod the pavement of the quiet street. There stood Mr. Fowler's house. He looked up at is for a moment, then following some irresistible impulse, he laid his hand on the latch, and once more stood in Lily's home.

He had closed the door behind, and stood listlessly gazing up the broad stairs, never dreaming that the house might have changed owners since he had known it, when a woman, attracted to the sound of the door and the heavy tread with which he had crossed the hall, made her appearance, not a little astonished to see what a rough sort of visitor had entered unbidden.

"Is Mr. Fowler in?" inquired Reginald in a voice well matched to his listless look.

"Mr. Fowler! why, bless the man, he's been dead these years!"

"And Mrs. Fowler?"

"Gone too; they're all gone!"

"All dead?"

"No, not all dead, but next door to it—all broke up and ruined."

Reginald sighed and asked no more, and the maid thought it was now her turn to make inquiries. "I suppose you're come from foreign parts," said she, "as you don't know all about the Fowlers?"

"Yes, I've been away from here these many years. Who does the house belong to now?"

"The creditors have taken possession of it, and it's to be sold when any one will buy it."

"How was it they were ruined?"

"The Fowlers?"

Reginald nodded assent.

"Oh! you see, after Miss Lily died, bless her,"—Reginald winced, and the woman paused, and lifting the corner of her apron wiped a tear away—"nothing seemed to go right. Mr. Fowler never lifted up his head after; and his son turned out unsteady, and worrited him and all of them most out of their lives, and people said bad things of him; how it was he that was to blame about the muskets (no doubt as you knew the Fowlers you knew that story), and not poor Master Reginald, as the folks called him, and how he had been the cause of Miss Lily's death, by falsely accusing her lover; and then—but it is too long and too bad a story to tell—he shot himself.

For a moment Reginald felt a feeling of triumph that the man who had been the cause of so much misery to him, had in turn been punished. But the feeling soon died away, for he knew in his own heart how much more he had had to do with Lily's unhappiness than her brother.

As he stood in the hall he almost fancied his past life was a dream, and that the Lily would come tripping down the old oak stairs, and he looked up as if expecting that she would appear. But no, the Lily is withered long ago, and the house is desolate!

"I must go up-stairs," said the stranger, after a long pause, "I want to see the room where—one of the family died," and slowly and lightly he trod, thinking of the spirit child, who was gone to her rest.

The blinds were down in poor Lily's room, and it looked mournful and sad enough. The room had been left pretty early as it had been when she had died, for none belonging to her cared to intrude there when she was gone. A long branch of a rose-tree she had once loved to train, had got loose from its fastening, and swayed hither and thither against the window, making a piteous sound, as if mourning for the dead.

The strong man—the skilful sailor—the undaunted pirate—leaned against the old bed, with its faded, dusty hanging, and his whole frame shook with suppressed sorrow. It was more than he could bear—worse even than it had been the night he knelt beside her new-made grave—that deserted room, that death-bed! He rushed from the room, and hastily throwing up the window on the staircase, eagerly inhaled the free, pure air as it came sweeping up the river. How altered was the view from that window! The river was there, and the hills were there, but the broad expanse of salt marsh was now rich fields, and the garden—poor Lily's garden—once so neat and trim, was a wilderness—tall, straggling, unpruned rose-trees, beds choked with weeds, untrimmed borders, grassy walks!—only here and there some poor solitary flower struggling weakly up amid the coarse intruders, like a frightened child looking for a face it had lost.

All told of death, desolation, misery; and, with a bursting heart, the weather-beaten sailor turned away. She was right, he muttered, when she said it was better for me not to be a sailor.

Poor Hortense! She had worked on these many years, she had grown old and plain, but she had still her only charm left—that marvellous neatness, so characteristic of Frenchwomen, and a certain unobtrusive kindliness, which made her truly loved when once known.

And then, instead of making herself out a martyr, or an ill-used woman, as many in her case would have done, she silently bore her sorrow, without a word or a murmur.

She was destined to have her reward, all the reward at least she had ever craved, the greatest happiness of which she had ever dreamed.

She became Reginald's wife. He made no violent professions of affection, and she wanted none; she knew his story, and told him what she knew, but she made him a good, true wife. His station he could never regain, that is to say, his position in society; but, minding the Lily' dying words, she watched over him, and kept him, as far as in her lay, from evil; and so, tending him for many years, she lived his wife, with Damaris and Will for her assistants—friends rather than servants.

What happy gatherings there used to be at Harscourt in those quiet autumn days of Reginald's life; quiet days they were to him and his kind foreign wife, but cheery, merry days for the younger ones. There were the vice-chancellor's sons with Sir Edward's children. "The young pirate," now one of the most audacious middies in his Majesty's navy, and Douglas not much better, and a little Grace, who bade fair to rival her mother. Yes, we were all happy, very happy, more especially when the elders of the family could be coaxed to spend a week or two at "dear old Harscourt," the enjoyment thereof being much enhanced by the necessity which compelled detachments of the party to rough it at one or two of the neighbouring farms, as well as at the cottage in Combe.

Then the delight it used to be when we could prevail on Lady Mountjoy, one of the noblest-looking ladies in all England, to tell us some of her reminiscences of "the olden days," with her friend sweet "Ocean Margaret" at her side. Nor were the Douglases always absent from these meetings, and, with the greatest glee, the admiral would listen to some new story of Tye's daring, and then rebuke her in his old tone, "Convicted, madam, convicted! How did you dare ever to interfere with my young pirate when you were such a character yourself?"

Sometimes the whole party would flit southward to Stoke Petrock, where Sir Edward still retained as owner the cottage of his early days, and to which he had added and added till there was but little resemblance to be seen between as pretty a villa as could be found, and the tiny building to which he had originally taken Grace. Nothing would have induced either of them to abandon a place consecrated by so many ties, and which no change of fortune could break.

At Stoke, Bellamy, who through Sir Edward's influence had obtained a position in the coast guard, was a frequent visitor, and while at Harscourt, Will turned all the girls of the family into horsewomen by his graphic descriptions of Lady Mountjoy's girlish achievements in that line. Bellamy at Stoke drew such lively pictures of Sir Edward's adventures, and the charms of the sea, that the navy seemed destined to be inundated not only by all the Mountjoys and Dawsons, but by half the boys of the neighbourhood.

Ah well! those days are past and gone, Frank Dawson's eldest son is owner of Harscourt, and the house, much reduced in size, and strangely altered from its original appearance, is now only a farm.

THE END

www.ingramcontent.com/pod-product-compliance
Lightning Source LLC
Chambersburg PA
CBHW020931310726
48980CB00007B/728/J

9781917113007